Reviews of DOG

'DOG' by EM Faustus
sure if it's due to its main character Pete and his side-
duck Sid or its cast of thousands of vampire, booty-full
women, quite crazed scientists and other extraordinary
out of this world types. but .. Anyway, I'd recommend
this book to anyone wanting something so different to
read and entertain that nothing else matters in high season
Summer or low season Winter. It's a book to romp you
through hours of laughs and raised eyebrows, the
dialogue's different to say the least, the pictures it paints
is.. well, read it, move to another country and like me,
laugh at it and feel alive .. or something!
***Emma Joy   Poet, Artist, Landscape Gardener, Model,
Nutter***

Oh my naughty little PI, you taunt and tease but just
enough to please. You unfold your tale with little
peeks…but I assume from those peeks only to be
surprised by the tricks of my eyes-The Blond and Ginger.
Oh jealously could linger over the attention of those
fingers. You had to be smiling when you finished that
first tid-bit, laughing at us, knowing 'HA I got you now'.
How I love your twisted wisdom and humor

**TK Bickel   Author of The Forever Hunting Series.
(Real big nutter)**

I don't understand the last one either, but it makes me
sound hot….

www.emfaustus.com

ISBN-13: 978-1478303817

ISBN-10: 1478303816

To Margaret

DOG
By Chris Davison

© Chris Davison 2011

For Gillian

Happy Nightmares —
Chris Davison
aka
E.M. Fawkes.

Once upon a Sometime Later…

"O.K. What if we kill her?"

"Well morally it is a mortal sin to take a life. On the other hand there are circumstances under which it is necessary to take a life in order to prevent suffering of oneself or others. Then…"

"Pete."

"…there are also the legal implications to be considered such as…"

"Pete."

"…..most of the major religions…"

"Pete. Look at her."

"You shoot her in the head and I'll dismember the body."

Chapter One: The Dick and The Dame

The Name's Faustus.

E.M. Faustus.

Best not ask what the E.M stands for. I get bored with that.

I'm a Private Eye. Not as glamorous as it sounds but it pays the bills. I have five simple rules.

Read them;

1) Respect the confidentiality of the client.
2) See the job through to the end.
3) Make sure you know what your client really is and never work for the Bad Guy
4) Always get paid in cash.
5) Never, ever, work for fairies.

I am not a psychic Private Eye. I am not a wizard, warlock, vampire, werewolf or any kind of supernatural Private Eye. I am a straightforward human P.I that's good at his job with an eclectic range of clients.

Simple.

It was a Tuesday in September and I was sat in my office looking out the window at the rain. Rains a lot here. Good for atmosphere.

You need atmosphere when you work my genre.

The corpse sat in the chair opposite me, with only my desk between us. She said thank you, paid her bill and left.

Got to love zombies. They pay their bills promptly.

It's a nice office if you go for the film noir, PI look. All wood panelling with an old fashioned oak desk, desk lamp and from the ceiling, a single light bulb with attached ceiling fan. Filing cabinets to the left and leather sofa to the right. Wooden chair in front of the desk. Name painted on a half glass door. Of course there are also Venetian blinds at the windows. Me, wearing a suit with a matching trilby on a coat rack by the door.

Image is as important as genre.

It was a Tuesday, at risk of repeating myself. You don't expect much to happen on a Tuesday. Mondays are good for busy, so are Fridays and Saturdays surprisingly, but Tuesdays…Same as Sundays but the shops are open later. So I sat there this particular Tuesday, feet up on the old fashioned desk, rolling cigarette number seven of the day, watching the rain.

That's when She walked in.

A dame to kill for, and by the end of it all I had.

There's a typical kind of dame that walks into a P.I office. Tall, leggy, slim brunette, wearing dark lipstick, killer heels and a dress that clings in all the right, (and some of the wrong, but nice) places. Those in the know also wear one of those hats with a veil. To accentuate rather than conceal.

In fact she was shorter than average, about 5'6" or 5'7". Blonde hair that had never seen a bottle or a stylist by the look of her. Natural. She wore blue jeans - a little baggy- and a dark green T with the logo 'Mel's' above the left…chesty bit. No killer heels but beat up trainers, and she was knocking on my door.

Gods, she was beautiful.

"Mr Faustus?"

6

I knew I should come back with some Private Eye Style banter.

"That's the name on the door Lady. Don't let your eyes wear it out." I put down the cigarette and gave her my full attention.

It wasn't hard.

"How can I help?"

"I brought you your change." She purred.

I have to admit I had expected something a little more intense than that.

"Can I come in?"

"Certainly. I'm sorry, come on in."

As I stood up she strode through the door in a not unpleasing fashion and placed a handful of coins on my desk. She looked around the office, and I was impressed she kept the look of disappointment from her face.

"So this is what a Private Eye's office looks like. It's like something from the 1940's." She said.

"I do try to keep up that look Mrs...?"

"It's Mel. And it's Miss, as you were fishing."

Yes! Result.

She sat down on the edge of my desk and looked out of the window, down onto the street below. The soft light through the blinds played upon her face like a glockenspiel and I began to drift back towards reality.

"My change Mel?" I said.

"You left it on the counter this morning when you bought your coffee."

Of course I had recognized her. This was the woman who served me a double Espresso with extra caffeine every morning for the past couple of years. I'd never had the nerve to say anything apart from put in my order. Damn shame because I'd been stunned by her the first time I saw her, and having watched all the younger and slimmer hopefuls floating around her thought it was best to just…order coffee.

"So I thought I would take the chance to come up and see what your office looked like. And," she paused and looked down at the floor before looking up into my eyes, blushing as she gazed at me. "And see if you were ever planning on asking me out. There I've said it. It's only taken me two years. I've made a total fool of myself and now I'll leave but please don't get embarrassed and stop coming in for coffee because I like to see you in the mornings and I had better go before I make more of a fool of myself. I'm sorry if I embarrassed you."

She slid off my desk during this and strode back towards the door.

Now this does not happen to me every day. I spend most of my life stood in alleyways, getting too cold, too warm, wet and bored. Yet every now and then you just have to act. Problem is I had no idea what to say.

"Wait. Food or Film?" Not good Faustus. Very not good.

Thank God she stopped and turned. Her kissable mouth was open. "Pardon?"

"Food or Film? I don't drink you see so I w…w…wondered whether you would want to get something to eat with me. Or go and see a film, because then you really don't have to be seen too much with me and start the gossip."

Damn. Looking at her she seemed more nervous than I did.

"Is it greedy to say both?"

8

"Oh that's perfectly O.K." I felt the relief wash over me. I had got it right. She was going to go out with me. A date. Bloody Hell.

"I'll see you…." She began.

"Tonight?"

"Tonight. 7 o'clock at the café then."

"Oh I'll be there then."

"See you there, then."

"See you then, then."

"See you then…Eh. What's you're name? First name that is. I know the Faustus bit."

Always something to spoil a damn good time. I hate my name.

"It is embarrassing. Could we just leave it at Faustus? My friends call me that. All of him."

She glowed as she looked at me. A smile spread wide over her face like butter on warm toast, and I went weak. "Is it really that bad?"

"Oh yes. Faustus is good." I said.

A serious look crossed her face as she looked down. She moved to the doorway and turned. "I have heard that "Faustus was good", from everyone. I could use some good, Faustus." A half smile played on her lips but it didn't spread to her eyes. All of a sudden she looked very scared. "I really could use some good. I'll see you at seven then."

And with that she turned around slid through the door frame and was gone.

I had a date.

Good Gods I had a date.

With a woman.

With a pulse.

First in over a year.

A real live woman.

Well a Vampire, but it still counts.

9

Vampires are good people too.

Then, as my little piece of heaven left my office, my own little bit of Hell walked right on into it.

Chapter Two: The Dick and The Daemon

"Mr. Faustus? Is that you? Am I addressing Mr. E.M. Faustus? I looked downstairs but didn't find you so I came up here. You are The Private Enquiry Agent? I have some work for you if you are willing to accept it."

It said.

A few years ago an old lady I did some skip tracing for did me a needle point tapestry of my rules. This, I took down from the wall and walked over to the Daemon who stood in my doorway. I slapped him in the chest with it forcing him to clutch it, before I turned and walked back to my desk dropping into the chair. I find with Daemons it's a good idea to keep something between you.

Shotgun maybe.

"Check out rule 5. It applies to daemonic individuals too. Have a good read then go. Or don't read it. Just go."

Hard Boiled time.

He was a big man. Not your typical looking daemon. Six foot plus, wiry, which was a bit odd as they tend to go for the muscle boy look. Thin and lost looking. He wore a simple pair of slacks and a jumper. Given the fact it was still summer that was a bit much, but given where he hailed from I'm not surprised he was a bit cold.

He looked down at the needle point then carefully walked over and hung it back onto the wall. Slow as treacle on a frigid woman in winter he walked over and stood before my desk.

I took the sensible precaution of reaching into the waste paper basket and taking out the office bottle. I may not drink, but a whisky bottle filled with Holy Water is handy to have around.

"Still here? I didn't bother looking at him. With his kind you keep up the front. Big guns are nice too but I had to settle for a front.

"Yes." He seemed surprised that I had asked him such an obvious question. "I do not understand your overt hostility towards me. I…I need some help and my friend told me to come and see you and you would help me."

I sat back in my chair and looked him over. He really was not your typical daemon. For a start he really was not that attractive. Daemons tend to go for the pretty boy or super model look. It endears them to whoever they are tempting. This one had moles on his face, was too thin and had really screwed up hair. Curly and muzzled. His teeth were also wonky and, well, not brilliant white.

Daemons 'grow' from the base matter of the universe. Their cellular nature is about as perfect as it can get. Foetal cells. Same as Angels. After all they were the same basic stock before the Fall. (Or as Satan likes to call it, the Corporate Restructuring). Their bodies are as physically pure as pure can be. This one looked as if he had picked up the scrapings from the vat after other bodies had been made. Even his clothes did not have the style Daemons and Angels have.

They wear Style. He wore Charity Shop.

Even so He looked basically Daemonic, with a bit of Angel about the hair and that spelled Trouble, with a capital TROUBLE.

I like my soul where it is.

"I don't work for your kind." I rumbled. "Don't take it personally; I don't work for Angels either. Now go to wherever it is you're going to from here."

"May I sit down?"

"It's your arse but my chair, so leave the chair where it is but take your arse out of my office, down the stairs and onto the street."

That was three times I had told him to go. A thrice bidding. Powerful juju if you got it right, which I had of course. In spirit, if not the fancy words.

He wasn't taking the hint.

"Please Mr. E.M Faustus. I need help and Mr. Peter told me that I could come and see you and get help. I need your help. Mr. Peter told me you would help me. Please help me."

Bugger.

Peter.

Bugger.

Peter is a bit of a legend around here. You could not ask for a nicer guy, but you don't mess with him. Get on the wrong side of Gods, get on the wrong side of Satans, get of the wrong side of anyone or anything but DO NOT, ever get on the wrong side of Peter.

Thank Gods he's my friend.

I let out a slow, resigned sigh.

"You sit and talk. That's as far as I go Kid."

He didn't need asking twice. He pulled the chair back and folded himself into it like an accordion into its case.

Just a few minutes before a beautiful blonde sat down here. Now I had him.

"I'll give you ten minutes of my time. After that you go. Understand?"

13

A look of poor gratitude swam over his face and he actually breathed a sigh of relief. "I understand. Thank you for giving me your time. I am aware that it is precious to you and I am sure that you have other cases to work on."

I picked up the cigarette and match from the desk, lighting it and taking a deep draw. I thought deeply on the situation and decided on really strong mouthwash before my date tonight. And a new toothbrush. Maybe one of those electric ones. I was aware that he was talking, but I wasn't exactly listening. I said I'd give him ten minutes of my time. I never said I would listen.

Maybe I should go shopping for some clothes. O.K money was tight at the moment, but a date like this only comes around…

"….dog was gone. I don't know what to do. I love him so much and Mr. Peter said I should come and ask for your help."

"What?" I couldn't believe what I might just have heard. Peter sent him here over a lost Dog!

"My dog has been stolen. Mr. Peter said you could help me. Please help me. Now."

I looked in his face and reeled. I had never reeled before and here I was reeling. Seemed like a day for trying new things.

"Someone stole your dog? Was it some kind of statue? Religious item? Something like that? A thing of worship?"

Now it was his turn to look confused. "No Mr. E.M Faustus. My Dog. He is gone. Stolen."

"Some kind of Hell Hound? Three Heads? Great big pointy Teeth?"

"No. He's just my little Teddy Bear."

Never heard a Hell Hound described like that before.

Ω

Excerpt from
Angels, Daemons and other realm beings.
By E.M Faustus
(unpub)

Hellhounds.

…..Hellhounds are nasty. Very nasty indeed. Sired by Cerberus, he of the three heads they are not just capable of ripping you to bits, they shred your soul just as willingly.   Then they do it all over again.

Typically they stand around four foot tall on all fours, Seven foot long, nose to tail. Their heads are an over exaggerated wolf, but with the body of a highly muscular Great Dane. If you get close enough to identify one, you're dead. If your dead and get close to one, you are going to suffer. If one is pursuing you, the only reason you are not dead and/or in unspeakable pain is because they are playing.

They tend towards names along the lines of Soul Ripper, Gut Shredder or Flesh Render (apart from one named Bernard. The Daemon doing the naming gets confused sometimes).

They are not easily distracted, so throwing a stick or grabbing their testicles does not work. They are partial to a fluffy blanket for some reason. If you have one. Don't hesitate to use it.

Never, Ever, try to pat one!

Ω

"Teddy Bear? You called him Teddy Bear?"

The daemon looked more confused by the second, as was I, and I jumped when the cigarette, utapped, burnt my fingers.

"No. I call him 'Dog'. I just think he's a bit of a Teddy Bear."

I looked into the Daemon's eyes. Ordinarily not something you want to do. But I have seen worse things than a Daemon's stare, so I helped myself to a good long look. I just wish I'd had a chance to do the same with Mel. She had great eyes.

"Are you alright Mr E.M Faustus?"

I think I might just have reeled again.

Nothing. Just eyes.

No Daemon stare.

Just Human eyes.

A daemon can take on human form, it can even possess a weak body and dance it around, but it cannot change its eyes. This one had Human eyes. Real eyes. Something was very wrong in the State of Denmark and the Prince was doing his laundry.

I stood up and walked round the desk. The Daemon sat still, hands on his lap, only turning his head to follow me.

There are many ways to check for Daemonic influence. One is the Aura and this guy was glowing like a light bulb. Others include The Stockdale Sigel, the Byron Codex or the Ducalli Reveal. Me, I prefer something a little more up close and personal. Besides I didn't have the equipment to do that other stuff.

I stood behind him and sniffed his hair. Long and deep.

O.K.

So it sounds a little pervy, but it works.

I should have got an unmistakable whiff of Brimstone. Instead I got Flowers and Chocolate.

Bugger Me.

The guy was an Angel.

Ω

Excerpt from
Angels, Daemons and other realm beings.
By E.M Faustus
(unpub)

Angels

Don't get me started on Angels.

They are bad news; never tell you the full story. Always chunder on about Gods ineffable plan and never pay their bills.

I hate Angels.

I also hate those people who wander around saying "Oh, I have a Guardian Angel that looks after me. Angels are everywhere. They are the nicest beings in the Universe."

They are stuck up, irresponsible, totally devoid of the concept of consequences and dress badly. And they never pay their bills.

I really hate Angels.

Oh, and they smell a bit like flowers and chocolate.

And they NEVER pay their bills.

Ω

I took a few steps back from him and looked hard.

I am either lucky (or unlucky, depending on your perspective) in that I see things as they really are. I see people in all their glory and depravity. I see buildings that are awash with love from the family and others burning with hate and fear. I also see those who walk the earth amongst humans the way they truly are. Vampires, Werewolves, Ghosts and Ghoulies. Angels and Daemons.

There's no special trick to it. No inherited trait or anything. Someone just showed me what to look for. Makes life easier on The Streets.

The People of The Streets, 99.9% of the time, are just the same as everyone else. People trying to get by in the world. They have jobs, families, hobbies and simply practice a bit of an alternate lifestyle.

They tend not to prey on humanity (normally it's the other way around). They tend to keep themselves to themselves and just get on with life. Same as all of us.

I see them all the way they are, Good and Bad. So far as I know I'm the only human that does. Most people block out what they think is impossible. They don't believe in Vampires so that guy over there with the long teeth can't be one. That woman has long hair and her ears are a bit pointy, but werewolves aren't real so she's just a bit hairy.

I see the truth.

This guy was wrong.

Very wrong.

He had the feel of a daemon, but the smell of an Angel. Still there's always the straight approach.

I took a step further back and made a couple of rudimentary passes in the air with my hands and elbows.

"I bind you by all the powers to speak of your name and true place of origin. I bind you to speak your name and place of origin with truth. I bind you now and require an answer. Stay still and address me. The Truth! Your name?"

"Pardon, Mr E.M Faustus?"

That's not the response you expect.

"Come on. Tell me your true name and place of origin."

He stood up and walked towards me, hand reaching inside his trouser pocket. I looked around for something to protect myself with, in case this turned nasty.

I found a comb and a packet of smokes.

"I have a card." He said.

He pushed an address card through the air and into my face. I took it from his hand and looked at it as he returned back to his chair.

Hello. My name is Pete. I do not have a last name yet.

I live with Peter at the antique shop. If I am lost please

help me back there.

I flipped the card over. If I knew Peter….. and there it was.

Faustus,

Stop being a silly boy. I don't know what he is either but he's a good man. He needs help Faustus, and I think you're the only one who can help him.

So help him.

Peter

PS. Be Careful of the Duck.
PPS. Sorry I won't make film night. I'm sure you
will understand.

Bloody Peter.

I handed 'Pete' his card back and walked back to my desk. I put the Holy water back into the desk drawer. I got the feeling it would be worse than useless against him. He had walked through a binding of words as if it wasn't there. It was the closest thing to magic I knew and useless against him. I had used it once against a Djin who'd skipped out on his child support. It held and I got it to sign off on a direct debit, but this guy...

He sat back down in the chair opposite me.

"Would you like to see Dog's photograph Mr E.M Faustus?" He reached into his trouser pocket and drew out a fairly rumpled photograph, holding it up for me to see. When I reached to take it from him for a closer look he drew it back at snake speed back to his chest.

"I get it. I can look but not touch." I nodded, but wanted to shake my head in disbelief.

"It's the only thing I have of Dog. I am sorry Mr E.M Faustus, but it is mine." He gingerly reached it out again. I gingerly leaned forward.

I don't know what I expected to see, but I wasn't prepared to see a clear photograph of this 'Pete', with his arm holding a mutt. Shot on a beach there were two figures in the background, a couple walking hand in hand down by the shore. Pete's hand was ruffling the mutt's head. The Daemon-thing was smiling. His whole face was lit up, even the eyes.

He was a happy little devil. The dog looked happy too. It seemed to be smiling. The dog was like a Jack Russell on elongated legs. The body was mainly ginger with a white belly and white legs. Both ears were ginger with a dark ginger patch over a white face. It was a scruffy little thing. Cute though.

"Look, first we will go and see Peter." I've explained to him quite clearly though, that I don't find lost pets. "You could use some copies of that though. If I can hold it for a little while I can run you some off."

"No. It is my photograph Mr E M Faustus."

This was beginning to get to me. "Look Pete, you need copies of that photograph to help find your dog. Come over here."

I stood up and walked over to the closed door. Opening it I revealed something you don't really expect to see in a Private Eye's office that smacks of the 1940's.

A high spec computer was straight ahead as you walk in. Three monitors were running continually with various programs and files on each screen. Two printers were to the left of it, with assorted technical gubbins next to them. A color photocopier sat on the bench next to the array of listening equipment I may have been known to use. I know it's illegal, but sometimes you need to bend the law a little.

To the right sat the hub of my operation. The one thing I cannot function without. An industrial 'Lincat' coffee maker.

I don't drink alcohol. Ever. So I substitute the booze with coffee. There is a whole array of coffee there, ranging from decent instant to the ultimate coffee beans you could imagine. The very kind that have passed through digestive tracts of animals.

I don't like coffee. I love coffee.

I lifted the lid of the photocopier.

"Do you know what this is?"

The Daemon-thing Pete looked confused.

"It is a copier." I said. "You put a piece of paper face down on the glass, press the start button, that's the green one, and a copy comes out of the picture you put down. OK?"

The Daemon-thing Pete, clutched the photograph to his chest.

"Look. I'll show you.

I picked a photograph up from a pile on the side, quickly running off a copy. I held the copy up to Pete. "See."

"Can I do that? I am sorry Mr. E.M Faustus, but I do not want this to be lost. It is…"

"I know. It's the only thing you have of Dog." I stepped to one side. "There you go. You do it."

The Daemon ran through the process and a copy came out the other side.

"If you press that button there" I showed him the numbers button, "you can run off ten."

He turned and thrust the copy at me.

"You only need one copy to find Dog Mr. E.M Faustus."

"Look. Call me Mr. Faustus, or just Faustus. You don't need to say the initials as well."

I led him outside the room and walked over to the coat rack, slipping my hat onto my head.

"Come on. We'll go and see Peter."

Pete walked up to me and put his hand on my arm.

"Are you going to help me find Dog?"

I tore my arm away, actually annoyed at being grabbed like that. I rammed my hat onto my head tight.

"First we see Peter."

I pulled the office door open.

"Come on."

I walked through the door and promptly went flying along the hall.

I had tripped up over a Duck.

Chapter Three: The Dick and The Duck

"Sid. Gods Dammit." I raised myself onto my knees looking at the Duck. "You're a Duck again."

The Duck looked down at itself, then looked me back straight in the eyes.

"What's wrong with Ducks?" the Duck said.

It was not a quacky type of voice, rather a deep bass with a slight growl to it.

"I happen to have come to terms with my identity as a Duck, and am considering changing my name, so I would be appreciative it if you accepted me as I am."

"Look Sid, it is always nice to see you, however you look, but the Duck thing is getting a bit extreme." I stood up, dusting the carpet lint from my trousers. Pete the Daemon thing peered around the corner of the door.

"Are you alright Mr E.M Faustus? Is that a Duck?" he asked.

The Duck gave Pete a look that could have melted concrete.

"Sid, allow me to introduce you to Pete, he's got no second name yet but I'm sure he's working on it. Pete. This is Sid."

I don't know why I was surprised when Pete held out a hand for a handshake. I was even more surprised when Sid held out a wing and 'shook hands' with Pete.

Sid was not a Duck. He is Sydnrthrr Chhryknds Krpr. Knight of the Fourth Vessel and general Fae dogsbody. An extremely gifted Troll shape shifter. There are not many forms, organic or inorganic, he cannot take.

Trouble is that Sid…Sid was born wanting to be a Duck. He loves the feathers, the flight, the swimming, The sex. All of it. He should have been born a duck. He is a Duck trapped in a troll's body.

"Ti wants to see you Faustus." Sid said.

"Busy Sid."

"This is not an invitation to debate. Come on Faustus. I don't have a choice in this." At least Sid had the decency to look shamefaced. As much as a duck can.

Pete came out of the office and put his hand on my shoulder. He gave a little squeeze that was either too tight or he was unaware of his own strength. I gave him the benefit of the doubt.

"Move that hand, now." I said.

"We need to go. Now." Pete said.

Sid eyed the Daemon-thing carefully.

"Working for the 'Downstairs' now Faustus? Shouldn't have a problem with Ti then." Sid was curious, but knew better than to ask till we were alone.

I knelt down in front of Sid so we were eye level. It's strange talking to a Duck but you do get used to it.

"I'm not working for anyone at the moment Sid, but you know the rules."

"Ti wants to see you Faustus."

"I can't be made to go Sid."

"Ti Demands to see you Faustus."

"I am not going Sid."

"Ever had a Duck attack your bollocks Faustus?"

"Ever got up close and personal with Orange Sauce Sid?"

I stood up and stepped back.

If you looked at it objectively, here was a man facing up to fight a duck.

Ridiculous. I know. However, in any shape Sid was a dangerous opponent. We had never talked about it, but Sid was a killer. He was not sent just to fetch people. He was sometimes sent to make sure they weren't seen again.

Sid was my friend. One of the best. A great bloke, with an encyclopedic knowledge of westerns and sixties science fiction. We often went to the cinema together (But I always insisted he looked human till we got inside. Management don't take kindly to Ducks in the auditorium).

We both knew that one day Ti would really want to see me dead. On that day Ti would send Sid. He is the best she has. I'll get that honor at least. Sid knows I'll fight back. He'll play by the rules. I won't.

I'm not a nice guy.

I hoped the day was not today.

Sid took a deep breath. "Here we go." Then he changed. There was no 'morphing', no 'shimmer', just one second a duck standing in front of me, the next a six foot plus man, wearing a brown suit and tie. Sid's reset to Human form. The shape was overweight to compensate for the muscle behind it. Then with no warning or chat he just let go a punch.

I saw Sid punch something once.

A car. Doing sixty. It stopped dead. The two in the front should not have worn their seat belts. It could have saved them from Sid tearing the roof off the car dragging them screaming from their seats and down an alleyway.

We take road safety seriously around here.

The car was a right off.

And here he was punching me.

I remember thinking how unprepared I was for this.

I was less prepared for the blow stopping half an inch from my face.

Pete had hold of Sid's forearm. Sid, confused, looked at his arm.

"My wing. You could have broke my fucking wing!" The blood drained from Sid's face. He went weak at the knees and slid down the wall to the floor clutching his limb.

"My wing." he wailed.

I pushed Pete to one side and crouched by Sid. "Take it easy mate. He didn't break it. He just caught it. Your wing's fine."

"Did I hurt him?" Pete asked.

I turned on him. "Don't be fucking stupid. You could have broken his arm."

"Wing." Sid managed through clenched teeth.

"Wing. He may never have flown again." I felt Sid's forehead. He was cold. "Who can I call mate?"

"No one. Take me to Ti Faustus. I am going into shock."

"Hell of a way to get me there. Your arm or wing isn't broken Sid. You'll be fine. It's just a bit of a shock."

Sid looked up at me, tears in his eyes.

"Shock can kill a duck Faustus. I can feel myself slipping away." Sid whimpered.

"Look at your body Sid." I said.

Sid looked.

Sid paused.

"Feel a bit of a pillock Faustus." He said.

"Look a bit of a pillock Sid." I said.

27

Pete leaned down. "He was going to hit you Mr. Faustus. We have to find Dog."

Now it was my turn to punch. I hit him square in the face. With the anger behind it, there was no pulling, no forgiveness.

Shame.

I think I broke my hand.

I slumped next to Sid clutching my fist.

"Bugger." I whined.

Pete stood up looking confused. "Are you both hurt?"

"Stupid bloody question." Sid said.

"Oh. I am sorry Mr. Faustus and Mr. Sid. Allow me to remedy this. It seems a simple dislocation."

Before we could stop him he took my hand in his right hand. The pain stopped. After quite a lot of pain from putting my fingers back in their sockets.

No pain. I looked down at my hand. I wiggled the fingers. They didn't hurt anymore. "Sid."

"Tk til tsa tsgn tsortit? (What the hell did he do?)"

"He's an Angel. Maybe." I slowly stood up flexing my fingers. I looked at Sid holding out my hand. He gingerly took my hand and pulled himself to his feet. "You were going to hit me."

"Can we go and look for Dog now?" the Daemon/Angel said.

"Relax Faustus. I had an audience. It would only have been a little love tap." He rotated his shoulder. "That actually feels great." He turned to Pete. "Thanks. I think."

"It was not a problem. Can we go and find Dog now?"

Sid nodded his head at Pete. "He's got a bit of a one track mind." Sid looked down then back at me.

28

"Sorry Faustus but Ti still wants to see you, even if I have to pick you up and carry you."

Pete was beginning to look irritated. "We have to find Dog Mr. E.M Faustus."

"Look Sid," I picked up my hat and rammed it back onto my head. "I need to go and see Peter. We can call in on Ti after, OK? You can come with us as an 'escort'."

Sid considered this for about a second. It was the perfect get out for him. Admittedly I would have to see Ti, never pleasant, but I could avoid a run in with Sid.

"Fair enough mate. Mind if I change into something more comfortable?"

Without waiting for permission Sid was a Duck again. He flexed his wing and looked up at Pete. "This feels pretty good. Thanks son."

Pete looked down becoming more annoyed by the second. Good.

"I am not you're son. We have to go now and find Dog. Let us go." Pete headed for the stairs.

"Very blinkered." said Sid. "What's his story Faustus?"

"Peter sent him. They want me to find…"

"A dog?" Sid was always a good guesser.

"His Dog. Must be some Dog."

"Got a picture?"

I showed him the photograph.

"Not seen it around, but I'll keep an eye open and ask the lads to watch out for him."

The Duck patrol. Useful to have when you need some eyes on the water.

"Thanks Sid. Appreciate that. Are we OK?"

"We're OK Faustus. Things got a little bit hectic for a minute but your friend seems to have sorted it, so no harm done."

I could relax with that. Pete stopped half way down the stairs ready to explode. "Are your coming or not?"

Sid looked out at me and stretched his wings imploringly.

"Carry?" he said.

I picked up Sid (Stairs and Ducks don't go well together) walked down the stairs and onto The Streets.

"Bloody Hell Sid. You're putting on weight."

Ω

Excerpt from
Angels, Daemons and other realm beings.
By E.M Faustus
(unpub)

The Streets:

After Bram Stoker published 'Dracula' in 1895 it became open season on any and every Other World person. You could even buy a Vampire Defense Kit in the more fashionable London Stores if you were travelling in Europe. Not just Vampires, but werewolves elves, fairies and even little old ladies who lived on their own, happened to own a cat and were not right in the head, were subject not just to persecution, but a stake through the heart and their heads lopped off.

At the Annual Accord of 1901 a solution was proposed by Lady Simone de Malsaunte. "We all live together".

This idea was unthinkable at the time. No one trusted anyone else. There were feuds between families and species that had gone on for generations. In many cases no one knew what had started them. But good old Simone was a very persuasive lady. She worked for a year on getting everyone onboard. Negotiation, argument, bribery and the occasional tactful assassination got everyone to agree to a trial period.

The richer families invested in property in every city. Big buildings, small buildings, plots of land, and families relocated from the country where they thought they were safe on their own, into the cities where they watched each other's backs. Slowly families grew and spread out from the centre so that within ten years a large percentage of other world people became urbanites.

The Streets all interconnect. You can cross from one side of a city to another without entering the 'Human' world, and people all get on. Sort of.

This is where I work.

Not perfect, but it works.

Ω

Walking down The Streets with an Angel/Daemon thing and a Duck is a bit disconcerting. Pete was getting a lot of glances and stares. He was a stranger and looked 'wrong'. On the other hand people kept walking past us while saying hello to Sid. His duck shape was making matters worse because every time we passed a reflective surface he could not help but stop for a moment or two to admire himself and preen.

I was not getting paid enough for this. Come to think of it I was getting no payment at all. Yet.

I also had a date tonight. I wanted to figure out where to go and what to wear. Not spend the time arguing and Dog hunting. Peter was going to have some explaining to do.

And then we were there.

Chapter Four: The Dick and The Dodderer

People called it 'The Junk Shop'or 'Peters'. The sign above the door was so faded that it was illegible now, but the shingle that hung from the L-bracket above the door was very clear in both advertising and warning;

Temptation allowed, so long as you are good Boys and Girls.

That shingle had led to the humans who shopped there calling the place 'Temptations', which really irritated Peter. Mind you in twenty years he still has to tell me the original name of the place.

Set in the middle of a busy shopping street, looking out of place amongst the plate glass, bright light and brighter window displays, the shop sits double fronted and dusty, it's surprising how many people don't notice it. Two enormous windows with Georgian Bar framework. The windows show everything from bicycles to rocking horses. Vases to buckets. Mirrors to medals. Each one of them came from somewhere, someone, something, and each had its own story behind it. Sometimes they were not pleasant stories.

The shop drew people to it. Some came because they needed a thing they could not get anywhere else, and for the price of the time it took to rummage around it and a few pounds they could have it. They got what they needed. Some came because they did not know what they needed, but in the shop they could find it. It would help them. They got what they needed. They often came back.

Some came because they needed a lesson but did not know it.

They got what they needed.

They never came back.

Peter's pricing structure was eclectic. He always knew what you could afford to part with. That is what you paid. That was for good boys and girls.

If you were Naughty, you always paid more than you could afford.

"Faustus?"

I turned to Sid who was looking around the street to see if anyone could see him.

"Do you mind if I stay outside? Wouldn't do my credentials any good at all if I went in there."

"Not a problem Sid. I love the man but sometimes I worry about going in here."

I turned the handle and was pushed to one side as Pete rushed in.

"Peter." he called. "Peter. Mr. EM Faustus is here. He wants to see you before he will look for Dog. I think he is being silly."

I walked into the shop, shaking my head.

The first impression you get when you walk in is that of gloom. The light from outside is slowly filtered by the carefully dusty windows. Then the light has to get past the varied webs of gossamer that frame the inside. It needs to be very brave light to brave Peter's shop. A row of carefully off-kilter light bulbs dotted around the ceiling, their low energy light bulbs actually seemed to make the room darker.

I was not looking forward to this. Peter was forever picking up strays, pointing these strays in the right direction to put their lives back on track. Advice, support and guidance to help you get your

life right again. Often he gave you a thing.
Something from the shop to remind you of who you
really were and what your life was about.

Strays like Pete.

Strays like Sid.

Strays like me.

Eighteen and drunk in an alley.

Eighteen and angry at the world.

Eighteen and angry at being able to see what I
could see.

Eighteen and a drunk.

A drunk since I was fifteen and found the best way
to mask teenage angst was to get too drunk to stand.
Left home at sixteen because I couldn't bear to hurt
my parents anymore. More like I Was a self-pitying,
self -obsessed arse. Living rough for two years.

Drunk, thief and thug.

Hard to tell where the emphasis was.

Peter found me when he was taking out his rubbish
one night, and he took in me and my rubbish.

He gave me a job, a place to live, did some strong
talking to me and applied a little reinforcement, via a
clip round the ear. He even applied my natural
cynical, nosey nature to the job of Private Eye. Only
one on The Streets, only human on The Street as
well. All thanks to Peter.

He gave me sanity and focus.

He also gave me a Trilby. Every Private Eye
should have one.

Thank you Peter.

"Peter, what the Hells do you think you're
playing at? Does my office look like the bloody
RSPCA?" I shouted.

"The problem with being the local good guy is that people will come to you for help EM. Pass me that brush will you?"

A heavy Scottish accent attached to a thin man, thin spectacles and a thick cardigan rose from behind a chest of drawers. Cloth in one hand, curious foul smelling bottle in the other.

"What do you think?" Peter gestured to the drawers, taking the brush from my hand and giving the drawers a light dusting. It was certainly old. Possibly 17th Century. But what would I know. "I have been told it belonged to the Marquis de Sade." Peter looked around distracted. "I've got his skull around here somewhere. Used it as a door stop last time I fumigated. I thought I should keep hold of this one for a bit. Imagine the stories it could tell us, eh!"

I ran my hand over the drawers. It felt cold and clammy. That could have been the sealer Peter had just put on of course. "I don't think I'd want to know anything this could say. Are those nail marks? Near the back there?"

"Oh yes. There are some teeth marks on the front as well."

And this is not the oddest thing Peter has.

Pete held up the brush in front of him and looked at it. It looked like an old battered shaving brush.

"Belongs to Richard Dadd you know." Peter said. "Used for dusting his brushes prior to painting. Mad as they come."

"I need to talk about him." I nodded my head towards Pete.

Pete put his hand gently on my shoulder. "I am here Mr. Faustus. If it hurries you up I will go and make some tea."

Without another word Pete walked through into the back room.

"Coffee. Black. Strong." I called after him. I turned to Peter. "What the Hells is He Peter?"

Peter took a deep breath. "I have no idea Faustus. I found him. Out in the alley eating from a thrown away fish and chip wrapper. He was even trying to eat the wrapper! Stark naked. He was feeding the best of the rubbish to his Dog." Peter walked over to an overstuffed chesterfield and sat down. He patted the seat next to him and I joined him. "He couldn't even speak any language when I took him in. Only grunt. I had to teach him to talk from scratch."

"I'm surprised he doesn't have a Scottish accent." I said.

"Not only no accent, he now seems to be able to speak any language to anyone." Pete let out a deep sigh. "He learns very fast. I know roughly what he is Faustus. Part Daemon, but part Angel. That's all. And all wrong. He is capable of who knows what, and I'm not sure that I want to find out. The trouble is that he is so…nice. He is devoid of the darkness and loneliness Daemons have, but also void of the supercilious nature of Angels.

"He wants me to find his Dog Peter. That's ridiculous." I rubbed my temples with stress.

"Why?"

"I don't find animals Peter. There are agencies for that, charities."

"Not for the people on The Streets there isn't. Faustus, your being an arse." I began to turn towards him, but Peter put his hand gently on my shoulder. "No. Listen. The last few years you have done well. You have made a decent business for

37

yourself and gained some important clients amongst Street people. You see what no other human, well save the odd one that's been burnt at the stake or locked in a mad house, has ever seen. You accept us all as we are now that you know and understand us. You see that we just want to be normal."

Then he hit me with the palm of his hand across the back of my head. After all these years it still hurt.

"Yet you are still narrow minded, bigotted towards Fae and The Angelic, fallen or not. Sometimes they are not plotting The Last Days. Sometimes they don't want to possess or tempt. They just want a cuppa and a bacon sandwich. Sometimes they just need one of their kind found. Sometimes they just need their dog, who seems to have saved them from themselves, found. You think you are something special…"

I did try to protest but the hand was applied again, possibly with a bit more force than needed.

"You do. You are developing an arrogance my boy. You think you are special, because you are." Peter put his arm around my shoulder. After all these years it was a new side to him. "I love you like a son, my boy, but you need to realize the truth. You stopped drinking and self-medicating. Probably. Good. Now it's time to accept that you are starting to be a prick. Time to stop being a prick. Rules are to be broken sometimes and you need to keep that in mind."

"Peter, I will not work for someone who is looking to put others at risk."

"I'm not asking you to, but you compartmentalize your life son. Your only let out is Film night and That Band, where anyone can attend. There you get you, me, vampires, djin, fairies, even Ti. Good God man. Even Stan comes to film night."

"As he pointed out more than once he did have a hand in writing some of them."
We both took a moment to think then both at once said,

"Home Alone and The Sound of Music." You have to know Stan to understand.

"I… I am asking you Faustus to take on this case. It is one you don't want I know, but as a favor to me and yourself, take this case. Find Pete's Dog and…"

"Now comes your agenda."

"I can hit you again Faustus if you like. For me. Find out who he is, if you can."

"You like him."

"Yes son. He reminds me of you. How could I not like him?"

"Except he's not an arsehole."

"Exactly."

I thought for a moment. I really did not like Pete. He was 'wrong'. All over 'wrong'. Yet I loved Peter like a second father. He saved me…and he could slap like a bull seal. I couldn't help but smile.

"You blackmailing sonofabitch. I'll do it. But you're the client, which means there's a fee."

"Oh that is naughty Faustus. I'm just a poor old man. I have such a small pension. I am disabled."

To his credit Peter did try to look just that, but I knew him too well. I simply sat and stared at him.

"How much?"

"Ten pound. It's a retainer. That means You are officially my client and I can't divulge anything about you or the case to any one. Clients rights and client confidentiality."

"Sneaky. I like it and oh look." Peter reached into the pocket of his cardigan and pulled out a bright crisp Ten pound note. "It was just the figure I had thought of."

I took the tenner from him and made a show of inspecting it against the light then quickly rammed it into my pocket.

"Coffee." Pete said. "The sooner you drink, the quicker we find Dog."

A small cup of black coffee was shoved into my hand. Peter and I both turned to see Pete holding a tray. It was Peter's favorite tray. The one with Prince Charles and Lady Diana Spencer on it, pre-wedding. Pete had arranged three cups and saucers on it with a silver sugar bowl, silver milk jug and a small cut glass bowl holding three silver spoons.

"Coffee. You can drink it." Pete nodded his head towards the cup he had pushed into my hand. The cup steamed with malicious intent.
I sipped it.

It was good.

It was damn good.

It was angelically good.

It was the best cup of coffee I had ever had in my life.

"What kind of coffee is this? It's great." I turned to Peter. "Have you started buying the good stuff?"

"It comes from a jar Mr. Faustus. It is called Kendo or some such."

I stared at my cup. This was wrong. The coffee was wrong. It was too good. I had not drunk instant coffee for five years. I felt strangely dirty. Erotically dirty. I looked at Peter.

"I think I hate this man." I smiled, but there was more than a little truth in it.

"Only for now Faustus. Only for now." Peter took his cup from the tray and sipped it. "He does make really good coffee."

Pete looked between the two of us. "Is it sorted between the two of you now? Can we go and look for Dog?"

I gave Peter the barest of nods then downed the coffee, more out of spite than enjoyment. I picked up my hat.

"I'll start pounding the streets and the animal centers."

"I shall try not to get in the way of your investigation." Pete said, putting down his cup, half drunk.

Philistine.

"Well I'll be in touch if I find out…" I started.

"No need. I will come with you."

For the third time that day I reeled. This was beginning to be a bad habit.

"No way."

Peter took my arm by the elbow.

"You should take him Faustus. You need him. Really you do." Peter looked at me with deep meaning and hidden communication in his eyes. I just wish I knew what he meant.

"Do I get any choice in this at all?"

"Not really son. Now be off with both of you."

Peter looked at me with a smirk barely concealed on his face. Pete looked at me with puppy dog pleading. I took a deep breath.

"You come with me and do what I say when I say it. We won't spend all of the time looking for your mutt. Understand that now. I finish work today at six. I have a date. No discussion. Understood?"

Pete nodded his head, "Understood."

41

"Come on then." I rammed my hat onto my head and walked to the door. I turned to say goodbye to Peter and Pete was hugging him goodbye.

"I will see you later and I'll bring Dog back with me. I am sure everything you told me about Mr. Faustus is true. He seems like a really nice man…underneath."

Oh for Gods sakes.

I took Pete carefully by the elbow and led him towards the door.

"Come on you. Time to go a hunting."

I took a smoke out and shoved it into my mouth.

"Light me." I said.

Pete looked at me as if I was insane, so I lit myself.

As we got to the door it opened and two men walked in. One was your average vampire heavy, tall enough, thin enough and muscular enough to pass off as impressive in the right situation, but he let it down with his clothes. Black soft leather shoes, black satin trousers, and a thin black cashmere turtle neck. All designed to help him creep up without making a noise. The jet black sunglasses and black beret were a bit much though. He had color to his cheeks as well. That meant he was a blood feeder. He fed on live blood - willing or not - it still raised my hackles.

The other man though was the problem.

Vampires are easy enough to deal with if you have faith. It is that simple.

The other man was human.

That was unusual. An average human with a vampire was either food or a hunter.

This man was in charge. In eighteen years I had never seen that before. Vampires are used to being in charge. They don't like the food to answer back.

And I was on a date with one tonight.

"So, Mr. EM Faustus. I have to admit I have looked forward to meeting you. You're shorter than I thought you'd be though. People talk like you're a giant of a man."

He was a giant of a man. He had to be six foot six at least. I'm five nine (and a bit), but this guy towered over me and took great delight in looking down on me. He was dressed in functional clothes. Grey suit, white shirt and blue tie. Nothing unusual bar his size. And his shoes. Not only did they look like canoes, but the edge of the soles were rimmed with metal.

This man liked to kick.

"I believe you know my friend here." His accent was European. At a guess, French 'something'. Around that area.

He gestured to the vampire. I took a closer look.

"You knocked my teethh out with a metal bar four yearth ago." The vampire lisped.

I could not help but smile. I remembered him now.

"I didn't like your choice from the menu." I said. "Nice teeth. Lisper."

"Thhey grew back nithe." The vampire bared his teeth to show me a full set of teeth, close up. He had sharp pointed incisors.

Ω

**Excerpt from
Angels, Daemons and other realm beings.**

By E.M Faustus
(unpub)

Vampire Teeth.

It is not like the films. Vampires do not have pointed incisors. Well, not normally. They have normal teeth, same as everyone. Biologically they are the same as humans, but with a severe need for additional life force. Those who choose to feed on blood, (Thankfully there are very few of them, mainly the Old Ones and gang-bangers) tend to use a razor blade to open a victim up then drink from the wound. Those who use their teeth tend to get messy.

They take great care of their teeth because they tend to be tender. A punch in the mouth to a vampire is like any human being kicked in the crotch. It hurts.

A lot.

Ω

"Bollocks. They're dentures." I said. "Nice lisp, Lisper."

"I could demonth…"

Before Lisper could finish The Big Man put a hand on his chest and pushed him back.

"Mr. Faustus. As I said, I am delighted to meet you. You are a bit of a legend. My name is Cadell. Pleased to meet you." He extended his hand. I ignored it. While I didn't like Pete much, I really disliked this fella.

"Well you know my name. Why are you here? Looking to improve your social circle?"

"Funny." Cadell smiled with a total lack of humor. "No. Just out shopping. Thought I might find something unusual in here. I think I will browse a while."

Cadell picked up an old glass bottle from the window shelf. It looked too comfortable in his hand. He held it too much like a weapon for my liking.

"Good place for the unusual." I said.

"Mr. Faustus. We should go." Pete tapped me repeatedly on the shoulder with his finger. Though it was irritating I had no plans to take my eyes from Cadell - or the bottle. Cadell didn't worry about taking his eyes from me though. I felt vaguely insulted.

"And who have we here? An interesting individual to be sure." He again held his hand out, this time to Pete. "The name is Cadell, and you?"

"He's just leaving sir. No bother to you." Peter came forward and held out his hand. Cadell took it and shook it. He made the mistake of trying to squeeze Peter's hand. Pointless. As I watched the tendons strain on Cadell's hand I knew he was onto a loser. Peter had spent too many years hauling furniture, crates and sculptures around. That combined with opening jars of those pickled eggs he likes so much, had given him muscles like an elephants.

"A strong grip. I like that sir." Cadell let go of Peter's hand and slowly massaged life back into his fingers.

"How can I help you?" Peter asked him.

"Oh, just browsing." Cadell gestured to Lisper and they began to wander around the shop. Pete put his hand on Peter's shoulder.

"Would you like us to stay?" He asked. Genuine concern for the old man was on his face.

"No son. I shall be fine. Now you go and find Dog. Look smart now and I'll see you later." He patted Pete on the shoulder and guided him out the door. He looked meaningfully at me. "Take care of him Faustus."

"I will old man." I gave him a quick peck on the forehead.

"Faustus.!" Pete called.

Cadell was standing holding a skull. He eyed it carefully.

"Nice piece this. Marquis de Sade. I'll take it." He casually tossed it to Lisper. "Faustus, I hear you're going on holiday. Good to hear. A man as busy in the community as you should take time out to have a break every now and then. Does him good to take two or three weeks away. Leave his worries and work behind."

Peter put his hand on my chest. He had never seen this side of my work. I do get warned off a case every now and then. It happens.

"Well I did think of a fortnight in Florida, but a case came up and it just seemed to need my attention so I put it off for a while." I eyed Cadell as he played with a sacrificial druidic stone knife. "I didn't catch who you worked for Mr. Cadell. You could give them my regards."

Cadell laid the knife down and picked up a blood bowl.

"Oh me? I'm an independent Mr. Faustus. Just killing some time. By the way what does the EM stand for? No one seems to know."

The name. Always with the name.

"Just EM. Like TS Garp."

"TS Garp?" He didn't get it and immediately moved further down my shit list.

46

"Famous writer. Mother more so, but I prefer TS's work."

"Oh." He smiled. "Never mind. Nothing wrong with affectation."

It was crossing my mind to hit him. Just out of principal. Instead I turned back to Peter. "See you later Old Man." I looked at Cadell. "I'm sure I'll see you around too Mr. Cadell, and Lisper." Lisper sneered. I have to admit the teeth helped him there. "Lisper, don't forget to floss now."

"Don't forget your duck Sir." Cadell called.

I turned and walked out, not a happy bunny. Plus he got the last word.

Bugger.

Outside Sid was ready for a fight. But then again he always is.

"Big guy looked easy enough. Recon I could take him?" Sid was looking up at me from the door way. We set off walking towards Ti's office.

"Depends on the body you use. Catch the shoes?"

"Too right."

"What was wrong with his shoes?" Pete asked, falling in step behind us. Sid looked at him with a degree of disgust on his face. Mind you it could have been lust. What do I know? He's a duck.

"You couldn't see the silver and iron rim?" Sid said. Definite disgust in his voice. Around The Streets you recognized dangerous metals quickly.

"I saw his shoes. Are they a problem?" Pete said.

Oh to be so naïve.

"The man is a kicker. He likes to kick things." I said making with a fresh smoke.

47

"People mostly." Sid piped in.

I had to grab him before he ran back to the shop.

"Let me go. Peter could get hurt." Pete snapped.

I had to struggle to hold him. He didn't look it, but this guy was as strong as a bull. As strong as Sid. Then I knew I had made a mistake.

He threw me off.

Fortunately a car was there to break my fall.

Unfortunately the car was a good ten feet away.

Fortunately, unconsciousness helped me to ignore the pain.

Unfortunately I was not around for what happened next.

Coffee. I wanted coffee.

And a smoke.

Not reality.

"He hit him."

I was awake, sitting against a lamppost and holding a cup of excellent coffee.

"Yep." If a duck could smile, Sid was smiling.

Pete stood next to the car apologizing to the driver, but as the driver had seen the throw, he was not keen on making a big deal of it.

"Was it hard?" I asked.

"I heard it from where I was." Sid said.

"Where was that Sid?"

"Right here. I didn't want to leave you alone."

The car owner drove off with a large fold of cash in his pocket. Pete came over to me.

"I am sorry Mr. Faustus. I truly am. I thought Mr. Peter was in danger from Mr. Cadell."

He did look very sorry. Very ashamed. Upset.

Good.

I used the lamp-post to raise myself to my feet. My back and head hurt, but my pride was more bruised than anything. My hand rose and rested on his shoulder.

"Pete. Let's make things better between us. We should sort this out before it damages our burgeoning relationship. Lend me one of your shoes." I said.

"Faustus!" Sid piped up, but I grabbed his beak and he simply spluttered. Pete, with his confused face, bent over and removed his right shoe. He passed it to me heel first. I reversed it so I held it by the toes. I gently pinched the bridge of his nose.

"Ow."

"You felt that? I asked.

"Yes. It was uncomfortable." He sounded confused.

"I just had to be sure."

I felt the sole of the shoe. It was soft enough. I didn't feel bad therefore when I hit him on the head with it.

Several times.

He didn't really react apart from look at the shoe in my hand. I handed him the shoe and he bent over to put it back on.

"Do you feel better now Mr. Faustus? Pete asked as he tied his laces.

I dusted off my jacket and shot my cuffs.

"Great." I said. "Now listen boy." I jabbed him in the chest with my finger and nearly broke it. "Peter is more than capable of taking care of himself. If Cadell worried him he wouldn't have got into the shop, let alone lay a finger on him. If He had needed your help He would have asked for it. You're lucky to have got away with a slap on the head." I took a deep breath "Now, let's go see Ti...and keep an eye out for Dog on the way."

I hate dealing with The Fae.

Chapter Five: The Dick and The Doldrum

We arrived at Ti's building about thirty minutes later. The walk was only about five minutes from Peter's shop but Pete ended up checking every alleyway, and people kept stopping to talk to Sid. Then Sid got the bug for alley searching and we ended up with three rugs, a couple of stuffed toy dogs, rank with rain and mold, and a street sleeper who got a surprise and a half when woken by a scruffy beanpole and a talking duck.

And then we were at Ti's.

Ti's building redefines Gothic architecture.

Ti's office was in an old deconsecrated church. She liked the atmosphere. Ti is big on atmosphere.

She had built onto the church, putting extra, ornate carvings above the doorway. Small and intricate. And judging by what the various men, women, animals and yourguessisasgoodasmine were doing with and to each other, were not appropriate subject matter for a Church. I spent too long looking at these carvings once and came away feeling dirty and with a distinct itch behind the eyes.

And a need for a bag of Sherbet Lemons.

There were twelve great stone steps leading up to two deep oak wooden doors. Set into one of these doors was a smaller door, just big enough to admit one person at a time. Given who could pass through these doors I suspect the big ones get opened sometimes as well.

I walked up the first three steps, Pete one step behind me. Not looking happy at all.

"Faustus!"

I turned around. Sid was still standing at the foot of the steps, holding his wings out in an exasperated manner. Sid always had problems with stairs and steps.

"Carry?"

I turned to Pete. Probably with an evil grin on my face. "Pete. Get the duck."

I trotted up the rest of the steps, with a bounce in my steps. Behind me I heard a lot of grunts and groans.

"You're a duck. How heavy can you weigh?"

"Thirty six stone. I'm big boned"

"You are a duck. You cannot be this heavy."

"Don't drop me. Thank you. I can't help my weight. Different shape same weight. Cannae change the laws of physics."

"Why the strange accent for that last thing you said?"

"Ye Gods. You do know bugger all, don't you?"

At the top of the steps I turned around. Pete had Sid draped across his back and was struggling up the steps. Well, he might be fast and strong, but it appears even he has limits. I turned back and knocked on the big oak door. As was the custom with doors like this, the sound echoed.
The smaller entrance in the big door slowly swung open, creaking with the obligatory groan. I know the handyman worked for days to get that creak just right.

Ah well. Time to enter the world of The Fae.

Ω

**Excerpt from
Angels, Daemons and other realm beings.**

The Fae.

The Fae posed a real problem for Lady Simone de Malsaunte. While almost all of the other people from The Other Life saw sense in The Streets, the Fae believed (and still do) that they could do what they want when they want with no accountability. They felt they had more of a right to this world than the apes that dwelt on its surface. It was their plaything. People; toys to amuse themselves.

Understand that The Fae are totally inhuman.

They are humanoid in shape, but can change it at will. They are cruel, heartless and devoid of morals. They control their actions purely by good manners.

Their manners. Their rules.

They exert a 'glamour' over humans and non-humans alike, projecting a picture to them of beauty.

They are not beautiful.

They project a feeling of desire to humans and non-humans alike, making them desirable.

They are not desirable.

If confronted by one of the fair folk…Do Not Run. They like the hunt.

Lady de Malsaunte extorted from the Fae a contract that would prohibit their acting within the human world and The Streets, without the courtesy of informing the local ruling body.

This, given the lazy nature of the Fae, meant that they could rarely be bothered to inform anyone. Their bounds of courtesy meant that they would not act without informing, so they rarely bothered.

A simple catch.

In return the Fae were granted properties on The Streets for free. A simple entrance to the 'real' world...

Ω

Inside the doorway it was gloomy enough to make me take a second to adjust my eyes. Pete struggled through behind me, placing Sid on the ground. A figure stepped out of the shadows.

"Thank you Sire. May I fetch you a drink to slake your thirst after your great exertions?" the male voice asked.

Pete opened his mouth, but I leapt in. "No. He wants nothing. Shame on you Reese."

Electric light flickered on, revealing an eight foot tall Centaur. He looked at my hands and stretched out his.

"Good to see you again Faustus. I had thought time would have taken you. I am glad it has not."

I nodded to the pile of straw in the corner.

"New sofa?" I asked.

"Now you behave F. No need to be the hard case around friends."

The new voice came from behind me. A dark sultry voice. It always makes me melt. Well, not all of me.

There she was. First girlfriends you never forget. Kat.

Five five in her bare feet, with a mane of red metallic hair down to her waist. Well, best to think of it as hair. Wearing a typical pinstriped business suit to conceal her slim figure, and a piece under her left arm by the look of it.

Ray bans shrouded her eyes as always.

"Hi there Kitten."

She came towards me and threw her arms around me, damn near squeezing the breath out of me. Her hair wrapped itself around me too, hugging just as tight. I guess it was pleased to see me too.

"What's the skinny on The Street F?" she asked

"SameO SameO Kitten. How have you been?"

She gestured behind herself to a camp bed opposite Reese's pile of straw. Spartan, but nice to see she was still using the Kitten cup I had bought her for her 21st. I nodded my head.

"Your manners have still to improve. No introductions?" Kat gestured to Pete.

"This is Pete. Has no second name yet. He lives with Peter." Still holding Kitten's hand I turned to Pete. "This is The Lady Christina. Call her Kitten and I will possibly tear your head off."

She hit me. People were doing that alot today. Good job it was playful.

"Pay no attention to F, Pete. I am charmed to meet you. Any friend of F's and Peter's is a friend of mine. Call me Kat. This gentleman is named Reese."

Reese took a low, theatrical bow.

"Any friend, likewise." He boomed. "You are here to see my Lady." A statement not a question. He held open the door that led to the interior of the Church.

I thought it appropriate to fill Pete in before we stepped inside. Peter would kill me if I let him get goosed.

"Pete. Before we go in, and you can wait here if you want, you should know a couple of things."

"I will come with you Mr. Faustus. Someone might know about Dog."

55

"Your choice. One, do not talk to anyone. Two, accept nothing from anyone. Even if someone trips you up and offers to help you to your feet. Accept nothing. Talk to no one. Three. Ask no one about Dog. Leave it all to me. Try not to look at anything." Then I remembered the potential for WAR. "Do you have anything on you made out of Iron? Sorry Reese."

Reese flinched at the mere mention of the word. Someone had shod him with iron nails a few years ago. If I hadn't got them out he could have died. He is still a little lame in his hind quarters. Must be why Ti has him doing guard duty.

"Careful with the "I" word there Faustus."

Sid cleared his throat. Hard when you're a duck.

"I will leave you now Faustus. I have delivered you to My Lady's care and benevolence." Sid shot a glance at the door to the church interior. He had no desire to go back in there. Couldn't be easy for him. I played the game and bowed low to him, sliding my hat off my head with one wide sweep.

"I thank you for your care and guidance Lord of Water and Air."

Sid bowed back. I tapped Pete with my hat.

"Oh yes. Thank you." Pete reached out his hand to shake 'hands' with Sid. I pushed his arm down.

"Bad manners." I stood up and turned to Kat. "Ring me and we'll catch up."

"Got it right there F. See you later." Kat smiled. Then I remembered Mel. I checked my watch. 11.30 I put my hat back onto my head, straightened my tie and walked through the door.

Oh Shit!

Oh Buggeration, Bollocks and Shit.

Ah. Fuck.

The Tree.

She had brought the Tree here.

To My Town.

Bitch!

"Ooo. That is so Pretty." Pete said from behind me. I turned to see his head peering round the doorway. He folded himself forward and came in. He gazed in wonder at the tree. "Look at all those pretty people in the branches." A smile of wonder crossed his face. "Ah. Those children. Look at them swinging on those branches."

Another flaw. Pete was subject to The Glamour The Fae projected. On the street that could pose a problem. In here it could get him killed.

If he was lucky.

"Look again. Carefully." I said, gently as possible, because this was not going to be pleasant for him.

I knew what he could see. I had heard it spoken about often enough.

The Tree would be growing from the stone floor of the church. A good hundred foot tall, its branches would fill the space. Leaves, every green you could imagine would spring from the end of each branch. The Tree's bark would be smooth, a beautiful russet brown, with an occasional knot hole to be seen, where playful squirrels would dive in and out, tidying their nuts away. A soft mellow light would filter through the branches, making you believe in long spring evenings and warm summer nights. A lush green grass would stretch between the Tree's root base, inviting you to lie for a while.

In the branches, Fae would be lounging; children would be playing, carving their names into the bark with silver blades.

57

So pretty an image. So Lovely and natural.
So glamorous.
Fae Glamour.
In reality The Tree is a deformed Oak.
Twisted.
Rotten.
Foul.
Parasitic.
Eternal.
Wrong.
Charnel.
Very Wrong.
A Twisted, Rotten, Foul, Parasitic, Eternal, Wrong
Leech...

It projects a glamour that draws you in, makes you
feel like you want to lie down, back against its oak
and relax in the sun.

Then it grips you.

Holds you.

Digests you.

Slowly.

It keeps you alive for years. Hundreds of years
while it slowly ingests your body.

Not your corpse.

You are alive the whole time you are being eaten.

You can't move, scream, fight. No escape. Only
slow digestion.

And that's not the worst of it.

Once it has you on the inside, ingested, your
consciousness remains. Aware and sane enough to
feel the fear and terror of never being able to escape.
Those lovers carving their names, that is not wood
they are cutting into.

It's flesh.

Those Children swinging on tree limbs?

Well they are limbs.

Those papery leaves. Skin between the branches.

They are not squirrels, and that's not nuts they're carrying.

Well…

Fae lie.

Fae deceive.

Fae are terrible.

Rule Five applies. Always.

"Oh no. We have to get them out." Pete began to walk towards The Tree. "We have to help them."

I grabbed him and spun him around. Fortunately he did not throw me off this time.

"We can't." I said as gently as I could. "They cannot be helped. I'm sorry Kid. If you go any nearer it'll take you too. Whatever you are, it is stronger. You can't help. Better than us have tried. Come on. Come with me."

I took him gently by the shoulder and led him towards the staircase leading to Ti's office. He looked back over his shoulder, tears running down his cheeks. He turned back to face me and used his balled fists to wipe the tears away. He looked so childlike and vulnerable at that moment I couldn't help but feel like a real bastard.

The alternative was to let him get lost.

No choice really.

Lounging in the stairwell were several nude Fae. Tall, muscular yet delicate they observed us with barely concealed amusement and disgust.

"EM Faustus." the one nearest us said. They all look the same to me. I recognized this streak of horse piss from the scar on his chest.

"Don't wear out the name Tkchll. I might need it later." I replied.

"Who is that delightful boy?" Tkchll nodded towards Pete. "Would you like to play a game delightful boy?"

The rest of the Fae giggled. I could feel them start to exude their glamour. They can't help it. Tkchll stood and stretched like a cat, stretching itself out after an hour resting in the sun. He ran his hands through his long dark curly hair, giving us a better view of his body. It was…unpleasant.

"I do not play games." Pete replied. He glanced back at the Tree. "Certainly not here."

Tkchll swaggered forward and ran a hand over Pete's cheek.

"I know some nice games delightful boy. We could have such fun."

I reached over and drew Tckhll's hand away. He let it fall to his side.

"Oh Faustus. You are no fun. We just want to play.."

"You know, you are the second person to try and brace me today. Believe me you're not even in the other guy's league." I reached into my inside jacket pocket and took out a packet of cigarettes and lighter. I put one between my lips and lit it. The reaction to the flame from the lighter was immediate. All of them drew back, except Tkchll. Give him credit. He had bottle.

"Put that out. Now." he said, both angry and fearful. Fae don't like fire.

"I thought you wanted to play." I said. "Playing my game now."

Oh dear. Tkchll smiled.

"If you don't want to play with us EM Faustus, then we can always find someone who will. Maybe the coffee woman would like to play our game."

60

OK. He pressed a button. I took the cigarette between my fingers and used the same hand to prod him in the chest. A mistake. Quick as a flash he had a silver knife pressed up against my throat.

"Or maybe the Old Junk Man would…urghh!

I didn't even see Pete's hand move. I smelled a rise in Pete's background odor of brimstone and he had Tkchll by the Adams apple and was squeezing.

"I do not like him Mr. Faustus. He makes threats that he may try to carry out. Should I crush his larynx? Do you think that would dissuade him?"

I shot a sideways glance at Pete. With no effort he had Tkchll lifted an inch from the ground. Tkchll was turning red. I pushed his knife away with my cigarette. Pete was looking at him with vague interest. Like you might have for a butterfly landing on the back of your hand. Tkchll looked duly scared.

The others however looked feral.

They rose to their feet and drew knives. Not threatening, just curious. So far. I tapped Pete on the shoulder.

"You know," I asked , "when I said don't talk to anyone? Don't touch anything, don't accept anything? Well it also extends to not picking a fight with armed men."

"He threatened us and our friends. Perhaps I should deal with him."

"Good point." I tapped Tkchll on the chest with the fingers holding the cigarette. Pointed the smoking end right next to his nipple. His chest tried to flinch away from the heat. "You might want to apologise. He's not big on self control like me. Earlier today I saw him lose it. Ripped a fella's lung out. Through his stomach. I found it hard to keep my breakfast down. He even showed it to him before he died. Made him wear it as a hat. Nasty boy."

Tkchll tried to nod, but he had limited movement. He was a lovely purple now.

"Drop the knife." I snapped.

He dropped the knife.

"Say you're sorry."

He mumbled "Thurrsss." Near enough. Not enunciated enough though.

"Do you know, " I stated, "He can be quite handy to have around. Strong as an ox. Quick as a mongoose. Now I'm not too shabby in a fight, but he's rather good. I think I'll ask him to let you go…"

"Do I get a say in this Mr Faustus?" Pete asked. I ignored him.

"Now, promise you'll behave like a good boy and not take any action against us or our friends and he won't pull your head off."

"That would be difficult from this position, but I am willing to try." It was the matter of fact way Pete said it that made a shiver go down my spine. It was becoming obvious that he was dangerous. I had begun to forget what he was.

Tkchll was drooling. He was also trying to nod. I gave in.

"Put him down."

"Gladly." Pete took me a little too much at my word. He put him down. Twenty feet away. I turned to the smiling group in the stairwell.

"Shift." They all moved to the edge of the stairwell, knives were beginning to slide back into the scabbards. "Come on." I began to walk up the

62

stairwell. The Fae moved to one side for me, but they flattened themselves against the wall for Pete.

The Fae don't frighten easily. They are hard to hurt, but Pete had achieved both.

That was bad.

Very bad.

At the top of the stairs was the minstrel gallery. Ti's office was off the gallery. Easy to find. It was the one with roses growing round the door. As custom dictates a knock followed by a long wait, I pushed the door open with one hand and walked straight in.

There she stood. Resting against her desk.

Veronica Bloody Lake.

Nice Tits.

Chapter Six: The Dick and The Divine

Not Veronica Lake, but as close as you can get,
But with larger breasts, nipples like bullets and legs
like a barber's scissors.

Ti loves glamour. She loves beauty. She loves the
movies. A regular at film night, her favorite film is
'Gone with the Wind." Always brings a tear to her
eye. She shifts her look frequently. Sometimes she
is Marilyn Monroe. Sometimes Elizabeth Taylor.

Today she was Veronica Lake. Famous Screen
Goddess of the Forties. Renowned for a blonde
hairstyle that hung over one eye. Damn she was hot.
I had to fight the urge to slacken my collar.

Ti always liked to meet me in film noir mode.
Hence Veronica Lake.
Ti was not my friend, but she and I were friends for
a certain measure of friendship. Makes sense to me.
I know her and know her well, but we are not
friends. We were just 'sort of friends'.

When she's not trying to kill me.

She was mad as a box of frogs. Dangerous as
sword swallowing with hay fever. Ruthless as a
horny dolphin.

I had to keep reminding myself what she was like
every time I met her. She was also as hot as a
volcano on the surface. The only Fae whose
glamour could cut through my control…apart from
one time. That one time I could never forget.

I wish I could.

The only time I saw her as she really was.

"Faustus. So lovely to see you again. Who is
your little homunculus?" Ti asked with a voice like
silk on an oiled straight razor.

"His name is Pete. He's a case I'm working. What's that fucking Tree doing here? It breeches every rule and you know it."

"An answer will cost you Faustus. So far you have nothing to bargain with." Still silk and oiled steel. Damn, it was getting hot in here.

"Hello Miss. My name is Pete." He strode forward and held his hand out to her. She looked at it as if she'd just found pubic lice.

"Do you like that hand homunculus?" she asked. I hated him more for not having any reaction.

"Well, out of the two, it is the one I prefer. Yes." Ah. Back to bemused.

"Then remove it before I rip it off." She beamed a smile as she said it.

Pete lowered his hand and surprised me by bowing. " I meant no offence your Majesty. I am unfamiliar with your customs. It is an offence that will not occur again."

Ti ran her index finger down Pete's face. Curiously intimate for a predator. Here came the razor's edge.

"If I were offended Homunculus, you would now be wishing for death" She glanced at me. "I do not like that cigarette" she purred, pointing to the smoke I'd recently introduced to my lips.

"That's all right Ti." I responded taking a drag. "It likes you."

"When will you stop this flirting and sleep with me detective?"

"When will you stop this flirting and get to the point?"

Fortunately she laughed.

"Sit." She gestured to two chairs in front of her desk. Chairs that were not there when we walked in.

"Standing is just fine Ti." I said. "I spend a lot of time sitting. I need to keep my legs busy."

"As you wish Faustus." And the chairs were no longer there.

"You wanted to see me for something Ti." A statement. You don't ask her questions. The answers come at a price. Always.

"The Crown of Ursula has been taken. I want you to find it for me." She tossed her head, revealing a flawless face and neck.

"I don't work for Fae Ti. Ever."

A petulant pout stole to her lips. Tears welled up in her eyes. Nice try.

"Please Faustus. You know how important it is to me. You must find it. My world will come to an end without it."

Chapter Seven: The Dick and the Diadem

"Fourth case on the right, second row from bottom."

Chapter Eight: The Dick and the Devious

Ti smiled.

My feet twitched. I stopped them.

Something else twitched, but I stopped trying to control that years ago.

"Nonsense. The Crown has gone. You will find it." she spat. Ti's not used to people contradicting her. You can lose your tongue for disagreeing.

Hell, you can lose more than that for blinking at the light when she sets you on fire. But Health and Safety rules won't let her do that anymore. Not indoors at any rate.

"Open the vault Ti, if you want to prove you're right." I said. Pete put his hand on my inner elbow. I think he was becoming a bit worried by the confrontation in my voice. He needed to be. They don't come much more powerful than Ti. I wasn't so much poking a wasps nest as shoving it down the front of my trousers and inviting people to kick me hard in the nadgers.

Ti slid from the desk and walked over to the wall to my left. She never batted an eye, just kept on walking towards and then through the wall.

The wall that had always been there, but never been there now.

Ti's Vault.

A collection that had taken her forty years to gather together, and like any collector the collection and vault would just grow and grow. It stretched one hundred yards square. Glass case next to glass case. Shelf next to shelf. Simple wooden plinths holding various artefacts of great importance.

I knew one obsessive collector who had a collection of psychopathic memorabilia in cases like this.

He had ropes, knives, gags, photographs, even death masks. From somewhere he had even gotten hold of one of the original Jack the Ripper letters.

I took great pleasure in passing him over to the right people. It might not have been illegal, but it was wrong. His collection was his reason for living. After it all burnt in mysterious circumstances he was a broken man.

Who says that fire Djin don't serve their community?

Ti had the same obsession. Hers was just more...Girlie.

I walked in with my shadow too close behind me, and on my right was the basket Judy Garland had carried Toto in.

My left, a sketch from Titanic. Ahead, a Marilyn Monroe dress. The room was filled with movie memorabilia. Ti was mad for films. Or maybe just mad.

The Crown of Ursula was a headband Ursula Andress wore in Dr No. No magic except it had been worn by a film star. Theft was a big worry for Ti, same as any obsessive collector. Problem was that Ti had so much, she was always misplacing things. Normally she didn't't call me to find them though.

We came to a stop at the case.
There it sat. A blue, faded headband on a stone head. The head looked remarkably like Ti.

Egotist.

"Hmm." Ti looked at the 'Crown' to hide her annoyance. "It has been returned by the thief. There is no need to remain. You may go Faustus."

"Nice to have been of service Ti." I said and decided to chance my luck. "Why the Tree Ti? It should not be in this realm and you know it."
She slowly turned to me. I was dancing with a nuclear whirlwind to ask her a question a second time.

"As you may have done me a favor I will tell you a little." She purred. "The Tree needs to be somewhere. At this moment in time it is here. When it is safe and prudent to move it on, so will it be. Now you may go."

Ti turned her back on us and gazed with wonder on her collection. She ran her hands over cases and gave a smile, not to us but to herself, in her own world. It was pointless to talk to her now. She had left us and everything else behind.

I took Pete's elbow again and led him away.

"But…" he began.

"Pointless asking her anything Pete." I said. "She's not in at the moment."

Chapter Nine: The Dick and The Debriefing

We left the church by way of a back door. Sid showed us out in silence. We passed by a few of the Fae who gave us a wide berth, or possibly it was just Pete they were avoiding. The business with Tkchll was unnerving them. I could stand that.

I reached inside my suit pocket and took out my tobacco and papers. I rolled one deftly, without even looking. I was more concerned with looking at the Angel/Daemon. Peter had saddled me with him and I didn't want to upset the old man, but things could have gone seriously wrong in there. He seemed a nice enough guy but Daemons could put up a good front. He knew his way around a punch up, but both Angels and Daemons were used to a good fight. It's genetic. This guy was trouble. Then he made matters worse.

"What were we being told in there?" he asked.

"No idea what you're talking about." I replied. That worried me. It was clear we were being warned, but I didn't think he would notice. I lit up, because I could.

"There was no need for us to be there Mr Faustus. We were being shown that the Fae are preparing for a fight."

"That's right." I said, taking a big draw. I was not happy revealing this. "They have 'gone to the mattresses'. The Fae are scared of something. Must be bad, otherwise Ti wouldn't have warned us."

"They won't be helping us?"

"No. They won't hinder us either. Ti won't come out until the fight."

"Then?"

71

"Then I will stay indoors with my head down. Possibly down the lavatory. You'll do the same if you have any sense. You made an enemy today. Any excuse to kill you and Tkchll will take it."

I saw no reason to dress it up. Tkchll will even avoid the oncoming fight to take care of Pete.

Oh well. I had only agreed to find the dog.

After that he was his own problem.

"Come on. Let's hit the dog sanctuaries."

One o'clock.

Three hours we walked, checking all of the dog shelters, dog sanctuaries, dog charities, dog homes, dog lovers and even the less savory restaurants, turning up nothing. Pete was getting more irate with every visit. Come the last takeaway I had to make him wait outside otherwise he could have caused a scene.

Well, we had exhausted the typical routes. Time to go back to basics.

"Where was it you saw Dog last?" I asked.

"In the alley behind Mr. Peter's shop." he replied with an uncommon jauntiness.

"OK then. Let's work it from there."

"So we go back to Peter's then."

"No. Just think back to that day. The last time you saw Dog."

Slightly unbelievably, Pete closed his eyes and lifted his head to the sky. Bit of a problem as we were standing in the middle of the Street. I guided him, eyes still shut to the wall of someone's garden.

"So was there anyone apart from Dog in the Alley?"

"Yes."

"Good. We're getting somewhere." I found myself getting excited. "Now, what do they look like? Were they male or female?"

"Male, Mr. Faustus."

"Tall?"

"Tall."

"Dark hair, light hair, no hair, covered in hair or scales?" This was The Streets after all.

"Dark hair."

"Was their body fat or thin?"

"Thin."

"What were they wearing?"

"Blue jeans and a nice warm jumper."

Bugger. Realization dawned.

"It was you, wasn't it?"

"Yes Mr. Faustus. I was there as well. I am always with Dog. Just in case I need to pick up a number two he may leave behind."

I let out a deep breath to maintain control and not kill him.

Didn't work, so I let out more till I got bored with hypoxia.

"Alright Pete." Round two begins, "Was there anyone else there? Apart from you. And Dog."

"Yes Mr Faustus."

"Tall?"

"Yes."

"Fat?"

"Thin."

"Hair?"

"Yes." Rules out Peter.

"Colour?"

"Blonde."

"Ugly or pretty?"

"Pretty."

"Wearing?"

"No Mr Faustus. I feel quite fresh."

It took a second or two to realise that he was not joking,

"No, you twonker. What was the man wearing?" I asked. Ye Gods. It was like interrogating a five year old. Only with less sense.

"Oh he was smartly dressed Mr. Faustus. A silver toned suit with a pale blue shirt. He had very nice shoes." He seemed quite proud of answering all my questions. As if he was in a school quiz and was getting all the answers right. Actually so far he was doing pretty well.

"What kind of shoes did he have? Were they flat heeled, like mine?" I lifted my foot so he could see. I didn't want any confusion.

"No. They had high heels. A slightly raised sole as well." He smiled. "He did say what a good boy Dog was. He left to go and buy some grapes for his poor white haired mother who is currently in hospital with a terminal illness. He is very kind to his mother. I even gave him some money so that he could buy her a bunch of flowers. Did I say something wrong Mr. Faustus?"

My mouth was open.

I know my mouth was open.

I could tell my mouth was open. Jaw didn't work that well, that's all.

"Jo-Jo Mar."

Jo-Jo Mar.

"Mother-fucking, bastard, shit bag, cock sucking son of a bitch…" I'm sorry, but I hadn't finished, "…fish shagging, clinge, tlacking bastard fucking Jo-Jo fucking Mar."

"You know him then?"

"A little."

I turned and started walking down the street. I was not a happy bunny.

Rarely am come to think of it

But now I was pissed off.

And walking fast. Pete scurried along behind me.

"Mr Faustus. I take it that we are going to ask him about Dog?" Idiot talking.

"Amongst other things." I managed through gritted teeth.

"It is just that you seem very angry, Mr Faustus." Pete managed. I was almost jogging now. "Is it a good time to try and question him when you are angry? You do seem to be personalizing a certain degree of anger towards this Jo Mar person."

I swung round at him. I jabbed him in the chest with my finger, a little harder than I intended. It hurt.

I rarely learn.

"Listen kid. Jo-Jo Mar is not a person. He's the sort of stuff that sticks to your shoe and won't scrape off." I may have been sounding a little aggressive. I'll admit it. "And as for being professional. Of course I'll be professional when I talk to him. I'll even remove my shoe from his mouth to let him talk back. OK?"

I made it back to the main Street in about five minutes and straight into Club Transco.

Chapter Ten: The Dick and The Dark

I promised myself I'd never go back there, but here I was back in the old place.

I'm sure they had forgotten all about it.

The insurance covered the damage, anyway.

In I walked.

"You're barred." A familiar Welsh baritone said. "As in, I said that I will hit you with a bar if you come back in here." The round deep voice said from the shadows. "Wait a few seconds till I get that bar I have with your name on it."

The Shade was serious. I was up for a kicking. I actually had this one coming.

"Hang on big man." I held out both hands, palms in front of me to show I was no threat. I really wasn't. "I just need some of Fatso's time. That's all. For old times' sake. What say Shadwell?"

"Just keep your arms out there. It makes it easier for me to get a clean break."

The bar came out of nowhere. I heard it rather than saw it. I dropped my hands and stepped back to avoid the second swipe that was aimed at my head. I'm so glad I did because if I hadn't, the bar would have took my head clean off. And I was so lucky. If I had not stepped back I would not have found Pete blocking the entrance.

The idiot was blocking my escape.

"Ooo. It is pretty in here." the Idiot said.

I was in no mood to appreciate the décor, (which had opted for the shiny since my last visit. Must have rebuilt it. Well, they had to really.), as the bar swung again. I rolled out of the way to the left. Straight into the second bar swinging from that side. Am I a lucky Faustus or what?

"Forgot to tell you I had two bars with your name on Faustus." Shadwell said. "Sorry. Think of it as two for the price of one if it helps."

Shadwell may be a disembodied spirit, but he at least has a sense of humour.

Ω

Excerpt from
Angels, Daemons and other realm beings.
By E.M Faustus
(unpub)

Disembodied Spirits

They hit like bastards.

Ω

The bar hit like a bastard and as my head snapped round I saw the second one coming in, aimed right at the bridge of my nose.

It stopped about two inches away.

My vision, already blurred, was blocked by Pete's back. He had caught the bar in his left hand and was blocking Shadwell's swing with his body.

"Please stop sir." he said. "This is wrong and I cannot…"

That was as far as he got. In one move Shadwell reached around him, lifted me from my feet and pinned me against the wall. Pete moved towards me but before he got more than two steps Shadwell grabbed him and threw him out the door. As a bouncer Shadwell has excellent aim for evicting people.

He was also superb at darts.

And babysitting. Go figure.

What I didn't expect was Pete to reappear in the doorway two or three seconds later. Normally when Shadwell throws you out you stay thrown. Yet there he was, arms down by his sides, the light from the outside world backlighting him.

Poser.

Problem was, he looked different. Taller. Wider. Muscular. Pissed off.

He walked towards Shadwell and I. A table flew out of his way with one backhand and landed on the DJ's stage.

That would cost me.

Teeth, probably.

I felt the wind from the punch rather than saw it. It scythed through the air and landed sweetly where Shadwell's head would be in the shadows. A blow that could knock a fist sized hole in the wall.

If Shadwell hadn't been made from the shadows it would have done some really serious damage.

"Is this guy serious?" Shadwell asked me. I felt his gaze on me. I tried to nod my head, but I did have limited movement, due to being a foot from the ground, grabbed by the throat and pinned against the wall.

Pete's punch turned into a neat backhand that was meant to distract, while his left came up in a lethal jab, just below Shadwell's probable rib cage.

All Pete managed to do was put himself a little off balance.

You try throwing two punches at once.

"Perfect." Shadwell said and grabbed Pete by the throat as well. The next second we were matching wall ornaments.

I am fairly sure that Pete threw me a glance that was filled with confusion, apology, regret and many more emotions, but I was so close to blacking out I didn't care. I delved my hand into my pocket and rummaged for my lighter.

Shadwell is a shadow being. He has no body. He relies upon the shadows to form a body he can use. As I saw him reach down with a third and fourth arm to pick up the two bars, I remembered he didn't have the typical humanoid shape either.

My hand closed around my lighter in my pocket and I dragged it out as quick as a torn pocket was allowing me. I flicked the flame alight and drew it along the 'wrist' of the hand that held me.

The shadow burned away under the light from the flame.

Shame the wrist was so thick, and the light so feeble that the shadow closed back an inch away from the burner.

"Please." Shadwell said with wounded pride. "You're putting up more of a fight than you should. Considering what you did."

I struggled to say something, but only succeeded in dribbling down my chin.

"Pardon?" Shadwell relaxed his grip a little and I managed one phrase.

"Jo-Jo Mar."

"Drop them Shadwell. For now."

The voice oozed over the clubs speakers like hot, liquid tar. From what I had heard it was just about as bad on the skin.

Shadwell obediently dropped us as a door opened in the wall at the rear of the club. I got to my feet rubbing my throat. I felt a good six inches taller. Fifteen point two centimeters if you're metric.

"Nice grip Shadwell." I croaked. "We really should get our little disagreement sorted out one day."

"Anytime Faustus." he rasped back.

"I must remember to bring my arc light." I moved quickly out of the shadows as I felt another slap on the head coming. I reached back and grabbed Pete, hauling him to his feet and towards the door. Shadwell dogged our footsteps. I couldn't hear, see or smell him, but a good Heavy keeps an eye on things. Shadwell was the best Heavy in the business.

"Is there anyone who likes you Mr. Faustus?" Pete gasped as we staggered on.

"Not many, but don't worry about Shadwell . He was only playing." I managed.

"Playing?" Pete squeaked. "That was playing? He almost pulled my head off. You would call that playing?"

"Didn't kill you, did I?" said a shadow an inch from Pete's ear.

And we walked on through the door into…the Seventies.

Chapter Eleven: The Dick and the Deviant

"Hmm. Pretty. Are all of its parts in working order Faustus?" The noxious liquid voice said. "It has been centuries since I deflowered one of his ilk."

The room was unbelievably tasteless. I don't often use the word festooned (I'm not even sure how to spell it), but the room was festooned with mirrors, painted to show men, women, animals, furniture, appliances and varied flora and fauna engaged in acts you couldn't even find on the internet.

Probably.

A giant kidney shaped, plastic and gold trimmed desk stood in the middle of the room. Psychedelic wall paper ran from the floor up to and over the ceiling. Large orange globe lights hung down lighting the room, but still gave plenty of scope for shadows. The biggest lava lamps I have ever seen stood dotted around the floor, dollops of multi coloured mucus rising and falling in an obscene manner.

Only Fatso could make an obscenity of lighting.

A large fur draped sofa sat opposite the desk. Fur also covered the working surface of the desk. I perched myself on the edge, drew out my smokes.

"Jo-Jo Mar is back in town." I said as I lit up. Pete sat down on the sofa. I should have warned him he could stick to it.

From behind the desk undulated the fattest man you could ever want not to see. Rolls of fat were concealed within rolls of fat crowbarred and corseted into a white linen suit. Around his neck a Ceres pink and gold cravat.

Never trust a cravat wearer. For it is the badge of evil.

"Really. Hard to believe he had the nerve to return." Fatso said. "There are so many people waiting to kill him." He sat on the sofa next to Pete and rested his hand on Pete's thigh. Never a slow worker. "You are such an unusual man dear boy, tell me, where do you hail from?"

"Can we keep our mind on Jo-Jo Mar Fatso? Ow!!" The slap on the head I was expecting came from the shadows. I glanced behind me with disapproval.

"Jo-Jo Mar will be found, sweet thing. Don't worry. Drinky?" This was addressed to a worried looking Pete. Fatso knew better than to offer one to me. I must have cost him a lot in repair bills.

"No. Thank you." Pete managed, staring at a fixed spot on the wall. Maybe I should have helped him. After all he did try to save me from a beating. But on the other hand I was on a ridiculous dog hunt, thanks to Peter.

I did what I do and lit a smoke.

"Hands off the client Fat Boy." I ducked and stepped into the light but felt the wind of the head slap miss by a fraction of an inch. I grabbed the orange globe light in front of me and shone it into the shadows. The shadows drew back away from the light. "And you can behave as well."

Light did not hurt Shadwell- no nervous system- but it did irritate.

Fatso removed his hand from Pete's thigh, slower than decorum should allow and turned his head to meet my eyes.

"Firstly young Faustus, I did not hear the boy object," he raised his hand to stop my reply, "and secondly, it is unwise to irritate Shadwell. You simply make his retaliation considerably more retaliatory."

"Firstly" I began, "he has a naivety you don't get to exploit, and secondly, I would not have trashed your bar in the first place if Jo-Jo Mar had not slipped a Mickey into my coffee. Thirdly, you're the best person to ask what the skinny is on dealers. You being low-life, drug dealing scum yourself. Let me know where you think he is, I'll take him a nice bunch of flowers and a fifty pence mix-up and we have a little question and answer time, just before I kick his teeth in."

"And fourthly," Pete said, "If you touch my leg again with the sexual intent you are expressing, I will hurt you."

I was shocked. I heard the most controlled threat come out of his mouth. Courtesy of Shadwell I was seeing another side to the guy. With Peter and the Dog he was loving and caring. Concerned about their welfare. Even Jo-Jo Mar got a degree of sympathy from him. Shadwell hurt him and if he'd been humanoid could have got a slap for it. Now, here he was threatening Fatso.

Suicidal, even for an Angel/Daemon/thing.

Not clever to mess with Gods.

Ω

Excerpt from
Angels, Daemons and other realm beings.
By E.M Faustus
(unpub)

Gods

Bastards.

Gods are funny things. They only exist if you believe in them. Bit like Tinkerbelle, but you don't have to clap your hands.

Gods are because people believe in Gods. Without the belief they stop existing. They fade away as belief fades.

They are amorphous personifications.

Problem is that because they come from the faith and belief of people, they come from the minds of individuals with personalities. If you are a vengeful and warlike culture you generate warrior gods. If you come from a group of farmers you generate agricultural gods, more peaceful but with a tendency to moan a lot.

If you're Greek you get a bunch of randy buggers.

If you're English, well pretty much the same as farmers but with an added air of depressive resignation.

If you're American, not so much Gods as parodies of celebrities.

As belief fades so do the Gods…unless they are clever.

Developing personalities also leads to the developing of intellect and some Gods, realising what would happen to them, adapted to changing circumstances. Hence Aphrodite, Goddess of Love, changed her nature to become the Goddess of Lust, Ladies/Gentlemen of Quantifiable Relationships, and Desperate Acts of Men who have forgotten that Special date. So next time you look at a member of the opposite sex and go "Oh My God. Look at that." She's listening and smiling.

Mars, the God of War changed to become Mars the God of War, Mass Destruction, Overly Dangerous Weapons of Mass Destruction and for some reason Chocolate Bars.

Ariel became A Slow Postal Service.

But the most successful was Bacchus, God of Wine. He simply expanded his range to include ALL forms of excess from drink to drugs and women. He catered for every bottle jockey, pill jockey and needle jockey there could be. If you could ride it, He was there, He even expanded into all forms of deviant behaviour. He now owns a range of exclusive bars, nightclubs…

Ω

Fatso smiled at Pete, but there was little humour in his eyes. And he was supposed to be such a nice God.

"Such aggression young man." Fatso said. "Were you human I would react quite badly to your lack of flattery. As you are whatever you are I'll forget it." Fatso stood up with surprising grace and sat on the edge of his desk. It almost screamed out. "So you want the Elf. Wait your turn Faustus. Others are in the queue, and it seems, I head it."

I dropped my cigarette on the carpet and ground it under my shoe, immediately improving the carpet's appearance.

"Simple reasoning Fatso. I do need to speak to him. Let me know what is going on in your world and who's doing what that might be of interest and I won't get the verbals." I knew I was pushing my luck, but I had played my hand and had to follow through. "You could draw a lot of attention and it that would put a hole in your wallet. Would you like people to find out what goes on in your little side rooms?"

I was bluffing but Fatso didn't know it. Who would I talk to after all? Fatso dealt in Booze, Sex and Drugs with such control and regulation that it was better to have him running things than freelancers or gangs. Everyone on the Streets reported back to him, eventually. I hated him, but he was useful.

"And what would you tell them? Nothing people do not already know Faustus. All is consensual. And Never the young."

"Thunderbird Six." Pete said. If my jaw didn't hurt I'd have dropped it.

"Pardon?" Fatso replied. He couldn't believe his ears, and neither could I.

"Thunderbird Six. Also known as T6, T, Bright house, and Bright Eyes. Also for a reason that abandons me Kelvin's Cake. It is a synthesized narcotic that activates dormant cells within human eyes allowing them to see the aura of those around them while simultaneously producing a state of euphoria and abandonment. A popular drug, with potential within the clubbing crowd. It could replace Ecstasy within five years as the party goers' drug of choice. You are also personally experimenting with it so as to engage men and women in sexual intercourse." Personally I think Pete played the hand too early.

Fatso took a deep breath. One word I knew would put out the lights and Shadwell would make sure we didn't say another word. At least I wouldn't have to worry about where to take Mel.

"There is," Fatso began, "a new house of negotiable awareness I have heard about in The Meadows. I have yet to establish who runs it, but they do not share the same goals in life as I. You may wish to ask there." Fatso leant forward until he was nose to nose with Pete. "You will say nothing about anything to anyone. I hope you understand."

"No. Not really." Pete said. "That sentence was riddled with tautology."

Oh Bugger.

The tension would have needed a thermal lance to cut. Then it happened. Fatso leant back and laughed.

"You have balls Sir. I will give you that." Fatso sniggered. "Not even Faustus here would be stupid enough to try and face me down like that. You may leave. Intact." The last part was aimed more at Shadwell than us.

"However next time Angel, I would allow Faustus to do the talking. He may go around the block a little, but it does reduce the chance of any terminality of confliction."

Pete stood up and walked over to me.

"Terminality of Confliction." I said. I wasn't about to be left out in the pissing contest. "Your making up words now Fatso."

We left Fatso's office and the Big Man laughing about our incredible bravery. For Bravery, read Stupidity.

Half way across the club's dance floor I felt my elbow tugged and I was turned around. I was face to presumably his face with Shadwell.

"Problem Shadwell?"

"You're going out tonight?" he said.

87

"You look after my social diary now? Let's face it somebody should so I can have one."

"Don't get clever Faustus." Suddenly Shadwell's voice sounded much more echoey. The sort of echo you get in a crypt. "She's a friend of mine. You hurt her Faustus and I'll slice you apart. Cast iron guarantee."

I don't know what surprised me more. The idea that Shadwell could have friends, or that one of his would be my...friend.

"Tell you what Shadwell..." I managed, "...if I hurt her I will come find you. I like the girl."

"Good. She's had a rough time with men. Believe me when I say you won't cause her any trouble."

I get threatened. A lot. Mostly it is like water of Sid's back, but this was a first. The first time a threat ever really scared me. It was the first time I thought anyone was able to carry it out.

"OK." I said, "But let's be clear straight off Shadwell. Personal, not business."

"Very personal Faustus." Shadwell replied.

"If you two have finished with this urination contest, may we leave now?"

We both turned to face Pete. He was adapting a pose of 'hard man'. Fists clenched, leaning slightly forward, balanced on the balls of his feet and a frown on his face.

"I have had enough," Pete said with a growl, "of faffing around with a fat man, a shadow and a PI who so far couldn't find his bottom with both hands and a road map. Please excuse my language."

"Faustus?" Shadwell smiled.

"Yes?"

"Is he serious?" I could sense Shadwell smile.

"I believe so."

"Then this is too good a chance to miss. Do you mind?"

"Be my guest."

"More talking Faustus?" Pete asked. "All talk and no action."

"Oh, here comes the action." I said, folding my arms and waiting patiently.

The blow hit Pete full on and sent him flying straight out the door and into the street. I turned to Shadwell. Probably.

"Good punch."

"Thanks. I get a lot of practice." Shadwell paused. "I hear you're a 'good guy' Faustus. Trustworthy."

"I have my moments." Rough waters this. We were being nice-ish to each other. "I hear you're not so bad yourself, given who you work for."

"I have my moments. Take care of her Faustus."

"I will." I looked out the door. "Now I had better go and scoop up my client." I walked out the door.

Outside Club Transco, at the edge of the pavement, was a wire mesh barrier, six feet long by four feet high. When Fatso applied for permission to fit it, his argument was that it would stop clubbers from wandering into the road and risking injury or death. He was right. There were no road accidents outside the club since it was fitted.

In reality it served as a catcher's net for the people Shadwell encouraged to leave. He could drop a semi-conscious trouble maker in any part of the net. He was good.

My client was lying on his back, with his head resting against the wire net. I crouched down next to him and tilted my hat back on my head.

"You OK?" I asked him.

"I think he broke my…everything."

"You can talk. You'll be alright." I stood up and reached down my hand. He gingerly took it and I pulled him to his feet.

"Sorry about what I said Mr Faustus. I thought it necessary to keep up the tough guy image."

"So you thought it was a good idea to insult both Shadwell and myself. You thought a slap wasn't coming?" I held up a hand to stop him saying anything else. "Look Pete, thank you for trying to save me in there, and for the other things you've done, but I am quite good at my job. I wouldn't have gotten hurt, badly. As for 'faffing around', I am following the standard process for searching for a missing person. You check the obvious places first. We could have got a lot further if you had told me about Jo-Jo Mar earlier."

"I am sorry Mr Faustus." his head was actually hung in shame. "I had not realized the import."

"Now let's get one or two things settled. Don't try to play the hard boiled character. That's my job and it doesn't suit you. Also when it comes to talking, leave it to me. You don't know the people we are dealing with. Some would hurt you a lot worse than Shadwell, and I promise you he pulled his punch."

"How do you know?"

"There's still a body to identify. If he hit you hard enough, that net would have sieved you rather than saved."

Is there anything else?"

"Yes. How do you know about Thunderbird Six? I thought there were only a few people who know."

"Mr Peter told me. He told me you could use the details, so he had me memorize them."

That figured. Sometimes I think he doesn't think I can do the job.

"Any other things he thought I should know?"

"Several, but he said they would only make sense at the time so I don't know what to tell you. Sorry."

I knew there was little point in arguing. Peter was a terrific old man, but sometimes he delighted in being enigmatic. I straightened my hat and tie.

"Come on then." I said to the Angel Daemon thing. I had to keep reminding myself of that.

"Where to?"

"The Meadows."

"That sounds so pretty."

"Delightful."

Chapter Twelve: The Dick and Dealer

Back in the Nineteen Eighties the Government of the time encouraged people who lived on Council Estates to buy their own homes. Give up renting and become part of the Home Owning Economy. Create estates of people who would in turn vote for them.

This worked to an extent, but after a while it became clear that something had to be done about those terrible people from number 42, who had loud parties, never worked and whose children ran about with the arses out of their trousers. They were letting the side down, responsible for all the crime in the neighbourhood and worse than that, lowered the property values.

So those people from number 42 were re-housed. Re-housed to an estate where people were all 'like minded', keeping all the let downers of the side, all born criminals and property lowerers in the same area. Much easier to police. Watch Escape from New York and you get the idea of how well that works.

Of course you do get some ordinary decent people mixed in with the bad lot. A small amount. Only about 95%, but they live on 'That' estate. The one with the bad name, so they must be up to something. Their post code makes them guilty.

In the words of one Mayor, "Fuck 'em. They're not our problem."

And it wasn't because the council to generate cash, sold all of the council houses to Private Housing Associations, who cut back on services and maintenance while raising rents and introducing Tenant Behaviour Contracts.

Then when the riots happened the council blamed their ex tenants, the Private Housing Associations blamed the lack of morality in today's society and the Police blamed...well, everyone else.

In this blameless society, no one is to blame.

So The Meadows grew to be a Sink Estate where 'Bad Things' happened. Gangs of feral children roamed the streets, which were littered with burnt out cars, broken bottles and needles. Crack houses were everywhere. Smuggled booze, cigarettes and guns could be bought as easily as sweeties. Gardens were overgrown and Hell had its own extension.

At least that was the popular myth.

The families who lived on The Meadows were happy to keep the Myth alive.

With no hope of help from the outside, people banded together, cleaned up the estate, 'encouraged' most of the dealers to leave, dug out the brooms, the paint and the lawnmowers and made sure the kids knew how to behave. Employment was 95% for those who wanted to work and training was there to help those who wanted it. A community developed that was tight knit, inter-supportive and didn't like outsiders. It became a good place to live.

They were careful not to let people know about it.

Cars were strategically burnt out in prime locations for media access, bottles broken and swept into careful designs and the needles to be found were clean and blunt. Everyone knew where they were and to stay clear of them. A stage managed rough place to be.

The crack houses were still there, but they had to be somewhere and everyone watched who went in and who came out. Community policing with zero tolerance.

The families were happy to keep the Myth alive. They had a good place to live.

I shouldn't have known all of this, but a little bit of straight work for people on the estate had brought me in. I wasn't accepted, but tolerated. A necessary evil.

A word or two in the right place always speeds things on and as I approached my most useful contacts Pete seemed concerned.

"They do look threatening and dangerous Mr Faustus."

"Too right," came the reply.

"Unless I am mistaken I count eighteen edged weapons amongst the ten."

"You are mistaken." I was enjoying this. "There's a lot more than that."

"And I am not to react to anything they say or do?" he asked. "Not even in self defence?"

"Not even in self defence. You turn and run away. Kylie!" I called.

"Thought I could smell a Dick." Kylie replied. For a twelve year old she certainly had a grasp of Noir dialogue.

Kylie was in pink. Pink tracksuit, pink trainers, pink ribbon in her hair, pink bicycle. Even the knife in her sock had a pink handle. She had ruled a gang of twenty three with a rod of iron for the last two years, ever since she beat the living daylights out of the sixteen year old prior leader. It wasn't that she was incredibly tough, or a good fighter, she just wouldn't stay still, stay down or play by the rules. She didn't play at anything.

Like me she had rules.

No drugs.

No booze till your eighteen.

No sex till your eighteen and old enough to know better.

No second chances.

We got on well, the vicar's daughter and I. She had been my last client here when one of her gang had been having problems at home. She paid cash and I didn't ask where it came from.

The gang members 'uncle' got religion and turned himself over to the cops with a full confession and explanation as to how he got the bruises.

"What you want Dickhead?" one of her gang asked, a mousy fifteen year old called Lawrence. A bicycle tyre slammed down on his foot and the Vicar's daughter smiled.

"Skinny." I said. "Looking for a dealer. Flash shinny suit, thin, wearing money but none to spend."

"Payment?" Kylie asked

"Thirty for a number, fifty for details."

"A tonne gets you an in."

"Working more on Seventy."

"Eighty."

"Call it seven five. Eight zero with result."

"Up front, sorted."

"Sorted or shanked?"

"Please. Shanks for playtime. Business. Accountant and everything."

"Pleasure."

I handed over a roll of notes. One hundred pounds. Of my own money. For a dog. Oh yes, and a pop at Jo-Jo Mar. I always paid Kylie more than she asked for, but quietly. It meant she had to work a little less rigorously to impress the other kids.

"Bing bong five at sixty three. Do one after." Kylie nodded at Pete. "Set the monkey in front. Do em the Dirty Skipper."

Hey. She had watched the film I gave her for
Christmas.

With that the whole gang spun on their bicycles
and road away.

I turned and looked at the monkey. I was
beginning to enjoy the puzzled look on his face.

"I know you were both speaking English." Pete
said, "but I have no idea what either of you said."

"Meadow-talk. It prevents outsiders knowing
exactly what the kids are talking about. She just told
us where Jo-Jo Mar's place is and how to get in. Oh
and you have to lend me one of your socks."

A few minutes later we were walking down the
right street to the wrong house. Wrong because of
the inhabitants, not the skinny.

"So Elves are afraid of socks?" Pete asked for
the tenth time. "Why again?"

"Because they constrict the feet. They have a
thing about their feet being free." I was on a bullshit
roll. Might as well go with it. "The socks remind
them that there is potential for constriction in cotton.
Big fear for Elves."

"But my socks are nylon."

"It's the thought that counts."

We stopped a few houses down from number sixty
three. The house had a community tag. A broken
refrigerator and worn out sofa dumped in the garden.
This tagged the house as 'Drug dealer. Watch and
report'.

That and the big spray painted logo 'Drug Dealer
Scum - Die.'

"So I ring the bell five times, pause and then ring
it again once. Correct?" Pete checked.

"Correct. It should be a reinforced door." We had to get in and this was the only way. Then I said something I possibly would regret...eventually. "The only other way in would be a battering ram."

"That would be quicker? We are somewhat pushed for time."

"I seem to have forgotten to bring one with me."

"I see."

Pete walked down the road with me keeping low behind the wall. He duly rang the bell five times paused then stepped back. I took position crouched down, beside the door, Pete's sock ready and dangling in my right hand. The weight was comforting.

Had I mentioned that I had pushed a half brick into it?

After a few moments a shutter in the door fell open. Piggy eyes stared out.

"Piss off. We closed white boy." Piggy said.

Oh good. Gutter trash heavies. Makes you feel better about hurting them.

"Open the door please. I would like to purchase some illegal narcotics" Pete was very polite, but not doing what I told him. Bad Pete.

"Piss Off. Yawl dent' wanna be yhere."

Piggy was talking the Patois of the white boy wishing he was a big bad black guy in a big bad black posse. Impossible to reason with. I wondered how long it would take to kick the door in.

I found out.

Accompanied by a strong smell of brimstone.

Pete stepped back and picked up the fridge from the garden. The last time I moved a refrigerator it took me ten minutes to walk it three feet. He picked it up like balsa wood and threw it square centre of the door.

It is a tribute to whoever fitted that door that it stayed in its frame. Fortunately for Piggy he was still behind the door when the refrigerator struck it. Unfortunately the frame came right out of the wall, door intact and flattened him. Running feet could be heard in the hall. Out came the obligatory three disposable bad guys.

Disposable bad guys tend to come in threes. Normally there is the collective intelligence and morality of a tapeworm between them. I did have time to register they had two guns and a machete between them, which was good to lower their intellect further and made me feel even less squeamish about what I was going to do.

I let the first one pass, then swung my Brick/Sock into the knee cap of the second. There was a very satisfying crunch-crack as his leg crumbled under him. The third got a backswing full in the face. I'm sure it did something unpleasant to his face but there was too much blood to tell.

One gun and one machete down.

I spun round to deal with the third.

"You'se dy fucker. Nwan dis mwy crib." The moron screamed. His gun inches from Pete's face.

Another white kid with dreams of being black.. He was a good six foot and change tall. Muscles rippled under a skimpy little silver T-shirt, contrasting nicely with the steroid rash and splits on his back. Regulation baggy silver tracksuit bottoms and long trailing laces in expensive silver. Little silver Chav hat perched on top of a shaved head.

Jo-jo Mar. Stupid bugger. Getting them all decked out in silver was like hanging out a flag saying "Yoo Hoo. I'm here!"

Silver drawers had punk gun pose number one going on. Left arm out, fist clenched. Little bit of jiggle in the legs but buttocks clenched so tight you couldn't swipe a credit card there. Right arm out, crooked at elbow and gun pointed sideways on. I didn't need to see his face to know he would be chewing on his bottom lip. Punk was so wired he didn't even notice the hypo was still hanging from his arm.

I had to do something for him. After all it's bad form to let your client tag along on an investigation. I could live with that for the old man's sake, but it is really frowned upon if you let them take a bullet in the face. I had no idea what would happen if he did. Angels and Daemons are tough, but they can still bleed. Back to work.

I mouthed to Pete "Keep him talking."

Pete slowly folded his arms and looked the punk straight in the eyes.

"You seem to have a lot of aggression." Pete said. "I wish to talk with a man called Jo-Jo Mar. Is he in there?"

The punk said something but it was wired patois so I can only assume it was a series of threats and insults. He didn't notice me bending over and tying his laces together. Very Hal Roach I know, but sometimes it works.

"You do realise that in attempting to shoot me you will engage the interest of the Police Force?" Pete was very cool. I give him that.

"Mumble mumble obscenity, mumble SHOUT mumble obscenity really bad obscenity. Mumble. Huh?"

The 'Huh?' was probably the result of me grabbing the waist band of his pants and pulling them down around his ankles. Idiot as he was he tried to turn walk and keep the gun on Pete at the same time.

I cannot punch. I may have a 'certain' reputation, but a swift right hook? No way. When I slammed my right elbow into Silver Drawer's chin he was out for the count before he hit the ground. Pete didn't move an inch.

"Were you aware that those people were in there and likely to attack us, Mr Faustus?" he asked far too calmly.

Not us, I thought. You.

Bad Faustus. Bad, Bad Faustus.

"I thought someone would need to be talked around." I snapped back. "I never expected you to throw a fridge through the door."

"I did not expect you to turn my sock into a weapon." He sighed. "I am disappointed in you."

"I'll get over it." I said and walked into the friendly neighbourhood crack den. "Pick up those guns. There's kids around here."

The décor left a lot to be desired.

The walls were covered with a multitude of invisible wards, sigils and magic symbols, effective to mask Jo-Jo Mar from the sight and scrying of gods, wizards and witches. It had worked too, but most of them would not bother to simply walk up to a house and have a look. They rely far too heavily on 'other senses'. And the pictograms are invisible, but the liquid they get drawn with does leave a watermark. Some people never think.

The door to the lounge was off the hall. I could hear frantic barricading going on behind it, but I seemed to have my own battering ram with me.

"I brought the big knife too. Was that right?" My little Juggernaut said.

"Fine." I pointed at the door. "He's in there. Open the door will you?"

"Is there a potential for physical violence in there Mr Faustus?" he asked.

"Well I do intend to kick his teeth in if that's what you mean."

"Then he won't be able to show us where Dog is will he?"

I got a little cruel.

"Jo-Jo Mar is an Elf, Pete." I said calmly. "Elves eat dogs, Pete. Alive, Pete"

The smell of brimstone increased as he carefully placed the weapons on a hall table.

The door came open and off its hinges in one blow. I looked down at the door and fridge to my left. Piggy's little silver feet and left arm stuck out under the frame. I could hear him groaning.

Poor little dealer.

"Faustus." Pete shouted from inside the room, sounding more annoyed than angry. "Should I take these guns away from him?"

Guns? Plural?

I hurried through the door and there stood Jo-Jo Mar. He was a little over five foot tall, thin as a lat, angular face, with a little tuft of beard on his chin. His jacket was brilliant silver, reflecting the lights that filled the room. Obviously he was worried about Shadwell calling by. He would have cut quite

101

a striking figure, were he wearing trousers. Even his boxer shorts were silver.

And he held two SIG automatic pistols, both pointing at Pete, until I walked into the room that he was kind enough to let me share.

"Faustus?" he said in his squeaky little voice. "How did you find me?"

"Big silver flag flying over the house." I replied. I sat down on the one sofa in the room and took out my smokes. "How do you think?"

The room was quite sparse, apart from a wide array of halogen lights keeping shadows out of the room. A beat up sofa, beat up chair and a table filled with assorted powders, smokes, pills and needles. Jo-Jo Mar was being safety conscious though. A nice painted yellow bucket was by the table for used sharps.

"How sure are you that you can get the guns away from him before he pulls the triggers?" I asked Pete.

"Positive."

"Now look…" Jo-Jo Mar began.

"Take him." I said putting the smoke in my mouth.

By the time I had lit it Pete slapped both guns out of J-Jo Mar's hands and grabbed him by the throat. He lifted him up and slammed him into the wall so hard the dealer's head left a discernible dent.

"Now," I lit up. "I was going to take some pleasure in tearing you apart," (True) "but I think my friend here would do a much better job of it. Take a good look at him Jo-Jo."

Through bulging eyes Jo-Jo Mar focused on Pete. Judging by his face he did not like what he saw. Not one little bit.

"Before he lets go of you let me just fill you in on your front door. This guy threw a fridge at it. Well, through it. Truth be told." Jo-Jo Mar was sweating so badly you could hear it. "He then took out all of your play pals." I wet stain appeared on Jo-Jo Mars boxer shorts, swiftly followed by one of his socks getting very wet indeed.

Jo-Jo Mar was a true bully, and a true coward. Put the pressure on him and he folded like a house of cards. I felt he was scared enough to talk now.

"Would you put him down please?" I asked Pete.

"But he is turning such a nice pretty colour." Pete replied. Jo-Jo Mar just gurgled.

"If he is dead it makes it hard for him to answer questions."

"Are there no Necromancers in the area?" Pete said. I'm not sure if he was serious or not. Wind this boy up and there was no stopping him. Slowly Pete lowered Jo-Jo Mar so that his feet touched the floor. Pete leant in closer. "You will tell the truth to us. You will be open and honest. If you lie, I will first throw you through a wall. The second time you lie I will tear off your favourite limb. Then I will begin to hurt you. Do you understand?"

Jo-Jo Mar looked at Pete with shocked fear but managed to nod his head. Pete slowly let go of his throat and stepped back a couple of paces. Jo-Jo Mar massaged his throat with his left hand.

"Was that necessary Faustus?" he croaked.

"Calling him off was necessary, otherwise he might have killed you. Eventually. Slow." I put my cigarette out on the floor. It was the cleanest place. "Now, you were seen in the vicinity of a dog-napping earlier this week. So where did you take the dog?"

"I'm no thief Faustus."

I should have been quicker, but I doubt I could have moved quickly enough. Pete grabbed Jo-Jo Mar by the shirt front and hurled him at the outside kitchen wall. Unfortunately for Jo-Jo Mar the wall that linked the lounge with the kitchen was in the way.

Pete, it seems is true to his word. Limbs next.

The wall was, fortunately for Jo-Jo Mar, plaster board, although there was no way Pete could have known that. I made a note to myself to have a word about anger management.

"That was a lie, Mr Faustus." Pete said.

I walked into the kitchen. Jo-Jo Mar was sitting in the sink, his head resting against the window. I leant close to him and whispered into his ear.

"And you were worried about me?"

"OK. OK. There's no need for this." Jo-Jo Mar was flapping his hands in front of himself. He looked left and right, probably trying to find something to defend himself with. The only thing visible was a pristine washing up sponge. "I'll tell you what I can." He looked up imploringly. "Please don't let him touch me again. Please Faustus." He struggled to get out of the sink.

"I like you fine where you are." I said. "You stole a dog. Where is it?"

"If I tell you, you'll leave me alone?" he pleaded.

"Don't be silly." I said, "It will just be better for you. Less of a kicking."

"OK." Jo-Jo Mar licked his lips and swallowed. "A man and woman said their dog had been stolen. They paid me a grand to get it back. They knew where it was and everything. All I had to do was pick it up and give it to them."

"Shall I hurt him?" Pete was by my right shoulder. Too close to the sink sitter for comfort. Too close to me for comfort. I moved him back gently with the back of my hand.

"Straight up. Simple as that." he slapped his hand onto the drying board. "Damn it Faustus. I thought I was doing a solid for a change, you know. No Law. No problems. I thought I was doing right. Now you're here and some soft shoed shit is sniffing around trying to find me. He hurt me!"

"This couple, what did they look like?"

"Ask him where Dog is." Pete interrupted. I flashed him a look that said 'Desist from this mode of enquiry for it fails to assist us in engaging a positive result.' Or something similar…with fewer words.

" What? Which?" Jo-Jo Mar shook his head and waved his hands. "Which question do you want me to answer first?"

I looked around and saw the kettle next to Pete. It felt full enough. I turned it on. For some reason, goodness knows why, Jo-Jo Mar saw this as a threatening gesture and went duly white.

"Both." I said

"Ok. OK. They were both tall. As tall as him." He flapped his hand at Pete. "But they were pretty. Both of them. Long blonde hair. Good muscles. Real nice clothes. They looked similar. Could have been related."

"Eyes?" I asked.

"Oh. Yeah. They had those. Two, both of them."

I gave him a tiny slap.

"What was the colour?" I stressed.

"No need for violence." Jo-Jo Mar winged. "I'm trying. I don't know what colour. They had sunglasses on."

"What did they smell like?" A long shot, but something was niggling away.

"Chocolate," came Jo-Jo Mars answer in a flash. "I know that 'cause I though it odd that two gym pushers would want to eat so much sweet stuff. Don't they eat meats and eggs and stuff? What's that look on your face for?"

Angels smell of chocolate.

You damn near have to snog someone to smell chocolate on their breath. To get the smell from someone in the open, and they would have been in the open as no one wants to get stuck in an enclosed space with Jo-Jo Mar if they can avoid it, it has to be really strong. It was on Pete but not as strong, and the mix of brimstone cuts it quite a bit.

I hate cases that involve Angels. They are always so damn, nasty. Angels are above human morality, codes of conduct, niceness or compassion. They leave all that to the Big Guy Upstairs.

"So where did you take the dog?" I asked, resting my hand on the kettle's handle.

"At last." Pete snapped behind me.

"A car park." Jo-Jo Mar snapped back. "One of those tall new buildings on Hartley Street. "The two of them met me in their car, took the dog, cage and all and left. Didn't even offer me a lift. Bastards."

"They were tall, blonde and pretty?" I said. Something was niggling again.

"That's what I said." Jo-Jo Mar said. He nodded his head down to the sink. "Look Faustus, can I get out of this? My pants are soaked through."

106

"Yeah. OK." I replied, distracted. I delved my hand into my jacket pocket and took out the copy of Pete's photograph. "Damn."

"What is it?" Pete asked, leaning in to look.

I showed him the photograph. I could hear Jo-Jo Mar dragging himself out of the sink. There in the background of the photograph, behind Dog and Pete, two people. One man, one woman, both tall and blonde. The photograph was too blurred to see, but I would have bet my eye teeth that they were both pretty and smelled of chocolate.

"Do you see them?" I asked Pete, pointing at the two in the background.

"Could that be them? You." Pete snapped at Jo-Jo Mar. I kept looking at the photograph. "Faustus."

"What?"

"I think we are about to have another incident." Pete said as water dripped onto my photocopy.

The water was coming from a freezer bag. Inside the freezer bag was a 9mm gun. Big and nasty.

What is it with criminals and 9mm guns? Is it some macho phallic thing I don't understand? I have a gun. It's a .22 target air pistol. I'm a good shot with it. Never felt the need to wave a big gun about. Besides, guns get you killed.

You go carrying a gun, people think it's fair to start waving one at you and pulling the trigger.

"Never thought I'd be prepared, did ya?" Jo-Jo Mar sneered.

I faked a lack of concern, even though I was bricking myself, and kept looking at the photograph.

"Jo-Jo," I began, "you're dripping on my paperwork."

"Well, let's mix it up with some…" Jo-Jo Mar said.

I don't know what the end of that sentence was, because the window exploded. I grabbed Pete and dragged him to the floor.

"Faustus?" Pete said.

"Yes Pete."

"Why is he dancing?"

I looked at Pete with a mix of awe and disbelief. It was preferable to watching Jo-Jo Mar being torn apart by bullets. By now he was dead and the only thing holding him upright were the impacts of the slugs.

Someone was using a full automatic on him. Very nasty.

I should have felt bad at the loss of life. Any life. The feeling I had was one of being cheated. Cheated of questioning him further and cheated of meeting out some limited revenge myself.

Difference was, I wouldn't have killed him.

I know many others would have, and obviously someone did, but I just wanted a little payback for myself.

The impacts stopped and Jo-Jo Mar slopped to the floor. His chest and abdomen were mostly left on the wall behind him. Scraps of bone and flesh almost held his chest together, but they deflated under the pressure of gravity.

He folded like a concertina.

No more shots came. The assassin having dispatched his target didn't seem too worried about us, so with consummate bravery I crawled out of the kitchen. Pete sat staring at the body. I turned and put my hand on his shoulder.

"Come on Kid. Time to leave." I said as gently as I could. It didn't work. He was transfixed by the corpse.

Jo-Jo Mar was beginning to decompose.

It wasn't horror movie decomposition, where the body turns to ash or goo in seconds, but the quick decomp that Elves go through. The body was sweaty and rank already, mere seconds later. The open eyes had fogged over and the flesh was in its second stages of rigor.

Elves rarely find their way onto a mortuary slab. Because of their physiology they decompose too quickly for a cutter to make any inroads. The body is normally soup after a day with a few bones adrift in the mess. It has something to do with accelerated metabolism.

Problem was that I was at a murder scene with a client.

Peter was going to kill me.

Chapter Thirteen: The Dick and The Dick and The Dick Head

The easiest thing to do was call the police, which is exactly what I did. I try to be an upstanding citizen after all.

The hard thing was to get rid of Pete.

No one likes the Private Investigators client to be at a murder scene, especially not the police. I convinced him through careful negotiation and lying through my teeth. I did feel a little guilty about promising that the police could be of help in finding Dog, but they would only talk to me. I sent him back to my office so that I could talk to my good friends on the force.

I was waiting in the hallway awhile.

"You shit-bag pervy peeper!"

"You're going to have a wee accident son."

Ah. My good friends on the force.

"Well. If it isn't Moulder and Schooly. You wearing long trousers as well Schooly." I came back and caught a jab to the stomach for my trouble. Fortunately the young guy could punch about as well as I could.

"Now, now." said the older, "It is impolite to hit the suspect like that."

The punch to the kidneys however, hurt. "You do it like that."

And Malder likes me too.

"You be nice Faustus or I'll staple your scrotum to the back of your head." he said.

The PACE rule hadn't quite reached Malder yet.

Malder and Schoone. Malder was the older one. An old style street monster who had been promoted to CID because the brass wanted him off the street. Big and heavy, he wore the regulation cheap suit, cheap shoes and beige raincoat. His face was that of a boxer. The dog, not the athlete. He knew every dodge, con and piece of nastiness and used them to get the job done.

We hated and liked each other in equal measure, but knew the other was useful, on occasions.

Schoone on the other hand was a fast track University graduate. Just on regulation height, with a big chip on his shoulder. He'd been matched with a street monster before he had enough discipline or experience to know any better. He'd meet out a beating if he could, but couldn't be trusted in a fight. Word was he was one step away from taking a bribe.

Hated him too.

"Young fella, go get me a cuppa." Malder said. The implication being that he was about to have a 'quiet chat' with me. The sort where you don't want any witnesses.

"Guv." Schoone replied and scurried off grinning to find a neighbour who wouldn't spit in the tea.

Malder relaxed his shoulders and took out a packet of cigarettes. He offered one to me. I took it and lit up. Cheap tobacco. Good indicator he was clean.

"How's Freak Street?" he asked

"Freaky. How's Straight Street?" I replied

"Equally freaky."

There are those who know and most who don't. Good enough.

"I like you for this. How much do you have to do with it?" Malder asked.

"Not much. He stole something from my client." Time to lie a little. "I was going to ask him some questions, but he looked about three days dead by the time I got round to it."

Malder took his time smoking and considering.

"This is Freak Street business?"

"So far as I know."

"What was the stiff?" Malder's compassion shone through.

"Dealer and petty lifter." I was about as compassionate about Jo-Jo Mar. "No loss to the world, but left a hole in my enquiries."

"You're a big boy. You'll live."

Another series of drags on the cigarette, close to being a dog end now.

"I'll give you some time." Malder said. "Find me a shooter, bit of proof."

"How much time you giving me?" I asked. "Oh, and anyone in particular as the shooter?"

A few seconds later I did wonder why people kept slapping me on the head.

"The guy who did it will do." Malder said. "Now piss off."

As I like to help the police as much as possible, I pissed off.

Not quickly enough though.

I had made it about ten yards from the gate when Schoone came out of a nearby house holding a large mug of tea. Filthy stuff. He moved to stand right in front of me.

"Exactly where are you going?" Schoone asked.

"I'm doing exactly what your boss told me to do, Schooly. Off I am pissing."

"You expect me to believe that?" Schoone sneered. He needed more practice, as it just made him look as if he had a wayward snot trapped somewhere in his nostril.

"Ask him."

"I don't like you Faustus."

"Not too keen myself sometimes." I said. "Maybe I should get some therapy to help me love myself more."

"What?"

"Though you look like the sort of man who spends a lot of time loving himself." I said.

"You calling me a wanker?" Schoone snapped, spilling Malder's tea.

"If the boxing glove won't fit."

I saw the punch from a mile away and simply stepped back. Schoone only managed to spill the remains of Malder's tea down his front. It served a purpose. There was a small ripple of applause from the other police officers and cat calls from the locals.

I stepped in and offered him my handkerchief. He snatched it from me and pointlessly tried to mop himself dry. I stepped in and looked down on him.

"Now don't stop, but do shut up and listen." My voice just above a whisper. "The only reason I haven't decked you yet is because you're with Malder. He maybe a thug, but he's honest enough and gets things done. You don't measure up and one day he'll realise and throw you to the wolves. This is advice and you take it or not. Be yourself and be honest, don't try to be a clone of him, and if you ever walk down MY streets and try this act I'll tear your head off."

Before he got a chance to respond I stood up and continued pissing off.

Chapter Fourteen: The Dick and The Deliberation

I was sat in the office chair, drinking coffee and trying to decide what shirt to wear tonight.

Pete wasn't there.

A relief in its way.

Troublesome cases are rare. Usually they take the form of complicated divorces. Rarely murder. I know Jo-Jo Mar was slime, but he was murdered. It made it worse that he was murdered right in front of me. That rankled.

There are very few murders on The Streets. People die, but mainly it's normal gang or blood feuds, occasionally food based arguments, but rarely criminal murder.

Currently I was sprouting cases.

A pair of Angels were interested in possession of an ordinary mutt.

An impossible 'man' existed, half Angel, part Daemon, big part pain in the neck.

Someone murdered in front of me.

Something going on between The Fae and another party.

The Fat Man developing some new drug. I wouldn't be letting that one rest.

I decided to ignore The Fae and Fat Man and just concentrate on the one that got it started. The Case of the Missing Dog. Pete and Jo-Jo Mar were linked to it and who knows what I'd turn up.

If in doubt, follow the money.

Though I didn't think I'd see any money on this case.

I opened my desk drawer and took out Jo-Jo Mar's wallet. It had accidentally fallen into my jacket pocket back at the house while I was waiting for the police. I had also accidentally had a good look around and taken a photograph or two and sent them via one of Jo-Jo Mar's mobile phones to my computer.

I may look old fashioned, but I work Hi-Tec.

The inside of the wallet was embarrassingly sparse. A bank card, a photograph of Dog, a library card (something of a surprise), an out of date condom (Who would be that desperate?), a left luggage ticket and a cash and carry card for a business supplier.

The condom and the left luggage ticket were pointless to look at. Jo-Jo Mar was not stupid enough to leave anything useful in a railway station. In good old tradition I dropped the library and wholesalers' card in my desk drawer, picked up the bank card and decided to follow the money.

It was but a short walk to my little cubby-hole, where the glow from the computer screens was permanent. A decent coffee in my hand and a few brief hits on the keyboard and I was into five totally illegal sites, chasing down Jo-Jo Mar's bank account.

One of the plus sides to being private is that I can cross the line and do things the police can't.

The down side to this is that if I get caught I do serious time and I don't really feel like going several years without using a shower.

The computers were beyond state of the art, constructed by a genius and programmed by a madman. I just flew them. Yet it never fails to surprise me when they talk to me.

"Faustus," the sensuous voice said. "It is six o'clock. Shouldn't you be getting ready? Now!"

Nothing scary there though. I had set up the thing to remind me.

I left the computers doing their thing while I went to my flat.

Americans call them apartments, Europeans call them Pensions. In England, it is a flat. Directly above the office. Not many people know it's there and I keep it very quiet. All post is delivered to the office; there is no telephone line to it, no modem, no television. Just a CD player and Digital Radio. I listen to two stations, Radio 4 and Radio 7. I used to listen to a jazz station till it went off air. I think I was the only listener.

I had the usual sofa, chair, wardrobe, table and the like. Perfect for when I had to stay in town. The rest of the time I lived...elsewhere. It suited me not to live where I worked. Not a good idea for too many people to know where you live.

Just because you're paranoid doesn't mean they aren't out to rip your still beating heart from your chest and consign your soul to enslavement.

Dressing with a coffee on the table and a nicotine patch on my arm, I opted for casual. Dark jeans, white T-shirt and light jacket. Money in pocket and I was ready.

I don't know why women make all the fuss. It only took me an hour...and five changes of clothes.

At least I lived close by if Mel was in a ballroom gown.

I drank my coffee down, rubbed my nicotine patch for extra effect and opened the door to an uncertain night.

"Mr Faustus?"

Pete.

Again.

And again.

And again and again.

He was like a tic with a homing beacon.

"Have you had any result?" he asked as he walked, uninvited, through the door.

"Not yet, but the night is young."

"Pardon?"

"I have a date. Remember?"

"What is a 'date'? Should I be there?"

"Not on your Nelly." I waved my hand to shoo him out the door. "Now go and I'll see you tomorrow."

Pete seemed confused.

"I am confused." he said

Told you.

"We need to find Dog. He could forget me."

Guilt crept up on me…but not fast enough to catch me.

"Look. I am going out to meet a young lady. Private time. You wait here. Read a book, listen to the radio. Drink some coffee. I'll be free about eleven. I'll see you then and we'll have a little chat."

With that I walked past him and onto…fun.

Chapter Fifteen: The Dick and The Date

When I got to the café I was early. The lights were out inside, but I could see some activity inside. I lightly tapped on the door. A door opened spilling light into the dark interior and a shadow moved to the front door. Briefly I thought of Shadwell, but then the door opened and I forgot all thoughts of badness.

Mel wore a brilliant smile. Her hair was down and hung to her shoulders, a touch of make-up, jeans and top that did justice to her figure, but the smile was the killer.

There were teeth and lips and the usual things you get with a smile, but it continued across her face, down to the chin and up, through the cheeks and into the eyes.

"Cat got your tongue?" she asked.

"Half my head along with it." I replied. "You look amazing."

"Thanks. Only took a couple of hours and many changes of clothes."

"It works."

"You look quite passable yourself."

"Thanks. You ready?" Damn. Too pushy.

"I'm ready. And no. That wasn't too pushy."

That threw me further than Pete had.

"I'm not psychic or telepathic." Mel said. "The worry was all over your face. This is a date. Not work. Jesus man. How long since you went on a date?"

"A little while." Oh, tell her the truth. "About two years to be honest."

Mel gave a little laugh, stepped out of the café and locked the door. She took hold of my left hand, stood up on her toes and gave me a kiss on the cheek.

I may have blushed. A bit.

"That makes two of us." she said. "So, where are we going? Please don't say for coffee. I get that all day."

This was the chance I was taking. Mel was someone different in my life, but I needed to know something.

"Mel, do you like Hardcore and Rave?" I asked.

She gave me a puzzled look.

"Can't stand it." she said. "I'm more of a rhythm and blues gal."

Halleluiah.

"Then you may just enjoy tonight."

The sax player was strangling a low note out of his machine, while the bass man was lost in the rhythm.

They were good.

Even their own band members were looking on in amused awe. The drummer had given up and was resting his elbows on his kit and his chin in the palm of his hand.

I had never heard them play better.

The Questionable Taste Blues Band.

They almost had a cult following. Well, the people in the room liked them.

One Wind player (Tim), a bass guitarist (Steve), acoustic guitar (Paul), demented drummer (Dave - the words demented and drummer always go hand in hand), a kazoo player (Tim again) and keyboards (someone called Sid). A great bunch.

If only the band wasn't made up of a golem, a werewolf, a vampire, another werewolf and an occasional duck.

Sid picked up the rhythm on keyboards and switched the plaintiff blues into boogie woogie with a couple of bars. The band all laughed and picked up the swing. A few of the audience got up to dance.

"Where did you find out about these guys?" Mel asked.

"Do you like them?"

"They're great." she said. "Don't I know them?"

"Probably." I said. "They all come from The Streets." I took a sip of my coffee. Mel took a sip of her pint. "They are all friends of mine."

Mel sat back in her chair, feigning surprise.

"You have friends Faustus?" She said. "Good God. Is that allowable for a Private Eye? Doesn't that ruin the hard boiled image?"

I laughed. That surprised me. No sarcasm, no bitterness. I just laughed. It had been a long time.

"Do you know," I began, "I have spent so long working, sometimes the front you put on for work takes over. Sorry if…"

"Faustus?" Mel said leaning forward and taking my hand. "Shut up and listen to the music."

Sid and the band rattled off the last few bars of 'Sidewalk Boogie' and sat back to enjoy the round of applause. Dave the Drummer lent forward to his mike. He had been doing brilliant vocals all night.

"Ladies and gentlemen. Thank you for your spontaneous indifference. I thought the band should apologize as our normal vocalist is not with us tonight. Them as know us know the line-up changes a bit from gig to gig, but our vocalist is actually out in the audience tonight contemplating a little tonsil hockey."

I was seriously considering killing the whole smirking band when the spotlight hit me.

A grin spread across Mel's face.

"You're the vocalist?" she said.

"Laugh it up lady." I wanted to crawl inside my clothing like an agoraphobic tortoise.

"Now, " Dave said, " with a bit of encouragement the work shy bugger might just get off his backside and get up here for a tune or two."

I shook my head, but Mel got to her feet and started chanting.

"Sing. Sing. Sing."

Within a few seconds the rest of the audience were on their feet chanting too. I leant forward to a grinning Mel.

"You are an evil woman Mel."

"I have my moments." she said.

I stood up and took her by the hand.

"So have I." I said, and with a good hard tug led her up and onto the stage. The audience applauded, I turned to look at Mel, who looked stunned but was still smiling.

"Can you play anything?" I asked her.

"No." She said. I'd seen this look before. Time to act before she realized what was happening. I led her over to Dave at the Drums. Dave was grinning wide enough to park a truck.

"Dave, this is Mel. Crash course on something if you please." Dave took her hand and led her behind the kit. "Oh. Dave?" Dave looked up, as much a picture of innocence as you could get. "I'll set aside some time to kill you later."

I walked up to the center mike and looked out at the audience.

The Band is popular enough on The Streets. The audience was mainly our usual crew and a few straights who'd wandered in off the streets and thought the musicians were wearing heavy make-up. We played for fun. Good enough.

Even P.I's need a hobby or two.

"Right. Let's dance." I shouted. I breathed in and stepped close to the mike. I held my hand up to the band. They knew I was starting solo.

"All around my hat,

I will wear the green willow,

And all around my hat,

For a year and a day.

And if anyone should ask me,

The reason why I'm wearing it," hold note for dramatic effect.

"It's none of their fucking business.

It's my fucking hat."

The Band picked up the cue and kicked in tearing up the old folk tune with a mix of swing, old fashioned R&B and rock. A few bars later and I started singing again, the odd snatch to keep the audience who were not dancing singing along with the last couple of lines. Audience members got up to dance as Sid picked up the tune and Dave hammered out a beat, with Mel being encouraged to hit the cymbal when Dave nodded towards her. The rest of the guys came in. We hadn't rehearsed the number long, but we all liked it so that was good enough.

We'd nicked the idea from The Bad Shepherds and it was becoming one of our favourites. People always got into it.

At the end of the number I looked over at Mel, who was shaking with laughter.

"Another one?" I asked the audience.

"YES!" They shouted back.

So we did a few more. Some fast, some slow. Some sad, some fun. After about forty five minutes I took a bow, applauded the band and all of us stood and applauded Mel, who did a little curtsey, took my hand and we returned to our table. A complementary coffee and a glass of wine were waiting. I waved a thanks at the bartender. She waved back, a grin on her face.

"You are a dark horse." Mel said to me. "Every day you come in for coffee, too worried about asking me out, and I thought you were just too shy for words. Then you turn out to be this detective who's got a reputation for being so hard boiled he's got bits of egg shell left in the pan. Then, it turns out you get up and sing with these guys at night."

"I also play a little guitar." I said.

"Who are you Faustus?" She asked. "There are so many sides to you."

I took a deep breath and sipped my coffee. Free coffee always tastes good.

"Describe me when I come in to get coffee." I said.

"OK." she said. There was the puzzled look again. "Shy. Average height, a little over average weight." I was pleased she blushed a little at this. " The sweetest eyes. Handsome in a knocked about kind of way."

"And."

"Oh Yes." She realized. "You always wear that trilby."

" How do you know I'm a Private Detective?" I asked

"Ah," she said, "you always wear that trilby."

"Who played the best Private eye to make the silver screen."

"Humphrey Bogart in the Big Sleep. Easy." Mel said, grinning. What a great smile.

"Describe what he wears." I said.

"OK. I see what you're' getting at." Mel replied. "You know he's a Private Eye because 1940's Private Eyes wear raincoats and Trilby's."

"Exactly" I was pleased (and a little surprised) at the speed of the uptake. Although Humph only wears the raincoat when it's raining.

"Everyone knows how a Private Eye is meant to look." I continued. "So when I wear the hat…"

"Everyone knows who you are and what you do." Mel interrupted. "So when you take the hat off…"

"I'm undercover and practically invisible." I finished.

"Wow!" Mel said leaning back in her chair. "I'm not sure if that's genius or totally mad."

"Both." I said. "But it works. So what about you?"

"Not so fast." Mel said. "One more question here. What does the E.M stand for Faustus?"

Predictably , I knew that she'd ask. People always get around to it.

"Later, lady." I said. "I got me a question or two first."

A serious look crossed Mel's face. She looked a combination of worried, scared and very tired.

"Don't Faustus." She said. "Please. No serious questions tonight."

I have no idea what came over me next, but I reached over the table and took hold of the hands that held the wine glass.

"I'm sorry Mel." I said. "I didn't mean to upset you. I just wanted to get to know you better. So no questions. I promise."

Mel visibly relaxed at this and pulled one hand out from mine in order to hold my hands.

"No." she said. "I'm sorry. It's nothing mysterious." She dove on in. "My ex used to drink. Not just booze." A feeder then. "I don't feed. I just get on with my life. He used to like to feel powerful. Do you understand?"

I understood. I had to suppress my anger. I had to stop asking who and where he lived. He used to like to hit her.

Not good.

A bad man.

Time enough.

"I understand." I said. "No questions. If you want to tell me anything you will. If you don't, you won't. Now I'm not going to ask you anything, bar one thing…"

I got in quick before she had time to worry.

"…and that's if you would like another drink."

Mel smiled and I pushed thoughts of the ex to the back of my mind, into the little file Jo-Jo Mar's departure had vacated.

"I would, and before you ask, he died."

Empty file.

"He had an accident in a dark alley one night." Mel said. "Drunk as a skunk and looking for someone to eat. Something found him first. I never found out who or what, but they never found the head. So that's it, minus the nutshell."

125

Mel sat back in the chair as the Band came to our closing number. Sid glanced at me in case I wanted to join in. I shook my head.

"Now." said Mel with relief, "This Lady is going to the lavatory. You can order another wine and a coffee. Back in a bit."

Mel stood up and moved through the tables and crowd to the toilet. I waved a thanks at the Band. They nodded back.

"Nice titties."

I looked across the table. Mel had been replaced by someone I did not want to see.

"Nice arse too. Had her yet? Vampires can be hell on wheels. She know about you yet Mr. E.M.Faustus?"

"Hello Cadell. Unpleasant to see you." I said, mentally slipping my trilby back on. "You too Lisper."

Lisper slid out of the crowd and sat down in the seat next to me. He smiled and leant forward.

"My name ith…" he began.

I never found out his name. I head butted him.
In the mouth.

I heard cracking noises as my forehead did damage to his dental work…again.

From the stage the Band clocked what was happening and shifted to a finale of 'Bad to the Bone'.

"You have a band on retainer for background music?" Cadell said, smiling like a shark who's just had its teeth whitened. "I'm impressed."

"What can I do for you Cadell?" I sipped my coffee and kept an eye on Lisper.

"Die." Cadell said, a little too honest for my liking. "Quickly. That's what I've been sent here to do. Nothing personal Faustus. Just business." He shrugged his shoulders. "Well, everything personal actually. I don't like being talked back to. Nor do I like the hired help getting a slap unless I'm the one doing it."

Bugger.

"To demonstrate, this is how you hit the help." Cadell's straight line punch hit Lisper on the jaw, making a recognizable popping noise as his jaw dislocated.

"Really. I prefer something like this." I grabbed the back of Lisper's head and slammed his face into the table. He whimpered a bit. Cadell smiled. Cadell's hand slowly reached out and rested on mine.

"I think that is enough, don't you?" he asked. "I don't want to have to carry him out. Now should we leave? I don't want to spoil your date's night by blowing your brains out in front of her."

All in all it was turning into a day of ups and downs.

"Are these men a problem Mr Faustus?" Pete asked.

Hooray. The limpet was here.

"Ah." said Cadell, his eyes never leaving mine. "The Daemon thing is standing right behind me isn't he?"

"Yep." I said, sipping my coffee and hoping Mel would take her time at the toilet.

"More friends, Faustus?" Mel said, complicating matters a little.

"Not exactly." Cadell said, smiling at her but looking at me.

"Not friends Mel." I said. "More assassins." I hoped Mel would take the opportunity to get out of there.

"Well you know your job." Mel said, sitting down. "I'll just wait till you're free. But don't take too long. OK?"

"OK." I said, possibly with more confidence than I felt.

"You know I have more men in the crowd." Cadell said.

"You might have noticed the band's stopped playing." I countered.

Cadell risked a quick glance around the room. The lads were wandering around chatting with the crowd and planting themselves behind people they didn't know. It helps to have a werewolf in the band with excellent hearing.

"Do you think my men are scared of a few musicians." Cadell said.

"Mr Faustus…" Pete began.

"Shut up Boy."

"Shut up Boy"

Both Cadell and I spoke together. He smiled at the verbal tie. I didn't.

"Oh." Pete gave a little burst of frustration. "Enough of this."

Cadell must have picked up on something in Pete's voice as he began to spin round with a knife sliding down his sleeve. Pete was quicker, grabbed the knife as it slid out and pinned Cadell's sleeve to the table.

Lisper got to his feet and reached under his jacket, but before anything could be pulled he slumped over the table. Mel stood behind him, holding a chair by its back. Throughout the audience various members of Cadell's crew tried to rise but found restraining hands on their shoulders and whispered advice in their ears.

Staring at the chair with surprise Mel said.

"I thought it would break."

"Only in Films." I said.

I stood up and took the chair from her. I put it down and encouraged her to sit on it.

"Alright!" Cadell exclaimed. A smile was on his face. "You can let me go now. Nothing is going to happen tonight."

Pete glanced at me. I nodded and he let Cadell go free. Cadell twisted to his feet. He nodded at Mel.

"Lady has a lot of spirit there Faustus." he said. "Got a job for her if she wants one. Truce for tonight, simply because that was fun. I really don't want to expend any more effort on you now. Small fish and all that, but you do get the pulse racing."

Cadell walked around the table and grabbed Lisper's collar. He slumped him onto the floor, holding him still by the collar and let him hang.

"So. I'll see you around E.M Faustus." Cadell said. "Face to face." Cadell lent in closer to me. "I had heard you were tough, so far no sign of it. Go on. Amaze me."

I picked up my coffee and took a swig.

"I do a mean soft shoe shuffle." I said. "See you later Cadell." I tipped my imaginary trilby at him, he bowed from the hips and turned laughing, dragging the semi-conscious Lisper with him. His men slowly stood up and followed him out. All neck biters. All same black uniform.

Ye Gods. Bad Guys in uniform. It was turning into a bad spy movie.

"Thanks Pete." I said. "Are you OK? " I asked Mel.

"The chair was supposed to shatter." She said.

"Cast steel." I said tapping the chair with a metallic clung. "Thank you. It was…unexpected."

"I really thought it would smash." Mel smiled. "Hey Faustus. I kicked his arse."

"You did that Lady." I said. I felt a very hirsute hand fall onto my shoulder. "Thanks as well Steve. The extra support is always appreciated."

"Anytime F." Steve said. Vampire bass player. The good thing about his claws are he never needs a pick.

The rest of the band came round and pulled up chairs. You have to love the way your friends always want to butt in on a date.

"Nice move with the chair Lady." said the cultured tones of Tim.

"Real nice tits too." said Paul, getting universal glares of distain.

I put my hand on Pete's shoulder and guided him to a chair.

"I understood you were coming back to work on the case." Pete said.

"It's touching you missed me." I said. "However, I've been busy."

Mel reached over and put a hand on my arm.

"You never said you were working tonight." She said. I had no idea if it was question or accusation.

"Mel. This is Pete." I said. "He's a little obsessive about his case."

"I am delighted to meet you Miss." Pete stood up and took Mel's hand and kissed it formally.

"You have been spending too much time around Peter." Dave said. "I recognize that greeting."

"Now before we go any further," Sid said, "there is one thing we need to clear up."

"Who the bad guy was." Mel said.

"Nah." Sid said. "Faustus attracts flakes like that like I have feathers." Sid changed into a duck just to emphasize the point."

"I agree with Sid." Paul said.

"You agree with anything that could get you a glimpse of breasts." came the witty retort from my friend Steve. Oh the fun. Oh the wit.

"She sang with us, so what we goanna call her?" Sid said.

"Are you serious?" Mel asked.

"I'm afraid they are." I said.

"Mr Faustus." Pete said. "It is important that we continue work on the case. You said you would help me."

I turned to Pete. He looked his normal worried self.

"Pete." I said. "I have a life outside of work. Now I have things in motion, but right now I'm trying to have a coffee with a beautiful lady. The case will wait."

Pete sat down, rested his elbows on the table and steepled his fingers in thought for a second.

"Would you say the same if it was the beautiful lady who had been kidnapped?" He asked.

Low blow.

"What is the case? " Mel asked.

"How about Miss Lace." Paul said. "We could get a lacy costume and…"

There was a clatter of hands striking the bald patch Paul does not like anyone to mention.

"What about Lady M?" Tim suggested. "It's kind of mysterious."

131

"You have a something." Sid said "What about just 'Lady'?"

"His Dog's been dog-napped." I told Mel. "Some very bad guys seem to be involved." I rubbed the bridge of my nose. "It has turned into a bit of an odd case."

Mel looked shocked.

"His little Doggy's been taken." she said.

"Yes." I was being honest after all.

"And you decided to come on a date with me?" Mel asked.

"Well, yes." I said. "After all I…"

"You should be ashamed of yourself Mr Faustus." Mel said, stern as someone being very stern indeed.

"It seems the beautiful Lady agrees with me Mr E.M Faustus." Pete said, daring to smile.

I sat back in my chair amazed the way things had turned on me.

Everyone at the table was glaring at me.

"So let me get this right." I said looking at my watch. "At eleven fifteen at night you want me to go out and continue to track down this guy's dog?"

A chorus from the table of 'Yes' said it all.

"Get your coat. You've pulled" I said to Pete and stood up. "Mel. Would you like me to walk you home?"

Mel stood up and faced me.

"I think these gentlemen should be able to get me home safely." she said. "They can probably tell me a story or two as well." she smiled.

Oh that smile.

"They better not." I said "So where to start?" I turned to Pete "How am I going to find out about pet dogs at this time of night? The local Pet shop?"

"Pog Mahon's Pet Food Emporium."

I turned to look at Paul. It had been his voice after all. He was sipping his tea.

"What?" I said. "There is such a thing as an all-night pet shop?"

Paul looked distinctly uncomfortable. He played with his cup and avoided my gaze.

"Well no. Not exactly." he said. I sat back down next to him.

"So what is it Paul?" I asked

"It's more a place to pick up food." he said. I sat still and said nothing. The rest of the band just glared at him. Paul played with his cup.

"Stop glaring at me." Paul said. "It's not like the rest of you haven't stopped by for a snack after closing time."

"It is a place that sells food for animals?" Pete asked.

"More like a place that sells food to people who...are...animals for some of the time." Paul managed.

"A Lycanthrope take-away?" I said incredulously.

"Not just Lycanthrope, vamperic, troll, skin walker, ghoul. Anyone who occasionally needs a little snack with a bit of life to it." Paul looked at me, wanting me to shut up. For friendships sake I did. I rested a hand on his shoulder.

"Paul." I said, "I happily eat steak, fish and chicken." I looked at Sid. "I have been known to consider Duck."

"Sicko." Sid said.

"Point is mate, I'd be a hypocrite to say things didn't die for my dinner." I said. "At least your way is a little more direct."

133

"I never kill to eat." Tim said. "But Golems are not renowned as big eaters." He patted his stomach. "No digestive system."

I stood up. Mel grabbed the front of my shirt and drew me down to her.

"If you don't call by for coffee in the morning, I will call by your office and give you such a slap." Then Mel kissed me. Not long. Not deep. Just a wonderful kiss. The kind you can still feel years later.

Years later I would also feel a repetitive tapping on my shoulder and Pete saying...

"Mr Faustus. Mr Faustus. We should go."

Mel sat down and waved her fingers at me, smiling that killer smile and leaving the memory of the kiss on my lips and brain.

Ω

Excerpt from
Angels, Daemons and other realm beings.
By E.M Faustus
(unpub)

The Kiss of the Vampire.

A lot has been written about the seductive power of a Vampire's kiss, how it is able to enthrall you, enslave you, to give up our life's blood for the touch of a predator.

Some people don't get out much.

Vampires have two lips. There is no special gland that secretes an hypnotic venom to rob you of your senses, nothing in the saliva that transforms you into Renfield. Most vampires are 99% human.

There is nothing in a vampires kiss but the kiss itself.

Ω

Damn. I was standing in the bar floating. One kiss and I was away.

I was quickly brought back to earth.

"Are we going or not?" Pete snapped.

I turned and looked at him.

"The next time you spoil my date," I said, "You will get such a slap."

"Faustus." Paul said. "Don't forget to change to your work gear. Pog Mahon can be…a bit of a challenge."

"A Bit of a Challenge." I said

"A Bit OF A Challenge." half the table said.

After the day I had just gone through a visit to a takeaway might be a chance to relax.

Chapter Sixteen: The Dick and The Delicatessen

That's what the sign on the wall said. Offering 'Ethnic Foodstuffs.'

The shotgun was a bit of a surprise.

The great steel door was a bit of a surprise.

The drop down flap in the steel door was a bit of a surprise.

The live cobra crawling down the length of the shotgun was a concern.

"I think I have broken my hand." Pete said as he sat to the left of the door nursing his sore appendage.

When the gun had come out of the slot Pete had tried to punch through it to grab…who knows what. Probably hurt.

I was more concerned about the shotgun two inches from my nose and the cobra that was getting closer by the second.

So I did the most sensible thing I could.

I struck a match on the barrel of the gun and lit my cigarette. I slid my hat back a little from my forehead.

"You Pog Mahon?" I asked.

"He's dead. Piss Off," came the clipped Belfast accent. A small gesture of the shotgun indicated the direction I should piss off in.

"I'm looking for Pog Mahon. Paul Greystoke sent me. Werewolf with a tittie complex". I tried.

"My hand really hurts." came the whinge. I duly kicked Pete quiet.

"All werewolves've got titties on the brain." Belfast said.

"This one suggested you could help me." I said. "Any chance you could call your friend off?"

"There's no telling Alison what to do. Wee poisonous bitch that she is."

"I really think it is broken, please don't kick me again."

"Magic on the door'll stop even his kind." Belfast said "Now, at the risk of repeating myself Piss off."

"I can pay for…" I stopped. The cobra had reached the end of the shotgun barrel. It raised up and spread it's hood.

"How much?" Belfast asked.

"Fifty?"

Alison swayed and hissed.

"One Fifty?"

"That'll get ye through the door." There was the sound of bolts being drawn back "Now stand very still."

When a cobra lurches forward and slides onto your shoulder, then around your neck, believe me you don't want to move. You stand very still indeed.

But your sphincter goes into spasm.

The gun withdrew and the door opened on well-oiled hinges. The room inside was brilliantly lit, but brighter than that was the smell. Fresh dung smell rolled over me and I would swear even Alison the Cobra used her tail to hold her 'nose'.

"Throw the money in." Belfast said. "Carefully." he added helpfully. With a cobra around my neck I needed no reminder.

I reached slowly into my trouser pocket and took out my pocket cash. One hundred and Fifty pounds in each pocket. Bribes, for the use of. I folded it in half one handed and tossed it into the shop. It landed with a slap on the floor. A booted foot came around the door and stood on it. The cash and foot

were drawn back behind the door. After a moment
Belfast called,

"Come in then if yer intentions are good to me."

I waved the fingers of my left hand towards Pete.
He slid back up the wall.

"After you." I said.

Pete steadied himself and slowly walked around
the door. I slowly walked up the step and followed
him inside.

The interior of the shop was brilliantly lit. Shelves
covered every part of the wall space. Cages sat on
every one of the shelves. Each cage held an animal.
A rat. A rabbit. A snake. Somethings I didn't
recognize, or would ever want to. On the front of
each cage was a price tag and a little guarantee that
it had been organically reared for a succulent taste
experience.

Best not to judge.

A few of the cage doors were open and various
creatures walked, slithered or oozed their ways
around the shop. Curiously though, no animal was
attacking the others, though I could feel Alison on
my shoulder eyeing it all up like a giant buffet.

"Ye like the shop then?" Belfast said.

"Nice place." I said. "Could use a few throw
cushions. Make it a bit more homely."

"Funny man" Belfast came round the door, still
holding the shotgun on us. He pushed the door
closed. Suddenly I felt like I was in a casserole.

Belfast was not a big man, about five foot six. He
made up for it with hair.. A ragtag explosion of
ginger hair spilled out from underneath a black
bowler hat. It was easily half way down to his waist.
He wore an old brown leather jacket, too small and

black leather trousers, too big. A red T shirt underneath the clothing explosion read 'Make Tea not War.' Large leather boots with Steel toe caps completed the ensemble.

"Here" he said, holding out his hand to Pete. "Give me your hand."

Pete, ever the trusting soul, reached out his injured hand. Belfast took it in his and shook it once. The pain vanished from Pete's face. Belfast held his hand out to me. I kept mine where they were.

"Thank you." Pete said. "I thought my hand was broken. It really…"

"Hurt." Belfast said. "That's the idea. Big fuckin' ward on the door. Stops anyone getting in I don't want to. Not planning on shaking me hand Big Man?"

I slowly reached out my hand to Belfast. Alison hissed a warning in my ear. I took his hand and shook it. It felt very…human. He held onto my hand.

"Won't take but a moment Big Man." he said and gave a little whistle. Alison uncurled from around my neck and slid down my shoulder and arm across to his. The cobra slid up his arm and settled around his neck like an especially vicious scarf.

"There. All friends like." Belfast said. "Pouge Mahone." he said giving me a little nod.

"And you can kiss my arse too." I replied. Pete just got his shocked look. He tapped me on the chest with his finger.

"You cannot talk to people like that." Pete said. "I am so sorry Mr Mahone." He turned to see a great grin spread across Belfast's face.

"Not many fella's get it Big Man." Belfast said. "They don't want to upset me ethnic nature ye see."

139

He relaxed the shotgun a little. "I got me an ethnic nature. Came in the post one day. Every other bastard round here's got an ethnicity so thought I better get me one sharpish, so sent off and it arrived. Next day I's a manna property an business all straight up an legal so don't go askin' about taxes, so what'll'' ye be after then? Bin here two years. Gotta reputation now to go with me ethnicity. Got a nice Wilder-beast out back. One careful user, only slightly gnawed."

"Hello. My name is Pete, no second name yet, and this is Mr E.M Faustus. Both Private Investigator and singer in a band."

"Ah. A shamus, a gumshoe, a dick." Belfast began again. "Could have used yew a few months ago, woke up one morning an me left foot had gone. Babylonian demon got it in the night. Had to go looking for the wee bastard with me shotgun and a baked bean tin taped to the stump, so it was to give credence to me ethnicity I like to throw in an odd Irish phrase, Beggorah. Never hurts to play to a cultural stereotype."

He was a Looney.

"I thought you could help me with something. I gather you know animals." I said.

"Could say, could not. Don't know. What you recon?" Belfast was getting very ethnic.

"There's cash in it." I tried. "Extra if you drop the charming Irish act."

"Ay well, fuck ethnicity then." Belfast said. He held out his hand. "That'll be another hundred."

I passed over another hundred and added the cash onto Peter's bill. I also passed over the photocopy of Dog.

"Ah, wee little charmer, isn't he? God love him" Belfast gave. "Not worth the fifty I charged, but he was a whitlow. Some buggers always daft enough to buy him."

Pete wasn't looking confused or relaxed anymore and the smell of dung had an underlying brimstone quality.

"Before you try anything me little Labradoodle there's rock salt an silver in me wee girlie here. As well as lotsa ball bearings." Belfast raised his shotgun towards Pete. "An' me other wee girlie'll have you Big Man."

"You sold Dog." Not a statement, or a question. A threat. I put my hand on Pete's shoulder.

"Wait up." I looked at Belfast. "What's your name Belfast?"

"Name's are power round here." Belfast said. "I'm not that stupid, Big Man. I notice I didn't get yer full name there.

I took a couple of steps back. There was a squish under my feet. I hoped I hadn't ruined his stock. This visit was pricey enough as it was.

"It's all right. That'll dry an wipe off." Belfast said. "What you want?"

"Just some information." I nodded to Pete to take a step back. "When did you sell this dog?"

"'bout three, four months ago. Tall prick, shinny shoes. Wanted something cute and vulnerable. Charged him more than it was worth."

"Watch what you're saying." Pete warned.

"What kind of dog is he?" I asked. "Just a mutt?"

"Not just a mutt." Belfast said. "Nothin' special, but he was the whitlow. Runt of the litter.

141

Shouldn't have lived but did. By rights I should've fed him to the…"

Grab.

Slap.

Bang.

I saw nothing happen, but the gun was out of Belfast's hands and in Pete's, a hole was in the roof, and Alison the Cobra was dangling from Pete's other hand.. about an inch away from my face.

I remember most clearly the look of sheer hatred in the cobra's eyes, that and the open mouth. With the fangs extended. Venom looks quite unpleasant up close like that.

Not nice.

"Get that snake out of my face before I beat you to death with it." I said to Pete through the tightest clenched teeth I have ever had. I could see a sort of rainbow in the prism of the venom.

The snake was nicely removed from my face…and thrust towards Belfast's face.

"It appears she wants to envenomate something." Pete said. He threw the gun away, disinterested.

I walked over and picked up the gun, breaking it and taking out the shells. I popped them in my pocket for safe keeping. I looked at Belfast, who looked trouser dampening terrified.

"Put the snake away Pete." I said.

Pete's head snapped round.

"We need answers, Faustus. This seems to be an effective way to obtain them."

"It's not right though." I said. I rested my hand on Pete's arm. "Please. Put the snake away."

The look on Belfast's face agreed with me. Not such a good pet after all.

Pete slowly looked around the room. An empty fish tank sat on one of the walls. He walked over to it, snake wrapped around his wrist. He flipped the lid from the tank with his free hand then slapped Alison hard on the head. He dropped her in.

I didn't know you could knock a snake out.

Pete put the lid back on the tank and turned back to us. Both Belfast and I let out visible sighs of relief. Belfast's jaw held open.

"Jesus, Labradoodle." Belfast said. "No one's as fast as that. Yer can't catch a cobra. Not in mid-strike."

I tapped Belfast on the shoulder. He jumped. I enjoyed it.

"You can't grab a shotgun like that either, but he did." I said. "Apologize."

"Oh, I'm sorry like son." Belfast said. "No harm done eh?"

"Now you." I said to Pete.

"I am sorry if I hurt your snake." Pete said. "All friends again."

I took my hat off and went to lay it on a table. A Meercat popped its head out of a drawer and looked at the hat with interest. I had second thoughts and put the hat back on.

"Like I said Belfast, we are looking for the dog. Can you tell us where it went?"

"I think he will." Pete said. The smell of brimstone was still an undercurrent to the smell of guano.

"He took the dog with him. I swear to ye Big Man. That's all I know."

"Fair enough." I nodded to the gun in Pete's hand. "Give him the gun back." There was a bang from the fish tank. "Leave the snake where it is."

"He could be lying." Pete said.

"He's not." I was right. Not a muscle in his face said anything but the truth. He even smelled truthful. Hard through the other smells.

"Nice to meet you Belfast." I said.

I nodded to Pete. He passed the shotgun back to Belfast and bowed his head.

"Nice to meet you to Mr...Pouge Mahone." Pete smiled.

A smile crossed my lips.

"You make a funny?" I asked Pete.

"Oh no." Pete said. "I would not be that rude." No smile hit his lips but there was the touch of a glimmer in his eyes.

"Let's go." I said.

Then things got a little worse.

"Here. Big Man. I hear how youse runs this film night. Any chance of me's commin' down?"

You can mess with me.
That's OK.
You can mess with my job.
That's OK.
You can even mess with my coffee.
I'm a big boy. I can take it.

You.
Do.
Not.
Mess.
With.
Film.
Night.

Understand?

I rounded on Belfast.

"What's Your favourite film?" I asked. You could not have missed the threat in my tone.

Belfast managed to miss it.

"Oh. That's easy. Fuckin' 'Blade'." he said. "All them chopped up fuckin' blood suckers. Fuckin' love it. Calm down there Big Man."

I must have covered the distance to him in under a second. Alison was banging Hell out of the tank. I stopped too close to him and he had to take a step back. This kept up till there was only me, him and the wall. You couldn't have fit a Christmas card between us.

"There are five rules about film night." I said.

"I'm bettin' the first one is youse don't talk about film night." he managed.

"Wrong." I said, jabbing him in the chest with my index finger.

"Big Man. Youse want to stop drinking so much caffeine."

"Rule One." Prod. "No eating or drinking during the film."

"Got that one."

"Rule Two." Prod. "What happens outside Film night stays outside Film night."

"No problem there."

"Mr Faustus." Pete said. I ignored him.

"Rule Three." Prod. "No talking during the film."

"Got that. Do youse wanna stop jabbin' me with your finger?"

Prod.

"Rule Four." Prod. "No copying of the film."

"Wouldn't know where to begin. Now…"

Pete's hand touched my shoulder.

"Mr Faustus. You..."

I shrugged his hand off with a flick of my shoulder.

"Rule Five." Prod. "No Shite video nasty bollocks. Got that?"

"Faustus." Pete barked.

"You could listen to your friend right now."

I took a deep breath. I stepped away a little and lowered my hand.

"They are the..." I began.

"Faustus." We are shortly to be in very bad trouble."

I turned and saw Pete looking out of the grimy front window. I moved over to him and peered around the corner of the glass.

I wiped the dirt away. Then I could see. What is it about men running small shops.......

..........don't they dust?

Outside the shop six men were in the process of getting out of a Land Rover. All were dressed in long flowing dusters. Leather, by the look of it. I recognized three of them as local vamp heavies. Meant the rest were probably neck biters too. Five were carrying very large, very black and very scary automatic shotguns.

The sixth was carrying...a long stick.

Belfast walked over and glanced out the window. He swaggered back over to his shotgun and reloaded. He brushed some imaginary fluff from his collar...well, probably not imaginary.

"Don't youse worry boys." Belfast said with confidence. "Wizard who put the wards on this place said nothing could get through lessin I wants 'em in. So..."

146

I relaxed a little.

Belfast got a worried look on his face and ran to the window. Alison banged hell out of the aquarium. The three of us peered through the grimy patch of window.

"That's the fuckin' wizard."

"I really hoped you wouldn't be saying that." I said.

"What exactly is it Youse two have done?" Belfast asked.

"I think we may be about to die." Pete said.

I turned to Belfast.

"Have you got a back way?"

"I'm a take away food emporium." he said with pride. "Course I got a back way. Through that door." He pointed to the door at the rear of the shop. "Past the Meer-cats, past the Elk and through the enclosure with the fuckin' tiger in it."

"A Tiger?" I asked stunned.

"What can I say? Me. I like a vindaloo when I've been on the piss, but a couple of customers like sometin with a bit more bite."

I turned to Pete.

"I was on a date earlier." I said to no one in particular. "Beautiful woman. Now it's a choice between death by vampire, death by wizard or death by tiger. Still. Got my health."

"You are being very strange Mr Faustus." Pete said.

"I'm about to get stranger."

"Oh good." Belfast said. "How can I tell the difference?"

There was a knock at the door.

"Hellooo." A voice twilled. "Is Faustus coming out to play?"

147

I turned to Belfast.

"Tuck yourself away somewhere. It's me they want. Not him. Not you."

"Can the lanky one play too?" the voice trilled.

"OK. There not after you Belfast. Hide."

"We could all hide." Pete said.

"They'll burn the place down." I said. "You hide Belfast. We'll be OK."

"Big Man." Belfast said. "Tough as you are. My shop. My rules. I stay. Got a spare shotgun if you want it"

"Don't touch them." I said. "Guns get you into trouble."

"Well that is somewhat ironic." Pete said.

"Ha-bloody-ha." I said "How many do you think you could take?" I asked him

"I would have to get close enough to grab their weapons." He said. "But I don't think they will let me."

"Getaway." Belfast said.

There was a tap, tap, tapping on the pet shop door. Only this and nothing more.

Apart from the whiny voice.

"Can we come in and play?"

Chapter Seventeen: The Dick and The Dying Time

Excerpt from
Angels, Daemons and other realm beings.
By E.M Faustus
(unpub)

Doorways and invitations.

It is notoriously easy to avoid attack from vampires, werewolves, daemons, witches and wizards and all sorts of other worldly predators.

You don't invite them in.

Simple.

The threshold is a sanctified place of power. It is a gateway, charged with the emotion of those who live or work there. When people who have a right to cross a threshold walk through it, they impart a small bioelectrical charge to the gateway. Over the years this gateway builds up the charge to the point where some become loaded with power. Places such as churches that see a great many people cross the threshold build up phenomenal amounts of power. Others less but it still counts.

People can charge the portals with love, hate, fear or joy. The portal just stores the emotion.

This can explain when why you walk into a building for the first time you can get an immediate feeling as to what it's like. You may feel sad, happy, relaxed or anxious. It all depends on the type of emotion the portal has been charged with.

Otherworldly people originate from a time when they all lived in the outside world. Forests, deserts, plains etc. They are extra sensitive to these man made portals. They can walk straight through them, same as anyone else, but they get one hell of a jolt from the power. Strong enough to stop a heart or fry a nervous system.

The way around this...Invitation.

Without an invitation from those who have a right to be there, the best they can do is hover around on the outside and try to persuade you or threaten you, to invite them in.

Simply put...Do not, under any circumstances, invite them inside.

Ω

"Oh youse can come right on in." Belfast shouted. "Doors open and we all friends here."

Bollocks.

Four burst through the door, shotguns raised and pointing center man. All at Pete.

I took that as a personal insult, and I'm sure that my new Celtic friend felt the same.

The taller of the four slowly turned his head to me and smiled.

My, weren't those canines long.

"Well. Mr E.M. Faustus." he said. "I am delighted to meet you. I would shake your hand but given the circumstances I hope you will forgive me for not doing so."

"I can live with it."

"I take it you will be aware by now there is a price on your head." smiler said.

"Still attached to my body I hope."

"That's not a requirement. No." Still smiling.

"Now no-one said he was worth money." Belfast said, snatching up his gun and pointing it at the centre of my chest.

I thought I saw a slight wink in his eye. Mind you under that face fungus it could have been a greedy little muscle spasm.

"Put the gun down Mr Maghone." Smiler said. "So far you're not involved. Best to keep it that way."

"He is worth enough to pay you for your inconvenience." Smiler said. "His friend is worth enough for us all to retire on. Intact."

"Oh good." Pete said. "I think this might be where we part company Mr Faustus."

"Looking that way. You never even paid your bill." I managed.

"Do you know what?" Belfast said.

"Oh please enlighten us Mr Maghone." Smiler said.

Belfast lowered his gun slightly, and the other shotguns came down a little too. Bit worse for Pete. They were all aimed at his groin now. The other vampires were keeping an eye on Belfast. They were thugs in the true sense. Hurt first. Chat later. Smiler was enjoying himself though. Let him chat.

"It's like this." Belfast said, getting too friendly for my liking. "I'm fuckin' sick o' dancing."

The shotgun came up a fraction of a degree, but swung around as Belfast fired. The first barrel took Smiler full in the face, while the second took out the vampire to his right.

The remaining two guns swung round on Belfast. Handy because they ignored myself and Pete.

Swift as Alison, Pete's hand smashed through the glass tank that housed the cobra and swept her straight towards the vampire closest to him. Alison landed fang first at the man's neck. Impulse alone caused him to drop the gun to try and get the snake off him, but she was wrapping her body tight around his throat and striking repeatedly at the same spot.

Needless to say. He pitched over twitching.

Number four didn't get off so lightly. I slammed the glass case that had been in front of me straight into his exposed face. The glass shattered and loose soil filled his hair and face, running down his clothes.

He swiped the soil away from his eyes as Belfast's reloaded gun came up and emptied both barrels into the window, ripping out the frame and leaving the vampire there having a bad head day.

Well more like no head actually.

The remaining vampire raised his gun and pointed it straight at my face. No point in trying to duck. I was bang to rights. One chance. A gloater.

"And you're meant to be the tough guy." Four said. "Move and I shoot bits off...."

And that's when I stopped listening to him to be honest. I was too busy watching the dirt in his hair and collar move. Then the little blood that was in the vampire began to run.

Then he began to scream.

The screaming did not last long.

Unfortunately, he wasn't dead. His mouth simply filled up with the 'dirt'.

Them his body began to smoulder.

He thrashed a bit.

It had to be ended. I stepped around the desk and picked up Smiler's ichor covered shotgun and pointed it at Number Four's chest.

Before I could find the, whatever you need to fire it, Belfast's hand slowly moved the barrel away.

"I wouldn't do that." Belfast said. "You disturb their new home, they'll come after you. They were growing too many for the cage anyways."

"You said they were fire ants." I said

"Sort of." he said.

"I do not think that was a nice thing to do Sir." Pete said.

"Don't forget they were going to kill youse."

"Point taken."

It only took a second to do a little basic math's and have a quick look about.

"So," I began, "got any more shells?"

"Box in the back shop." Belfast said.

"Would that question have anything to do with the very annoyed looking Wizard standing in the doorway Mr Faustus?" Pete said, too calm for my liking.

"Yeah." I said, then looked up to the wizard and held up a finger for a moment. "Excuse me. Belfast."

"Aye?"

"Never tell me what eats those things."

I might have tried to raise the gun, but invisible hands ripped it from my hands and embedded it, barrel first, in the back door.

Bloody Wizards.

Actually, Bloody Telekinetic, Power Crazed, Cruel as Fuck, Mad as A Box Of Frogs on Helium and Speedballs, Mercenary, Bastard Wizards.

I think that sums them up.

I hate going up against Wizards. Partly because they can rip you apart with just a thought, but mainly because they look too damn smug while they're doing it. And I'd seen this one around. Real scum. Sort of guy who'd burst a kid to see what the balloon would do.

Nasty wee bastard.

But up closer than I wanted to be…The Wizard was…just embarrassing. If this was an undercover operation, he would have looked less out of place with long flowing robes and a pointy hat.

He was wearing a long flowing leather duster coat, custom fit by the look of it. Black. A wide brimmed leather hat sat on his head, set forward at an angle to shroud his eyes. Black. Black leather gloves encased both hands, and black leather trousers rested atop black leather cowboy boots. On all leather surfaces were stitched fine silver sigils that glowed in the light, reflecting his level of magic. He carried a stave, easily his own height, covered with intricate runes that glowed in sympathy with his clothing.

Mind you the battery pack powering the glow was visible in his right hand pocket.

The man was a pervert's wet leather, biker boy dream.

He had the obligatory wizardly beard, but shorter and darker than normal, with odd looking bare patches. He looked the sort to say it was scar tissue. Looked like creeping alopecia to me.

"My name is Harringcour Milius Bergan Trachaneus." he said, extending his hands for dramatic emphasis. Pratt. "I have come for the head of the Detective Faustus. No other body parts required."

"He already did that line." I said, gesturing to the vampire Smiler. I would like to say I had a plan, but apart from trying not to soil my underwear not much was happening in my head.

"Ah. Fuck this." Belfast brought up his shotgun, but a wave from Harringcour's hand slammed the barrel into his face, driving him down to the ground. A faint blue glow shone on the barrel.

"Bet you never need a remote for the television." I managed.

"Ah, the famous Faustus humour." Harringcour said. "Your turn."

I was 'picked up' by unseen hands that dragged me across the floor and pinned me down onto the island in front of the wizard. My Meer cat friend stuck his head out of the drawer, decided that discretion was the better part of valour and vanished back in.

"It is time to stop this now Mr Trachaneus," a little voice said. "I do not wish to see anyone else get hurt."

"I second that emotion." I managed.

"Ah. The homunculus," the wizard sneered and gave a little wave. I would have moved over to allow Pete to join me, but I couldn't even move a finger. I got ready for company.

None came.

Just thinking back to the way Pete walked through the wards on My Door I came to think Harringcour Milius Bergan Trachaneus was in for a great deal of trouble.

He was beginning to realise that too.

"Get his Jewellery." I grunted.

"I am not a common thief Mr Faustus." Pete said. "Sir, you are injuring my friend. Please desist. My. That is a pointy sword."

Harringcour had drawn a blade from his staff. It was indeed pointy and sharp looking. Harringcour held it to Pete's throat.

Why was everyone pointing weapons today?

Why can't villains just give me flowers and a nice box of sweeties?

Harringcour slowly walked around Pete, keeping the blade to his neck. The pressure kept me pinned to the bench.

"Don't let him walk around you." I tried, but Pete was too busy trying to figure out what was going on. A wave of Harringcour's hand and the circle he had traced on the grubby floor with the end of his scabbard/staff was complete and sealed, trapping Pete inside its walls.

"Now to the decapitation." Harringcour said, walking towards me. He jumped up and sat himself down on the bench next to my head. For comedic value, he then farted.

"Mr E.M. Faustus." Harringcour said. "Allegedly the toughest man on The Streets. You look more like a fat bastard to me." He leaned closer. "So tell me Faustus, what does the E.M stand for?"

"Enviable Musculature." I said, wishing it was true as I struggled against the increasing pressure on my back. Bloody hell. This guy was treating me like a puppet and not even breaking out in a sweat.

Harringcour laughed and slid off the desk. He raised the sword and held it in front of my face so I could see it up close. Nice of him.

"No one told me the Homunculus was so powerful. What is he? Daemon or Angel?"

"Don't know."

I could see Pete out of the corner of my eye, pushing against the walls of the binding Harringcour had laid down.. Maybe they were giving, just a little.

Maybe.

A bit.

OK. Lying to myself.

"Want to see how tough I am Harringcour?" I said. "Face me down. Your sword against anything I can find."

Harringcour placed his face on the table next to mine.

"Nice idea Faustus." He said. "However I would have to have the brain of a gnat to fall for that. Now, short back and sides time matey."

Harringcour stood up and raised his sword. Sharp looking as well as pointy. It began to fall.

There was an explosion of orange and black and incredible pain shot across my back as the pressure increased ten-fold. It felt like someone was trying to kick my spine through my chest, the table and floor.

Then I heard the crunch.

The pressure released and I guessed my spine had gone. Funny that I could still feel my legs. A warm, wet feeling ran down my neck and round to my throat and chest.

My first thought was that Harringcour had decapitated me. The bastard had cut my head off.

During the French Revolution the executioners at Madame Guillotine would lift the severed heads from the basket immediately after the blade had fallen and look directly into the eyes. This was because very occasionally the head would take up to ten seconds to die after it was separated from the body. It gave a chance for a good look around just before you died.

At least you got to see a blood enraged crowd giving you a little cheer.

I was still alive. Headless but still alive.

It could take an Elastoplast or two to sort this one out.

Then the pressure came back on my shoulder.

"Told you I had a tiger." Belfast said.

"Yes you did." said Pete, taking hold of me under the arms and lowering me to the floor. "A Tiger."

"Tiger?" I said.

"Tiger." Belfast said.

"Tiger." Pete said.

"Hairy man eating cat?" I said

There was a crunch, followed by a gurgling noise.

"Definitely man eating." Pete said "Definitely."

I ran a hand over my neck and looked at it. Blood. The good news was it wasn't mine.

"The Wizard?" I said, sounding more idiotic minute by minute.

"Proving that it's a man eater." Pete said to the accompaniment of a ripping noise that wasn't exactly fabric. I might not forget that noise.

I sat still with my back to the centre aisle. Belfast sat on my left and Pete sat down to my right.

On the Streets, where werewolves, vampires, Gods and fairies all rubbed shoulders with each other, we were three very unwise monkeys indeed.

I looked to my right, beyond Pete, and saw the Tiger.

It was eating Harringcour.

Harringcour was not totally dead. His eyes were open, mouth moving and his right arm extended towards us in a hope to be pulled free. Not a chance.

158

One of the tigers' paws clamped down on the arm and drew it back by way of added emphasis.

You see animals on the television. Red in tooth and claw. It does not prepare you for the actual experience.

The smell was 'rich' in its quality. Musky.. Feral. Like an old carpet that could use the attention of a good cleaning company.

Then there is the size. I never expected a tiger to look so 'big'. Its size was easily twice that of its actual measurements.

As for red in tooth and claw, it fails to mention all the other colours. The red, obviously, but also the greys and gingers in its hair, the nicotine brown of its claws and the deep amber of the eyes.

The noise. Not just of it's eating, but the sound of it's breathing. Slow. Rhythmic. Hypnotic.

As it ate, it was looking at me. Straight in the eyes. Not a challenge or threat. Just waiting to see what I would do, before it decided to ignore me or kill me. They were the only two options it gave me.

Over the years on The Streets I had seen many things. Many half animals, half beasts and humans who were more animal than they should ever have been, but until that moment, three feet from a tiger, I had never seen a true animal. Something that killed simply to eat. Everything else had been pale shadows.

I nearly wet myself.

When Pete tapped me on the knee Gods know what muscles I had that stopped me.

"We should really go now." Pete said. "I really think we should go now Mr Faustus."

"Yeah." I managed, still locking eyes with the Tiger.

"Could you stand up first please?" Pete asked.

"I don't think I want to do that." I said. "No. After you."

"Ah. You big fuckin' girls." Belfast said, as without warning, he stood up, walked over to the tiger and started tickling it between the ears.

On the tiger's part, it swallowed a little more of Harringcour.

"It's only Tigs." Belfast said. "Little wee kitty."

"If that's your idea of a kitty, never show me your idea of a tiger." I said.

"Better than havin' a guard dog." Belfast said, trying to haul Harringcour's body to one side. 'Tigs' was having none of it. "Be a good girl. Save some for later."

With that Tigs let go, stood up and walked back towards the rear of the shop. My eyes never left her as she walked through the doorway and into what looked like an open yard. I couldn't see a single cage.

"I thought you said people came here to eat the animals." Pete said. "Not the other way around."

"You know what it's like." Belfast said, but I was beginning to loose my grip on reality a little so I affirmed that I did not. "Some lycanthrope wants to show off to his girlfriend that he can handle the biggest meal on the board. Turns out he can't."

Belfast started going through Harringcour's pockets.

"Thing is with caterin'. Food might not always agree with the punter."

"We're going now." I said to Belfast.

"Better get off the floor first then." he replied. "Hey. Twenty Pence."

Belfast held up the small prize and grinned.

160

"Few more of these I'll be able to come to film night."

Back on The Streets, Pete held my arm and helped me limp to the corner. Times Like these I wish I owned a car. Or could even drive properly. Then I could steal one with a good reason to and have a good sit down.

A warm wet feeling was starting to grow in my elbow. I moved Pete's hand and felt the elbow through my jacket. Definitely wet. I looked at my hand. Blood, as expected.

A mix of causes ran through my head, from Belfast's buckshot to tiger claws, considering snakebite and burning sands as two other possible, horrible, options en-route. I took off my jacket and rolled up my sleeve to confirm whatever the worst was.

Much better than I thought, actually. Not even a bruise. Just a red smear. I looked down at Pete's shoes. There was a noticeable amount of blood splattered there. Drops running down his fingers making the splashes bigger.

"Let me see your hands." I said.

"Oh. The hole." Pete said, holding up his left hand for me to see.

Lo and behold, there was a nice hole right through the centre of his palm.

"Ow." my initial reaction probably didn't do the hole justice. "Who did that?"

"Oh, it was Mr Maghone." Pete said. "One of his pellets went a teensy bit wide." He was far to calm for my liking.

I found it hard to understand this man. One minute he could be filled with rage and anger,

161

capable of Gods knew what, the next, calm as a cucumber (a phrase I have never understood), dripping blood and with not even the slightest annoyance at the man who had shot him.

Still, best get him sorted.

"Come on." I said. "Let's get that stitched."

Then Pete fainted.

"Great." I said, looking down at his prone body. "Let me guess. You don't like needles."

And for one blissful moment, the first in what seemed like a lifetime, no one replied. Oh the blissful quiet.

We were near enough to the vampire's car to make use of it, so I bundled Pete onto the back seat. He was surprisingly light, considering his strength. I duly climbed into the front.

It had been many years since I had stolen a car, but old habits die hard. With a fair bit of gear crunching and more weaving than a blanket factory we were underway. Admittedly at twenty mile an hour but I was a very timid joy-rider the couple of times I had tried it. Besides, when I stole cars in my youth I was really stealing somewhere warmer to sleep in the winter.

After a slow start and a slow progress we arrived at the hospital.

Pigglum Hospital.

It should have been Pilgrim Hospital, but by cutting corners during the renaming, the hospital management hired a company run by an embittered ex-patient who had lost one eye to the surgeon when he went in for an NHS nose job. An overly enthusiastic consultant gave a chisel a good whack and the end result was that every-thing, from the signage to the notepads now said Pigglum.

Odd days we live in.

I pulled into the special car park. The one next to the bins, for an audience with Frankie the Fly.

Chapter Eighteen: The Dick and The Doc

There are always places in any town or city where the 'Invisibles' can go for medical care. It might not be brilliant, but it's there. All you have to do is find it.

I had found Frankie through word of mouth, resultant from a claw wound to the ribs that needed what turned out to be sixteen stitches and a series of anti-biotics. The man was a genius with a needle and knew just what med's to prescribe each condition and variation of person.

He did have his 'little quirks'.

The side door opened and a weasel faced man peered around the corner.

"Gee whiz Faustus. You're bringing me corpses now." Frankie said. "What do you want me to do? Cremate it?"

Frankie's voice alone was…indescribable. It was like someone dragging their nails down a blackboard, while simultaneously belching and doing that thing where you try and suck the snot down into your throat from your nose. But much worse.

"Bring it in. I'll get the saws out." Frankie said. "Bloody fly."

And with that Frankie turned on his four inch heels, skirt swirling and teetered off down the corridor. I swung Pete up onto my shoulder and staggered after him.

Frankie was…unusual. Even by Streets standard.

Frankie wore women's clothing, even though a good six foot tall, but he lacked any kind of dress sense. To him a skirt was a skirt, a blouse a blouse. No need to coordinate. I never asked him about his underwear, but as transsexuals go, he was the most unconvincing I had ever met. Too heavy makeup on his face and hands clashed with his fake tan and heavy, heady, cheap perfume. Poured on, rather than just a dab behind the ears.

Frankie hadn't had a lot of choice in his gender reassignment. An over ambitious orderly, during a wait in the morgue had provided Frankie with a novelty hat.

Frankie provided the orderly with a cardiac arrest when he sat up and complained.

Frankie was one of the more successful Street people to integrate into the 'normal' world.

He had done this, and risen to the position of consultant in the hospital by creating a total fiction about himself, to explain his eclectic behaviour.

Heavy makeup, lots of perfume, looking like a man in a dress, flirting with every woman in sight. So far as everyone was concerned, Frankie was a post-op transsexual lesbian.

"Does that look healthy to you?" Frankie said shoving a now bared forearm, grey and flaking.

"Of course not Frankie." I said. "You're a zombie."

Ω

Excerpt from
Angels, Daemons and other realm beings.
By E.M Faustus
(unpub)

Zombies.

Zombies do not eat people. They have no digestive capability.

Zombies do not walk the streets moaning. Unless it's about the state of the country.

Zombies do not look like dried pink prunes. Unless they looked like that before they died.

Zombies are basically a nice group of people. After all the worst has happened, things can only get better.

What Zombies Do is;

Excellent needle-work. Essential for keeping things together.

Excellent cosmetics - to disguise the greyness: You would be surprised how many zombies work on cosmetics counters. Or maybe you wouldn't be.

Superb taste in furniture. No idea why, but they do.

Zombies' skills are varied, from consumption of concoctions in Haiti to magic in producing cheap labour for Cornish tin mines.

Wherever a zombie comes from, whatever their past lives were, when they die, they tend to become incredibly altruistic. They just want to help and be a productive member of society. Consequently they turn up in all sorts of caring professions from medicine to bar work. None in Social Services though. That's more the province of downstairs.

Ω

"Faustus," Frankie said. "You know I prefer…Bloody Fly…differently alive."

"I'll use the word alive about you Frankie when your heart starts beating again."

"I'll let you know Faustus. Watch it if you like. It's in that Jar over there."

Frankie pointed to a jar of specimens on a shelf. Even after all these years, internal organs send a shiver down my spine. Especially if I'm talking to the owner of those organs at the time.

"So what do you want me to do with him Faustus? I'm not getting rid of any more bodies. That last one tried to get out of the oven."

"He's been shot in the hand Frankie. Stitch him up will you?"

Frankie lifted up Pete's wounded hand.

"Through and through." Frankie said. "Pop him on the counter and I'll get the needle and thread. Don't suppose you'll tell me how this happened?"

"He stopped someone from making money."

"How?"

"Decapitation."

"Of whom?"

"Yours truly."

Frankie shook his head. A small shower of probable dandruff fell from his head. It had to be dandruff. Wigs don't shed and Frankie had been bald for twenty years at least.

"Bad Days Faustus. Bad Days."

A thought crossed my mind as I lowered Pete onto the table top, placing a pile of paper under his head as a cushion.

"Could you do a blood test on him? Real fast." I said. "I need to know...what he is."

"You don't know that?" Frankie asked as he began to clean Pete's hand.

"No. I..."

"Bloody fly." Frankie said, walking over to his handbag and taking out a spray which he liberally squirted all over himself. It didn't smell too bad.

"New perfume?" I asked.

"Fly spray."

Frankie lived in fear of the imaginary flies. Something called 'Fly Strike'. Look it up. I began to feel queasy when he tried to explain it to me.

"Not too bad. A through and through." Frankie said. "Few stitches and some out of date anti-biotic should do the job."

I idly picked up a thin metal tube from the table and began twiddling it. Several grooves along the side looked curious so I pulled the little lever at the base. I was a tad surprised when four razor blades popped out.

"Jesus Frankie." I said staring at it. "What do you use this for?"

"Cleaning my pustules since you ask. Cleans the scabs out a treat. Used to be used for treating syphilis. I'll let you figure out where it used to go."

I hurriedly put it back down and stood up, putting my hat back on.

"Frankie, can you keep him here for a while?" I asked. "There's something I have to do and I'd rather not have him around."

"Trouble is he?" Frankie asked, pausing with his needle in his hands.

"Not in himself." I replied. "He just attracts it."

"Fair enough." Frankie jabbed the needle into the back of Pete's hand and walked to his desk. He opened a desk drawer and took out a small bag. From it he took a small vial and a hypodermic. He filled the syringe from the vial.

"How long do you want him to go Bo Bo's?"

"Couple of hours?"

"Call it three." With that he walked back to Pete and pushed the needle straight into his carotid artery. Ow!

"Back soon." I said, glad to be leaving Frankie's little world.

"Laters F." Frankie said as he busied himself in Pete's hand.

Chapter Nineteen: The Dick and The Delicate Discussion

A cool breeze blew through the trees and bushes in the garden. I pulled my jacket closer and lit up my third since I got there. The other two stubs were in the ashtray on the table.

It hadn't taken too much to make four out of two plus two about my visit to Belfast's special little shop. That some-one, had tipped off the neck biters and the tiger snack as to where we were going.

Long shot to be here, but it was three in the morning, and we were staring though a set of French windows into a happy home. I was tired, pissed off and had a mouth like an ashtray. I also hadn't had a coffee in hours so I'd play a long shot and hope I was wrong. I dug the chocolate out of my pocket and took another bite from my 'Marathon'."

I refuse, point blank to call them 'Snickers'.

I grew up calling them 'Marathons'.

I will continue to call them 'Marathons'.

If the spotty little tit in the all-night garage can't understand, then he can…well, refuse to serve me as it happens, but fortunately there was more than one garage on the way here.

I heard the car pull up out front. I had been waiting long enough to be cold and annoyed. Hoping against hope I was'nt about to make a fool of myself and get my arse kicked.

A key went in the lock and a light came on in the hall. Keys were dropped onto a side table and a face I knew well was framed in the door-pane, peering through into the garden, watching me take a long drag on my cigarette.

A surprised look crossed the face, and after a second a smile spread, lighting up the place.

Feet on the carpet, a door being unlatched and expensive odour.

I wish I didn't know I was right.

"Hello Paul."

"Bloody Hell Faustus. You must be freezing." my friend said. "What you sitting out here for?"

"I didn't want to wake Cecile and Andre." I said

Cecile. Nicest werewolf you would ever want to meet. Paul's long suffering wife. Andre. Beautiful little Andre. I'm one of his God-fathers.

I hated myself. Two weeks ago I had been at a barbecue here with all the band. Paul had even got me some special Iced Coffee.

"They're not here Faustus." Paul said. "They went to visit Cecile's mum in Paris last week."

"Not you though."

"Got to make the money mate." Paul said turning. "Come on. I'll put the kettle on."

"Paul?"

"Yeah?"

As Paul turned I hit him over the head with the spade he kept in the garden shed.

"Son of a bitch." I said.

Paul went down like a sack of potatoes. As he hit the ground he started to change. I couldn't take the chance of dealing with a pissed off werewolf so I did the kindest thing and hit him in the head a few more times. Paul's about my size and weight, but tough as any werewolf you care to name. I kept going until he was too groggy to stand.

Blood ran down his face from several cuts I'd opened up on his scalp. I added insult to injury by kicking him under the chin and knocking him out cold.

I dragged the limp body over to the elm tree and propped him up against it. I carefully cuffed his right wrist and bent the arm around the tree. I bent his left arm behind the tree and cuffed both wrists together.

I hit him once more with the spade.

It's not excessive force if your opponent can change into a two hundred pound werewolf and rip your throat out by reflex. It's prudent.

I went through his pockets. A wallet. Three mobile phones. Some loose change and a guitar pick. Just the normal stuff in the wallet, a little cash, couple of business cards, a prescription for Andre and a photograph of Paul, Cecile and Andre, all crowded into one of those picture booths. Paul camping it up for the camera, Cecile looking embarrassed and Andre grinning like a Cheshire cat.

No. I had no feelings of guilt at all.

"Wake up."

Slap.

"Come on. Wake up."

Harder slap.

"Wake up, or it's a kick in the face again."

The change was fast.

The face sprouted hair as the nose and jaw elongated into a muzzle while the teeth suddenly became longer and noticeably pointy. The eyes changed in a blink from human to canine, but still retained the blue tint Paul was convinced caused the ladies to swoon.

The jaws lunged at me.

It is both logical and prudent to draw back, so I shoved my hand with all three mobiles in it, deep into his jaws.

Paul's jaws should have crushed the tech and my arm to unrecognisable pulp. Instead he paused, teeth just holding the mobile phones. His tongue ran over them.

"Or ukth sak theth. Tk mm ooww." Paul managed. Muscles were beginning to shift inside his clothing.

"Stop that." I said, flicking his nose with the end of my finger. "Cecile bought you that jacket last Christmas. If you wreck the stitches she'll kill you"

I reached into his mouth.

"Open wider."

I reached in and took the mobiles out, dropping them into my jacket pocket. I sat down on the ground opposite Paul. His features went into reverse, creeping back to human. He shook his head and was back.

"How's my hair?" he asked

"Fucked up and bloody. How do you think?"

"What's…" Paul began.

"Stop. Don't pretend you don't have some idea of what's going on." I said. "You pointed me in the direction of Belfast's shop. Next thing I know there are people after me with guns and swords. Apparently there's a contract out on little old me. I know you told someone. I just want to know why."

"Why ask if you know what happened?" Paul asked. Paul was serious. Not something that happened often, so I decided honesty was the best policy.

"Because I don't want to loose my friend."

173

Paul looked stunned. Then again I had hit him with a spade. I got to my feet and walked around the tree, bent over and unlocked the handcuffs. I walked back to the garden bench and sat down. I heard Paul get to his feet and do the wrist rubbing everyone does when handcuffs are removed.

"Can I sit down? Paul asked.

"Yeah."

Paul sat opposite me. Both in silence for a long while. Paul picked up my packet of cigarettes. He rolled the packet round in his fingers for several minutes, then snatched the flip lid over took out a coffin nail, lit it and took a long drag.

"I'm supposed to have given up." Paul said.

Me. I said nothing.

Often, when you're interviewing someone you know is guilty, the best way is just to sit still and do nothing. Say nothing. Limit your movements to a minimum. People cannot stand the silence. They have to fill in the blank space, so they talk. They talk about anything, but they do come around to the subject of what makes them have the guilty weight nuzzling in their chest.

"Remember that time I was on my first date with Cecile?" Paul said. "The lot of you filled that restaurant. Just to make sure I behaved. You even followed me back to her place. Well, I suppose I did have a bit of a reputation, but from that minute, that first date, I knew Cecile was special. I behaved like a perfect gentleman. You all took me out afterwards for a drink. What you didn't know was that Cecile gave me a key to her front door for later."

Paul took a drag on his cigarette.

"We laughed a lot about you. She thought you were great. She thinks you are terrific man. She considers you our big brother. Did you know that? Prays every night for you. Thinks you should get out of the business. After that last time, with the Oni, she was worried sick about you."

Drag on cigarette.

"Andre thinks the world of you too. Gets this big grin on his face when he knows you might come around. Loves to play with you. I love you too man. I do."

There was a pause. Frankly I didn't know what to say so I left him to do the talking. My sole contribution was to place the three mobile phones on the garden bench.

Paul looked at the telephones. He reached out and slid one to one side.

"Home phone." he said.

He slid the second to the other side.

"Work phone."

Paul picked up the third phone and looked at it, disgust playing across his face.

"I had no choice." he said.

I reached out and took the phone from Paul's unresisting fingers. I dropped it into my pocket. I lit up a cigarette myself and slid the pack back towards Paul. He greedily took the pack, dug out a smoke and lit up.

"Thanks." he said. We fell back into silence.. The silence lasted a long time, until Paul finished his second smoke and lit up his third.

"Andre was ill a few months ago." Paul said. I controlled the anger on my face. If he was going to use Andre as an excuse I might just pick up the spade again.

"Pneumonia. Really hit him hard. Cecile had to take three months off work to look after him."

Why not you Paul? You are his dad.

"Session work and teaching isn't too much money you know?" Paul looked at me imploring understanding. He got none.

"So I borrowed a couple of grand to tide us over. Bare Faced Charlie
was more than happy to loan it. Interest wasn't too bad, then all of a
sudden he sold the note. Next thing I know I've got one hundred percent
on it and it's due the next day. I told the collector he could have my Gibson, or Les Paul. Even my Martin, but he told me the money or my hands."

Paul sat back a little and raised his hands dramatically.

"Without these I couldn't raise a penny Faustus. Not a penny." Paul threw the remains of smoke three away and lit up number four. "Then he turned up. That big guy from tonight. Cadfael or something. Shinny shoed bastard. He came here. Here. To my home. Gave me the telephone and this."

Paul dug into the recesses of his jacket pocket and took out a battered photograph. I looked carefully. The image was a little blurry, but there, looking wilder than I had seen him so far was Pete. A close up photograph. Pete snarling at the camera and blood in his eyes. Just shy of an animal. I took the photograph from Paul and dropped it into my pocket. It felt considerably heavier than the phone did.

"He told me that my debt would be written off if I could find him. I didn't have to do a damn thing, just phone him and say where he was. Gave me some bull about the guy being a runaway from an old, mad family who just wanted to get in touch with him again and it was worth a lot of money to them to pay whoever found him."

Paul paused. He looked worried now, ready to run or fight worried. I was sympathy itself. I brought the spade up and dropped it on the table.

"OK. No need for that." Paul said. "So I looked for the guy. I didn't want to bring you into it. I knew you could find him, but this was my mess and I didn't want to get you involved. I felt… I should sort it."

Paul swallowed hard. A big fat truth was on the way. His eyes flicked towards the spade and he took a frantic drag on the cigarette.

"I'd looked everywhere I could think of for a solid week. Nothing. Then a couple of weeks ago I was dropping some stuff off for you at Peter's shop and out he comes. Happily walking this little mutt. Barely recognized him from the photograph, but there he was. Same guy who was at the gig tonight." Paul paused and took a drag on the cigarette that had died. He didn't seem to notice. So I called them then, and when he showed up again tonight I called them again."

There you go.

Got to the point eventually.

I can't help but turn the screws when I have someone on the hook. Yes, Paul was a friend. Yes, he was sorry as hell, but he had brought himself into my world so I would be dammed if I'd treat him like a tourist.

"Who was at the end of the phone?" I asked, breaking my silence. I knew the answer, but it's good to follow the script.

"That big guy from the bar." Paul said.

"Call him." I said sliding the phone towards Paul. He looked at the mobile like the chalice from the palace it was. He picked it up and pressed whatever buttons you need for speed dialling. Don't own one. Don't really know how they work. Don't care.

"It's ringing." Paul said. I reached over and took the phone from his hand and held it to my own ear. I could hear a scratchy ringing toney thingy.

"Hello doggy. You after a treat?" Cadell's voice sounding far away and echoing.

"Missed me? I said.

"Aww. You found out about my doggy." Cadell said. "I might have to tap his nose with a newspaper."

"Told the RSPCA about you." I said. "They rehomed him with me."

"And he cost me so much money Mr E M Faustus. So much money. I will need to be compensated."

"Where do you want me to send the cheque Cadell?" I tried.

"Ah well. I do move around a lot. Just let him go and I'll pick him up." he said. Ooo a tad frustration in his voice. I liked that.

"Funny thing about you and me Cadell," I said, tightening the screws, "is that I'm like a road runner, and you're some wormy coyote. You keep trying to catch me but keep falling off that damn cliff. Why not call up Acme and get them to save some time and shove a giant rocket up your arse? Lend you a match to light the fuse?"

"No Faustus" he snapped. "You are more like an annoying little mouse and I know the right pussy cat to chase you down."

"Beep Beep." I said and hung up the phone. Paul was looking at me askance.

"Did you upset him?" he asked.

"I bloody hope so." I said. "Go pack some clothes. You're moving in with me for a while."

While Paul was packing I should have sat in the garden and waited, so I went through all the papers I could find. Nothing unusual. Cecile kept all of her bank statements neatly in a file. Paul kept his wedged in a pocket of a guitar case.

Predictably several large amounts had been paid in from someone else. The details seemed familiar so I pocketed the statement for later. I heard Paul's tread on the stairs and looked up. He said nothing, so neither did I, just picked up his laptop and shoved it into its case, then led the way out to his car. I sat in the back with his clothes and laptop. He always kept a guitar in the boot so I knew he wouldn't be bored.

I knew how scared he was, not so much for himself as Cecile and Andre, and I wasn't making things easier. But if you want easy you don't get mixed up with loan sharks let alone psychotic bastards like Cadell. I needed to check something out so I silently reached over and took Paul's SatNav from the dashboard. I tapped in the address. I tossed the SatNav to Paul.

"Drive." I said.

"OK." He said.

We drove in silence for about fifteen minutes. A record for Paul. Then he couldn't last any longer.

"Are we still friends Faustus?" he asked.

"Never stopped." I bluntly replied.

"Good, because.." he said, getting ready to start a chat.

"Never stopped but shut the fuck up and drive." I said, leaning back in the car, pulling my hat over my eyes and grabbing a few minutes sleep.

Chapter Twenty: The Dick and The Discovery

I woke up about fifteen or twenty minutes later as the car jumped to a halt. I got out and looked at the street, then checked my watch. It was three in the morning, so not surprisingly it wasn't busy. Even the Police Constable on duty outside Jo-Jo Mar's house looked sleepy. I leaned into the car.

"Stay here." I said.

"Can't I…?"Paul started.

"No you can't." I said. "If I don't come back…You're fucked mate."

"I hope you come back then."

Strictly speaking, I thought as I walked towards Jo Jo Mar's, I didn't have to be so rough on Paul, but one ounce of sympathy and he might forget the mess he was in. With players like Cadell about it wasn't such a good idea to be nice.

Be nice he'll fold.

Be nice he'll expect me to sort out this mess for him.

Sorry, but when I'm working I don't do nice.

I opened the gate at Jo-Jo Mar's and walked up to the door, stopping when my progress was blocked by a large and very thick arm.

"And where are we going at this time of night sir?" the PC said.

I kept looking straight ahead, down the corridor.

"We are not going anywhere constable." I said with pure bred conviction and arrogance. "I am going to continue in my job, while you stand in the cold, possibly even the pissing rain if the weather forecast holds true. A job you could find yourself doing for many nights to come, depending on the outcome of the next minute or two."

I turned my head to look at the unfortunate copper.

"If I have to take my ID out officer, then things will be very bad for one of us."

Yep. You'll find out that my membership of Blockbuster Video expired two years ago.

"Sorry Sir." He said, arm snapping down to his side, rocking to attention and head staring straight ahead.

If you have enough arrogance, are quick, look the part and turn the tables on someone, anyone, you can bluff your way in a great many situations. It helps if you're dealing with an out of favour idiot.

I passed straight through the house and after throwing a few bolts and braces was out into the large, overgrown back garden at the rear. I took a few steps into the garden and took off my hat, holding it out from my body and both arms out to the side. I slowly turned around, keeping my head raised and as visible as possible.

Someone would be watching, possibly even filming. I wanted them to get a good view and a good idea that I was no threat. I held up one hand with my fingers outstretched, indicating I would be no more than five minutes, then popped my hat back on my head and began to walk around the garden.

The grass had been flattened by size ten boots and those interesting plates forensics put down to preserve the scene, but prior to the police someone had come in here and sat with an automatic weapon, waiting for Jo-Jo Mar to make a cuppa and...there it was.

A small indentation in the ground, where someone had knelt down to take aim. About a foot in front of it a small hole in the earth, about the size of a little finger where the shooter had rammed in a Y-rest to balance the barrel for greater stability while they fired.

A Pro then.

The weight of indentation on the knee pointed to someone light. A small indentation in front of it showed where they had buried their heel when shooting.

Pointless to look for shells, the police would have been thorough enough to find them all, if the shooter left any behind. Likewise anything else.

I put my knee into the indentation and foot where the heel had been, both legs close together. Tight. The hole was close to my body. Put the shooter at a little over five foot.

Someone slight. They must have been in that position for a good long while.

I stood up and walked back to the house, peering through the broken window. No one had got around to boarding it up yet. Probably tomorrow.

The splatter pattern against the wall was quite pronounced, but a walk back to the shooter's position showed that if they had wanted to take out Pete and I it would only have taken one squeeze of the trigger.

Someone wanted us alive.

Then.

I strolled back through the house, giving the constable plenty of time to get back to attention. As I came level with him I slowed down a little. He tried to get further to attention than he was already. Boy was going to break his spine if he wasn't careful.

I stopped on the step next to him. I could hear him sweat.

"Cigarette?" I said. He visibly relaxed.

"Please. Thank you sir." he said.

"I didn't ask you if you wanted one. Have you got any?" I said. Paul's chain smoking had seriously depleted my store. The PC frantically rummaged in his top pocket and produced a packet of ten. He slowly handed me the packet. I opened it. There were three left. I took one and passed him the pack back.

"Light up if you want to." I said, doing just the same myself.

"Thank you sir." He did just that.

We stood.

We smoked.

My, weren't we all palls together!

"What's your name Constable?" I asked.

"PC Kenneth Lloyd." Straight back. No hesitation. I like someone who doesn't't have to think about his own name.

"Been on the door long?"

"Since start of shift sir." So. Since ten o'clock.

"Had the chance of a cuppa or a pee?"

"No sir." Liar. "Been on the door the whole time." Still lying.

"Good. I hate to think what could happen if anyone got in here."

"Who should I say visited Sir?" He asked. "For the log."

He wasn't totally stupid then. He had enough sense to get my name at least. So I thought I'd play a little.

"No one." I said. "I was never here. You never saw anyone. No one crossed the door. No one invited you into their house to get a warm and have a cuppa. The house over there with the red door."

I pointed to the house where I had seen the curtains move earlier in the day. She seemed like the kind to do that. Be nice to the police…and find out as much as she could about what was happening.

"It was only for ten minutes Sir." He looked scared. Looks like I got it right. "It was freezing out here."

"It's alright son." I was being comforting. Wasn't that nice of me? "The house was being closely watched. Relax."

He relaxed. "Who was…?" PC Lloyd was asking all the right questions. I'll give him that.

"Some questions don't get asked." I said. "Some answers never happen, and some departments do not exist PC Lloyd." I stubbed my cigarette out on the sole of my shoe. "Watch your post laddie. Watch your post."

I pocketed the stub - after all I don't want to leave any DNA at a murder scene- and walked away.

I'd learned a few things, not the least being that some people would believe secret government agencies existed and would recruit them if they were good boys and girls.

Secret Government Agencies don't exist.

So it was impossible for me to walk across the road and talk to one.

So I didn't.

Interesting to know they were watching though.

I got back into the car. Paul jerked awake.

"I wasn't sleeping. Just resting my eyes."

Liar.

"Hospital." I said. "I've a package to pick up."

Chapter Twenty One: The Dick and The DNA

"If he was a dog, I'd call him a mongrel." Frankie said.

"I never told you to do a DNA test on him." I barked.

"I. Was. Curious." Frankie came back.

Frankie was holding a set of completely unintelligible papers in his hand. We were standing either side of a prone Pete, still out cold on the bench. The papers were DNA tests. Tests that are supposed to take weeks to produce.

"I thought those tests took weeks to produce." I said, predictably.

"Oh, bollocks." Frankie said, waving the papers at imaginary flies. "That's just what we tell people to make it seem harder than it is. Takes about thirty minutes with the new machines."

I had always thought that.

"I'd always thought that." Staying predictable. "So what do they say about him?"

"Well, I'd gotten curious about him when I realized that he was healing himself as fast as I was stitching him up." Frankie was now walking around the room expounding to his audience. "By the way did you know he'd been bitten by some snake? Anyway, the test came back and it was impossible because…"

"Stay in English Frankie."

"OK. DNA reveals the parentage. It shows the DNA of the two parents. That simple."

"I follow that."

"Except he seems to have three parents. Two of whom are non-human"

Frankie paused for dramatic effect.

"OK. You knew that didn't you? Bloody fly."
Frankie sounded deflated. I nodded my head slowly.

"But did you know that on a genetic level several
proteins and amino acids are seriously corrupted, by
the introduction of HUMAN DNA?"

You could hear Frankie's voice reach up to get the
uppercase letters. All that was missing was the clap
of thunder, wolf howling or crash of dramatic music.

There was an uncomfortable pause.

"Sorry." Frankie said.

"It's OK mate." I said, as comfortingly as I could.
"What does all that mean?"

Frankie leaned on the bench over Pete.

"He shouldn't exist." Frankie said. "His DNA is
so biologically corrupt; he should never have been
born, let alone lasted 'til his thirties. I guessed his
age. He is the waste of a litter. The runt. The
Whitlow. The fact his parents DNA are all
corrupted doesn't help."

I had to sit down.

When the Big Guy produces Angels, or Him
downstairs gets himself a Daemon, they utilize
human 'patterns' to generate the body. Difficult to
do apparently, but it makes them perfect human
specimens. Perfect in every way. Some argue better
than perfect.

"Is his DNA Angel or Daemon?" I asked.

"Wait a minute." Frankie checked his papers,
occasionally swatting at the imaginary flies. "I think
so. I think so. Right kind of neutral markers."

"Which?"

"Both." Frankie said. "One of each."

I had to sit down.

"That's impossible." I said. "They don't share the same room unless they have to, let alone…" I waved a hand at Pete "their DNA."

"I wonder if they shagged?" Frankie said.

"Bloody hell Frankie. I thought I left Paul in the car." I picked up Pete's hand and looked at the wound. There were no stitches. "I thought you stitched him up?"

"I did. Twenty minutes later his body spat them out. Give it another half hour and I'm guessing there won't even be a scar."

I took a smoke out by reflex. A look from Frankie was sufficient to make me put it back.

"So what is he?" I asked the world in general.

"Pete. My name is Pete."

I have to admit, I nearly jumped out of the seat.

"I have of course heard everything you said." Pete opened his eyes, sat up and slid from the bench.

"In short you have no idea what 'species' I am!" Pete said. More a statement than a question.

I looked awkwardly at Frankie. Frankie, The Professional. Looked more awkwardly at me.

"Well. No." The Professional said. "I mean you are…" Frankie consulted several sheets of his papers. "…Fifty eight per cent human, that accounts for your physical nature and your brain, but the rest of you, and I'm guessing here…"

"Guess away." Pete said.

"OK. I would guess that the rest come from a nominally male and nominally female Angel and daemon."

There was one of those dramatic pauses. I looked at Pete. Frankie looked at his feet. Pete looked at a point on the wall.

There are no books, no DVD's, not even a newspaper article on how to deal with finding out your mum was an Angel, your daddy was a devil and your other daddy was a human. Maybe there was an American talk show in it, but I defy a psychologist to give any kind of help.

"Well that's cleared that up then." Pete said. "Shall we go?" Pete stood up and held his hand out to Frankie. "Thank you very much. You have addressed some unanswered questions in my life, but in truth have generated more that I must think upon."

Pete shook Frankie by the hand and walked to the door. He turned to me.

"I do have one question you could answer for me immediately Mr Faustus." He said.

"Yeah." I said, amazed at his seeming simple acceptance of the news. If I can."

"Where are we?"

Chapter Twenty Two: The Dick and The Drugs and The Detection

With Pete bundled into the back seat, Paul drove back to the office. We went upstairs to the flat. I threw Paul a sleeping bag and told him to crash in the back room. He could have used the bedroom admittedly, but I needed sleep myself and Pete was going to be on the sofa. I gave Paul a nice cup of tea to go to bed with. It would help him sleep.

Oh. And it would assist with rapid bowel movements in the morning.

Very Rapid. With the capital R.

Wolfs bane tea. Wolfs bane doesn't exactly repel werewolves, but it can really upset their stomachs.

After me nearly getting killed that night, I was entitled to a little revenge.

I put a toilet roll in the refrigerator and stood in the kitchenette making a night time coffee. Pete walked in and got himself a cup from the wall cabinet.

"I'll only ask you once." I said. "Are you sure you are alright with that news?"

Pete let out a slow sigh.

"Today, Mr Faustus, I have beaten up people and in turn been beaten up myself. I have watched people die, quite horribly, and am culpable in some of those deaths myself. I feel sick to my stomach about this. And all I want is my dog back. Against all of this my petty concerns of my parentage mean little." He poured himself half a cup of coffee. "I just want Dog back Faustus. I just want my little

Teddy Bear." He picked up his cup and turned to leave.

I have no idea why I did it. After all he was just a client, and I'm not paid to make anyone feel better about their lives.

Maybe it was because he had saved mine, but I put my hand on his shoulder.

"You just proved you're human Pete. Whatever the genetics say. No Angel or Daemon would think that. Ever. You're human. I hope that's a compliment."

He turned and gave me a violent hug.

His head rested on my shoulder as he cried his human heart out.

Now, I am against casual drug use.

I have seen too many friends be destroyed by a wide variety of drugs from spliffs to the more Street orientated Ba-Bou.

Sometimes though, sleep gets in the way.

Oh, there's payback. There always is, whatever you take.

So you pay it. Grit your teeth, don't complain, hope you don't stroke out or have a heart attack.

I popped two white pills into my mouth. Mainly Caffeine adrenalin and sugar concentrate.

Mainly.

I took a swift slug of really strong espresso and began to creep downstairs. By the time I got to my office door I was wide awake and likely to be for the next forty two hours.

Hey. Who needs sleep?

I walked into the computer closet to find the machine humming quietly to itself. I wiggled the mouse (can't abide those touch screen mousey paddy thingies) and the screen came to life. A series of bank details. God bless the internet and insecure banks.

I took out the bank statements from Paul's and checked his bank account.

Healthy.

Not quite the whole truth? Well, you get used to it with Paul.

Several payments had been made, funnily they matched the times he had rung Cadell. Now for the complicated stuff.

I tapped some keys and did some mouse wiggling and clicking. I took out a packet and before I could light up heard the magic start.

"When you gonna marry my Dorothy? Skinny Boy." the magic said.

"Once I meet her I'll tell you."

"Excuses, excuses." Mojo lady said.

A large brown skinned face filled the screen, a big smiling face. The background showed a wonderful tropical scene. I was, as always, immediately envious.

"Hello Mammasayra." I said. "How's the latest husband doing?"

"I think I broke him." Mammasayra said. "Ain't seen him in tree days. He went into town with Dorothy and he didn't come back."

"Girl get hungry?" I asked. I'd seen photographs of Dorothy. She was a big girl. Mind you not a patch on Mammasayra.

On the screen was my friend Mammasayra. An immense personality, heart and spirit surrounded by a body you have to take a good ten minutes to hug. Working your way around slowly. A big Fijian woman with a heart of gold and knowledge of computers and hacking second to none. It has even been rumored that she can hack a computer with no internet connection.

"What you need Skinny Boy?" Mammasayra said. "I tell you what you need. My Dorothy to cook you a decent meal. Y'need some meat on them bones. Dorothy would break you in half on your wedding night."

"I'm not marrying Dorothy Mammasayra." I smiled. Same attempts to marry Dorothy off every time. "But I could use your 'special' help."

"What you need boy?" Mammasayra said, spreading her arms wide.

I held up the account number details I had from various bank statements.

"If I give you an account number, could you tell me where the money came from. It's origins."

"Bad case, skinny boy?" she asked, her face betraying her concern for me.

"People dying, and a contract on yours truly." I said. "I need to stop it."

"Why it always come down to you?" Mammasayra said, leaning into the camera on her machine. "You think you're a superhero or something?"

"I'm the wrong man, in the wrong place, at the wrong time." I said. "And I'm the only one who can."

"I send you a cape an tights inda post."

"Look. There are some-things I can do, others I can't." I said. "I walk these streets at night time. I work out problems and get answers. Sometimes I get a kind of justice. I'm honest and don't take bribes to look the other way. I see the job through to

193

the end. On this case I think I'm the only one who can finish it."

"I doubt that, but give me the numbers."

I read out the numbers of the account I had, along with Paul's and Jo-Jo Mars, so she could cross check and do whatever she did.

"Any idea how long this could take?" I asked.

"Go make yourself another coffee boy. Smoke some, then I'll tell you something." Mammasayra said. "Get something to eat too. You could use…"

"Some meat on my bones. I know." I smiled and stood up. I walked back to my office desk and opened the bottom drawer.

Traditionally a Private Eye keeps a bottle of whisky in the bottom drawer.
I keep a bottle of Holy Water and a big bag of chocolate. I unpeeled a Marathon (they were Marathons when I was a kid, they're Marathons now-no matter what the wrapper says.) and bit a good third off before I got back to the screen. Mammasayra was peering at another screen on her window.

"Have you minimized me?" I asked her. "How could you?"

"You got a big case Skinny Boy?" she said.

"Well, it started out as a dognapping." I began before Mammasayra interrupted.

"No. I'm telling you, you got a big case Skinny Boy." Mammasayra sighed. "You wait a minute. Someone stupid enough to attack me."

I could see Mammasayra furiously tapping away at her keypad. She reached into a drawer and slipped something into her machine, then sat back and smiled.

"Some God Botherer just downloaded a hard drive full of Goat Porn." Mammasayra said, smiling so wide her head was in danger of falling off.

"I'll not ask where you got that from. So, what people after you?" I have to confess concern. Mammasayra was only doing a trace for a few minutes when she was under assault.

"You go to church regular Skinny Boy?" Mammasayra asked. "'Cos someone at church got an interest in you."

Mammasayra typed away for a second or two. In a small box on my screen appeared a large symbol. A papal mitre with two crossed keys. The keys each had an intertwined snake on them.

"They arrogant enough to put their logo on their firewall." Mammasayra said.

"I half recognize that picture." I said. "Any idea what that is?"

"Detection is your line there Skinny Boy. But I can give you a clue."

"Ooo good." I said taking another bite out of the Marathon. "I love clues. They make a case so interesting."

That is true.

Sometimes clues just get in the way. A nice simple case becomes more complex the more clues that turn up. Sometimes it's best to ignore the clues and go with gut instinct...and a sock with half a brick.

"Was that sarcasm or irony Skinny Boy?"

"Irony."

"In that case, it's the Holy See, Skinny Boy." Mammasayra started to laugh. "It seems the Vatican are paying to get you killed."

I sat back amazed.

Mammasayra laughed her tits off.

"Are you going to be alright?" I asked her. If someone was trying to kill me, for discovering Who knows what, they could go after her for tracking their money down.

"I'm perfect safe Skinny Boy." she said. "If they do track me down on line they gonna end up in a tittie bar in Hamburg. Don't you worry about me. You look after yourself. Hello there…"

Mammasayra leaned closer to her screen, reading fast.

"They just offered me a whole lotta money to tell them how I got as far as I did." Mammasayra sat back "I'm gonna go an' delouse my drives. You take care of yourself Skinny Boy an' if I can help you just let me know. Give yourself a big hug from your Mammasayra."

Mammasayra blew me a big kiss. I blew her a kiss back and the screen went dead.

See what I mean about clues?

They just make a simple case complicated.

I sat for a few minutes trying to get my head around everything. Ignoring the homicidal intent of a bunch of neck biters, possibly financed by The Vatican, the case boiled down to a few simple points.

1) Pete's dog had been stolen.
2) Someone had silenced the thief.
3) The thief had been paid by Angels or possibly Daemons.
4) The same people were interested in getting their hands on Pete.

5) Someone had declared war on the Fae.

I'm not too sure how much the last has to do with points one to four, but I like my lists in fives.

So.

Find the money tree for the theft, get the dog, find out what they want from Pete and stop the same from cutting my head off.

Simple.

Sometimes I do wonder why I no longer drink.

Oh. I'm a drunk. That's why.

Sometimes, knowing you're a drunk from not being a drunk in this line of work is the difference from being sued by Robert Rankin and not being sued by Robert Rankin for stealing one of his catchphrases.

Then the computer went bing.

I opened the screen and there were the results from Jo-Jo Mar's bank accounts I had set running before I had gone out with Mel.

OK. I forgot I'd done that, but in my defence it was a busy night.

From the start it was obvious that a lot of money had come into Jo-Jo Mar's account. Not just your average drug dealer amount but hundreds of thousands of pounds over a year and a bit. A quick run through my high tech calculator (a pen and bit of paper) revealed…

Two million and fifty thousand.

Bugger.

More clues.

I sent an email to Mammasayra, asking her to find out whose accounts were debited. I recognized the account number that had paid in the money. The Vatican.

The thing that confused me was that the Church was very much against The Streets. After all the very presence of Greek, Norse, Balinese and all sorts of Gods upsets their preaching that there is only One True God and his son Jesus, or Mithras or any other of the sons of God. One of them runs the local chip shop and does excellent fish and chips, as my waistline can vouch for. THE CHURCH does not like competition.

They ignore The Streets so long as they don't draw their customers and their customers' money away from them. A handful of people worshiping Derek, the God of Broken Sat Navs, does not impact on their customer base, but thousands of people worshiping Kali does tend to get noticed. Especially if Kali walks in and it turns out she runs a dress shop in Peterborough.

However much the Church was against The Streets, they seemed to be ploughing a lot of money in its direction.

Still, better to concentrate on simple things such as my new list and...

"Good work Faustus." A deep baritone voice whispered into my right ear.

In that moment I knew I was dead.

No arguing, no fighting, no chance. I would be dead in seconds and they would never find the remains.

"Cup of coffee Shadwell?" I asked. No sense in forgetting my manners.

"No thank you. I do wish you had left Jo-Jo Mar for me though." There was a feeling of movement behind me and my space chair creaked slightly.

"Putting on weight?" I reasoned that as I was dead, he couldn't hurt me more.

"No." came the voice next to my right ear. "I just thought you would like a location to talk to. Gives the impression I'm sat down."

"Nice trick." I thought I might as well gamble. "Here to collect on my head?"

There was a low chuckle from my left.

"Really Faustus." Shadwell said. "If I was here to kill you, then I would not be having such a nice chat. No. My employer simply wished to thank you for bringing Jo-Jo Mar to his especially violent end.

"While I appreciate the thanks, I didn't kill him." I said, feeling nervous. A small bead of sweat ran down the back of my neck.

"I don't believe for one minute that you did, but rumour on the street is that you ripped his guts out with your bare hands." Shadwell laughed again. "I would stick with rumour on this one Faustus. Those who were considering collecting the bounty on you are somewhat warier now. People seem to think you are psychotic. Personally, I would've liked to have gotten my hands on him myself. Metaphorically speaking of course."

"Of course."

"Any old how, to business." Shadwell paused for needless dramatic effect. I took a swig of my coffee. "As payment for being there at Jo-Jo Mar's unfortunate demise, my employer would like to offer his thanks."

A large brown envelope dropped into my lap.

My bladder remembered how much coffee I had drunk recently.

"Where did you hide that?" Well it was the obvious question to ask. "Besides, I don't accept payment for being at a murder scene Shadwell."

"It is not money Faustus, merely a little help from one concerned citizen to another regarding the recent tumult to be found on The Streets."

Weight shifted unnecessarily from the chair.

"Would you like me to open and close the door on the way out? Give the impression that I need to?" Shadwell asked. Damn sporting of him I thought.

"Do you need to?"

Shadwell chuckled again.

"Not in all these Millennia. But if it makes you feel better, I will."

"Whatever is easy for you Shadwell. And thank you."

There was a brief pause. Imagination could see Shadwell turning his head and looking bemused.

"What for Faustus?"

"Talking." I said. "Just talking."

"No problem." Shadwell said. The door opened. It paused slightly in closing. "I may come back, one day. OK?" For some reason that didn't quite seem like a threat. Not quite.

I turned my chair to face the door.

"Any time Shadwell. You'll be welcome." I said. "Just knock on the door first. OK?"

"Agreed." Shadwell said. The door closed.

I had thrown Shadwell by inviting him back.

I had thrown myself by inviting Shadwell back.

Time to go for a walk. I would look at Shadwell's envelope when I got back. I stood up and left my cubby-hole, closing and locking the door behind me. I picked up my spare hat from the filing cabinet drawer, where it was filed under 'H'. For Hat. Then I stepped out of the office.

Thinking time.

Chapter Twenty Three: The Dick and the Decoration

Excerpt from
Angels, Daemons and other realm beings.
By E.M Faustus
(unpub)

On the Subject of Hats.

Hats are important on The Streets. They are indicators as to 'who' and 'what' you are. Witches wear pointy hats. Wizards wear pointy hats. Enforcers wear pork pie hats. The hats of the Fae tend to be bright and colourful. And made of dead things. Some of which have been gutted and cleaned. Satanists tend to wear wide brimmed hats.

Hats are almost mystical. They are passed down from father to son. Mother to daughter. They are not supposed to be bought on EBay. Hats themselves gather knowledge from the heads and actions of the wearer. Their personality shapes the nature of the hat.

Every hat has its own magical secret. Some convey wisdom. Some hold great danger.

Even my hat holds a secret.

Just one. Let's not get carried away.

Chapter Twenty Four: The Dick and The Dominatrix

"Mister."

When I'm on The Streets, I wear my hat and people tend to give me a wide berth.

"Mister."

They know roughly what I am, and some who I am, know I'm working and don't bother me.

"Mister. Want a date?"

I stopped walking and looked down.

"Fifty quid for twenty minutes Mister. I'm really worth it."

She looked all of fifteen, which meant she was probably twelve. Short skirt, short jacket, push up bra that couldn't do its job on one so young. Dyed blonde hair that needed washing, conditioning and attention to the roots. Make up too heavy and too weathered and too old.

Brand spanking new to the street. She'd be lucky if she made it through the night without becoming a victim or a meal. Or both.

"Show me your arms." I said.

She sighed and obligingly rolled up her sleeves and showed me two clean arms. White and covered in Goosebumps, but not a needle mark in sight.

"Your teeth." I said.

"What? "She said, genuinely puzzled.

"Show me your teeth." I repeated. She sneered and peeled back her lips. Perfect white teeth. Young teeth. A child's set of teeth.

"Come on. You some kind of dentist?" She said. "Fifty quid. Hundred for the night."

The paranoiac in me immediately assumed this was an attempt on my head. Still, the girl was human.

Probably.

You walk the streets late at night, or in this case, just before dawn, you see things.

You see the Night People. People whose lives are inverted. They sleep during the day and surface when the sun goes down. Not just Vampires. The whole crumbling to dust in the sun is a myth anyway. There are Others who choose to live in the dark.

I like to walk The Streets at night.

There is a clarity to it you don't get in daytime. People are exactly who they are. No side to them. There is nothing to hide. You can't afford to be anything apart from who you are.

Hard to find even in the best of friends.

There is great threat on The Street at night, but also great compassion. Shame I wasn't the compassionate kind.

I reached down and took her small, child's hand in mine. It was cold and clammy.

"Come with me." I said. "I'll show you value for money."

She was unresisting as I led her down the pavement, though I could hear a pair of feet padding along behind us. Soft soles. Trainers. We walked in silence for about five minutes until I found the alleyway I was looking for.

"No way." She said. "I'm not doing it in an alley. I got standards. Let's get a room. I know a place."

"I'll bet you do." I said, grabbing her by the hair and shoving her into the Alley. "I'll show you a trick or two."

Her scream was stifled by the knife that appeared at her throat. She had the common sense not to scream.

I too had the common sense to almost keep my mouth shut when another blade pressed against my Adams apple and a second rested against my groin.

"Mistress." I said.

"My Lord." Came a voice of satin to my left.

A scream just began in the throat of the girl on my left. She suddenly realized she was in a dark alley with a strange man and a knife against her throat. In other circumstances she would have been in trouble, but in this alley she was probably the safest she had been in days.

A hand came from the shadow on her right and gently caressed her hair. A gentle touch from a gentle, almost female, almost hand. The fingers were a little too long, a little too thin. A soft dark down started at the knuckles and drew along the arm. A smile appeared in the shadows. Not a predatory smile, but one of understanding and sympathy.

"Relax my darling." said a voice like warm spring fog. "Safety is here. Be calm."

The knife came down from the girl's throat. A smile appeared on her face. As she relaxed she looked all of her twelve years. I couldn't stop a smile crossing my face. Briefly.

I did notice that the blade was still against my throat.

Funny what a price on your head will do.

"Quarter of a million." Satin said. "The price on your head."

"So little? I am offended." I replied. I must have pissed someone off really badly to get that sort of money on my bonce.

"Relax my Lord." The blade at my meat and two veg vanished into the darkness. From said darkness stepped a tall blonde, dressed in tight fitting leather work of such quality your average dominatrix would kill just to get hold of one glove. Neck to toe, there must have been a good three cows on her body, tight and shiny. Like Black coffee in an addicts cup.

Now I have three leather coats. One long leather trench coat (It's a P.I thing), a loose jacket and a flying jacket (It's a Biggles thing). They all creak when I wear them, even the flying jacket that's a good twenty five years old. Her body suit didn't even whisper.

Skin tight, with leather lacing up the arms, all the way down the sides and exposing just a hint of flesh to show there were decent muscles under those laces.

She kept the blade held tight though.

"Mind if I move the blade?" I asked.

"It is very sharp." she said.

"Oh. I believe it." I said taking three steps backwards.

"Very Good." She said, laughing in a voice like champagne over ice. "Most people try and push it away. Personally I think they like the attention that comes from the bandaging afterwards."

I gave her a deep bow, sweeping my hat to the floor. I wasn't worried. They keep a very clean street down here. She in turn gave a low curtsey.

I nodded at the girl. Shadow Woman was stroking her hand. The child looked relaxed.

Mistress nodded her head.

"This girl cannot return home." Shadow Woman said. "I shall arrange for her care. She will be safe here Inquisitor. But there will be a price. One day a price."

I nodded my head in agreement. Good deeds always come at a price. In this alley, you pay them fast.

"Coffee My Lord?" Mistress asked me, sweeping her sword onto a sheath on her back without even looking. Me, I need to check I put my socks on the right feet.

"As is your pleasure Mistress." I swept my hat back onto my head in an equally deft movement. OK. It's not a razor sharp sword, but it does take practice.

Mistress walked back into the shadows and a door opened. A warm glow came from the doorway. I walked over to it and stopped gesturing her forward with my right hand.

"After you Mistress." I gave a short bow.

"My thanks, My Lord." Mistress herself gave a low bow to match the depth of my own.

Exactly. To the nanometer. You could bet on that.

With the archaic formality out of the way we walked into her rooms.

Ω

Excerpt from
Angels, Daemons and other realm beings.
By E.M Faustus
(unpub)

Ladies of Leisure.

Prostitutes.
Hookers.
Slags.
Whores.

And many other inappropriate names. Call your average working lady any of these, you may get anything from a filthy look to a slap. Almost certainly some abuse.

Call a Lady of Leisure a name like that, if you're lucky they'll just chop your head off.

The ladies come from all walks of life, and all forms of life. All are consenting adults and all are in charge of their fate and clients. All are specialists in one form of domination or another.

They get paid very well. They do not have sex, (unless they have someone special). They maintain a centuries old tradition with its own precise language and formality that reasserts their control at all times. No man is their equal.

Ω

Mistress and I were equals. She was being at pains to point that out to me in her movement, but when we entered her room and the door shut, things changed.

Drastically.

The room was threateningly and claustrophobically blue. A bright red fire burned in a grate, with a set of branding irons resting in its coals.

Different strokes for different folks. Delivered with care, precision and professionalism.

The slap was hard and duly hurt. Maybe I should grow a beard. It could soften blows like these.

A small table was set with an exquisite coffee pot and two small espresso cups. She knew my tastes. Maybe she had been expecting me.

"Fie, Sir. Thine art an imbecile." Mistress shouted.

"Been said." I replied. "And it should be; Fae Sir. Thou art imbecilic."

I caught the hand before it hit my face and slapped her with the back of my free hand. Hard enough to sting. Or maybe a little more.

As her head snapped to the side her right foot came up to my head. I ducked and punched her in the stomach, thanking the Gods that I punch like a drunken spaniel.

I thanked the Gods some more as the pain shot through my hand. If I could punch properly I could have broken it.

"How does eighteenth century corsetry feel My Lord?" Mistress said, throwing a punch at my throat.

In my defence I was growing tired of the foreplay, so felt only marginal guilt in hitting her across the head with the drinks tray.

By the time she had hit the floor, she had changed. She rolled to the side and to her feet, raising herself to her full seven foot.

I could see where those laces came in now. The leather had expanded and that tantalizing glimpse of flesh was now an expanse of auburn hair. Accompanied by a distinct doggy smell. The ears had moved up the head to the top and become noticeably pointy and her sweet little nose and lips had developed into a nasty looking muzzle. Still looking good in black lipstick though.

Two clawed hands grabbed me and did what I am beginning to think of as a Shadwell. Lifted me from the ground and pinned me against the wall.

It hurt. A lot. I didn't let it show.

The Mistresses werewolf head leaned in until her nose was touching mine and I was looking deep into two unforgiving amber eyes.

Wolf eyes.

"So Faustus." Mistress said. "Give us a kiss."

She licked my face from chin to forehead. Then she let me go and dropped me to the floor. She turned her back and walked over to the table, putting it back on its feet. As she moved her shape shifted back into that of the dominatrix.

"The last time you hit me like that we didn't surface from bed for three days." she said.

"I know. I still have the scars." I wiped the blood away from my lips with the back of my hand.

"Stop complaining and take off your shirt." she said.

I did as I was told. Mistress slapped some very cold cream on my back and rubbed it in.

"I could smell those bruises from the alleyway." She purred. "What's the story with the girl?"

I told her and she laughed.

"You fell for bait?" she said. "You are getting old."

"That makes two of us." I pushed things there as she gave me a slap on the back. "Should I put the shirt back on?"

"If you came here to relive old times Faustus, I'm sorry." She gathered the coffee pot and cups back up and put them on the table. "I have a client in an hour. Pass me the tray, will you?"

I looked at my hand and realized I was still holding the tray I had hit her with. I passed it over.

"Five men tried to collect her while she was waiting for you." She said.

"Odd." I said. "No one knew I'd be out. What happened to …? never mind."

"They'll not be going home. We cater for most tastes but not short eyes." Mistress smiled. Her lips showed a little more teeth than they needed to.

"I'm not asking a thing."

"Why are you here then?" she asked, folding her arms, not defensively, but surprisingly suggestively.

"Just wanted to get that girl to safety. I figured The Oracle could show her what she has in store if she continues. Damn you hit harder than you used to. Are you working out or am I really getting old?"

"Both." She smiled. "A knight in slightly tarnished armour. Are you seeing that café vampire yet?"

"Maybe." I replied. "Very early days."

Mistress looked hard at me. Our history was…complicated.

"Do you know why you and ladies never work out luv?"

"No." I said. "But I think you are about…"

She stepped forwards, put a hand on either side of my head and silenced me with a long deep kiss. Friendly like. Slowly she pulled away.

"It's because there's a point where you always think they deserve better that you. And there's not a damn thing wrong with you luv. Now piss off and do some good."

She let go of my head and stepped back.

"I wish I knew where to start darlin'." I said. "I really do."

"You normally find a way." She crossed over to the fire. "The girl."

For a minute I had forgotten how I ended up there.

"You'll all take care of her?" I asked. The answer came as a short nod.

"Her pimp has real short eyes. He's worked four girls out of our territory in the last six months. The other three just …stopped being seen."

The rest of the conversation hung in the air.

"What's he look like?"

"About sixteen. Spotty with BO. Wears a red hood."

"Yeah. Figures the law can't touch him because of his age." I took out a smoke and lit it. Her nose wrinkled. Pretty nose. "I had best be on my way."

On my way to the door, I turned and smiled.

"Can I borrow your poker?" I said.

Chapter Twenty Five: The Dick Detects

Physical violence does not solve the problems of street violence and law breaking in the young.

But it can be quite stress relieving, especially when he pulls a knife. More so when three of his older mates turn up in a car and you leave the remains for The Street People to find. It's sort of therapeutic. Like a good back rub.

In the office I opened Shadwell's bundle.

A mass of photocopies. Each one of them the deed to a property on The Streets. Each one of them bought for a song from the owners and purchased by the same company. Avatar holdings.

An Avatar.

As a Private Detective people expect you to spend lots of time working bad guys over, sleeping with women who will 'do ya wrong' and sitting in cars, with a dashboard covered in doughnut and coffee detritus on 'stake out'.

The last bit is always embarrassing. I have to find someone to lend me the car. Must get one for The Office one day. Yeah. When I get rich.

Nowadays it is more like working over a keyboard, dealing with an internet connection that 'does ya wrong'. The coffee and doughnuts are still true though. Detection is wading through evidence and coming to a conclusion. Clues just get in the way.

Shadwell had given me evidence.

Avatar is a Sanskrit word meaning 'a form of self'. If you have much to do with gaming, it's the character you create to represent yourself in cyberspace. There are millions of fit twenty year old

bodies on cyberspace that actually belong to fifty
something overweight couch potatoes.

In this case for Avatar read Alias.

Someone was hiding.

Someone was 'encouraging' people into debt.

Someone was buying their property.

Someone wanted me dead.

Decapitated.

I like my head. We've grown up together, and I
know its curious ways.

I did a check on Avatar holdings. Not a thing on
any data base I tried, bar a registry at Companies
House. Two trading addresses locally and several
internationally. A nice little business. Sounds like it
could be run from the back of someone's house.

If I didn't recognize one of the addresses, I
wouldn't have believed it myself.

The main company address was so exclusive that
people going to work there needed a credit check
just to do the cleaning. The other address was on the
outskirts of town. A small village. About two hours
walk.

Well. I was feeling great and…

"You bin takin' them pills agin? Ya gunna get
such a slap I see you."

The voice of Mammasayra brought me out of my
hiking mood. On the screen in front of me was her
big round, and angry face.

"WhatdidItellyaaboutakenthemthins? Hmm?
Answer me boy!"

Yeah. She was angry.

"I…" I began

"Gotnodamnexcuse." she barked back. "Got
nodamnbusinessbeenupadistimeanight.."

I managed to get one word out of that. She was calming down a little.

"You listen to me Faustus." she said, "Those pills do you no good. You wanna stroke?"

"Mamma." I tried. "There are a lot of people wanting me dead right now. I could solve a lot of problems to someone's bank account. Not just me either. I'll take the risk and pay the price."

"You might be savin' them the time boy." Mammasayra snapped back. "Them bad boys wanna cutoff ya preddy head."

"You get my Email?"

"Yeah." Not happy with the change of subject, but she had said her piece. One of the things I loved her for.

"I'm willing to bet the money all links back to a company called Avatar Holdings." I said.

"Than what you need me for? Goddamncomicrelief? Hmm?"

"I've been busy detecting. That OK?" Damn that woman could make me as angry as I could make her.

"Oh. Big shot detective humourin' big old fat lady who know more shit than he could ever begin to imagine. I take ya head meself. Not for the money but to go under the bed. Save me a walk to the head."

"Well face it old lady. The only head you could get is if you hacked it off. I'll slap you shitless you come around here." I was shouting now. If she had been there…well. I might not have behaved as a gentleman should.

Mammasayra sat back in her chair and laughed. A big old belly laugh. The contagious type that had me forgetting my own anger for a while and laughing with her.

"Jesus bitch." I said. "We should never have more than one conversation in a day. Always ends up the same."

"Cos you an' me is de same." She rested her elbow on the desk and her chin in the palm of her hand. "But you better get mad boy. Crazy mad. You made a hit list on the web."

I was quite controlled. Quite relaxed really. I took the news with grace.

"Hells teeth." I said, immediately looking around to see if anyone was in the room or about to shoot through the window. I closed the plywood door to keep any bullets out.

"Relax boy." Mammasayra said.

"If you say so." I replied. Funnily I did a little. If Mammasayra said relax, you could relax.

"But know this. I went to take it off, but turns out someone beat me to it." She said. "It went on ten minute after we talk earlier. One minute later. Gone."

"But someone put it out on the internet . They wanted me dead?"

Mammasayra waved a dismissive hand.

"Oh. Happen all the time boy." she said. "How's a hit man gonna tender for a contract if he don't know who want who killed?"

"Fair enough." A short laugh escaped me. "Thanks for taking it off."

Mammasayra sat quiet for a moment then lifted her head.

"I didn't boy." she said. "Someone else did, don't know who, but same originatin' address.

Someone in same organization either want you alive, or…"

"They want all the money for themselves." I finished her sentence.

Her finger pointed at me.

"For two million I'd be tempted." Mammasayra said.

There was one of those silences. One of those special, quiet moments in life, where you cannot quite believe what was being said, and what was happening. In this case I had just discovered what my life, or more accurately, my death, was worth. I also knew that for two million pounds, my friend would not kill me.

Personally I value my life at a lot more than two million.

"If you need some muscle, boy, I can send Big John over." Mammasayra brought me out of my shock.

"Pardon?"

"D'yall wan me to send Big John over?" She repeated. "Be with you in twenty four hours."

"No thanks." I managed. "Best no one else gets roped into this. I have some muscle here. If needed."

"That Sidney is a good man." She smiled. "A little confused, but a good man. His brother, not so confused. Might need him too."

We were quiet after that for a while, then Mammasayra waved at me.

"I'm goin' now. You be OK?"

"I'll be fine Mammasayra."

"I'll be fine." She repeated. "You better be. You might want to consider getting a gun y'know."

216

"Got one. Never use it." I said. "Guns get you killed."

"Take care Skinny Boy. Call me frequently, let me know ya not dead."

"Call you later today."

Then we hung up.

I sat for a few moments contemplating the women in my life. None of them was 'average' but I wouldn't swap any of them for the world. As I considered the nature of womanhood I opened the door leading to my office.

I was met by the arrow smashing through my window.

Chapter Twenty Six: The Dick Dives and Discovers Detestation

The arrow slammed into the edge of the door, burying itself half way down the shaft.

Oh Good. He was playing with me. I had a chance.

It is surprising what thoughts go through your head when someone is shooting at you.

I noticed the cup on my desk. An old metal camping cup, stained bitter chocolate brown due to lethal overdoses of coffee and a total unwillingness to clean it.

The coffee tastes better that way.

I noticed the glow, cast by my computer screen that lit the office with a low blue glow, making it seem cold, unwelcoming and slightly alien.

I noticed the man in the office across the road, drawing back another arrow in his bow. My. What an ethnic looking bow.

I reached around the doorframe and flicked the light off while throwing myself to the floor. The arrow slammed into the wall to my left. A half second earlier and it would have impaled my shoulder.

It had to be someone I know. A serious assassin would have had the decency to kill me by now.

Problem was that I knew so many people. Only most of them would kill me for two million.

I wondered if it was dollars or pounds.

I could make it to the door. I would only be in his sights (do bows have sights?) for a few seconds.

I scrambled for the bathroom.

At the first hint of movement an arrow slammed into the office door, just where my arm would have been had I been reaching for the handle. I shut the bathroom door behind me and crouched by the pan. In succession three arrows struck the door, pushing through almost to the flights. That was my first chance to see them a little closer.

Fae arrows.

While not on my side, I at least thought the Fae wouldn't actively try to kill me.

Double bollocks.

Vampires to the left of me, Fae unto the right. I looked at the toilet pan.

"Here I am, stuck in the middle with you." I said.

The reference was lost on the ceramic.

Safe enough to stand, and warily I did, raised the bathroom window and was on the fire escape in a few seconds.

A minute later found me in the alleyway, looking across at the archer's window. I was sure I saw a faint glint from Fae jewelry from the shooter's window. To tell the truth it could have been anything, but the open window with the arrow pointing through it was a real giveaway.

Raymond Chandler used to say that if the plot was slow, or he didn't know what do with a plot he would just send in a thug with a gun.

Oh for a thug with a gun.

Please give me a thug with a gun.

I dream about the joy of a thug with a gun.

Me?

I get psychotic vampires, killer tigers and lunatic fairies.

Mind you, I was having fun. I felt more alive than I had in weeks. Fully aware that that could change any second, I waited.

After a few minutes nothing happened. The arrow was still tightly focused on my bathroom door. Hopefully very focused, as there was nothing to hide behind on the street.

I ran for it. Straight for the door of the office building. Three arrows struck the pavement. One behind me and two in front. The next one would go straight through me, so it was with relief that I slammed into the wooden door and felt the lock give way. I burst through the door and rolled to the side.

I expected to see the room filled with Fae. What I got was a room filled with compost, spades, seeds and other gardening 'stuff'. I know all the horticultural technical terms.

One of the benefits of having an office on a shopping thoroughfare is that there are lots of different places to get 'things' from.

Like weapons.

I saw my weapon on the third shelf down. Grabbed it and headed out the back way. A flight of stairs led upwards, In deference to the laws of Pursuing an Armed Assassin, I ran up the stairs, keeping close to the wall. The laws of Being a Pursued Armed Assassin meant that arrows occasionally slammed into the stairwell.

Out of breath I paused on the second flight, right below his floor and got sorted.

I got my breath back and slid a smoke into my mouth and made flame.

I lit up.

Sorted.

Then I slowly began to walk up the stairs. A slow, careful tread, praying the stairs would creak under my weight. They let me down. They were creak free. It helps to intimidate the opposition if they can hear you're not in a hurry. I rounded the corner near the top and saw his ankles, then his knees then the rest of him.

He was fully clothed for the Fae.

He wore a rabbit skin jockstrap.

That is quite a lot for the Fae Lords. I wish he had taken the head and legs off though. And the squelchy rabbit bit out. Basically I wish he hadn't just tied a rabbit to his todger. I was finding it hard not to giggle.

Yep. It was him.

Good. He was a gloater. Improved my chances no end. I like gloaters. They make mistakes.

"My Lord Tkchll." I said. Not too surprised.

"Hu-man." Witty repartee. He sounded a little horse. Pete must have done some serious damage.

"Answer me this Tkchll, why try to kill me? I might not be on your side, but I'm not on the opposition."

"Lots of jingly money Hu-man. Why do you think?"

"I thought it was because you are a psychotic twat looking for an excuse to kill me." I smiled. "Can't take me in a fair fight so you fire your little sticks at me."

Tckhll's muscles rippled as he held that arrow, his last arrow in the string. He was not about to tire soon. He gave a long, slow grin.

"You can die fast or…"

"Oh for God's sake fluffy bunnykins. You want to kill me so get on with it. Time is ticking."

"Night Time. My Time."

"Been practicing that line have you?" I said. "Do you know you have a bit of a lisp there? Had any vampire inside you la…"

221

It was my turn not to finish the sentence as he let go the arrow.

I didn't see it leave the bow, but by Godfrey I felt it hit my belly. I was lifted from my feet as it hit but I was fortunately slowed down by the wall when I hit it.

I slid to the floor, the arrow sticking out front. My mouth opened and shut, fighting for air that the blow had forced out of me. I could feel something warm and wet trickle down the sides of my belly.

No!

It wasn't supposed to go like that.

What happened to him falling for the old fight like a man trick, so I could hit him with a crowbar?

Tkchll was next to me. Leaning over, his head tilting from side to side as he appraised his kill. He grabbed the arrow and twisted. My face duly twisted in agony. He leaned into my ear.

"Make joke EM Faustus. Make Tkchll Laugh." He whispered. Getting not a jolt of response he twisted the arrow more. "NOW."

I don't normally do stand up - or lie down in this case, but I thought I would give it a go.

"A white horse…" I managed then he twisted. I grimaced. "…walked into a bar."

"Good EM Faustus. I like horse stories"

"The bar man said we have a drink named after you." I whispered. He twisted. I drew my cheeks down to my ears. "And the horse said…"

"The horse said what?" Tkchll said as he twisted the arrow more, with that annoying giggle and smile.

"The horse said…" Twist. Grimace.

"What?"

"What? Eric?" I whispered.

Tkchll began to giggle, then laugh, his mouth open wide.

That's when I rammed the bottle into his mouth and slammed my hand under his bottom jaw.

The bottle broke and immediately smoke began to rise from Tckhll's mouth. He probably tried screaming but as his mouth was on fire, it came out more of a gurgle. I pulled the arrow from the front of my shirt with a cracking noise. Nasty looking flint head, which fortunately shattered when it hit the body armour.

Kevlar and chain mail.

Well I don't face down these heavily armed hoods and killers without some secret weapons.

On this occasion it also included fertilizer. Iron sulphate fertilizer. Oh yes. I rummaged under my body armour and produced weapon two.

Thank God's Tkchll broke in above a hardware shop.

A nice cast iron frying pan, which I hit Tkchll over the head with.

Just for fun.

When the Fae touch iron, it burns. It burns them a lot.

I have no idea how much Iron Sulphate is in a bottle of fertilizer, but it was working well on dissolving Tckhll's lower jaw. Flesh was dissolving in his cheeks and his bottom lip had almost gone. It hung by about a quarter inch of flesh. He was trying to push it back into place with his fingers. His fingers in turn were burning from contact with the melting flesh. 'Bone' was showing visible through the dissolved skin and flesh. Not white, but more like twisted brown root. It was smoking away.

While Tkchll had tried to kill me, I didn't expect this sort of reaction. The least I could do was help, so I grabbed hold of the remains of the lip and ripped it off. Cruel to be kind.

I straddled Tkchll, pinning him to the floor.

"Tkchll, I have to admit, you have annoyed me. I don't take kindly to people trying to kill me, but I have a question or two, so if you answer, I'll let you go on your way. If not…"

I pressed the Iron frying pan into his shoulder.

It smelled a little like an autumn bonfire. With a pig on it. A great big hairy pig. With an odour problem.

Tkchll may have tried to scream, but I think he might have swallowed the remnants of his tongue, so it was hard to tell.

"Now, just nod or shake your head."

Tckhll's head thrashed from side to side. I pressed the pan into his leg.

"Stop thrashing about."

With great difficulty Tkchll managed to stop thrashing. He went for spasms instead.

"Near enough. Did Ti send you to kill me?"

Tckhll's head rocked from side to side.

"Sure?" I pushed the pan harder into his leg. A guttural scream managed its way out.

Tkchll nodded his head up and down.

"Vampire?"

Tkchll shook his head.

"Big man with shiny shoes?"

Frantic nodding.

"Sure?" I said holding the pan above his groin.

Oh, was his head nodding.

I don't approve of torture as a means of getting reliable information. I despise it. I could reconcile

224

it with having enough evidence on Tkchll to prove him a rapist, murderer and paedophile. I could, but I'd be denying the truth. Part of this was revenge.

You play the hand your dealt.

Tough.

I lifted Tckhll's top lip. His canines were definitely a little longer than they should be.

A Fae with Vampire blood.

Not good.

Very not good.

Very not good at all.

I reached into my trouser pocket and took out a little packet of sherbet I had been saving for later.

I get peckish in the early hours.

"Ground up Communion wafer Tkchll. Burn a vampire worse than that iron on you."

OK. I was lying, but I was relying upon Tckhll's current state of gullibility.

"You have had some work done on you. Yes?"

A slow nod. Tckhll's lower jaw fell off. Tears welled up in his eyes. Surprising as I didn't believe Fae could cry.

"Cadell?"

More slow nodding, accompanied by a wheezing gurgle.

I knelt down next to Tkchll.

"I'm not going to kill you. Ti will be able to fix you up. After a fashion."

I reached into the string around his waist and drew his knife from its scabbard. I placed it next to his head.

"Any other choice you make is down to you."

I stood up. Tkchll reached for his knife with burning fingers. I tossed the frying pan onto the floor and headed for the stairs.

I would have a lot of explaining to do to the owner in a few hours.

Or maybe I would pretend I had never been there. Much better idea.

"Hello again Darling."

Chapter Twenty Seven: The Dick and The Drop Dead Delectable Dame

Walking up the stairs was a vision in silver chain mail. How Ti did not manage to trip up over such a flowing dress I have no idea. The dress was low cut, with a train flowing a good five steps behind her. Cut nearly to the navel, the chain mail in theory would provide some protection, but a decent shot could make one hell of a mess.

The blonde hair was now ink black and running behind her down the back of her neck. A white gold headband held it in place.

Considering I'd just spent a few minutes torturing one of her favourites she was being unusually pleasant. I based that idea on the fact I was still alive.

Ti got to the top of the stairs and looked down at the twitching mess that was Tkchll.

"Was he very naughty? She asked, kicking the knife out of Tckhll's stumps of fingers with a beautifully manicured foot in glass slippers.

She'd been reading Disney again.

"In general or in the last few minutes?" I asked her, jamming a cig in and lighting up. Last cigarette I was guessing. "Because when I told you all the things he's done in the past you just laughed and said, "What do you expect? He is Tkchll."

Ti stepped up close to me and placed a hand on my chest.

"I never realized you wore metal my love. Clever. Is your homunculus not with you?" Ti could rarely maintain concentration for too long.

"He has a name." I said

"I am sure he has, somewhere." She ran her hand across my chest and onto my back as she walked behind me and wrapped both arms around me. She nuzzled into my neck.

Not unpleasant.

"You have hurt one of my favourites darling." she purred. "What should I do with you?"

"You'll think of something, I'm sure." I started thinking about Nuns. Old, wrinkly nuns.

Ti playfully bit my ear.

Nuns, smelling of sweat and pee.

"Remove him. Take his feet so he cannot run away again." Ti whispered.

From the shadows, I hadn't even noticed were there, stepped four hulking Fae. Muscles rested uncomfortably on top of muscles. They had somehow managed to squeeze some more muscles on top and crowbar a few more in-between. And they were going to cut my feet off. Oh dear.

They bent over (given that they too were nude, not a pleasant sight) and picked up Tkchll. Then quickly dropped him before they got burnt. One produced gloves from Gods knew where and picked him up again. He was still struggling. A gloved hand reached down and picked up the frying pan and dropped it onto his stomach. A few twitches and it slid off. He stopped struggling.

"I did not ask him to hurt you My Love." Ti said. "I would never hurt you. Unless you asked me to."

The Fae picked up Tkchll and carried him off into the shadows. Leaving behind a leg and lower jaw. I waved a half- hearted goodbye.

"What's going to happen now?" I asked.

"To him?" Ti said "Nothing. Why? Would you like it to?"

Ti walked around so that she was face to face with me. She inhaled the collar of my shirt. Well that's what I told myself. Old Nuns. Kissing.

"Not especially." I said.

"And you? What would you like to happen to you?" Ti breathed, her breath raising goose bumps on my neck.

"I plan on living and solving the case." I managed, while taking a deep swallow.

"There is an option." She breathed. "Take his place. Command his men. Think of the good you could do."

"No thought needed Ti." I said. "I stand more chance of living as I am now."

Ti stepped back and leaned against the banister. Her hair and dress were noticeably shorter. The hair short and spiky, the dress now a tunic revealing a lot of leg. Thigh length silver leather boots embraced her legs.

"There are fringe benefits." She said giving me a look that would melt mountains.

I wasn't exactly melting but I was rather warm.

I took a step towards her and held my face a fraction away from hers.

"We can only ever be friends Ti. Never lovers." I said.

"Why? I can be anything you want me to be." she said, her hands finding their way around my neck.

Good question actually. Don't think Faustus, just wing it.

"Because I would destroy you, darlin'. I could never live with that." I said, resting my hand on her cheek. "Not that you'd let me."

"True My love." she said leaning her cheek into my hand. "But one day….."

Then she kissed me.

That was wrong.

That was so wrong.

Ti seals her contracts with a kiss. She never bestows them lightly. But I had made no contract with her. Agreed to nothing. Yet she kissed me.

Oh shit.

I cannot begin to describe the kiss, but none before was ever like it. I could use all sorts of words but they wouldn't do it justice.

Why can't I just get a normal girlfriend?

What is it about me that attracts dominatrix werewolves, barking mad Queens of The Fae and ancestral Gorgon killers?

I mean they are all wonderful, but just once in a while, a quiet night in, watching 'Arsenic and Old Lace' would be brilliant.

Maybe.

Ti stepped back. A look of shock on her face that must have equalled mine.

Then she was gone.

The taste of her lingered on my lips, the pressure of her hands still on the skin of my neck. Her heady musk still hanging in the air.

Oh Shit.

One of us had crossed a line.

One of us had done something very, very bad. Very Bad indeed.

If anyone found out I had been kissed by the Queen of The Fae, at best no one would trust me. At worst I'd be burnt at a stake.

It would be much worse for her if anyone found out she had kissed a mortal with no contract.

There are things worse than Tree food. Just ask Ti's predecessor. She's still around, somewhere.

My legs shook. Problem was that my stomach was doing an impression of a salmon going up-stream. I had enjoyed the kiss. I was stunned and ran my fingers over my lips to check they were still there. They tingled.

I was totally alone on the stairs as I walked down, unable to think of anything but that kiss.

There had to be a reason. She couldn't…No. Not Ti.

She was mad.

Totally, box of frogs.

Wasn't she?

I stepped outside and walked across the street, back into my building and up to my office.

Looking around the office I was fairly unconcerned by the arrows sticking out of walls, floors and doors. I took my jacket off and hung it on the one in the office door.

Ti had kissed me.

If I made it to the end of the day, with all limbs intact, organs on the inside and still alive, I was going to have had a good day.

I prised open the door to my cubby-hole. Arrows were buried into the monitor. I picked up my coffee from next to it and walked back to my office desk. Above me was the sound of feet on the floor. Four feet, or six if Paul had forgotten himself. They would both be down soon, both wanting answers, both wanting help.

I rubbed the bridge of my nose and blinked my eyes to reassert I was awake.

Her perfume was still on my jacket.

"Ooh. Visitors."

"Are you alright Mr Faustus?"

I looked up and framed in my office doorway was a half- naked werewolf and a fully clothed and unshaved Angelic Daemon Man-thing. Not a phrase you find yourself using every day.

I had to laugh, and I did.

Both of them came in and stood in front of my desk. I laughed. Maybe it was hysteria.

"Are you alright?" Pete asked

"He look's fine." Paul said. "Are you fine? He looks fine." Paul sniffed the air. "Ah. You have had a Lady in here. Dirty Boy. Ooo."

Paul placed a hand on his stomach.

"You feeling OK mate?" I asked him in-between chortles.

"Stomach's a bit upset. Must be something I ate."

"Or drank." I said.

He straightened up as a bowel twitch went through him.

"Oh Bugger. I thought that tea tasted funny." Paul said as he turned and headed back out.

"There's toilet paper in the fridge." I called after him.

Pete sat in the office chair, facing me.

"You gave him a laxative?" Pete asked.

"I'm allowed small revenges." I said and took a swig of my cold coffee. I spat out the bits of monitor.

Pete waved his hand around the room as I lit up.

"I heard some commotion a while ago." he said. "I did not realise you were in danger or I would have assisted. Like Paul, I assumed you were breeding, noisily, but smelling that perfume on your jacket I understand that The Queen of The Fae has been here."

Damn. Have to burn the jacket.

I put my cup down, fag out and faced him.

"I've been busy." I said.

"Doing what?" It wasn't an accusation, just a straightforward question so what the hell.

"Yes. I've had visitors." I began. "I had a visit from Shadwell, who opened up a nice can of worms for me, Ti gave me a little question or two to answer, and that Fae we had a run in with this morning tried to kill me."

Pete opened his mouth to talk but I held up my hand and stopped him.

"It turns out that this whole thing has bugger all to do with you, me or Dog. Sorry, but that's the way of it. Someone is buying up The Streets, The Catholic Church is financing a contract someone has out on me, someone is buggering about with genetics where you kind of come into it, and they are experimenting on Fae. Tkchll, The Fae you hurt, had real long fuck off canines. Stop me if I'm going too fast"

Pete sat impassive and simply nodded.

"I do wonder if the swearing was totally necessary." he said.

"Best thing you can do is go see Peter, get some cash and bugger off somewhere, don't tell anyone where you are going, not even Peter. I'll sort you out a mobile and you can ring me in a week or so. If you get me I can update you, if you don't reach me I'm dead. OK?"

Pete slowly shook his head.

"I will be looking for Dog." Pete said slowly. "I will help you and look for Dog. You are my…friend."

It was a childlike statement. A simple statement, but a simple man (man-Angel-daemon thing). It surprised me.

I liked the guy, but he was still a client.

"I do not know much about you Mr Faustus…" he said.

"Look. Just call me Faustus." I said. "I keep telling you."

"It seems impolite."

I had watched this man throw fridges, throttle Fae, and manhandle a cobra, yet he was worried about being impolite.

"It's OK if I say it is." I said. "Now I'm hungry so we'll go and get something to eat. OK?"

"I will stay here." he said standing up and looking faintly embarrassed.

"Why?"

"I have no money." he looked down at his feet. "I spent the five pounds Mr Peter gave me." He reached into his pocket and took out a small sponge ball. "On this."

He gave the ball a squeeze and it made an asthmatic squawk. "Dog likes them."

I laughed. Really laughed. I laughed so much I had to sit down. Whatever he was, whatever he had done, he would rather spend his lunch money on a squeaky toy for a mutt than eat.

"What is funny?" Squeeze, 'Squeaaarkkfffpp.'

"Sometimes, I get my faith restored in human nature. C'mon. Let's go eat, but first I need to change my clothes."

I lured Paul out of the bath room with the promise of Kaolin and Morphine (the old ways are the best), sprayed some air freshener about, took a shower and a shave. Then I was ready to boogie.

Chapter Twenty Eight: The Dick and The Damage

"I thought I would have had a call at least." Mel said, a little pouty. What a pretty pout.

"I am sorry, but this is what happens." I said. "Sometimes work gets 'busy'."

"Are you alright?" Mel asked. "What happened?" What pretty questioning.

Oh, I went to a psycho take away, was assaulted by vampires and a tiger, beat up my good friend Paul here, had various people try and kill me and oh, best not forget, got a slapping from a dominatrix werewolf, who then kissed my face off and all topped off by a Fae assassin and The Queen of the Fae snogging me better than you and curling my toes up to the knees."

"Ah, just normal P.I stuff." I said, thankful that I didn't say everything that came into my head. "Could we get six bacon baps and three coffees please?"

"I am rather hungry." Pete said from my left.

"Oh yes." Paul said from my right, his eyes glued on Mel's breasts. I didn't need to look. I just knew.

"OK. But we'll talk in a bit." Mel said, "And Paul?"

"Yes?" Paul said dreamily, resting his forearms on the counter and leaning forward, making it much easier for Mel to shove her pen up his nostril.

"Keep looking at my tits and I'll rip your nose off." All said with a smile. What a pretty smile. What a pretty threat. "Go sit down and I'll bring your breakfast over."

"Have you eaten?" I asked, hoping she would join us.

"I had some muesli." She said, shooing us off with a wave of the pen as she pulled it from Paul's nose. "Now, shift."

"You're sure we aren't intruding?" I asked her. After all we had not got to know each other that well.

"It's a café Faustus. You'll get a bill." She smiled. "Sit."

I would swear Paul's knees bent just a little. Mine did.

We turned and walked over to the table in the far corner. We kept facing the door, hard when it's a round table and there are three of you, so we had Paul with his back to the door.

"Sorry Faustus." Paul said. "But she does have terrific tits. Are they real?"

"I can go buy another spade." I said, gesturing towards the door.

"Sorry. Sorry. No offence. Great tits. And her…"

Pete tapped Paul on the forehead. Hard.

"You are talking about someone I have respect and a liking for. Please desist." Pete said. There was the faintest whiff of brimstone in the air.

"OK." Paul said, rubbing his forehead. A werewolf should not have had any trouble in catching that smell.

Mel's Café was great. I rarely had the nerve to spend a lot of time there.

A great long and wide room, it had two big windows that looked out onto the street. A large 'Open' sign flashed to all the passing trade. Each window had a brass rail crossing it at waist height.

A long metal and neon counter ran across the length of the room, separating the tables from the kitchen. The kitchen was all open plan so you could see everything that was cooked and what was going on. Out at the counter, Mel was taking orders with another woman I didn't recognize, but I only ever had eyes for Mel. It could have been my own mother working there and I would not necessarily have noticed her.

The tables were all low. At the tables Mel served sandwiches and steaming cups of coffee. I'm sure other drinks were on the menu but why would I be interested in any drink but coffee. Large, heavily padded leather sofas replaced chairs, giving it a relaxed feel. Although it came across upmarket, it catered for everyone, from workmen to yuppies (do they still exist?). Muddy boots. Jimmy Choos. And one pair of charity shop brogues. All graced Mel's Café.

"So, why we here?" Paul asked.

"I was hungry." I said.

"We should talk about what is going on." Pete said. Serious git.

"Not on an empty stomach, alright?" I said. "Besides, I think I got a bridge or two to mend here."

"Why did you sell us out Paul?" Pete asked casually. "Death has resulted from your actions."

There was a bit of an awkward moment. Paul looked straight down at the table.

"How did you know?" I asked. I was damn sure I hadn't told him.

"I worked it out." he replied. "Perhaps, deduction is communicable. That was a joke."

The tension would have needed a thermal lance to cut it. I had the feeling someone was going to kick off. I might not get to eat my bacon sandwich and was about to get barred from my possible girlfriend's café.

The day wasn't shaping up too well.

There is a Jools Holland track called 'Tranquil Passage', maybe jazz, maybe spaghetti western, but I could hear it playing away in my head and I couldn't say a damn thing.

How had he figured it out? I had had the benefits of going through Paul's dustbin. That and a bit of elementary deduction. Cos I'm really a detective, not a walking target.

"I didn't think I had a choice." Paul said. "I am sorry."

"It's alright." I put a restraining hand on Paul's arm. I didn't want him to say he was sorry about Dog. It was possible Pete would kill him. "It's going to get sorted."

Pete was looking at me, very confused.

"Can you forgive him so readily?" he asked.

"Got to." I said as matter of factly as I could manage.

"Why?"

"Yeah. Why?" Paul asked.

"You forgive a friend, because one day you'll need them to forgive you." I said. I was cooking with gas today.

And that's as true as it gets. Especially if he ever found out about me and his wife. And his sister. And his mother.

I looked up and Mel was coming towards us with a tray.

"I'm actually not too sure I can eat, F." Paul said.

"It's alright. I'll have yours. You're paying anyway." I said as Mel put the tray on the table.

Three steaming mugs of black coffee were placed in front of us.

"I'm broke Faustus." Paul said.

Paul broke into a grin, so did I. Even Pete managed a smile.

Things were looking up.

Mel winked at me and walked back to the counter.

I took a sip, burning my lips and tongue, but it was worth it. The smell alone of Mel's coffee was worth the price.

Maybe I was going to have a good day.

I really didn't want that car to pull up out front.

I really didn't want those four vampires to get out the car.

I really didn't want a second car, or Cadell and Lisper to get out, with two more back up vampires.

I didn't want them to go to the boot and start loading up with shotguns.

I didn't want it, but I got it anyway.

Must be my lucky day.

"You. Kitchen." I said to Pete, pushing him to the floor. He scurried towards the counter, keeping low.

At least something was going right. I had told him to do something and he was doing what I told him to do.

And he'd left us alone.

Bastard.

I swallowed hard, but before I could warn Mel, Cadell and Lisper walked in, both waving their shotguns about like…

Well, they were as intimidating as hell.

240

Four vampires filed in with them, two taking station at the windows, one covering the toilets, the other the counter.

"Hello, everybody." Cadell said, loud enough to be heard, "Now everyone who wants to live can leave. You want to die. Stay. The management thanks you for your custom, but the cafe is closing for renovations."

Cadell rested his shotgun on the counter and walked through the departing customers to our table.

"Hi Cadell. Got you a coffee." I said smiling at my new friend.

"Thank you." he said , Taking a sip from Pete's cup and sitting next to me. "Where is your little friend?"

"Around and about somewhere." I said "I think he nipped home for a shower. Wanted to smell sweet as lace panties just for you Lisper." I blew Lisper a kiss.

Then I remembered.

I wasn't wearing my vest.

I had showered and being in a hurry to see Mel had left my Kevlar/mail vest by the wash bin.

"Then I am sure we will pick him up there." Cadell took another sip of his coffee. He waved his left hand as he sipped again. "This is exceptional coffee. I am so glad you brought me here. Thank you."

Cadell put down his cup and clamped his right hand onto Paul's shoulder.

"What's the matter doggy? Not used to cups?" he said.

Cadell reached over and tipped a small amount of coffee into Paul's saucer. Then he placed the saucer on the floor.

241

He looked up at Mel.

"Ah Young Lady. You should not allow doggies on the furniture."

The barest glance at Lisper was all it took. A couple of steps and Lisper buried the butt of his shotgun into the base of Paul's skull. Paul went down to the floor, sending the saucer flying.

I began to rise, but Cadell's right hand gently held me down, while a heavy jab in my ribs let me know that he had a gun digging in there.

Even with body armour I doubt I could have survived at point blank range.

Cadell took a sip of Pete's coffee.

I took a sip of my coffee.

Paul wriggled so he was lying on his back, half up against the wall. Cadell's foot stamped on Paul's chest. My imagination heard a couple of ribs break.

"Leave him alone Cadell. Your argument is with me." I said gently.

"Ah, that is true." Cadell nodded his head. "But the doggy did upset me a little, you see I told him he would need to keep his mouth shut, but he barked to you. So I need to tap his nose with a newspaper. You know how it is when you house train them." He removed the gun from my ribs and casually placed it on the table.

I tried to calculate my chances of getting the gun and saving the day. More chance of waking up next to Marilyn Monroe. Actually the way it was going I had a very good chance of seeing her soon.

Cadell steepled his fingers in front of his chin.

"Now let me see." he said. "This is, from a narrative point of view, where you and I engage in verbal reportage, attempting to discern what the other knows, prior to.." he paused searching for a phrase. "Prior to something happening."

"That's generally how it goes." I sipped my coffee.

Then it got worse.

"Refill?"

Mel was next to the table with a steaming jug of black coffee.

"Oh that would be lovely, thank you." Cadell said lifting his cup up with his left hand and pressing the barrel of his gun into my temple.

Fast. Very fast hands.

"I know you were thinking about throwing that coffee at me, hoping it would distract me sufficiently so Mr Faustus and the doggy could escape, but all that it will result in is the three of you being killed. You will have to watch me blow his head off before my men literally tear you to a stump."

Slowly Mel refilled Cadell's cup to the rim. Her hands hardly shook.

"I just refill cups sir. It is my job in my café. Any trouble, take it outside." She said, cool as ice. She was doing well.

"A fair point Madame." Cadell said. "Any damages will be paid for. Now, you may want to move away. I'm about to shoot the doggy. I'm sure it would contravene some Health and Safety code if you get blood on your nice apron."

"Now, hang on there…"Paul said holding his hands up, to try and calm things. A safe, non-threatening gesture.

Cadell shot Paul in the wrist.

When the bullet hit, it tore into the flesh, not just blowing a hole in the arm, but taking the wrist away, and removing the hand totally. It took a moment or two before the blood began to pump, but when it did, it gushed.

Paul rolled onto his knees clutching the stump and staring in disbelief at his hand twitching on the floor.

A flick of Cadell's eyes and the counter goon came over taking a pressure bandage out of his pocket, moved Paul's seat out of the way with one push, and bent over Paul, expertly applying the bandage to the stump.

Mel came running through from the counter with towels and the first aid kit. Her way was blocked by Lisper's shotgun.

Me? I stayed perfectly still. I reached forward, picked up my coffee cup and took a sip. I kept my eyes on Lisper.

"Good control Faustus." Cadell took a sip again from his cup. "Others would have grabbed for the gun. Bravo."

"One of your men would have shot me. No use then."

"No." Cadell put his cup down. I put my cup down. "We will not need the towels my dear."

Lisper brought up his shotgun and Mel began to walk backwards towards the counter.

"Oh, I nearly forgot my dear." Cadell waved his free had in apology. "I have a mind like a sieve today. Pardon my rudeness. Newspaper time."

Lisper pulled the trigger.

The blast hit the towels, sending up a cloud of white cotton snow. The impact threw Mel four foot backwards till she slammed into the counter and came to a halt. She lay still, her mouth opening and closing. Blood began to seep through the toweling.

Lisper looked down at her, licking his lips. Hungry.

The Magic Hour.

Frankie The Fly once explained to me that any major gunshot wound gave you a Magic Hour to get treatment in.

I had one hour.

They had one hour.

Cadell and the rest were dead. They just didn't know it yet.

"My God." There was actually admiration in Cadell's voice. "I shoot your friend, I shoot your girlfriend, and you sit there. I even kick an old man to death and what do I get? Nothing. Bravo. You have Ice Water for blood my friend. Ice Water."

Movement outside, on the street. An audience.

"Cadell..." I sipped my coffee and put the cup down. "Cadell. I don't think you and I are ever going to be friends." I reached into my jacket pocket and took out a packet of smokes. I lit one up. "We're just not compatible. Must be different star signs."

Cadell laughed then sipped his coffee.

I felt bone crunch along with the china as I slammed my elbow up into Cadell's nose. The cup shattered as did the nose. My arm moving as fast as Cadell's hands, I slammed it back into his throat. Something crumpled and collapsed.

The front window shattered.

The Medic goon next to Paul fell back clutching for a throat that wasn't there anymore. A fully grown wolf man, minus paw was chewing something wet, warm and bloody, rising to its feet and looking for trouble. It found it.

Lisper turned around to find the shotgun being pulled out of his hand by an angry P.I.

Pete reached in through the window and separated one Vampire from its head, by simply pulling.

I pulled the trigger. As the gun was pressed against Lisper's stomach, he flew across the café.

Pete stepped into the café, swiped the gun out of the second goon's hands and drove it through his face and out the back of the skull. He twisted the goon around so the barrel was pointed at me, and pulled the trigger.

I felt the bullet pass over my head as I ducked, at the same time the pellets passed the other way. There was the sound of a body slamming into the wall. A glance back showed Cadell sliding down the wall, a large hole in his shirt.

One vamp still stood. He held out his shotgun, not knowing who to aim it at.

The Mad Window Breaking Decapitator.

The one handed, pissed off Wolf man.

Me.

He didn't go out well. Not well at all.

All three of us ran to Mel, though in Paul's case it was more of a lope. More blood was seeping through the towels. I cleared them away and lifted her T-shirt.

Six small wounds puckered in her abdomen. Blood was oozing from all of them, slow, dark and nasty looking.

"Stay still darlin'." I said, trying to stop my voice from shaking. "We'll get you sorted. It will be fine."

There was a sound of a gunshot behind me from a shotgun. A soft thump followed. I could feel no holes in me so I ignored it.

"We need to get them both to hospital." Pete said. "Fast."

I looked at Paul. Still wolf shape, pain was evident on his face as he sniffed at his stump and whimpered.

"Go pick up his hand. Stick it in a plastic bag, then stick that inside another one, filled with ice. Hurry."

Pete scampered away. Mel looked up at me.

"Is your world always like this?! She whispered.

"Only sometimes." I said. I couldn't lie. Though I wanted to. I pressed down on the wound to stem the bleeding. It didn't seem to be working.

"You know how to show a girl a good time." She gasped, in-between waves of pain.

"Stay still. I'm going to go steal a car." I turned to Paul. He had changed back and was looking pale and drawn. He was losing blood too. Pete came back with a bag rattling with ice.

"Done." He said.

"Stay here. Keep pressure on her wounds. I'm going to deal with those two outside and get a car."

"Dealt with them." Pete said matter of factly as he took over from me keeping pressure on.

I stood up and walked to the window. Cadell was missing. Lisper was missing.

My own stupidity and arrogance didn't allow for them wearing body armour.

One of the cars was also gone, but the second remained.

The first goon I found was next to the car. His head was across the Street.

The second was by the boot. More Fae arrows than I could count had turned his body into a porcupine. He was making weeble weeble noises. I kicked him off the boot.

Screaming was happening somewhere. I ignored it.

I was going to get into so much trouble for this.

Last Man Standing and all.

I got into the car. They had been good enough to leave the keys in the ignition, so I started and drove the car as close to the café door as I could.

I got out the car, ran into the café and picked up Mel. Pete kept pressure on the wound as we walked to the car and loaded her onto the back seat. Paul limped behind us and sat down in the passenger seat.

We drove fast.

There was traffic.

It could be ignored.

I ignored it.

Chapter Twenty Nine:The Dick and the Dying

When we burst into Frankie's lab Pete was carrying Paul over his shoulder and I held Mel in my arms. Both had passed out en-route, which meant the pain had stopped for them, but worrying as it suggested blood loss. We placed them both carefully on the table in front of Frankie, after taking a moment to sweep all of his paraphernalia to the floor.

Frankie was pretty good, considering.

"Get them the fuck out of my fucking lab. I'm fucking working."

"Gun-shot wound to the abdomen and gun-shot amputation of a hand. She's Nosfu, He's Lyca. They need immediate help. Now." I shouted back.

"And I'm in the middle of a fucking lecture." he screamed.

Pete and I slowly turned round to see ten wide eyed junior doctors, all holding notebooks, all open mouthed.

"You are all doctors then." Pete shouted. "Yes?"

Ten heads nodded in unison.

Pete reached forward and grabbed the closest, dragging him forward so they were nose to nose.

"Then doctor. Help them." Pete said, letting the doctor go.

There was a mad flurry around the desk as Mel and Paul were both stripped and examined. I grabbed Frankie by the arm and led him to one side.

"Make sure they understand." I said.

"Understand what?" Frankie snapped back. "They are about to unofficially work on two completely different species? Perhaps You'd like to explain that to them. Get out and let me work. I'll

249

figure out something. Come back in two hours and I'll update you. Now fuck off."

I fucked off.

From the hallway I looked back inside. Both Paul and Mel looked so vulnerable. All those hospital shows my mother watched when I was a kid came flooding back. Two patients go into a hospital, only one walks out.

I tried to think of a God I could pray to. None came to mind. So I prayed to Humphrey instead. Patron saint of washed up detectives. I let the anger soak through me till I was thoroughly wet in it inside. Bottled it up for when I needed it. Then turned to Pete. He looked impassive.

I watched him. Totally different from the mad being I had seen in the café, tearing vampires apart with his bare hands.

"I thought I told you to wait in the kitchen." I said.

"You were wrong." he said calmly. "I went out the back door. There was some unpleasantness with four of them. When I had finished I went over the roof and thought it prudent to dispatch those who were trying to hurt you and my other friends." He took a deep breath. "We need to go to Mr Peter's shop. Those in the alley in provoking me, told me…"

I put my hand on his shoulder.

"I know. Cadell happened to mention it." I said.

Blood would happen for this. But later.

"What do we do Faustus?" his voice was cracking. I looked at him. Tears were running down his face. "What do we do?"

"We finish the job."

More traffic happened.

We abandoned the car a street away from Peter's. He never approved of me bringing stolen vehicles home. We ran the rest of the way, reaching the shop to find the door was locked. I fumbled in my pocket for the keys. My hands were shaking so badly I couldn't get the key into the lock. Pete took the key from my hand and slid it into the cylinder. He held the door open. I went in.

My heart broke.

Peter was sat in an old wooden chair from the kitchen, facing the door. He was wearing his same polyester trousers, collarless white, shirt, scarf and old grey cardigan. He needed a shave, but he always did. Blood had dried around his mouth. Broken teeth could be seen through his open mouth. His shirt front was brown with dried blood. Both arms hung broken by his sides. His legs were not at the angles they were meant to be. Colour had drained from his face.

One look and you knew the body would be cold.

He had been set there for our benefit.

I would remember that.

"You two took your time getting here." Peter said. "I've been dead for eight and a half hours, and you two off gallivanting. I do not know what kind of boys I raised. I really don't."

Pete rushed over to him and started stroking his face. I have no idea what he said to him. He was gibbering. I walked over to Peter and knelt next to him.

"Any pain Old Man?" I asked.

"Not after the first two hours. They broke my spine, which helped." Peter said.

Peter's mouth was not moving when he talked, but his voice was quite clear. His eyes were fixed and cloudy, but his penetrating gaze never seemed to leave me. The most vibrant dead man I had ever seen. But definitely dead. I checked his pulse and he was short on beats.

"I'll call an ambulance. " Pete said standing up.

"No you will not." Peter snapped. "Bloody pointless waste of time. I'm dead. Can't bring me back from that. Stiff as a board."

"First time in fifty years." I said.

The shop rustled. A tin chamber pot fell from the roof and hit me on the back of the head.

"Ow." I said rubbing the head. "There was no call for that."

"Stop complaining. It's the last chance I'll get." Peter said.

Pete was pacing backwards and forwards.

"Who did it?" Pete said. "Tell me who did it and I'll kill them."

"No lad" Peter said. "No call for all of that. Something has been sent to see they don't get away with it. Now go and pack your things. It's time to move on."

Pete fell onto the floor next to Peter, He held his hand up to his cheek, wetting it with his tears.

"I want to stay here with you." Pete said.

"Not a good idea son. I'll make poor company and be a bit smelly after a day or two. No air freshener will deal with it, besides, it's time for me to move on. Same for you. Now go pack your things."

"But I…"

"Go." Peter did not shout, did not snap, but gently said the word. It couldn't have been worse for him. He turned and walked through to the back room. I heard him begin to ascend the stairs and go up to my…his room.

"I am so sorry Son." Peter said. "There were so many things I wanted to tell you. So many things you need to know. Are you alright?"

Do you remember that time you made me sit up all night watching 'The Jungle Book', 'The Green Mile' and all those other weepies?" I said, holding back the catch in my voice.

"How could I forget?" He said. "You went from stoic to crying like a baby."

"Well, that's how I feel."

There was a brief pause. Everyone knows how to be sympathetic around the bereaved. You're gentle and comforting.

No one ever knows what to say to the Dead. You certainly don't expect them to answer you back.

"You have to take care of Pete." he said.

"I had a horrible feeling you were going to say that."

"You have to look after him. You have to. You must." He reiterated. "He could be so dangerous if others take him on. You have to bring out the good in him. Keep the Devil away. I have tried, goodness knows I have tried, but there are so many who want him. That's what all this is about. Teach him about right and wrong and justice."

"He's pretty good at looking after himself." I reassured him.

"No." he snapped. "No. He's not. And neither are you. Right now I'm telling him to look after you. But Pete? Pete is far too dangerous. He could do untold damage to The Streets. People, straight ones, will notice him. If that happens they will ask questions, ask questions about here. This place. The Streets. You must keep him unnoticed."

"What do you want me to do? Take him to the Mountains? In case you haven't noticed It's as flat as a pancake around here."

Another chamber pot hit me on the back of the head.

"Don't be facetious." Peter snapped. Miserable old bastard. I dodged the next one. I had forgotten he could hear what I was saying. Thinking.

"Now listen to me son. Two things you need to know, so shut your mouth, metaphorically speaking." Peter took a metaphorical deep breath. "Firstly from my digging I know that there are six of them. The first two are Cadell and that vampire you dislike so much, but they are nothing. Not worth bothering with."

"You are kidding." I said. "They blew Paul's hand off and gut shot Mel."

"And killed me. They're tough. They'll survive. They are only tools boy. Little more than guns or crossbows. Point and fire. Point and fire. Oh they get the job done, but they make a mess of things. Mind them, but don't think they are clever enough for all this."

"OK." I said. Death was making him eloquent.

"The next two are the Angel and the Daemon that brought young Pete into this all of this. I don't know what they did, yes I know I'll be there soon. Oh yes." His disjointed conversation threw me for a second, then a realized he was talking to a third party. "The Angel and the Daemon. I don't know what they did or how they did it, but you shut it down." Peter was talking faster now. Time was running out for him.

"You don't go all Hopkirk on me, you hear." I said. "If you need to go, go."

"Soon, and please stop using that kind of jargon." Peter was fighting now to stay for a few minutes. "The last two are dangerous. Might not kill you outright, but they have power lad. Real power. Money power. They might not get their hands dirty, but they know people who do. You're playing in the big leagues now. You stay safe."

"It's time for you to go Old Man." I could hear the voices on the edge of my consciousness. They were calling to Peter,

"I have waited centuries for them," he managed, "so they can wait a few minutes for me. You still have my Will don't you?"

"In my files." I said. I couldn't care less.

"I'll save you reading it." he said. "You get the lot. Everything I own. Take your fee out of that."

"Bugger the fee." I said, welling up. "You can have this one gratis."

I felt an empty hand rest on my cheek. A thumb wiped away a tear.

"I love you son." Peter said. "You have always been a son to me."

"And you have been like my father Old Man." I said.

"That'll keep me going till I get to where I am at." I felt a turning towards the stairs. "He's coming."

"Peter." There were so many questions to ask, but I'd settle for the one practical one I needed. "What did you send after them? I don't want to get in Its way."

"You won't." Peter gave a short laugh. "I sent the nastiest most persistent bastard I could think of."

"Who?" I asked.

"You son." Peter said. "I try to be good, but I think if you have to be bad, be really bad. Like I said, don't worry about Cadell and the Vampire, but take 'em out for me."

Pete got to the bottom of the stairs.

"Keep him out of that." Peter whispered. "Now put on some Robert Johnson and let me go."

I stood up, shocked. Peter had a great many things he could have sent after Cadell and Lisper. He could terrify them to death, or turn them catatonic, with an eternity of fear to enjoy. The badest, nastiest thing he could do was send me.

Was I really that bad?

If I was, how could I bring out the good in anyone?

Pete came into the room and picked up a Robert Johnston album from the floor. I just managed to notice that he didn't even look to see where it was or what it was, but still got the old man's favourite album. Straight off the mess on the floor.

Without a word he swept the shattered remnants of a Chinese vase from Peter's Radiogram, lifted the lid and placed the album on the turntable. He lifted the needle and set it on the vinyl.

Nothing happened.

"Hurry up boys. I've got to go." Peter said.

"Hang on. You're going no-where." I said. "It's not like you are about to get any older." Keep it light. Make it easy on him.

I walked over to the radiogram and plugged it in.

"I was going to do that." Peter said. Given the smell of Brimstone, Pete was doing well to keep in control.

Robert Johnston's "Kind Hearted Woman" began to play. I took Pete by the arm.

"Time to go." I said.

Pete walked over to Peter, kissed him on the cheek and whispered something in his ear. I put my hand on his shoulder and drew him back to me.

"Goodbye Father." Pete said.

"Goodbye Old Man. Dad." I said.

"Goodbye my sons. Pete stay out of trouble." Peter said. "Faustus, go find some trouble to get into."

With that all three of us left.

Chapter Thirty: The Dick and The Discovery

"Ok." I said. "You can throw a car thirty feet. Bravo. No Angel or Daemon can do that. Do you remember what I said about us? Specifically you? The part Angel, part Daemon and part human, needing to, and I emphasize the words, needing to, maintain and perpetuate a low profile. Now put me back down on the floor before you get into serious trouble. With me."

I was dangling about five feet from the floor. Again.

Still, it could have been worse.

He could have thrown me thirty feet and still lifted up the car while he let rip a silent scream.

I was lowered to the floor by the old fashioned technique of letting go. The practice I had gained over the last couple of days saw me land on both feet.

Pete had fallen to the ground and curled up in a foetal position and was crying uncontrollably. His screaming might have been silent, but it was heartfelt.

He lashed out with his right arm, causing structural damage to the butchers. A nice little building alarm let me know it was time to move on.

The distant mating cry of a police siren, meant fast.

"C'mon." I said, risking life and limb by hauling him to his feet.

I looked at him, eyes shut and watery, mouth open and reeking of brimstone. I jabbed a finger in his vicinity.

258

"Alright." I said. "You're in a tough guy, Mr Captain invulnerable phase. So I'll say sorry now."

I don't see a point in visiting a lab or hospital without picking up a few souvenirs. Normally it's bandages and anti-biotics for me, but precipitously on the last occasion…

I jabbed three needles into his neck. Right in the vein. I had the sense to attach the needles to syringes with a good dose of morphine in each.

Down like a sack of potatoes.

I did try to lift him, but it had been a long day.

A minute later the brakes and flashing lights introduced me to my new social companions.

"What happened here?" The obligatory policeman asked.

"Oh. Big. Oooo. Car. Screechy screechy. Bumpy. Ooo. Fly. Splat. Slidy slidy. Ground. Helpy upy feetdamode." I said.

God bless you Professor Stanley Unwin.

"Are you Polish?" The second policeman asked.

"Neit." I said. "Ambulance?"

Might as well get a free trip to the hospital.

Some questions were asked.

At the hospital.

Where they saw the two of us covered in blood, strapped us down and tried to identify where we were bleeding from.

They were not very happy.

Some questions were asked.

At the Police Station.

Where they saw the two of us covered in blood, They strapped us down, locked us in a cell and tried to find out where the drivers of the stolen car had gone.

Leaving a severed human hand, in ice, on the back seat.

They were not happy.

It took a phone call to Malder to get us out.

He wasn't happy either.

We still had to walk back to the hospital.

"Do you have to keep hitting the back of my head?" Pete asked.

"It makes me feel better." I said. Hitting the back of his head. Again.

"I have said I am sorry."

"Oh? What for?"

"Losing control."

"And?"

"Throwing our ride down the street."

"And."

"Leaving Paul's hand in the car."

"And."

"Being a heavy, stupid out of control,…fricker."

"It's not exactly the word I used now, is it?" I asked, playfully wagging my finger. And hitting the back of his head again.

"I don't like to swear." he said. "Mr Peter does…did not like it."

Let that one pass.

We walked in silence, apart from an occasional slapping noise.

"People are staring at us."

Which was true. Both of us have blood splattered all over us, torn clothes and one of us was walking with a pronounced limp as the result of an over enthusiastic set of questions from a policeman who seemed to take it as an insult that I wasn't a copper, but doing copper stuff like walking into crime scenes.

He would be spending a lot of time guarding doors and checking ID.

"Really?" I asked him. "Could it be because we are worth millions dead? We trashed Mel's Café and are covered in blood, and I don't know about you, but my bruises are starting to come out."

A few known players had looked at us and were trying to figure out how to do things quietly, without attracting any attention. One of them was even carrying a hat box for my head.

Still, it was quite a pretty hat box. Nice to go out with some style.

We stayed very public.

When we got to the hospital it was almost three of the clock. People were still trying to negotiate the parking meters. At the end of the queue was an ambulance driver, tapping his change, waiting to get a ticket so he could park.

And people wonder why the 1940's hold such an appeal for me.

We got a few hostile looks from the reception staff when we entered the hospital.

Ah so nice to leave an impression.

I gave Pete a slap on the head ……. just because.

"You idiots." the voice screamed.

"Hello Frankie." I said.

"Hello Mr Fly." Pete said.

We both turned around to see a very annoyed looking Frankie, in a red floral dress, carrying a fly swat. The fly swat was duly used on both of us.

"Do you have any idea how much trouble you caused here today? No of course you don't because

261

you are both idiots, arseholes and morons." Frankie vented.

"Are Mel and Paul alright?" I asked snatching the fly swat from Frankie's hand and, well, hitting Pete with it.   Just because.

"Walk with me."   Frankie took off along the corridor. We both scurried to catch up. "Firstly, Paul was too badly injured to keep downstairs. Not that I could have shut those students up, you fucking idiots. Oh yes." Frankie stopped and rounded on both of us. "What happened to the hand? It's possible it could have been reattached. He could pick his nose given time, but never play the guitar again."

"I am…" Pete began.

"I am so sorry Frankie." I interrupted, "but there wasn't enough left of it to save. Just a couple of finger nails. The guy used some sort of explosive round."

"I've heard there's been a few of them through here recently." Frankie sighed. "Paul's the first one to survive." We carried on walking. Pete gave me a puzzled look.

"How's Mel doing?" I said.

"Well. Here's her room." Frankie stopped in front of a doorway and opened it. On the bed, there were…bed sheets. There was no sign of Mel.

"Are you taking the piss?" I said.

Twenty minutes later, after I had been calmed down and given a set of hospital scrubs to wear, I was drinking coffee in the staff canteen.

"So she just got up and walked out?" I asked.

"But she was badly wounded!" Pete said.

"Still, she just got out of the bed, got dressed and walked out the front door". Frankie sipped at his Skinny latte decaf. Wimp.

I downed my espresso in one then reached for my espresso chaser.

"I know vampires are tough, but even so she had a serious injury." I said.

"How much do you, Bloody Fly, know about the Old Ones Faustus?" Frankie said.

"Well, they are more legend than real, from what I've heard." I said. "They are, as the name suggests, old. Really Old Vampires. From amongst the early tribes in Egypt. Rumour has it that the really powerful vampires in their circles are the Old Ones. They have skills and abilities that none of the modern day vampires have. Also while modern day vampires feed by simply draining degrees of life force from people, the Old Ones were the real McCoy. Blood drinkers."

"That's right." Frankie said.

We all sat in silence for a while. Empty espresso. Skinny decaf latte and a glass of fizzy something.

"Are you suggesting that Miss Mel, maybe one of the 'Old Ones'?" Pete asked, saving me the worry of saying it. I guess he has his uses.

"All I know, " Frankie said "is that anyone, Vampire, or werewolf , if they get a gut shot, do not heal that fast. They need surgery. They need rest and recuperation. A bit of a lie down for a couple of hours does not sort out their problems."

"And the Old Ones? Could they survive that and walk away?" Pete asked again.

"If you believe the stories they could." Frankie said. "Bloody Fly" He snatched the swat from me.

"The only way to kill an Old One, according to legend, is to drive a stake…"

"Through the heart?" Frankie slaps Pete. Pete should learn when not to interrupt.

"Through the brain, sever the arms, legs and then the head." Frankie finished.

"And that…" Pete was glared into silence by two pairs of eyes.

"Then you burn the remains on separate fires, and bury the remains at least one hundred feet apart." Frankie finished. "Get it wrong, even by an inch, and they will, repeat WILL come back and your ancestors will know all about it."

"Oh dear." Pete said.

"I find it hard to believe Mel could be an Old One." I said. "She was too…vulnerable. Too gentle."

"Then she probably isn't." Frankie said. "The Old Ones are also supposed to be as Mad as a box Of Frogs. That's a medical term."

"Is it possible Cadell could have taken her? To use as leverage against you?" Pete looked at me.

"No." Frankie said. "First part of the protocol when a patient goes missing is to check the CCTV. There she is large as life, walking out under her own steam and alone."

"Nice idea Pete."

Frankie passed Pete a ten pound note.

"Go get Faustus another double espresso will you please?"

"Why?"

"Because I want to talk about something private, and with all due respect, I barely know you." Frankie said very calm and pleasant.

"Then I will go and buy some more drinks." Pete said. "May I have another coke? I have never had coke before today. Peter would not let me. It is quite stimulating and…bubbly in my head."

"That's the caffeine kicking in." Frankie said. "Certainly."

When Pete was a fair distance away Frankie leaned in close enough for me to smell the overpowering fly spray and see his makeup had need of a touch up.

"What's wrong Frankie?" I said. "You must be worried as you hardly bothered with flies for the past ten minutes."

"I took blood from your girlfriend Faustus." Frankie said.

"Isn't that normal?"

"It is. It's not normal for it to evaporate." Frankie said. "No Vampire blood evaporates from a sealed test tube."

"I understand that…" I started, but never got the chance to finish.

"No you don't. You really don't. I never got the chance to test hers but I know it's wrong. Hers isn't the only one to evaporate. So did his."

Frankie nodded his head towards Pete in the queue.

"It took his blood longer to evaporate, but by God it did. Whatever is happening old matey, watch your back. Do you trust him?"

That was a difficult question. He had saved my life, but he had got me into the trouble in the first place. I get on with him. Sort of. Trust. Well, Peter trusted him and that was good enough for me. But the blood?

Bugger.

Another clue.

I needed Coffee. Badly.

Ω

Excerpt from
Angels, Daemons and other realm beings.
By E.M Faustus
(unpub)

Coffee.

Gods bless The Oromo people of Ethiopia who are said to have been the first to recognize the energizing, blessed nature of the wonderful coffee bean.

Years of close observation has produced a clear definite recognition of the 'Nature' of coffee.

There are three kinds of cups of coffee.

Good coffee.

Average coffee.

Evil coffee.

Good Coffee you get once or twice a week. It's that special cup you make for yourself and is always at home. The cup you can sit down and enjoy, with no distractions, no worries and no rush to drink it. Half way through you find yourself wishing that you could have another one straight after it, just as good. But there is no chance.

Average coffee is the coffee someone else makes for you. A friend, family member and occasionally in a coffee house where they know your tastes and cater for them.

Then there's Evil coffee. Caffinus Satanicus. EVIL COFFEE!

266

Evil Coffee you buy, or are given in fast food places, motorway service cabins, take-away food outlets. The places where people with no sense of taste congregate. It has no taste of Coffee. No smell of Coffee. It does not even look like Coffee. It is little more than Satan's Urine, with a splash of milk.

Coffee should be good, or at least average. Evil must be rejected.

All decaf coffee is Evil.

Don't argue.

Ω

Chapter Thirty One: The Dick and The Delectable

We left Frankie spraying himself down. The fly had come back.

Both of us were now showered, shaved and wearing suitable attire, courtesy of the consultants changing room and a couple of dodgy locks.

Pete was a junior consultant, in a Marks and Spencer three piece, while I had hit the Jackpot.

I had never even dreamed of owning a Saville Row suit before. Technically, I was quite aware that I didn't exactly own it, but I was sure I could come up with some justification for holding onto a suit, 'borrowed' from someone I didn't exactly know, but almost certainly knew someone who knew them. If not exactly knew them, knew of them. If they didn't exactly know of them, was aware of the existence of consultants and that consultants wore Saville Row suits, so that's ok then.

It fit. It went with my hat. It was mine till they asked for it back.

Things were getting a lot more complicated. Too many clues. Too much going on. I needed a high tech bit of paper and a pencil.

Every dog the taxi passed drew Pete's attention. That's what called me back to reality. The incessant grabbing of my arm and Pete going "Look Faustus." He had a tight grip.

The thing was, at the end of the day this case was about Dog.

The deeper I had looked the more complicated it had become, so maybe it was time to simply find the damn dog. Ignore the rest, find the dog, get paid and take a holiday.

Yeah. Right.

The taxi pulled in next to the office. Then I realized that this case was costing me a lot of money.

"Eh. I'm sorry mate, but I seem to have…" I started.

A baseball bat was shoved through the open glass panel separating the driver from the passengers. The look he was giving me said;

"Sir, while I appreciate that you may have recently discovered that you are financially limited and may be unable to afford the reasonable tariff that is placed upon this journey I have afforded you, it may be beneficial if you consider altering your sentence in order to afford a solution to the problem you are experiencing. I appreciate your taking the time to think about this matter. My, I was not prepared for your friend removing my sports equipment from my hand and breaking it in half. Under these circumstances I will consider this transportation a pro bono journey and wish you well to the end of your day."

I dug into the consultant's pockets, and came out with a gold pen and a small sealed bag of some kind of herb.

"I could let you have this extremely expensive pen?" I asked.

"I'll take the skunk mate." he said, his hand snatching the bag out of my hand before I could say anything.

A few seconds later we were on the pavement, feeling good that we had made someone happy.

"D'you know Pete….?" I said. "Violence is not the only way to address a situation."

"At least I did not ask to borrow your sock." he said.

Fair point.

"Come on." I said. "I need some sweeties."

The Old Fashioned Shop's bell gave and Old Fashioned tinkle as we walked through the Old Fashioned door, into an Old Fashioned Sweetie Shop selling Old Fashioned Sweeties.

Though not those coloured by arsenic. Not that Old Fashioned.

"Never eat these after dark." The shop keep was saying to the five year old. "And never, never eat these before a meal. An hour before a meal would be safe, young sir, but no, definitely no later. Promise me that young sir. Oh. Promise me that, if you value your ears. Promise me."

"I promise." said the five year old, crossing his heart with a sticky finger.

"Then here you go." The shop keep handed a small bag of sweets into young hands and received a few coins from a smiling mother, who seemed amazed at the look of fascinated awe on her child's face as he opened the bag and looked inside at the jelly babies.

"What would happen if I did?" The young boy asked.

The shop keep took a few steps back and held his knuckles against his mouth for a moment.

"Oh. Too terrible to mention. But never risk your ears young sir. In years to come you may need spectacles and if your ears have melted... No. I have said to much. Ask me no more. Enjoy your sweeties, but responsibly."

The young boy took a jelly baby out of the bag and carefully put it in his mouth. After a moment he turned to the shop keep, smiled and began to chew. He took his mum's hand and they left the shop with a tinkle, leaving the owner grinning.

"Nice work Chris." I said.

"I thank you." Chris said, taking a small bow. "How's business Faustus?"

"Complicated."

"Always. Who's the Angel? Not your normal clientele. Smells of 90% dark slab chocolate. Maybe with an almond rich fondant in the next vat. Hint of brim, but only a hint. This nose never lies."

"Like I said. Complicated." I sniffed. "What's new on the street?"

Chris took a step back and lapsed into serious mode. He came around the counter, locked the shop door and turned the sign to 'Secret Tasting.' He turned to face Pete and leaned down.

Chris was tall, thin and angular. Even his face was a collection of Angles. These angles extended throughout the whole shop. The counter, shelving, even the sweet jars were set at precise angles. Sharp edges everywhere. Or maybe that was just me after an encounter with a wizard's sword. Chris's hair was jet black and slicked down, naturally formed into an angular widow's peak. His accent was old European. One of the Rumanian states. Take a guess which one. Just check the teeth.

He would have made a natural undertaker, but found out in the late 1890's that he liked working with kids.

On the run (Courtesy of Mr Stoker), he found himself as a teacher for a few weeks. After that he owned a toy shop for a few years. Then in 1938 he moved here to get away from the Nazi threat, did some war work and was 'helpful' in reducing the number of Mosley's crew.

Permanently.

Then in 1948 he bought himself a sweet shop and never looked back.

"Firstly." Chris said to Pete, "Be aware, that anything that is said in this shop never goes any further. I only talk to Faustus because he is my friend and he buys large amounts of chocolate from me."

"I understand." Pete said.

"Secondly, some may suggest that I conduct certain questionable deals that could draw attention to me if noticed. You must not talk about anything you might see or hear, as it would not prove beneficial for your health. Do you understand that?"

"I understand that." Pete said nodding seriously.

"Thirdly." Chris said, tapping three fingers on Pete's forehead. "There is significant word on the Street amongst those who know."

"And what is that?" Pete asked, leaning in closer. Chris turned and put an arm about Pete's shoulders, drawing him towards the counter. He got to me and placed his other arm around my shoulders and drew us both in close to whisper.

"Cinnamon and Cranberry bombs." Chris whispered. "Try one and every other chocolate is second best. Trust me. I am a confectioner."

Pete threw Chris's arm off while Chris stood back and laughed in his deep baritone.

"After everything that has happened I do not find that funny." Pete said.

"I am sorry my young friend, but you did look so serious. Like you had the cares of the world on your shoulders." Chris said, walking back to the business side of the counter. That's why I like Chris. He does like a good laugh. "But here, you will see that I was not joking."

Chris reached under the counter and produced a large white cardboard box. Those of us in the know would recognize it as the start of a dream. He lifted the lid and the smell of cinnamon and 'proper' chocolate hit me.

I looked into the box at the individual domes of delight, a rich chocolate with a red circular mark pressed into the top. Chris took a pair of tongs and lifted three onto a plate.

"Invert it and eat the base first." he said, placing the plate on top of the counter. I did as he said and the smell of cinnamon and fruit hit me as the taste of the most incredible chocolate melted onto my tongue and was transmitted directly into my brain telling me that I wanted the box. The dream had started. The look on Chris's face said that he wouldn't part with the box. Both of us turned to Pete who was sniffing the bomb with suspicion. We nodded to him. He popped the whole thing into his mouth, chewed eight times (I counted) and swallowed.

"Very nice." Pete said. "May I have another please?"

Chris and I both stared at the chocolate we had in our respective hands, then at Pete. Notably chocolate less.

"NO." we both said in unison. "You bloody philistine." Still in unison.

"If you were not with Faustus, I would throw you out." Chris said.

"Chris." I said warning and reminding.

"Relax Faustus." Chris said. "I didn't threaten to rip his throat out. I am still mostly on the wagon."

"Mostly?" I asked.

"Well." Chris said, looking down. "Every now and then some racist idiot calls around with a baseball bat and some friends. I keep them around for… 'company'"

"You got any Renfields kicking about at the minute Chris?" I asked. Chris held up his hands.

Ω

Excerpt from
Angels, Daemons and other realm beings.
By E.M Faustus
(unpub)

Renfields.

See Stokers biography.

Ω

"Only the one Faustus. Only the one, and he did try to burn the shop down while my grandchildren were staying."

"That's fair enough then." I said taking another bite. It was exquisite. And it was fair enough.

"What's a Renfield?" Pete asked.

"Suicidal human." I said.

"Suicidal?" Pete was suspicious. Good sign on a case, not around my friends.

"They are if they try to burn my grandchildren alive." Chris said, and that was that.

I bought fifteen of the chocolates, a box of Spangles and a box of Marathons. Also one full size, 1970's Curly-Wurly. All highly out of date, but tasting bigger and better than you can buy now.

Amazing the currency that's in a solid gold pen.

"Keep your head down Chris." I said as I moved the blue carrier bag from hand to hand to try and find a way for it not to dig in. "There're bad things on the street."

"I know Faustus." he said. "But not my kind of people. Did you hear, someone actually tried to buy my shop. My shop! I advised them that it was not for sale. I had to do that quite…forcibly. I'll keep my ears open. Amazing what a shop keeper hears."

"Thanks Chris. See you at Film Night."

"Give Peter my best." Chris gave a wave as we left the shop. "Tell him he still owes me for his Sherbet Lemons."

As Pete and I walked back to the office he was obviously confused.

"Who was that man?" he asked.

"He used to be a Count in the 'Old Country'. He's my friend. He owns a sweetie shop." I said. "I wanted some sweeties. That simple."

"I thought we were going to put the squeeze on a snitch."

"Please." I said. Actually Chris had told me a lot. This bunch we were dealing with were working outside of the normal Vampire circles and freelancing their activities. He was worried. Someone had actually tried to pressure him into selling up. Stupid. If he wasn't worried he would never have given away a tester. Worried enough to give away two testers and eat one himself. Even during the Vampires own civil war (1999-2002) that did not happen.

Most importantly Chris was willing to keep me, an outsider to vampire politics, up to date on what was going on. That meant no rumours, but straight talking truth.

He was worried. That meant I was worried.

I don't like being worried, but there was a solution.

I turned to Pete.

"Spangle?" I asked

Chapter Thirty Two: The Dick Declines Defending

I had experienced a few surprises over the last few days, not the least the sight that greeted me when I walked into my office.

My Office.

I would like to emphasize that it is MY office, nobody else's office, but MY office. Mine. Even though it was beginning to bear resemblance to a high street in a war zone.

The band were all sat around. All bar Sid, who presumably had other business, courtesy of his Fae Queen. Tied and gagged, sitting in my office chair, the one I used for clients, was not a client.

More of a vampire really.

The pump action shotgun he had intended to use on me was sellotaped into his mouth.

What is this thing they have with shotguns these days?

"Hello lads." I said. "Bit early for a rehearsal isn't it?"

Dave The Drummer stood up and crossed over to me. For a second I thought he was going to hit me. For a second he thought he was going to hit me.

"How's Paul?" Dave asked.

"Fine. I suppose." I said.

"Will he keep his hand?" Steve and Tim asked in unison.

"No." Pete said. Nothing else to say there.

"Right." Steve said, now promoted to lead guitar.

"We came to help." Dave said. "It seems you've gone to war and could use some muscle.

I took off my hat and hung it on the remains of my hat stand. I was touched by what they were offering, but these were my friends. We had gone through good and bad times together. Seen a lot of each other and knew each other's private lives.

We knew each other's personal life inside out.

But they knew nothing of my working life.

I felt like shit.

"If you want to help, you can start by killing him." I said pointing at the vampire. The vampire's eyes were looking around, desperately looking for a way out. The band were all looking at each other, trying to decide what to do.

"He came here to kill me so if you want to help, kill him, then get rid of the body." I said. "Oh, strip him for other weapons first. We'll need them. He probably has a spare gun at his ankle."

Eyes danced around friends, not knowing what to do.

I did. I reached down, took the stock of the shotgun and pulled the trigger.

Clack.

The vampire didn't wet himself, but he did wince and whimper. Surprising because he must have known he hadn't chambered a round.

Dave stepped back and nearly tripped over Tim, who had just tripped over the sofa. Steve winced. The only one who hadn't reacted was Pete.

"Empty." I said, taking up the shotgun and putting a round in the chamber. "There all fixed now. Anyone else want to try?" I asked. Lots of heads were shaken. All bar Pete.

"I'm sorry lads. You are all tough as they come, and in a bar fight there isn't one of you that wouldn't back me up. I know that, but the rules here are different. This is playing for keeps."

The lads were still looking confused, so I pushed it.

"Pete." I said. "Break all the fingers on this guy's hand will you?"

Take a carrot. Wrap it in several processed cheese slices. Break it in half. That's the noise you get when you break fingers. Now amplify it and times it by three. Or is it times by four? And don't forget to drag your nails down a blackboard at the same time.

"Does a thumb count as a finger?" Pete asked.

"Technically I don't think it does." I said

The vampire stopped screaming behind the sellotape.

"I'd just dislocate it." I said.

There was a distinct popping noise. Then some more screaming.

I never claimed to be a nice guy.

"You know why I did that. Don't you?" I said leaning in.

The vampire nodded his head slowly as he breathed through the pain.

"Untie him." I said. I had nothing against the guy. He hadn't actually tried to kill me, and with his hand broken, I had done him a favour. He would never get to hold or fire a gun again. Well, not without serious pain.

He had just been retired.

As Pete snapped the bonds that held him to the chair, I noticed what the guys had tied him up with. I looked at them. Tim proudly tapped his chest, the shirt was peppered with bullet holes.

"Don't worry Faustus." Tim said. "I know what you are thinking, but I'm OK." He tapped his chest. "Ceramic might not be bullet proof, but a little clay and glue and I'll be fine. Why are you staring at us like that?"

"You used all my computer cables to tie him up?" To emphasize my shock, Pete continued to snap the cables as he freed the Vampire.

"It's what we had." Steve said.

"You don't exactly have rope lying around your office." Dave chipped in.

"In the filling cabinet. Under 'R'. For Rope." I came back. Well. You never know when you'll need some.

I turned back to Pete and the Vampire. The free Vamp was holding his broken hand and had removed his gag.

"Need some codeine?" I asked.

He nodded, I passed him some from my desk drawer and he dry swallowed. I sat on my desk, lit up and passed it to him. He took it gratefully. I lit one for myself as Pete perched himself on the next corner.

"Will you answer questions?" I asked.

"Too right he will." Steve said.

"Shut up Steve." I said.

"Within reason." The Vampire said.

My weren't we all getting on well!

"What's your name?" Fifty-fifty chance he'd answer.

"Lawrence Le'Roux." Fifty-fifty chance he was telling the truth.

"So Larry." I said. "You Private or do you work for a big man with shiny shoes?"

"Those amateurs? Please give me some credit."

"Fair enough." I said. "Where did you hear about the contract?"

"Trade secret." Larry said. "No offence."

"None taken." I replied. "Best go get that hand looked at."

I stood up and moved round sitting at my desk. Larry stood up and moved backwards to the door. He nodded at the lads as he was leaving.

"You can't let him leave!" Steve exploded.

"He was going to kill you." Dave leapt in.

Tim looked down at the front of his shirt.

"Nothing personal gentlemen." Larry said. "Believe me, the experience hurt me much more than you." Which was true. From the way he was walking and sweating he would be lucky to make the stairs without passing out.

"Hey. Larry." I called out, as he reached the top of the stairs. "You forgot your gun."

I emptied all the cartridges out of the gun and went to slide it towards him.

"Keep it." he called back. He looked down at his broken fingers. "I just retired." He kept on walking.

"What the hell was that all about?" Tim asked.

"Simple." I said, "I said kill him. No one moved. I told him to break his fingers," I nodded at Pete, "he broke his fingers. You are all good guys. Damn it Steve, Dave, You are both vegetarian. Tim, it's physically impossible for you to kill. It's written into you. None of you could do it."

I spat my cigarette onto the floor and ground it under my toes. I lit another one.

"If I thought any of you would or could do it I wouldn't have asked. There will be blood. There will be killing. Paul wanted to walk in my world and got lucky. He lived. Peter didn't and Gods' know what happened to Mel. People are dying and somehow I have to stop it. I don't want you hurt. If I have to bruise your feelings then I will." I was almost shouting now. "If you want to be useful, go and sit with Paul till his wife gets there. He's got protection. What he needs are friends."

"And what about you Faustus?" Dave shouted back. "What do you need?"

"A Coffee, a Curly-Wurly and a smoke."

Chapter Thirty Three: The Dick and The Daemon/Angel/Human Debate

After the lads and I calmed down and they left, I made myself a coffee. I put one on the desk for Pete. He ignored it. His choice.

"And now?" he asked.

"Now we solve the case."

"Which one?" he snapped. "My lost dog? Who or what I am? Peter's murder? The war between the Vampires and the Fae? The induction into serfdom of large sections of The Streets? Or perhaps why your office has been redecorated in a pleasant shade of Arrow?"

Kid had a point.

"Let's start with Dog shall we?"

"Oh Good." he said. "The case I am actually paying you for."

I looked at Pete. Sarcasm was not something he displayed when I first met him.

"How do you feel?" I asked. I didn't need an unexploded Daemon on my hands on top of everything.

"In control. I believe I have even controlled the smell of Brimstone." he said, folding his arms in defiance.

I sniffed the air with tobacco insulated nostrils. He was right. No Brimstone. No Chocolate. Just...sweat.

"Alright then." I said. "We work this through." I dug into my desk drawer and pulled out some paper and a pencil. At last. Progress.

"One. Paul, and probably lots of others are given the task of finding you."

"I thought this was about Dog." he snapped.

"It Is." I said. "Now work with me. Paul finds you and tells Cadell where you are. They could have snatched you off the street… if they had an army big enough. Instead someone snatches Dog. Jo-Jo Mar. He gives him to two unknown Probably Angels. You go looking for Dog, and instead of tracking him down yourself, going through the normal routes, you come to me. All because Peter sends you here. Then it all kicks off. Why did Peter send you to me?" I asked him. "Why not the normal Dog Rescue? This county is lousy with them."

"He said that you would be the only person who could sort everything out." Pete said, sitting in the opposite chair.

"Were they the words he used? 'Sort everything out'?"

"The exact words. Yes."

I took a last drag and ground it to death in the ashtray.

"Son of a bitch set us up." I said. Not believing what I was saying.

"I beg your pardon?" Pete said, sounding more like his usual self.

I lit up again. A nagging throb was beginning in my head. The boost I gave myself earlier was coming back to haunt and hurt me.

"Peter. Our friend. Our surrogate father. He knew 'something' was wrong. Something on The Streets. Something with you. He used Dog's kidnapping as the excuse to stir things up. Try to get things sorted. Put right."

"But why?"

"It's what he did." I replied. "He loved The Streets. He saw them as a haven and a sanctuary for those who needed protection from persecution. He knew something was wrong, and for his own reasons didn't act himself. Instead he gets the only two Outsiders on The Streets to do his work for him.

"No. No. No." Pete was shaking his head. "He wouldn't do that."

"Really?" I said. "He once tricked me into going into Loftspace after a lost girl."

"Loftspace? That's not so bad."

"Really?" I still wake up at night in a cold sweat, occasionally screaming a little over the nine minutes forty seven seconds I spent in Loftspace.

"He would not kidnap Dog. He knew what he means to me." Pete was sounding unsure.

"No. He wouldn't. However he was not beyond taking advantage of any situation that came up. That's how he ended up...owning..."

"What? Come on say something. Don't just sit there staring."

Back round it comes.

This case is like Find The Lady. You know in your heart and soul where the card with the Queen is. You watch it closely. See where it lands then it turns out to be somewhere else.

Find the Lady.

Well maybe the lady has gone into hiding.

Maybe the Lady was never visible at all.

Maybe the ...

It was half there but I couldn't get to it. I mainly kept seeing Peter's property portfolio. He owned thirty five properties on The Streets, rented out at cheap rates to people like me or exorbitant rates to those he didn't know.

Old Timers like Peter didn't worry about money. It was just paper or metal.

Gold or Jewels were the tools of exchange.

Old Timers like Peter didn't worry about peoples' respect. You owned their houses and businesses. You got their attention.

Property were the tools of influence.

Old Timers like Peter didn't worry about dying. It just happened and when it did they embraced it.

Old Timers dying sent up a property scramble that was not exactly friendly.

Old Timers like Peter knew they were going to die and manipulated things.

Bastards.

Ω

Excerpt from
Angels, Daemons and other realm beings.
By E.M Faustus
(unpub)

Old Timers

I have a friend who is an Old Timer.

He is a pain in the arse.

Old Timers are exactly who it says they are. They have been around a long time. A very long time.

Some Old Timers have been around for up to two thousand years. They have seen so much and done so much that the only way they can fit in is to keep a low profile and engage in small and pointless little vendettas against each other.

They wage petty campaigns lasting for years, based upon the insult of who beat whom to the last ginger biscuit at their annual meeting.

They are one hundred percent human and are subject to the same rules every human obeys. They get colds, fall in and out of love, grow old and die. They simply take a lot longer to do it.

Anyone under a thousand years old is either a Boy or Totty. Anyone under five hundred years old is an infant.

They are very much like the miserable relative that comes around on Christmas Day, complains about everything, and insists that you pick them up from their home - even if they live miles away- and wants to go home just after they have created the volcanic tension that erupts just after you have left and you walk back into.

You don't know why you invite them, but you do. And they are vicious in their dealings with others.

Ω

"He simply wanted to help?" Pete said. Definitely more of a question than a statement. He wanted reassurance.

"Yes." I said. "I think he wanted to put things right. He knew his time was coming to an end, so probably wanted to put us in the right place at the right time to do something. Probably wanted to know something would get sorted because he knew he wouldn't be there. It would have been a help if he had told us."

"I have not seen you upset. That surprises me." Pete did look worried.

It worried me too.

"The best I can explain it," I said, "is that THIS, what we are doing now, is work. This is my job.

This case. My friends and family have been hurt and killed. Part of it, is to get at me, make me act without thinking. If I lose my temper now, go off looking for revenge, I will make mistakes. That will get me killed. You too probably and all the people we know will be marked for 'attention'. So. I stick to doing the job. Seeing it through to the end. I'll fall apart later. Right now, I'll see the job through. Does that make sense?"

"Enough." Pete put his hand out for me to hold. I looked at it and all the emotion and support it offered. I tapped the ash from my smoke into it.

"Best toughen up kid." I said. "We have a case to solve, ass to kick and buckets of coffee to drink."

"And the Curly-Wurly?"

"Eaten it. Get your coat. We're leaving."

Pete stood up and looked around for the coat he was wearing.

"Where are we going?" He asked.

"Off to kick arse son. Off to kick very large arse."

Chapter Thirty Four: The Dick Delivers Demands

The door to Fatso's office was temporarily locked. Club Transco had been locked as well, but careful negotiation with a brick had opened that door. My size eight opened Fatso's. We walked in.

Fatso was sat behind the desk, enjoying a light dinner of sushi served on the naked body of a twenty something young lady. Where there should have been delicate slices of fish and vegetables, Fatso had lumps of fish and whole veg. The end of an entire cucumber stuck out of the side of his mouth according to comedic narrative.

"Hi F." she said, giving me a little wave. "Can't talk now. I'm busy. Call me later?"

"Hi Jen." I said, taking out my smokes, because it annoys Fatso. "Might want to take a shower."

"Sorry F. I'm booked for the next hour and he's just started."

Fatso said nothing as his mouth was now filled with raw fish and cold rice. Lovely.

"Take a shower and I'll call you later." I passed her a dressing gown and she stood up, showering the carpet with food. If you could call it that. The view was pleasant though. She looked worried as she shrugged the dressing down on.

"It will be fine." I said kissing her cheek. "He'll pay for the full two hours." Jen smiled and skipped out the door.

"Hi Fatso." I said.

Fatso tried swallowing and grabbed some warm wine to wash down his raw fish and associate parasites. Some people know how to live.

"Move the desk please Pete?" I asked.

Pete grabbed the desk corner and slung it across the room, trashing some contemporary designer stuff on its way.

Fatso was sat there, with his trousers around his ankles, wearing baby pink drawers. His ankles were bigger than my waist, and that's not small. The thighs were larger than some tables. I began to think I would turn vegetarian. No. Vegan. Maybe anorexic.

"My, my Fatso." I said. "Planning on being a naughty boy? With a dear close personal friend of mine? Hmm?"

Fatso was beetroot red as he swallowed the last of his meal, part anger, part embarrassment, but there was also some fear in there. Just a little. He could not believe that any human would come into his office and play the hard case.

Or see him in his drawers.

One of the Rules: You don't face down a God unless you have something very big and nasty with you.

I had Pete. Not quite the same really.

But Fatso didn't know that.

"No Shadwell?" I asked. I was surprised that I had gotten that far.

"I fired him. He refused an order. What are…?" Fatso said, but I needed to keep him off balance.

"Shame, because I wanted to thank you both for your help, and those nice little clues you gave me." I said. "I also thought that I should give you a warning."

Fatso rose to his full height of eight feet. I think he was trying to intimidate. Didn't work.

"Best keep all your scum off the Streets. Fat boy." I said looking up. "You lot, whoever you are, decided to get me in on this, so here I am. Get out of my way or you will be squashed."

Fatso's mouth opened. I shut it with a bread roll I'd picked off the floor.

"Now before you start screaming about racism I will be calling on everyone. And before you start banging on about how you are a God and how you should be worshiped and revered, bear in mind that you and your kind are only here because, in any society, everyone needs scum they can look down on. Everyone wants to know that, whatever they are, they are better than that scum there. Even scum needs scum to look down on. You and your friends are that scum Fatso, and I have enough friends who are bullet proof, fire proof, God proof and arsehole proof. We can bring you lot down and out through fire, water and belief that you don't exist anymore. I can set it off so your very existence is removed. I can make Dawkins look like an imbecile. Now you all get out of my way or I'll take you down. So sit down, shut up and find a crew to help you pull your drawers on."

"Eh?"

With that, Pete, wearing rubber gloves, grabbed Fatso's drawers and pulled them to his ankles.

"My, what a small penis for a God." Pete said.

"And it's warm in here too." I said.

Then we left, without looking back. Outside Pete turned to me and said;

"I thought you were simply going to ask him a few questions?"

"So did I." I said. "I told you I've got a bit of a temper. But I'm working on it."

"Good." He said. "I would hate to think that you were annoyed in there."

291

Leech was the next on the agenda.

Loan Shark and Leech.

The term Leech is not so much a summary of a person who applies exorbitant interests to small loans, though he did do that.

No. Leech was a leech. Long black tube with sucker mouth. Slimy and makes you feel ill to look at him. Best description I can give.

"OK Leech." I said. "Thirty seconds and it's the bucket of salt." Waving said bucket with menace.

Leech's office was in a dark, damp cellar, from where it ran Its 'Empire', just the right side of criminal. When it sent round his collectors, you paid, one way or another. Leech was where you turned to when there were no other options.

When you threaten an invertebrate you get them really squirming.

"No need for that Mr Faustus." She said in her wheedling squelch voice. "What do you need to know? I'll tell you."

Bad Guys aren't just Guys.

"Where do all my socks go at the launderette?" I asked.

"What?"

"Wrong answer." I flicked a few grains at her.

I cannot explain the effect, but it was almost but not quite like a burn. Almost but not quite.

Sort of a bubbly, melty, squelchy, screamy thing.

I of course, took no little pleasure in inflicting it on the worse scum we had around here. The wrong words in the sentence being 'no' and 'little'.

"Been selling loans lady?" I asked.

"Kill him, kill him, kill him." Leech screamed at her bodyguards. The only answer they gave were little bubbling noises as they lay clutching their groins.

"Is this violence and intimidation necessary?" Pete asked as he pulled his socks back on.

"No" Leech squirmed. She's a leech. They do that.

Normally I don't approve of torture as a means of interrogation, but sometimes it can be fun. I flicked a little salt at her.

"Oh yes." I said. "So, have you been selling your loans off?"

"Yes, yes, yes, yes, yes, yes. Yes!"

I took up a good handful of salt.

"Man with shiny shoes?" Obvious question but I like to go with obvious. Nice and quick.

"Yes. Yes. Yes."

"Met with anyone else?" I threw a handful of salt past her 'head'.

"No. Bkruthra Faustus. I swear to you. Just him and the vampire. Just him and the vampire. I swear"

"OK." I upturned the bucket of salt so it spread over the floor. "See you."

I dropped the bucket and turned to the cellar stairs. I paused briefly to kick one of Leech's bodyguards in the head, then trotted up the steps, whistling a happy tune. Pete scurried up the stairs behind me.

"When you said we were going to see a 'leech loan shark', I did not expect an actual leech." Pete said. "And was that the right way to treat a lady?"

I lit a smoke. "The only way to treat her. I've never been able to prove what she's into but I know it's drugs, women, men and all sorts of bad stuff.

She gets people so far into debt that there's a limited amount of ways to pay off the debt. Except she keeps cranking up the interest so it never gets paid off. Believe me. She is worse than Cadell and his lot. Just don't have proof. Yet."

"In that case…" Pete stood still and thought for a moment. "Do you think I should kill her."

I rounded on him hard and slapped him full in the face.

"You listen." I said, getting so far into his face I was almost up his nose. "If you kill someone in self defence, or to save someone else, that's sort of acceptable. Murder isn't. Even if it's scum. You're talking about cold blooded premeditated murder. That's beyond wrong. That's becoming the very thing you're trying to get rid of. Do it. They win."

Pete took a step back, shocked, and held up both his hands.

"I just thought I would be doing good."

I walked up to him. He back pedaled until he was up against a car.

"First you kill the body guards. All five of them, because by now she'll have a lot more in there." I began. "Then…It gets worse."

"I get the idea." he tried.

"No you don't. Then you have to kill her collectors, because I guarantee you at least one has plans to step into the power void you just created."

"I…"

"Then it gets worse, because you have to track down her thirty five children, who want you dead because you killed their mother, and because they want to take over her business and money. You have to kill their bodyguards as well."

"…"

"Then it gets worse. Then you have to kill all of the administration staff, because they will know you are clearing house and could give evidence against you."

"Stop."

"No, because then it gets worse. Then you have to kill any witnesses. You stop them from telling anyone what you did, how you did it or what you look like. You kill them quick and painless because at they are innocents after all. Then it gets really bad for you."

Pete pushed me away and walked around me to face me again.

"Stop it. I understand. I understand."

"No you don't." I said jabbing a finger into his chest. "Your brain works and processes, but you don't understand. Learn fast, because that's the difference between right and wrong. Not just knowing it, but feeling it, and if you don't get it, then it gets really bad."

"How?" The Kid asked, snuffling his tears back.

"Because then you have to deal with me. I won't give you a break. I won't treat you nice. I will take you down hard, and I'll bury you. Now pull yourself together and get a shuffle on. We've good to do."

Chapter Thirty Five: The Dick and The Dead Dearest

A few more calls, The Kid pulling himself together and the same story replayed. Pete played a heavy well. Sort of Bad Cop, Worse Cop routine. No-one expected it, so we got away with it. It should limit the amount of scum getting caught up in what was going down. That just confused things.

"Has there been any point to this?" Pete asked as we walked down the street towards Ti's church office.

"Some. But didn't it make you feel good?" I replied. "Limited aggression and no-one dead."

"In a curious way it was quite cathartic. You seemed a lot less aggressive towards that lady in the leather body suit. The aggression seemed fake, even when you threw each other around. Why?" Pete asked.

"Old friends." I said massaging my bruised back.

"What is it with you and women?" Pete stopped dead in the street, looking not accusative, but curious. "They seem to have an 'interest' in you that transcends friendship."

He really does ask the strangest questions.

"Well, I guess as the only human around here I'm 'different'." I said. "People like the unusual."

"You certainly have a way of approaching things." Pete said. "Why the provocative behaviour? It seems as if you are looking for a fight."

"I'm just shaking things up to …"

I froze in mid-sentence as I saw the police cars and vans that were parked around the entrance to Ti's church. Policemen and scene of crime officers were scurrying about.

I ran. Policemen tried to block my way. I pushed past them. At the top of the steps I could see the door was off its hinges. In the gloom I could see a body on the floor. Flashes from cameras were illuminating the scene.

A pair of hands pulled me around, a rat face stared at me.

Schoone. Malder would be around somewhere.

"Well, if it isn't 'Prime Suspect'." Schoone said. "Revisiting the scene of your crime again? You're…"

I don't know what he would have said, as my forehead slipped and broke his nose. I pushed him to one side and stepped into the entrance lobby. A flash lit up the hallway.

The shotgun blast had left a hole.

The hole was surrounded by the remains of a body.

The remains that had once belonged to Kat.

Another friend.

Another love.

Another reason.

Another reason to be calm.

Then Schoone tried to place handcuffs on me.

When they pulled me off him, I had added a black eye, broken teeth and a wrist that went the wrong way to his broken nose exhibit. A few seconds longer and he would have had the full set.

It was Pete who held me up against the wall this time. Malder's face was an inch from mine. His forearm rested lightly across my throat with the implication that pressure could be increased at any time.

"Calm down son." he whispered to me. "I can see your upset, but so is the arsehole on the deck, so you relax and we'll let you go. Kick off and I'll beat you unconscious meself. You have no favours or friends here." With that the pressure came off my throat and Pete let me go.

I began to walk towards Kat's body. A hand on my chest stopped me and I halted, unresisting. Words were spoken around me and the scene of crime officers stood back to let me near her.

"Don't touch the body Faustus." Malder said gently into my ear. "I am sorry, but she is evidence."

I knelt down by Kat. Her heart and lungs had been ripped apart by a shotgun blast. Her red leather jacket was soaking up the remnants of the blood they had left in her.

There wasn't much.

Puncture wounds were not in evidence. They had ripped out her throat.

Simpler for them. And much more brutal.

I burned the image into my brain. It joined that of Peter. That of Paul. That of Mel.

I scanned her from top to toe. Seeing all the dirt. All the tears. There were large, finger sized puncture wounds to her wrists and her boots. Two holes through the top of each foot.

I turned to a scene of crimes officer and pointed at the holes in her boots. The man leant closer.

"She was crucified." He whispered gently from behind his mask. "When we found her, she was nailed to the door."

"I see. Thank you." I said and stood up. My legs wobbled. Pete's arms were around my shoulders. He half led, half carried me to the front door. Malder came up to us.

"I'm sorry about…" was as far as he got.

"You bastard." Schoone screamed. "You'll go down for that. I'll stick you in a cell with arse rapists, you broke my nose and I'll make you suffer." Schooner was standing just outside of my reach and knew it.

He wasn't outside of Malder's reach though and the older man reached out and grabbed the broken nose. It made for some interesting noises as he twisted.

"Fuck off and see the doctor you tit." Malder said, continuing to help me outside.

When we reached the top of the steps Malder stopped and turned me around.

"Listen Faustus," he said, "I'll be honest with you. You screwed up hitting a copper, even a piece of shit like Schoone. People were not exactly in a hurry to pull you off, but everyone will want to see you do some time for that. Can't hit a copper son."

"I know. Sorry I lost it." I said. "We were close." I met his eyes with mine and he almost winced. "Very close."

"I understand that. Here." Malder passed me a packet of cigarettes. With shaking hands I took one out. He lit it for me. "This is all Freak Street, isn't it?"

"Yeah." I said.

"What's happening?"

"That's what we will find out and resolve." Pete said.

"You'll shut your pie hole if you've any fucking sense," Malder said to Pete. "Him I know." he said pointing at me, then he turned his finger to Pete. "You I don't. Shut it and get him out of here."

Pete nodded his head and began to lead me down the steps.

"Faustus." Malder called. I looked back over my shoulder. "Sort it. Quick."

I gave the briefest of nods and kept walking.

"I will take you back to your office. You need to get some rest." Pete said.

"Bullshit." I replied.

"Faustus. I don't think you are in a fit state to continue. It would be unfair of me to ask you to." Pete took my weight as we rounded the corner. "However I am glad you were able to let some of the pain out. I wish I could help you."

"Well get off me kid." I said shrugging his arms off my shoulders. I stood up, straightened my tie and put my hat on my head.

"Yeah I'm cut up." I said looking Pete square in the eye. "But I couldn't think of a better way to get a closer look at the body with so many police around. Besides, Schoone always needed a slapping and that was a good excuse."

"I thought you were upset." Pete said.

"I am. More than you could ever know, but I needed to check Kat. She's the one who shot Jo-Jo Mar. I found her boot impression and some strands of her hair in the garden. There was dirt and a wet stain on the leather of her trousers. That's from where she crouched down to get a steady aim. If I've worked it out, Malder will work it out. He'll have his shooter and put this down as a drug war retaliation. He'll be half right."

"Are you sure?"

"Positive." I said. "Those little things and the fact that she let us live. Never thought she'd take a contract like that though."

"We did not issue such a command, nor sanction her death."

I spun around and Ti was standing behind us.

She had opted for a more typical look for the street. Dark blue velvet jeans and a pure brilliant white collarless man's shirt. Dark crystalline trainers. Mens' heads were turning and those driving nearly getting into road traffic accidents that they would never be able to explain to their wives.

"The girl was someone I thought I could trust." Ti said, looking this way and that, not wanting to meet my gaze, which was probably a tad hostile. "I had high regard for her, we were close and talked about…things." Ti swallowed hard. "I thought she was a friend."

With the word friend Ti looked up at me. The look was both confusion and a search for confirmation and understanding.

Mr Gentle had left me for a holiday when Paul lost his hand.

"You're an idiot Ti." I said. "You made mistakes."

"I do not make mistakes human. I am a Goddess." Ti drew herself up haughtily, but the eyes showed it. She had doubts. Doubts in her people. Doubts in her decisions. Doubts in herself.

"You tell me what is going on Ti, and you tell me now, or I promise you I will burn down your little house of fun, and I'll buy every iron nail I can find and strew the world with them."

As threats to the Fae go, the threat of iron is about as bad as it gets. I was taking a chance, but I didn't care. Ti pursed her lips.

"It began five months ago. Several of our 'offices' in Tokyo, Vienna and Paris, were raided and destroyed. Then the London office fell. Scourged. No survivors. We had found a prior interest in the purchase of property on The Streets by a company. Then the same company began to buy property here. We felt it prudent to invest. We thought it appropriate to bring a retinue of armed assistants."

"What a shame the Vampires had predicted it and got their own people inside your little retinue. Kat took that contract for the Vampires, and they used her as a trigger skirt and a way to get in." I could feel that I was talking through gritted teeth.

"I am sorry my love."

"Don't give me that." I snapped. "This isn't a time for feelings. What else do you know?"

"We cannot find out any more." Ti let out a heartfelt sigh. "We had placed Jo-Jo Mar with them, but he could find out very little. Then he was killed. All he knew was that the Vampires were escalating their game. They were planning something on a grand scale." Ti drew close and placed a hand on my shoulder. "Whatever else is happening I can do no more until I know where they are. They came out of nowhere and were gone just as fast. We could not kill them Faustus. We even burned one alive and it still came for us. It kept coming even when torn apart. And there were many." A tear welled in her eye. Just one real tear. "And they would not stop. We the Fae have been forced to run."

Part of me wanted to fold her in my arms and tell her it would be fine. Part of me wanted to run off with her and never return.

I was in over my head. Friends were dying and the only one I could even come close to relying on was some Half bred, Half fallen Angel. Half tuned in and Half tuned out.

I was fucked.

Might as well go out standing.

Even if I ended up begging for my life I'd go out standing.

Time to finish the job.

"Get all the Fae out of my way Ti." I said. Mr Gentle is still on holiday. "I see them I'll take them out. The average human is ten times worse than a Vampire when it comes to nasty. I need you, I call you. Not the other way round." I jabbed a finger in her chest. All things considered, suicidal but not an unpleasant experience. "Now." I took out a fresh smoke and slipped it in the right place. "Light me." Without hesitation Pete lit my coffin nail. I tilted my hat slightly over my eyes. "Now. Get off my Streets."

I turned and walked away.

Cursing that she smelled so good.

Must be a trick.

Chapter Thirty Six: The Dick and The Driver

Back at the office three phone calls. One to
Mammasayra, who tore me off a strip for letting her
know I was alright now and not sooner. The other
two went to the top and bottom. They sulk unless
both get involved.

Big Guns Time.

Pete came in as I finished the last call. He sat on
the sofa, slightly out of breath.

"She was upset Faustus.." He said.

"And?"

"You upset her more."

"Don't care right now. I'll make it right later or
she'll cut my head off, shrink it and wear it as a
necklace." Not just a turn of phrase that. "Come on
kid. No time to sit around. We are off to check on a
lead."

"About the War?" he asked.

"No." I said smiling. "About your Dog."

Outside a blue Morris Minor pulled up in front of
us. A cardboard sign on the Dashboard said 'On
Hire'.

"While I appreciate that on occasions we may
need to drive places, I was under the impression that
either you would have a car, would rent one, or
indeed steal another one." Pete was
becoming…ironic.

I pointed down at the car with its highly polished
paintwork.

"This one you cannot destroy. Make sure you don't touch the outside though" I said getting into the front seat.

"Why not?" he asked.

"Because it's minus three hundred degrees. It'll freeze you solid in less time than it takes you to blink. Pete took this as his cue and got into the back. Very carefully.

Inside the car the seats felt very comfortable. Very soft, almost woolly.

The driver looked up from her knitting.

Enid can come as a shock the first time you use her cab.

It is not the semi-transparency. She is a ghost. That can be part of the territory. Age brings solidity.

It is not the glasses. A good half an inch thick, magnifying her eyes to twice the size. She tells me she only needs them for driving, knitting and seeing. Fair enough. She's cheap.

It's the mole.

That big mole.

That big mole on her nose.

With those five, long hairs.

That mole.

Those hairs.

They call out to you. "Mention us. Acknowledge we exist. Say something about us. We won't mind."

General rule of thumb in Enid's taxi is don't mention the mole. Ever.

"What an unusual mole Miss. It is quite striking. My name is Pete. May I ask your name?"

Maybe I should have told Pete about that mole…Rule.

"Enid, Pete." Enid said. "Nice to meet you." Enid turned her head to look at Pete. "Do you know young Sir, no one has mentioned my beauty spot before. I was beginning to think it was invisible." Enid turned back to me. "So where to deary? It's your dime as our colonic friends say."

"Suttintin." I said. "Small village outside…"

"Oh I know where it is 'buddy' as our consumptive friends say." Enid said. "Now strap in. If I had seat belts in my day I would still be alive."

I hurriedly turned around to Pete, while rummaging for the two lengths of rope that served as Enid's seat belt.

"Do it." I said. "Now!"

"Tippe Kayak mither fooker." Enid shouted as she tore away.

I did regret lending her 'Die Hard' on video.

Then the World blurred………….a lot.

Enid had only encountered one accident in her lifetime of driving.

I knew that because she had been one of my first cases.

It had been in 1956.

It was the accident that killed her.

A lorry transporting pigs from Kings Lynn to Blackpool had the temerity to break without the due care and attention that allowed Enid the quarter mile of breaking distance that she required for an emergency stop. Enid had survived the accident unscathed with only slight bruising to her chest region.

However the peg that held the back gate of the lorry closed did not survive. Years of neglect had produced a weakening of the metal, which duly snapped, allowing the gate to fall backwards onto the bonnet of Enid's Morris Minor. It did however miss her, producing no more than a bit of a scare and a sharp intake of breath followed by a deep sigh of relief.

The last breath Enid ever took.

No.

What did for Enid was the stampede of fifty scared and angry pigs, all determined on escape. All rushing down the gate. All running over the roof of the Morris Minor. It was the twentieth one who fell through the roof, landed on Enid, who had been pushed closer to the floor of the car. Porky, now trapped inside the car with Enid became so stressed he (or she, this point is unclear) had an immediate heart attack.

Edith was duly suffocated by a dead pig.

Vegans would laugh their tits off.

I had found all this out at Enid's request, she having no memories of her own departure from the land of the corporeal. When she saw the death certificate and read the words 'Death by Porcine Misadventure' she took it quite well.

Actually it was quite a turning point for her. She stopped driving around in her ghostly Morris Minor, and started renting herself out. She started the Taxi firm specifically for those of us who experienced difficulty in getting hold of normal transport. After all, if a werewolf is caught short and naked in the park after a night out, they may not have money for a normal taxi. Nudity has no pockets. But Enid always understood peoples little ways. Just as all of her regular customers accepted Enid's driving.

You just had to accept Enid's driving as eclectic.

And tie yourself in.

Pete was on the floor. Screaming. That last lorry had come really close.

"Shut your eyes." I said. "It helps." I personally had my eyes screwed tightly shut.

A screeching noise came from my left and I risked a brief glance out of my left eye. With my head about two inches from the window, I was about three inches from the spinning wheel of a very long, very big truck.

"Oh My." came a voice from behind me.

Oh My indeed.

Then the worst part of the trip happened.

Enid pressed the brake.

Ever since the accident, Enid admits herself, she has become a little heavy footed when it comes to braking. Hence I ended up with my face through the windshield of the car.

Times like these I am glad it's the ghost of the car, otherwise I'd be looking at surgery.

"Ow." came a noise from the back seat. Pete was beginning to lift himself from the floor and get straightened up. A visible bruise on his forehead was fading before my eyes.

"Do you want me to wait sweetie?" Enid said, hands half way to her knitting.

"Please Enid." I said. "We may be coming back with something. I don't know yet."

"That's all right." She said. "So long as it's not a refrigerator. I won't touch those. Recycle properly I say. Don't just dump them." With that she picked up her knitting and began to knit a scarf. I had watched her knit that damn thing for ten years now. Apart from it getting long enough to gift wrap the car, I don't know if it will ever end.

Ω

Excerpt from
Angels, Daemons and other realm beings.
By E.M Faustus
(unpub)

The Religion of Enid's Scarf.

A curious cult or religion developed in early 1990.

It was based around a very long scarf, being knitted by a very slow knitter.

Common to many small religions that grew up in the 1990's it was based around Millenarianism. The concept that the world would reach Apocalypse at the end of 1999. The start of the New Millennium. And the End of the Old. The END OF THE WORLD.

The idea was that The Great Knitter took each year the world had known, and knitted it into a scarf. The Scarf of Years was more than an accumulation of the history of the world. It Was The History of The World.

If the time ever came when The Great Knitter unwound the 'wool' of The Scarf of Years then not just The World, but all Time would be unwound and The Apocalypse would unwind all of time and the Chaos of The Unwound would occur and we would all do The Apocalypse conga to the next plane.

This religion attracts a small, but fanatical following, who wear their own scarves, even in mid-summer. They are known as The Scarfini.

Or more accurately, tossers.

WARNING: THIS IS WHAT HAPPENS OF YOU TAKE TOO MANY DRUGS.

Ω

"Come on kid." I said. "If I have this right, you are about one hundred yards from Dog."

In retrospect, all things considered, hindsight always being a wonderful thing, maybe that might have been the wrong thing to say.

Chapter Thirty Seven: The Dick and The Devilishly Devious, Diabolicaly Deranged DVN Doc.

"How fast did she go?" Pete said, trying to stop shaking.

"Fast." I said. "She covered seven miles in about two minutes. I did tell you to cover your eyes." I took a Marathon from my pocket, took a big bite and passed it to Pete. He waved his hand. "It helps." I said to him. Shaking hands reached out and took it. He wolfed it down.

We chewed.

We swallowed.

One of us made fire to a smoke.

The other one whimpered a bit.

Both our shakes stopped in a minute or so. It seems to be something to do with the sugar. I looked around.

This was all very wrong.

Correct that. WRONG!

The lab was owned by Avatar. I could see the little, little, tiny writing at the bottom of the sign. A subsidiary of. But to call the lab 'Faust Genetics' was a little near home.

And its position.

This was a small rural village. I turned around and I was looking at a duck pond. A small school. A playground.

That's not the sort of place you have a 'Laboratory Of Evil'.

It should be at the top of a mountain. It should be in a castle. Bats should be circling and wolves howling in the distance. There should be clouds at least.

I checked my watch, 7.30 (ish) pm. At least the clear night had the decency to be dark. Cloudless, but dark. A neighbourhood dog tried its best by yapping in the distance.

So much for atmosphere.

Amateurs.

"Why are we here?" Pete asked.

"Well, I thought that this particular genetics laboratory was using an unusual amount of foetal stabilizer." I said sounding clever. "And recent entries for dog food on its bills. God bless internet hacking." I didn't sound quite so clever there.

Pete began to rush towards the lab, but I restrained him with a hand on his arm. Bit of Daemon whispering there.

"Kid." I said. You don't just go rushing in. Remember you're A, B, C.'

"It is a little late to instruct me on spelling techniques Mr Faustus." He said. "I have read one of your files and if it wasn't for spellcheck, you would be lost at sea."

"ABC Kid." I flicked the remains of the smoke into the ornamental fishpond. "Always Be Cool."

Good Line.

Slick hat.

Shoot cuffs.

Listen to sigh from comedy relief.

We walked up the block paved drive and cabbage palms in flower beds (while it should have been muddy cobbles and a blasted oak) up to the double glazed front door (not the oaken double doors and portcullis accessory Evil merits).

"After you." I said. Again to regret.

I don't know why I was surprised when Pete tore the door, frame and all, out of the wall, throwing it over his shoulder. It landed in the flower bed, seriously pruning two cabbage palms en route. Pete began to move forward. I put the back of my hand on his chest.

"ABC." He said. "Access Begets Canine. Come on."

"On second thoughts, after me." I said. I pushed him behind me. If I was wrong about this place I had just run up at least a grand in repairs. If I was right, well at least I'd slow the bullet down.

When we walked into the reception, I have to admit I was doubly surprised.

Firstly, by the exquisite taste that was evident in the décor. The reception was painted a soft lilac and relaxing photographs of sunsets hung on the walls. I even recognized the photographer, Mervyn Kelly. Expensive originals. A glass and wood wall separated the reception from the laboratory itself. A kidney shaped wood and chrome desk sat by the doors to the lab. It was one of those clever jobs, with a computer that has a touch screen keyboard built into the surface. The kind you have to be at the perfect angle to notice it's there at all. Behind it sat a tall, thin, beautiful blonde, probably very expensively dressed, in a loose white shift, with delicate embroidery and smelling of lots of perfume. Her long hair flowing over her shoulders and accentuating certain curves.

She was the second surprise, because you had to look hard at her. Not difficult to do. But if you concentrated, albeit really hard, you could see it.

Firstly, she was projecting 'glamour' to blur the senses. She was so good at it she could have given Ti a run for her money. Secondly, if you looked at Pete, removed the moles, gave him blonde hair, a

313

decent meal and a decent wardrobe there was a distinct family resemblance. Thirdly, if you ignored the smell of that perfume, you got chocolate…and brimstone.

"Can I help you gentlemen?" she said, either oblivious to the wreckage we had just caused or she was the coolest receptionist I had ever seen.

"Pete." I said placing a hand on his shoulder. "Meet your sister."

There was a total blank look on his face.

"Sister, meet your brother Pete Nosecondnameyet." I carried on. "Now the family reunion's over, where's his fucking dog?"

"Do you think she knows where Dog is?" He asked me.

"Well, ask her." I had expected more of a reaction than that.

"Where is Dog?" he said, that tell-tale hint of Brimstone in the air.

Bugger.

"We do have some dogs here, for experimentation purposes only. Allow me to get our Director. He will assist you." She picked up the telephone on her desk. Then the desk was no longer there. Pete had stepped forward and swiped it across the room. A few sparks flew up from the electrics that had fed into it. The receptionist was still holding the hand piece to the telephone, which must have been some high class model to still work. Given that the base set shattered against the wall.

"Father. The gentlemen you were expecting are here." She said into the hand piece.

Expecting. That was not a good thing.

Also, nice body aside, this girl was stupid.

I felt a reduction of the breeze at my back, then an arm went around my throat. As I drove my left arm back, the forearm was caught before it made contact with anything and was twisted up my back. There was a moment of pain, followed by some long minutes of much more pain indeed. I realized that I was standing on tip toe to breathe. I drove my right arm back, made contact with ribs and felt something crunch. My elbow. It felt like I was hitting concrete.

I looked to Pete for help, but as he turned to me, he found himself in the same vice like hold of his sister. Pain crossed his face as his arm was twisted back.

I hated this case.

The door to the lab opened on electric hinges, the whine of a motor giving it away. (Sorry, but a motor whirl is not the same as a good old iron hinge squeal.) Through it walked a short dumpy fat man. Balding, with moles on his face and black curly hair. I just knew he was going to say something like "Ah-ha. Mr Faustus."

"Ah. Mr E.M. Faustus. I have been expecting you." Bingo.

I gave him a little wave.

"Amusing." he said, looking around the reception. "I see my little whitlow has been busy. Tell me Mr Faustus, does he still exude that smell of brimstone when he is angry?"

I would have nodded my head, but couldn't move it. Instead Baldy sniffed the air.

"Ah. I see he does." he said. "Let them go, let them go. They won't do anything here. I have their answers after all."

Damn. He was cocky and arrogant. Not only did he hold the answers, but he knew it. There wasn't much we could do apart from play this out and see where it went. Although that was not the thought running through my head as I was let go. It was more 'Oxygen. Hallelujah.'

Baldy walked over to Pete and looked at him. He lifted up his chin and inspected his face.

"Someone taught it to shave. Dress itself as well I see. Had I known it could do that, I would have charged more for its use. It seems lucky it escaped. Ask it how it escaped" he said to me.

"I am perfectly capable of talking to you." Pete said.

"And it speaks." Baldy said. "In sentences. Does it do any other tricks Mr Faustus?"

This was the time for diplomacy. But as I was having trouble talking I simply gave him the two fingered salute. He laughed.

"Ah. Defiant until the end." Baldy walked over to me. "And this is the end for you my friend. The proverbial end of the line. You have brought me my whitlow back. A few aberrant behavior patterns but a little shock therapy and a quick lobotomy should cure that. After all, I do need him"

Ooo. Goody. Nutter. Nutter and a gloater. That gave us a fighting chance of being alive-ish a minute from now.

"Why do you need him?" I managed to rasp out.

"Well, for all of those lovely little cells in his body of course." Baldy smiled. "I am a geneticist after all. Do you think I need him for hot sex action? Oh forgive me. Would you like to see the laboratory?"

"Why not." I said. "Mind if I smoke?"

"Around all of that wonderful oxygen? I don't think so Mr Faustus." He said leaning close so I could smell his halitosis. "Nice try though."

Baldy snapped his fingers and walked into the laboratory. We were pushed towards the doors. The blonde pushing Pete and my unseen friend shoving me. Pete turned to me and whispered;

"And your plan is what?"

"My plan got us as far as the front door." I said. "Currently I'm winging it."

"What did they say?" Baldy asked. Our companions repeated every word. Even mimicking our voices, which was really strange. I'm sure I don't sound like that.

"Do they do tricks?" I asked Baldy.

"They do anything I ask." he said. "In the case of the female that can be quite enjoyable. Is it incest? I'm not sure, but it certainly is fun."

Baldy stepped back and rested his palms face down on the central bench. The lab looked like... a lab. Large glass fronted refrigerators were refrigerating. Large freezers were freezing. Things were going pop and bubble, and there was that medical smell that hangs around your nose for days. Two lab assistants were doing 'things' with glass tubes.

Science was never my strong point.

"Where is Dog?" Pete asked. "I want my Dog."
Baldy smiled.

"Now if it talks again Mr Faustus, I will have the Male dislocate your shoulder." He smiled as he said it. Ah. Maybe I was making a new friend. "I assume you understand."

"I do. Pete, please don't say a word." I turned and looked at the Male. He was a blonde, pretty version of Pete. Light white shirt over muscular frame, light white trousers over muscular legs. Bare footed. Show off. "Hello." He ignored me.

"Can I try something?" I asked.

"By all means." Baldy replied, spreading his hands magnanimously and smiling.

I drove my elbow into the Male's ribs and kneed him in the groin.
Pain happened, very quickly, in my elbow and knee.

"I removed all their pain sensors, increased their musculature and cellular density." Baldy said. "You can shoot them and the bullets stop half an inch in. Totally invulnerable. And self -replicating cells means any damage is repaired in seconds. Nice work if I do say so myself."

"And are these the ones you sent after the Fae?" I asked. Rubbing my elbow and limping.

"Oh no. I did a little work on some of the Vampires. Short term of course. Don't want an invincible army on the streets, do we? The vampires don't last long. The body rejects the cellular grafting after a while, then they have a little problem."

"Hayfever?" I asked. "Would you like to expand?"

"Well, you have to scoop them up in a bucket." He dusted off his hands. "Well, it has been nice to chat…"

"I have had enough of this. Where is Dog?" Pete said.

"Dislocate his shoulder."

At this point someone shoved a live electric cable, covered in live, wriggling, burning razor blade maggots into my left shoulder. The pain spread down to my chest, giving me pause to think I could be having a heart attack, down to my retracting testicles and causing my toes to curl up in sympathy.

It hurt.

Baldy said something, but a combination of tears running down my face, the screaming in my ears and the noises I was making made it hard to hear. I did the decent thing.

I passed out for a second. Alright. Maybe two.

I felt considerably worse when I came to on my knees a moment or so later. Worse because I knew that if we survived this mess, it would hurt just as much to put it back in place.

"Are you all right Faustus?" Pete asked.

"Warn it Faustus." Baldy said. "You have plenty of other joints and bones. Break a finger for daddy."

The male bent over and took my hand. Nice and romantic like.

There was a hollow snapping noise, but against the pain I felt in my shoulder I didn't even notice it.

"Please be quiet Pete. Please." I said holding my arm to the side with my good arm. That felt better.

"Not your own you fool." Baldy shouted. "One of his."

I watched while the male's broken finger re-set itself. Very odd.

"You made your point. What the hell do you need the dog for if you have them? It's certainly not guard duty."

Baldy smiled and beckoned the woman towards him. She stood next to him and wrapped her arms around his neck, nuzzling into him.

"Tell you what Faustus." Baldy said. "I'll make you a deal. That runs in your family, doesn't it? Deals with the Devil? I was going to have you beheaded, I always have a use for brain tissue. However, you taught it to talk so you must have something. Come and work for me, and I'll let you live and you can keep the female for your pleasure. Believe me," he ran a hand down her front, "there is nothing she won't do. Nothing."

Baldy looked at me. Definitely human. I hate power crazed mad human Loonies. He'd threaten Pete next.

"If you don't, I'll let you watch him choke until the point of paralysis, so I can use the cells, then I'll kill you slow." Told you.

Mad as a box of Frogs didn't even begin to sum this guy up. A good ten boxer if ever I saw one.

"What, work for scum, sleep with my friend's sister and sit still while you cripple him?" I took a deep breath in. "Been there, done that, bought the company."

"Mr Faustus, do you really think that thing is your friend? " Baldy said. "He is a product. A prototype. The first off the line, which explains his faults."

Baldy crouched down in front of me and gave a long sigh. "No snappy comeback? No witty repartee? Frankly I am surprised. Have you no respect for the genre?"

"How did you…?" I managed through gritted teeth.

"Well, that is a fascinating story." Baldy said, standing up and returning to the warmth of his blonde. "It comes as the result of a trip to New Guinea. Back in 1973 it was. Happy days. Filled with self-medication and sultry cheap prostitutes. I know, I don't look that old, but what can I say? I am a brilliant geneticist. A little self-surgery, of the plastic kind, does no harm."

He took a pause to turn and kiss the blonde. It wasn't just the pain making me feel sick.

"Well, I was conducting a little expedition gathering medicinal plant life for the manufacture of what became very expensive cancer medication. I found myself on a rather large plateau, brimming with some wonderful and financially rewarding specimens. That is when I discovered what I understand is called the 'mother lode'. It was at the base of a large tree. I had never seen its ilk before, nor since. It was gigantic. Around and about were dozens of bodies in various stages of decomposition. Some covered with a black mould. Or so I thought. I ran a small test or two in the field and was just a little shocked. I can tell you. Scraps of flesh and skin held the bones together, but the flesh was alive. The bones were alive, and the mould was keeping it alive."

Baldy paused for dramatic effect.

"Are you waiting on a drum roll, or wolf howling or something?" I said.

"Testing revealed that mould to be some sort of membrane. It was slowly ingesting the body while providing it with life. I did try to remove the bones of course, but the wonderful membrane took hold of both my porters and simply wouldn't let them go. I must have sat and watched them struggle for a good two months, but they couldn't get free. Probably still there. I suppose they should have starved but…anyway. I did manage to acquire a few samples of the membrane. Even in its separation from the whole, the damn stuff would still try to digest flesh and continue to maintain the life of its 'meal'."

"Look. I get the idea. It tried to eat everything it could."

"True. But it would keep them alive. For a very long time. And it never grew. I tested some cells and they never divided, and never died. They just were…Eternal. Until I gave them a good electric shock. Then they went crazy. Metaphorically they curled up and died. I am keeping this very simple for you. I hope you are following?"

I gave a nod, all the time thinking how madmen always feel the need to blather on. If he had been even partially sane he should have killed me a lot sooner. I got the feeling he didn't have anyone to talk to.

Poor chap. Middle child syndrome I guess. He was still a loony.

"Well imagine my surprise when my backers approached me and gave me the opportunity to take my research to a totally different level. Cloning. I was able to use the dead cells to activate cloned cells and create…, well eventually him." A finger jabbed at Pete. "I was able to increase longevity. Develop cellular repair second to none. Instant rejuvenation of damaged tissue. And once I had been given suitable genetic foetal material to work with well…"

"I get the idea." I said. Time to push. "You're a loony Mad Doctor, who gets access by accident to The Tree of the Fae, which they will kill you for by the way. Then you do some genetic alteration to it. You get your hands on a Daemon and Angel, generate a clone using a mix on their cells and your own. Perverted in the extreme, but that's just your jollies. End result is my friend here. You need his cells as they produce the best chance of producing nice, subservient clones like these two."

Baldy had a really sulky look on his face. Bingo. Right again Faustus.

"Well I gave you a chance to listen." Baldy waved a limp wristed hand at the male behind me. "Asphyxia to stroke." he said.

The male moved behind Pete, locking his arms around his neck as if to break it. Pete's hands immediately came up and grabbed the fore arm. His face started going red.

"Dog." Pete gasped.

Baldy waved a hand at the Male who cranked up his throttling slightly. He smiled at me.

Ah well.

"Pete." I said. "I'm going to have a little rest now. You just do what you do. Get your freak on."

"Finally." Pete said gasping for air.

Pete's hand sought out the Male's hand and pulled the fingers back until they snapped.

Now that would have made me let go. Unfortunately the Male's genes that let him heal fast were a little better than Pete's. A flex of the fingers and they were working again.

Pete leaned forward, lifting the Male off his feet and Pete powered back, driving the Male into the wall.

The Male held on, even when Pete repeatedly head butted him with the back of his head, he hung on.

I tried to help. I stood up. I threw up. I got back down again. Safer that way.

Pete dropped and rolled forward, slamming the Male into the floor. At the same time he grabbed and twisted the arm.

The smell of Brimstone began to rise dramatically.

The male's arm popped. Then it popped off. Pete simply threw it away, the Male's blood spurting all over the floor and walls.

Pete leaped to his feet, turned and came down heavily on the Male's chest. Not only could you hear the bones crunch, but you could see Pete's knee sink in a good two inches.

Then it got nasty.

Pete grabbed the Male's head and pulled.

It seemed such minimal effort as he pulled the head forward, twisted and popped it clean off. Pete threw the head in the opposite direction to the arm.

He stood up and turned to Baldy and the woman.

Baldy scratched his head.

"I have to confess you have surprised me Mr Faustus." he said rubbing his pate. "You have taught it to fight remarkably well. Bitch. Kill it."

With that the Woman was striding forwards. She reached out and…that was that. Pete grabbed the wrist, spun her around and decapitated her with one swift movement.

"That is simply not acceptable." Baldy bellowed. The last words he ever spoke. Pete punched him in the face.

More specifically, through the face.

And out the other side.

Pete simply gave his arm a twist, put his left hand on Baldy's shoulders and pulled his arm back. Then he turned to me, blood, brain matter and bone still dripping from his right hand.

I did think about throwing up again, but decided to save it for later.

Pete helped me to my feet. I gave him a bit of a slap on the head.

"Idiot. You're meant to leave them alive enough to answer questions." I said. "Such as who is bank rolling this little number."

"I am sorry." He said, mopping bits of brain from the back of his hand. "I sometimes find it hard to control my temper. I should re-position your arm."

Well that came out of the blue.

"Eh. No thanks I'll wait for Frankie and a big shot of morphine." Then I noticed the two lab tech's again.

I saw the two lab tech's, completely oblivious to us, still filling vials. I walked over to them. Their eyes were wide and semi-vacant, fixed only on their work. It was as if the outside world was completely tuned out.

I lifted the plastic cap from the head of one of them. Blonde, shorn stubble was under the cap. I walked to the other one. More blonde stubble. On each a livid scar, badly stitched ran across the top of the head. Right over where the temporal lobe would be.

"Faustus." Pete said.

"Wait." I replied, running my hands over the skull of what seemed to be a woman. Drawing the medical mask from her face showed a perfect nose and an equally exquisite mouth. Hung open and drooling. I leaned in and sniffed. Daemon.

"Faustus."

"Wait."

I leaned into the other and removed the mask. Male. Very male, exuding pheromones and chocolate. Angel. On his temple more scars while a small sigil I didn't recognize had been cut into his cheek. Just above the mouth. A check of the woman revealed the same.

325

"Who would zombie an Angel and a Daemon? Who would be strong enough?" I asked no one in particular.

"Faustus." Pete said, laying a hand on my good shoulder. "Remember what Ti said about the assailants not stopping even if they were hacked apart?" Pete turned me around. The body of the decapitated male had gotten to its feet. The female was struggling to hers. Blood had stopped pumping, the head was dead, but that didn't seem to faze them.

I looked down and the severed arm was dragging itself towards us. The head of both had somehow rolled onto their faces and were using their chins and lips to drag themselves along. Straight towards us.

"I don't fucking believe this." I said. Hey, I like good horror movie lines.

I just don't like being in them.

Typically, in a horror movie, when people are confronted by the living dead, they freeze. It seems that not until one of them dies in a grizzly manner does one of them react. Depending on the style of the film, they all die or one alone survives.

But as some of my good friends are the living dead and this is reality, I looked around for a weapon, and there it was on the wall.

Nice, friendly, heavy duty electric cable.

Not so much inspiration as Baldy's babbling on.

"Pete, rip that cable off the wall will you." I said, walking over to the head of the Male and picking it up one handed by its ear. The head tried to twist and bite me. I ducked as the woman's hand grasped for me and side stepped the searching hand of the arm on the floor. I then had to lean forward to avoid the grasp of the Male again.

Bit like Line Dancing really.

"Shove the cable in the mouth, but mind the teeth." I threw the head to Pete, who caught it one handed. He slammed the head onto the bench and pushed the cable into the Male's mouth. He stood back and raised his arms in triumph. Pity he hadn't left the cable attached to a power supply.

"You pillock." I said. "Push live electric cable into his mouth. Wire still attached to the mains. Then turn it on " I added the last bit for good measure. Pete can be quite literal sometimes.

Pete hurried back to the wall and ripped more wire loose. He duly did the right thing and turned on the mains.

I didn't expect the head to explode.

Hard for him to come back from that.

Big dry cleaning bill though. Shame because I really liked the suit.

I reached down and scooped up the arm by the soggy end and threw it to Pete.

"Shove the wire in the soggy end."

Wire shoved in soggy end.

Power turned on. Power turned off.

Bigger dry cleaning bill.

I grabbed the male's blundering headless body and shoved it towards Pete. He grabbed the remaining flailing arm, twisted it around behind its back and rammed the cable into the neck stump. Pete stepped away and turned the mains back on.

I may as well just right this suit off.

Those stains would never come out.

I looked up at Pete who was looking suspiciously clean.

"One down, one to go." I said. A smile of relief may even have crossed my lips. But don't bet on it.

"That may be considerably easier to say than to do." He said, nodding behind me.

I slowly turned around and wished I had stayed at home.

The female (I was so glad Baldy had not bothered to name them) had found her head, picked it up and was holding it onto the neck stump. The raw meat was knitting itself back together. Tendrils of flesh and bone were reaching both up and down to lock and fuse together. It was not proving to be a finger snap fast business, but nor was it painfully slow.

"Owh. Buggeration." I said. I turned back to Pete and grabbed the cable from his hand, thrusting it deep into the knitting wound.

"Turn it on…" was as far as I got, before both her hands fastened about my throat and tightened in a vice like grip.

The rest of the sentence went… "when I get clear."

Then Pete turned on the power.

Then the Female exploded.

Then the suit was a total right off.

The electric shock that hit me wasn't too bad. In comparison to being hit by a truck I suppose. The fillings in my teeth sang and itched simultaneously. All of the muscles in by body seemed to want to dance to the song my fillings were singing. My eyes enjoyed the light show that went with the song and dance number, then everything went on a water slide and little blue birds started whistling Dixie, while Louis Armstrong was singing The Sex Pistol's entire back catalogue.

Maybe I should lay off those little white pills.

The Detectives Dark Black Pit approached at light speed and smothered me.

Then something like consciousness hit. Hard. Very hard indeed.

A toe, neatly encased in a steel toed boot was tapping me gently in the ribs.

This just kept getting better and better.

With the muscular equivalent of trying to jack up a seven ton lorry by tongue, I opened my eyes to see a face of ancient angelic wisdom.

"Hello Stan." I said, staring into the face of Satan.

"You are alive then?" said a cultured voice out of my vision.

"Hello Mickey." I said to the Arch Angel Michael. One of Gods best enforcers.

A hand was outstretched and I looked at Stan (Well, he's got so many names at some point I just fell into calling him Stan. He doesn't mind.). I shook my head. That was a mistake. It hurt.

"No thanks Stan. Might cost me something I can't afford to lose."

"Don't be silly Faustus." Stan said in an equally cultured voice. "I'm only offering to help you off the floor. Not make claim on your soul. You seem to have done us both a favour, so we can call it quits. Fair enough?"

I put Stan's hand through my good arm and was half pulled upright and half stood myself. Not too shabby.

"You two took your time getting here." I said.

I looked at the two of them. Neither of them were my friends, but they were not my enemies either. At the moment that seemed to be as close to friends that I had. Mickey had Pete pinned to the floor under his black leather brogues. Dressed in his customary Saville row suit, with white shirt and black tie, he looked mid thirty's. Distinguished enough to give you a face to trust, but dangerous enough to ensure your daughter didn't date him. A Man's Man.

Stan was a similar kinda guy. Dressed in a pale khaki green suit with brown penny loafers, a pale blue shirt and bright National Gallery tie. He let it down a bit with the grubby cream trench coat though. His hair was brilliant white and worn at collar length. A white goatee gave an extra bit dash to his face. You wouldn't let your daughter in the same city as this man. One look could deflower your daughters, granddaughters, great-granddaughters etc for centuries. But Stan didn't do that anymore. He stayed within THE RULES.

Ω

Excerpt from
Angels, Daemons and other realm beings.
By E.M Faustus
(unpub)

THE RULES.

The name speaks for itself really.

At some point The Angels and The Daemons realized that if they kept up their War on Earth, they would proceed with tedious inevitability towards Armageddon.

The final Battle.

And redundancy.

After all not even a microbe will survive Armageddon thanks to mankind's incredible skill of Inventing ways to kill things. Including itself.

While it was impossible to change THE SCRIPT of what was to come, the Angels and Daemons realized that by either not influencing Mankind, or by actively stopping the race from blowing up the planet or indeed the Universe, the Final Battle could be delayed.

Possibly indefinitely.

Consequently men and women of potential sin that would encourage THE END, (believe me the capital letters are merited) suddenly found certain friends of theirs started giving them very good advice indeed. It had even reached the point where staff at certain reactors under certain mountains (doing very dangerous things indeed), found that small nuts and bolts were missing from the set, or someone hadn't put the plug into the wall to turn it on.

End result. Stalemate, and the world goes on to live another day.

Ω

"Any chance you are going to take your foot off my friend's chest Mickey?" I asked.

"No."

That simple.

"Thank you for trying Faustus." Pete wheezed. "I seem to be unable to overpower this gentleman so I have desisted. I shall rely on your experience." Pete was talking calm but smelling Brimstone.

"Coffee?" Stan was holding out a cup of strong black instant. It would taste great. "No trick Faustus." The good doctor had a kettle and a jar on the bench. It seems he shares my addiction. "Instant espresso."

"Always preferred Earl Grey and lemon myself. Perhaps a nice piece of cake." Mickey was such a snob, but that's Angels for you.

"Thanks." I said taking it and sipping. "You always put sugar in." I put it down and left it.

"It takes the edge off the bitterness."

"I like a hint of bitter."

"That seems to sum up your life." Mickey's attempts at humour never made me laugh. He's never been the same since he started hanging around with Jane Austen and Oscar Wilde.

"Move your foot Mickey."

"No."

A cinema chair slid across the floor. Stan lowered himself into it, placing a tub of Popcorn into one armrest and keeping a carbonated beverage in his other hand.

"Don't mind me." Stan said. "I do love a good action scene. I'm rooting for the underdog Faustus. Woo, as the Americans say." Stan took a long slurp and began to eat his popcorn.

"Move your foot Mickey."

"It will not happen, Faustus."

"Do I need to get nasty, Mickey?" I said. "Do I?" A lit cigarette appeared in my mouth and I took a long hit. Stan was helping things along. He had a low boredom threshold, but he did appreciate the genre.

A pipe appeared in Mickey's hand and he slowly drew a lungful. As he exhaled the cloud of smoke formed into a swan floating on a mirrored lake. The swan flapped its wings and flew away.

I blew a smoke ring.

"You are physically injured. Even if you were not, you would not physically be my match." Boastful, but right.

"Take your foot off him or I'll ban you from Film night for a year." I could play real rough sometimes. "And when I let you back I'll make you sit next to Percy." Real. Rough.

Mickey's foot stayed still.

"Percy's got a new itch you know." I said, smiling.

Slowly, snails' pace, Mickey slid his foot from Pete's stomach, leaving a muddy trail behind. Clever as there wasn't a spot of mud on Mickey's shoe.

"No hard feelings Faustus." Mickey said, standing right next to me. He could move really fast. "To prove it, let me fix your arm. Before I could say anything, Mickey grabbed my dislocated arm and twisted the arm back into the socket.

It hurt a lot more than being dislocated.

"Jings, that stung a little." I should have said. What I did say was totally unrepeatable. Mickey pulled me up close, so his mouth was next to my ear.

"Don't try to be clever." he said. "I don't like you apes. I don't like you. Always think you know better than The Devine and can do whatever you want. You should have been left as lizards. Crawl back under a rock, ape. Don't try to get involved in our affairs. We decide right and wrong. Not you. We tell you what to do and if you don't do it there are always sanctions that can be applied. Maybe I should hurt you a little more. Do you think?"

"Kick his bum Mickey." Stan shouted through handfuls of popcorn. "I'll turn off the telly for you. Make sure the big man can't see. Promise." Stan drew a finger over around where he presumed a heart would be. One day I'll tell him it's not in the stomach.

"Thanks for fixing the arm." I whispered, "But if you don't let me go we will see who kicks whose bum." Mickey let go and gave a little shove. He walked over to the kettle and made himself an Earl Grey. With Lemon. And grabbed a bit of cake.

I walked over to Pete who was slowly rising to his feet. He brushed at the mud on his suit. He glared at me.

"I. Want. To. See. Dog." he was controlling that temper quite well. Only a hint of Brimstone now.

"Be patient mate." I said. "Currently we are so deep in the brown stuff we should have snorkels."

"If one would breathe whilst in the brown stuff one should first invest in an oxygen tank Faustus." Mickey said, sipping his Earl Grey, little finger outstretched. Bloody Oscar Wilde.

I gestured a hand towards Mickey and Stan.

"Allow me to introduce the Arch Angel Michael, he's the effete snob with the tea, and The Falling Star, His Satanic Whotsit, whose name is Lucifer. Or Mickey and Stan as I call them. Pet names."

"Given by our pet." Stan stood up, brushed popcorn from his lap and gave a little bow.

Pete gave a bare nod of the head in their direction then headed for the door where Dog was. Stan's cinema seat slid across the floor and blocked his way. Pete gave it a slap and it sped away again. Mickey was suddenly in front of the door, still sipping his tea, but with 'that' face on him. 'That' face that said, 'You cannot beat me. I will win. Yet

334

I'm willing to confront you, because it amuses me and annoys Faustus. 'That' face.

Well I'd had enough.

I crossed over to Pete and I shoved him out of the way. I stood face to face with Mickey, who deliberately grew another six inches to force me to look up.

I hate Angels.

"Listen you effete budgie, in the past few days I have seen two of my best friends dead, watched as another was maimed, been beaten up, shot at, been attacked by vampires, Fae, horny Werewolves, headless Angel Daemon thingies, been electrocuted, beat up, beat down. In fact the only thing that hasn't happened is being blown up, so if you want to go up against me, go for it, but the second I reunite my friend with his dog, this damn case closes and I can go on holiday. Now. Fucking shift."

I said.

"Would you like me to disable the bomb then?" Mickey asked. "The one on the door? That bomb?"

Have I mentioned I hate Angels?

"Don't bother." I said, pushing Mickey out of the way and using my special size eight Sterlington shoe on the door.

I impressed even myself as the door came off its hinges and vanished into the room. I turned to Pete.

"Go get your dog." I said. "But be careful in there."

Pete ran forward, then stopped, turning back to me.

"Aren't you coming?." Pete said. "You should meet him too. He'll want to meet his new friend Daddy Faustus."

"No." I smiled at him. "Go see him. You probably have some catching up to do. But be careful in there. OK?"

The last was lost on Pete as he vanished into the dimly lit room. I turned back to Mickey and Stan. They were both on their feet now, standing next to each other.

I took out my cigarettes and lit one up.

"So. This is where we get it on then." I said.

They both smiled.

Fallen or Flying, I really hate Angels. A lot.

"Oh, you have a beating coming Faustus." Mickey said. "Not quite yet though."

"Time to discuss the Dog lover. Daddy Faustus."

At least they didn't call him 'It'.

"You mean my client?"

"Your client then, Faustus." Stan said. "He presents a 'problem' for us."

"He is a golem Ape boy." Mickey said. "A soul free shell. A flesh and bone anathema. He cannot be tolerated. He must be…"

"No." I said, quite calmly. Peter would kill me if I let anything happen to Pete. It would not happen.

"He has no soul, Faustus." Mickey said. "He is not clay. He is flesh and blood. Human in some respects, but the rest of him is not. He is angelic and daemonic, all at once. That makes him very dangerous indeed."

"He could bring about the End of Days all on his own." Stan said. "He needs to be removed from this plane. I will take him…"

"No." I said

"No" Mickey said. "I will take him. He will be safe under Our Lords Protection."

Stan smiled. He took several steps away from Mickey and looked at him.

"My dear old friend, surely you would not expect me to agree that you should have such a potential warrior? Come the end he will prove an unstoppable adversary."

"Similarly," Mickey said, "to allow you such a warrior would be inadvisable on my part. He should come with me."

Then the guns were out. At a guess Heckler and Koch Big Boys. Both with silencers to be considerate to the neighbours. I pulled the cinema seat round and sat down. Then they started shooting till the clips were empty. About two seconds. They reloaded and fired again. This went on for about a minute.

The front of both shirts were shredded as they lowered their guns. In the blink of an eye the bullet holes had never been there. Mickey lifted up his gun and looked at it.

"I don't know." he said. "It was 'different' when we had those flaming swords. More style, more finesse."

"Face it Mickey." Stan sighed. "It was better in the old days. You got proper battles then. Harder to tempt. Now I don't even have to try. They just turn up on the doorstep, sinned to death in some cases. Have you heard what they do to each other now?"

"Never mind these wars they keep having." Mickey said, throwing the gun away. It vanished before it hit the ground. "So many bloody Hero's, expecting a Hero's welcome and all we do is say, 'Right there's your harp. There's your cloud. Now piss off and stop bothering me. And, with all the cut backs we've had to stop the harp lessons so the poor buggers plink away on their own. It's depressing really."

"You think that's depressing. I've had to buy two extra dragons, just to keep the Lake of Fire on the boil. And...and, get this. They are family. Brother and sister. So they both want holidays together and I have to get temps in."

"Don't tell me about temps." Mickey said rolling his eyes and head. "Got three in to help that bloke on the gate with the influx. Well they didn't understand the paperwork, now the Heavenly Warriors are chock a block with Pacifists. Bloody pacifists. I ask you. What good are they in a ruck?"

"Good." I said. "Do you really need another one up there. Especially him. He's so 'nice', and as for down there if he loses his temper you won't be able to keep him in. You'll end up with another break out."

Mickey and Stan exchanged a long look.

"There is a third option of course." Stan said. "We just destroy him now."

"No." I shouted standing up. "I won't let you do that."

Both of them gave me quite a patronizing look.

"How exactly would you stop us?" Stan said.

Now there was a point. Physically I can hold my own in most situations. I'm a sneaky nasty bastard in a fight, that's how I've managed to stay alive as long as I have. That and some top flight medical help. Against these two, or one or even half of one I wouldn't last a blink of an eye.

Guile or persuasion. These fellas had millennia of experience on me. Begging for mercy. They are familiar with the concept, but don't apply it.

I was pretty stuffed.

OK. When all else fails.

Get desperate.

"What's your biggest objection?" I said.

"He is an unstoppable warrior." Mickey said.

"He has no soul and is unaccountable for his actions." Stan followed on.

"Both of you are unstoppable, and neither has a soul. You just are." Like I said, desperate.

I got that pity look again.

"We are accountable to The Lord." Mickey said.

"So what's his stance on Pete then?" I asked.

A simple question, but it floored the pair of them. They didn't know how to answer.

They hadn't asked.

Angels and Daemons work on their own. They spend a lot of time away from 'Home Base', but that shouldn't be the case with Mickey and Stan. Mickey has a direct line to Him, while Stan is the Final Word downstairs.

"Probably would have been a good idea if they had asked me." said The Voice.

Chapter Thirty Eight: The Dick and THE Dick

Oh Bugger.

That Voice.

Him.

The Big Guy.

Standing behind me.

God.

I turned around and looked at him.

Why did he always look like Humphrey Bogart?

Maybe it was some kind of homage to my hero?

"Because it's fitting to the situation." God said. "Besides, if you saw my face, the Real Face, you would…well, let's just say it wouldn't be pleasant. You would probably go very 'sane'."

God tilted back his fedora and looked at Mickey and Stan.

"You still here?" A flash of fire and they were both gone. "Pyrotechnics seemed appropriate. Now, the clone."

On cue, Pete walked through the door, holding Dog in his arms. On a thin green lead, walking behind them, and jumping up for attention was another dog. A soft blonde lurcher. Tall and gangly. Gazing up in awe.

"Look Faustus. It's Dog. And he's got a new friend. I'm going to call him Sol because he's bright like the sun. They were cuddled in together in a small crate. What bad people they were Faustus. I'm glad their dead."

With that Pete sat down on the ichor stained floor and began to play with Dog and Sol. Neither could get close enough. I watched as a fully grown man giggled as two dogs licked his face and demanded attention. After everything a lump still came to my throat and I was ready to go to the wire for him.

Had to.

Peter told me I had to.

Just because he was dead didn't mean I was out of reach of a slapping.

"Have a seat at the bar Kid." God said, as he sat at a bar that was suddenly there, a bar that had been there but hadn't been visible all the time. He was God. He can do that sort of thing.

He rested one arm on the bar as he looked at Pete. I sat down facing him, between them. A whisky and a coffee appeared in front of me. I chose the coffee. God picked up the whisky.

"He loves those Dogs." He said. "I can feel it burning inside him. Love. Odd though. You only get to feel love if you have…"

"A soul." I said.

"Don't finish my sentences Kid." God said, drawing on his cigarette. I drew on mine. We sipped our drinks.

"He's my friend. He stays."

"No soul. He goes."

"Give him one. He stays." I was in such trouble.

God took a drag then stubbed it out. He looked far too carefully at me to be comfortable. Really, you don't want God taking a serious look at you.

"I like you Kid." God said. "Know why?"

"Soft hearted?"

"Not likely. No. It's because you know the difference between right and wrong. You'll fight for what's right, even though it costs you. That and you don't bother me with fuckwit stupid questions."
God put on a high squeaky voice. "Why do you

allow all these terrible things to happen? You could stop it. Why don't you?"

"Simple answer to that one." I said. And it was. It's not too hard an answer to figure out.

Don't ask. Try.

"Want to make a deal kid?" God said.

"What's the price?" I replied.

"Your soul."

I'm used to Stan trying to make deals with me that will cost me my soul. Damnation for a few moments of joy. To have God do it…Well that's just a little bit different.

"What do I get?"

"Not a damn thing." God said. "Fact you lose."

I swallowed hard. I wanted to back down. I wanted to go find Mel and take a long holiday on a long beach.

But what would I come back to?

"Keep going." I said with a brave heart that was getting nearer tachycardia by the second. But I looked like ice on the outside.

"Give him your soul."

"Fuck Off."

Now that was a reflex action. You DO NOT tell God to Fuck Off. Certainly not when he's sitting opposite you. Not given his track record of getting people swallowed by big fish, turning them into salt cellars etc.

He laughed. Thank Him.

"Not stupid enough Faustus." God said. "Good. So the deal is this. He gets, oh let's say ten percent of your soul, just to start him off growing one of his own. Oh, and a little taste of Hell to let him know what's coming if he's not a good boy." He reached over and placed a finger on my chest. "You get nothing, but you do lose ten per cent. You might even grow it back. It's easy enough if you know how."

"You wouldn't care to enlighten me as to how?" I said.

"Fuck off Faustus." He said. And then he was gone.

I looked down at my chest for some reason. Then my hands. Arms, even tried to look over my shoulder at my back.

Apart from a really neat dry cleaning job (I must thank him for that one day) I looked no different, but I felt.. I felt.. Lighter.

It is like when you go shopping and end up with pockets of loose change. You get home, empty the change out of your pockets put those heavy carrier bags down and you feel, for a moment or two, instantly lighter. Missing something.

Different.

Guilty but without the guilt.

Then he was back.

"Oh. Forgot to say. It means you two are tied. He dies. You die. He commits a sin worthy of damnation, you get damned to. Teach him well Faustus. Otherwise you're both fucked."

God said.

And he was gone again.

Then he was back.

"Oh. Silly me. I'll give you a couple of days to clear up the Vampire issue. Congratulations. You just became a soldier of God."

And gone again.

That passes for a sense of humour in Heaven.

Ha Fucking Ha.

I looked over at Pete. He was frozen in the process of playing with Dog and Other Dog. Sweat was running down his face, a look of sheer terror on a face that's just not used to it.

"Oh My." he said. He turned his head to look at me, a tear running down his face. "Oh my, Faustus. What have you done?"

I put a hand on each shoulder and slowly helped him to his feet. The dogs danced around us.

"I saved your life Kid." I said. "You saved mine enough. Call it even."

"You gave away your soul?" His face was awash with disbelief.

"Just a bit of it." I said. "It was either…"

"I know. He told me." Pete pushed away from me and walked towards the door. Don't know why but the dogs stayed with me. Pete turned to face us. His face was white.

"He showed me what would happen if…what would be…things…" He simply couldn't find the words. He stood stationary for a few seconds then raised his hands and stared at them. "I feel…"

"A little heavier. I know." I said, trying to find something we could use as a lead for Sol.

"Fuller." He said, lost in his own private revelry.

"Well, while you contemplate that, do you mind if we finish up here first? You see," I said turning and walking towards the doors the dogs had come through, "I get the feeling this evidence of creation won't be around that long."

I walked through the doors.

Sometimes I hate being proven right.

Chapter Thirty Nine: The Dick and The Dynamite

I don't know if it was a big bomb or not. It was certainly impressive. It had everything you expect from a bomb. Big sticks of dynamite. A ticking clock face. Ten big containers of petrol surrounding it. Lots of blue and red wires. A really nice looking bomb. Even had a small note pinned to it.

'A present from your friends. M&S"

Ah. How nice of Mickey and Stan to think of me.

And destroying all the evidence.

After all they didn't want the whole science of creation being so easily accessible.

I looked around the lab. A laptop sat on a workbench, two filing cabinets stood to the right of the bench and three crates stood against the far wall. Two of them were open, in the third sat a small black kitten, purring for attention.

A rack of four refrigerators stood near the crates. Again I didn't want to see what was in them. I thought I saw eyes bobbing in a jar.

Damn kitten kept purring.

I'd deal with the kitten later, first I needed evidence.

Oh, and to the left were several benches, each with a body on it and various tubes going into it. Mouldy, manky bodies, that were in a slow process of regeneration.

I'd deal with them before the cat. Must be a power socket around here somewhere.

I opened up the filing cabinets. No research notes, just patient details. Not too many. A rough count showed that forty three had gone through Doctor Baldy's programme of Cellular restructuring. Five separate files contained info on subjects one through six.

I quickly picked up around fifty files and piled them on the bench next to the laptop and called for Pete. I got him to take the files out to the car. I wanted him out of the way while I looked at the laptop and bomb.

And those bodies.

Amateur job on the laptop. Smelled of almonds. It was closed so I left it that way.

No one uses CEMEX any more.

A quick check on the bomb showed I had eleven minutes before boom time, so I grabbed a length of cable that ran into the back of the refrigerator, ripped it out and took care of the self-resurrecting corpses on the table.

Twelve of them.

They went on their way. I hope to peace.

I couldn't take the chance they were like Doctor Baldy's playmates.

And I ruined my suit again.

Dripping, I walked over to the kitten cage. Seven minutes to go. My hands covered in goo they slipped on the catch and I frantically tugged on my shirt to wipe them dry. I went back to working my way through untwisting the metal wire that had been used to seal the catch. Kitten just sat watching me.

I very nearly had it open when a large hand clamped down on mine.

I spun away from the hand falling onto my back and twisted around to come face to face with Him.

Not Him, Him.

Another Him.

Him.

George Formby.

Minus Uke.

George was slowly retying the wires onto the catch. He was saying something but the pounding in my head made it hard to hear.

"Gods' damn it Sid." I snapped. "It's like a railway station in here. Could you not have coughed? Let me know you were there. Nearly stopped my heart."

"Sorry F." George/ Sid said in a perfect Formby impression. "You nearly let 'im out. Still…"

"Don't say it." I said waving my index finger at him. "Just don't say it. And why's it always George Bloody Formby?"

"I like the music. Sue me." Sid/George gave a little laugh. I hate it when he does that laugh. "Best go." Sid reached out a hand. I took it and he hauled me to my feet.

"The kitten?" I said giving a nod towards the crated feline.

"No kitten Faustus. Grimalkin."

There was the briefest of pauses.

"Fuck the cat." I said. "Let's go."

Quite a bit of really nasty, hatred filled noise filled the crate. I could have glanced back, but I had encountered Grimalkin once before. I owed her.

"So what's she doing here?" I asked as we passed through the lab. She really could scream a lot.

"At a guess she was with the Daemon I saw in here." Sid said. "Just a guess mind you."

We quickly walked through the entrance and out onto the lawn.

"So how come you're here then?" I asked.

Then the bomb exploded.

It was indeed, a very neat bomb. Very specific to the building, and guessing from the smell of my hair, very hot too.

Sid stood up and looked at the car.

"We should get out of here." Sid said.

I didn't say anything. Just thought I'd have a lie down for a while. I seemed to have gone a little deaf and big elves were playing bigger drums in my skull. I didn't like the music very much though. It was a little repetitive. And I could smell wet dog in addition to something burning. Oh, that's right. The burning smell was me. That's alright then. Then I heard someone say "Ow." Then they swore a lot. Then my cheek really began to sting, the world lurched and I threw up.

Once I'd gotten to the dry heaves, where you think your sphincter is coming out of your nose I realized that I was on my knees next to the car. Pete was rubbing my back, while George Formby stood over me. The two dogs were watching me from the car's windows. Enid was doing her knitting.

Just another normal day at the office dear.

"Anyone got any water? Or coffee for preference?"

"There you go." said Sid/George to Pete. "Just like I told you. Turned out nice again."

I threw up some more.

Back at the office Sid helped Pete and I carry all the files upstairs. Then we chased the two dogs into the building and upstairs. Then I drank coffee and smoked until the taste had gone from my mouth.

Pete had set up a bed for the two dogs on the floor. So naturally they were both fast asleep on my sofa.

I checked my watch. Still over a day to go. I'd be fine.

Sid carried in a plate full of anonymous meat sandwiches, from where I know not.

"So why were you there?" I asked between mouthfuls.

"Everyone vanished!" Sid said. "I checked all of our property and no one was there. I had been unceremoniously dumped. A small gly remained in my pigeon hole saying that all debts had been honoured and my observance to the Fae was no longer required."

"I am sorry. What does that mean?" Pete asked.

"He was made redundant," I said.

"That bit I got." Pete replied shoving the last ham into his mouth. "What's a gly?"

"Small little painted thingy. Sid, how come you ended up at the Lab?"

Sid grabbed the last probable beef with horseradish.

"Well, I'm unemployed, and I wanted some answers." He let go a tremendous burp. Still a troll. "As everything seems to be centred on Cuddles here, yes Pete I am talking about you, I figured if I followed him I might find out something. Don't know what, but I might have got my old job back."

A hand beat mine to the tuna and cheese. I love tuna and cheese.

"Find out anything?" I said, nibbling a crab paste.

"Yes. You're in serious shit." Sid said biting into my Tuna and Cheese. What sort of friend eats sandwiches with both hands?

"Gee. Thanks mate."

"Faustus." Pete asked. "Do you have a twenty four hour laundry around here?"

"What?" I said, totally bemused.

"Well I have just noticed that you have a small piece of dried brain matter clinging to your shoulder. That is one of the more pleasant stains on your suit. I would suggest we both change into clean clothing. Assuming you have any. You seem to have had a busy few days. A lot of it seems to have generated… 'splatter'."

Kat was dead.

Peter was dead.

Many others had died.

And it came again.

From the pain.

The laughter.

Starting off with a chuckle, building into a chortle and moving straight on to a big old belly laugh.

This time the laughter had the company of two other voices.

Chapter Forty: The Dick Delves into DNA Rejuvenation

Once the laughter had died down Pete and I showered and changed. I made damn sure both of us were wearing body armour. I didn't especially want to be a statistic in this war of body counts. While Pete was getting to grips with how to feed left overs to dogs and Sid was rearranging my vinyl blues into chronicle / geographic order I snuck downstairs and picked up the phone. I didn't bother dialling. Dialling her was just for effect. She was always on the end of the line when she wanted to be.

"Hello My Love."

"We need to discuss that soon."

"We do. Do you need me?"

"Well, it seems you're stuck in my head, but no. Not yet." There was one of those slightly uncomfortable pauses. "The uninvited guests you had?"

"Yes. The rude ones who would not leave."

"They don't respond too well to electricity."

"Very badly?"

"Explosively."

There was another long pause with neither of us knowing what to say. I took a pack of smokes out of the drawer and looked for a pack of matches.

"Under your telephone. The spare ones."

I lifted the phone up and sellotaped to the bottom of it were my emergency matches. I tore them free and lit up.

"Sid. He's found a side."

"I hoped he would. I didn't want to endanger your friends. He is a good soldier."

"He's a better friend. You OK with his side?"

"Very happy. Take care my dear."

I had no idea how to end the call. I had no idea why I had made it.

"You be careful and we'll…soon." I said.

"Bye." she said

"Bye."

"Bye."

"Bye."

"Bye then."

"Bye."

"Bye."

"Look, I'm going to say goodbye and then hang up. OK?."

"Yeah."

"Goodbye then."   There was a pause. "Are you still there?"

"No."

A pair of lips brushed my cheek, a swirl of perfume and she'd hung up.

I'm thirty eight you know.

Pete walked in as I was hanging up. I'm giving up on privacy. I jabbed an index finger to my office door.

"There is a door, correction the remains of a door, and it's polite to knock." I said.

Pete walked back out, turned around, closed the remains of the door, knocked, came in, picked bits of the door up and stood them against the wall. There they duly snapped in half.

"Just come in and sit down." I had stopped counting how much he had cost me since I started this.

And now the case was done.

Time to walk away.

"I wanted…" Pete began.

"Shut it Kid." I said, very P.I. "The case is done. You have your Dog, and a friend for him. Time to walk away. I'll do the mopping up."

Our old friend, the significant pause, came back.

"No." Pete said. "If you die, I die. I believe that was the deal you made, so I would like to try and ensure your longevity. I owe you more than you can…"

"OK. So shut up and get me a coffee will you?"

"Yes." Pete got to his feet, slightly stunned. "Are you feeling…?"

"Look. I told you. When this is over we can talk, we can grieve. I'll even buy you an ice cream. Till then, just make me a coffee and I'll look at these."

I got Doctor Baldy's files and spread them across my desk. Fifty plus files, all in red folders, data sheets part stapled in, part paper clipped in place. Untidy filing. Great. The sun was up again when I had finished them. My head hurt, if a paracetamol on top of the magic pill wouldn't kill me I'd take some.

Most files related to his Vampire subjects. A mix of Vampire, Old Vampire at a guess, Daemon, and Angel DNA had been used to re-sequence the Vampires own DNA. All combined with DNA combinations from The Tree of The Fae. Presumably to add strength, regenerative abilities, and senses. There was one other element present in one Vampire. DNA from a subject 'W'. Doctor Baldy referred to him once as Waste product.

I was guessing I knew who he was.

He had been classed as a reject for one simple reason. According to Doctor Baldy's aesthetic, he was ugly.

He had been kept in a cage, not given any contact apart from when harvested for cells or experimented on to test recovery from injury. There was a very long list of things they had done to him.

I really hoped that he didn't remember.

The Vampire subjects were all injected with a series of aggressive virus, viruses or viri. Depending on what the plural of 'virus' is. Over three weeks it realigned their DNA, making them faster, stronger and invulnerable - save for a jolt of electricity. Some it made as thick as a brick, others far too smart to be trusted. It also made them aggressive, cruel and totally devoid of all compassion.

To make sure they didn't get too big for their boots they were given a five day lifespan after they came out of their 'alteration'.

Bit Phil K. Dick that.

Well, you don't want to create an army that might turn on you. There would always be a supply of scum willing to fight.

Especially if you encouraged that kind of attitude on the street.

All you had to do was encourage a feeling of despair.

Recession had hit England hard, and there were plenty unemployed on both sides of the Streets. One good push into the fringes of crime, then straight into thugery. Pass Go and collect two hundred pounds - by robbing a Post Office and shooting or knifing the manager.

Nice world we live in.

There was a cold black cup on my desk. I hadn't even noticed him put it down. I downed it in one.

354

Even cold his coffee was great. Maybe I'll get a flake for his ice cream.

Pete worried me. I felt lighter since the soul share. Thinner. Less 'there'. Not a good way to explain it but the best I could do.

I had gone out on a limb for him and I don't know why. Certainly I had promised Peter I would take care of him, but I had committed myself to someone, who at the end of the day I didn't really know. He didn't seem concerned that I had sealed his fate without discussing it with him either. I was also worried as to why the Big Humphrey had done it. Logically it would have made more sense to remove him, but he had let him stay.

The biggest nag of all though was Ti's kiss. That scared me, and seemed to have the same effect on her. Although she was an excellent actress. Common sense said not to get involved with The Fae. But how did it work if you got on with one person, not the species? Trouble, any way you look at it.

Not for the first time since I quit I wanted a drink. I sipped the dregs from the coffee cup instead and checked my watch. Time to do something. Anything to stop these nagging worries.

I scrabbled among the papers on my desk until I found the paper with the other company address on it. Time to do some snooping.

After all it is what I do for a living.

But I would need a weapon. Going up against an army, you need protection. I opened up the desk drawer and took out the biggest firepower I had in my small, but effective, arsenal.

Chapter Forty One: The Dick Deceives Delectably

"Health and Safety Audit?" The security guard said. His name was Richard. I knew that from the metal badge pinned to the front of his uniform black jumper. Maybe it was upside down so it could remind him of who he was.

There is nothing like an audit to put the fear of Humphrey into people.

"Yes." I twittered. "Our records show that you are one month late submitting your P11Z349Q." Pause for effect. "119476 stroke 14. 27, and as security operative your duty is to compile the record so do you have it available?"

"I…" All credit to Richard for trying to get an answer in.

"Then the answer is no." I opened up the brown folder I held in my hand, took out a red pen and marked a big red cross inside it, right over my offer of thousands of pounds from Readers Digest. "I require your BFBB file immediately, your P14, your B52 and OO7. In addition I also require a 1411 and Plan Nine FOS. Your GA14 and of course your temperature checks."

"Temperature checks?" Richard said. He should have known better than to ask.

"I take it you have a coffee room here?" I machine gunned at him.

"Ye…"

"With a refrigeration unit, not exceeding sixty cubic litres?"

"Ye.."

"Then you have been keeping temperature checks on both the interior and exterior of the unit using a laser and internal probing medium, but not utilizing disc medium that are renowned for inefficiency and failure to register within. I take it from your lack of response you are in the process of delaying me while the aforementioned are being fabricated by your accomplice?"

"What? Sorry. Pardon?" Richard said, actually taking a step back from his state of the art reception desk.

"You are seeking to hinder my checking relevant paperwork. Can I be more specific than that?" Damn I was Evil.

"I'll go get them." Richard turned and made a B-line for the elevator. He stopped after three paces and turned around. "Where would they be?"

"Really." I sighed. "Do you want me to issue you with a B9?"

"No. No. I'm sorry." Richard said.

"Go. Go." I waved the folder in his general direction and he scampered off.

Richard hadn't been picked for his brains, or his looks. A large hooked nose, broken sometime in his youth, protruding and hooked jaw and a forehead that would have put a Neanderthal man to shame. Combine this with sticky out ears, steroid acne, in his mid-thirties and hair that wanted to grow in all directions at once and you just know he thought of himself as Gods' Gift to Women.

Women probably thought he was a tosser.

I needed to check the computer's hard drive, so I stood at the desk and checked the signing in book, making the odd note in my folder. I had made three cameras in reception, which meant there would be at least another three well hidden, all watching me. That didn't concern me. I was in disguise. Wearing a car coat, pair of spectacles and no hat. About all the requirements for people not to notice who you are.

That's one of the things about being a P.I. Unless you wear a big sign saying 'I am a Private Detective and I am investigating you!' people tend to see just the surface. If you look as anonymous as I do it's easy to blend in. Especially if people want to ignore or get rid of you.

You only wear the hat when you want people to notice you. Then they start looking for the hat.

No hat. It's not you.

The signing in book showed me nothing, but the kind of people I was looking for would hardly worry about the nicety of fire regulations. It was more important I got close to his terminal. I couldn't sit down and dig into it, but nestling in my pocket was a beautiful bit of kit. No idea how it worked, but so long as I was close enough to a terminal with wireless interface it would build a solid link that would do some sort of doodly flip and beam hard drive access to a lap top. Then the clever bit.

I get Mammasayra to check it for me.

Richard came scurrying back, clutching arms full of box files. I peered at him over the top of my glasses.

"I got everything I could find." He wheezed. Like so many body builders, any real exercise and they're out of breath. "Where do you want me to put it?"

Oh the temptation.

"You don't expect an audit out here do you?"

"Well Mr Campbell said…"

"Oh. Mr Campbell said did he?" I whipped out the threatening brown folder and red pen. "And what would his first name be."

"Bill. William."

I scribbled furiously.

"Then you can tell Mr William Campbell I shall require an office made ready for my audit and will return to these premises in two days. Until that time I am serving a restriction order on your staff room and I notice you have a flask under your desk that you will surrender at once for tests. Failure to do so will result in an Order 7."

Richard frantically grabbed hold of his flask and passed it over. All credit to him. His hands were not shaking too badly. I took out a pair of rubber gloves and held the flask at arm's length.

"I can tell just by looking an Order 12 will apply to this." And with that I turned around and strode from the building, knowing that Richard and Mr William Campbell would spend the next two days working on fabricating documents and double checking every Health and Safety requirement they could find.

A perfect distraction.

Outside, sat at a bus stop, was Pete. I hadn't wanted to bring him, but I couldn't take the chance he would get himself into terminal trouble if I wasn't there.

Given his track record that would happen anyway, but at least I would be able to do something to get him out of it.

He had a supermarket carrier bag clutched to his chest. I wordlessly took it from him and took out the other office laptop. Opening it up it flared into life and I double clicked on Mammasayra icon.

"You do it Skinny Boy?" Mammasayra's face filled the screen.

"Give me a minute." I took out the MP3 Thingy and connected it to the laptop. Both of them purred for a moment. I poured myself a drink from Richard's flask.

Urghh. Tea.

I passed the cup to Pete who sat there happily drinking it.

"You did it Skinny Boy. Their hard drive, your hard drive. Now what you need?"

"Evidence." Pete said. "We need evidence to prove that they are…"

"Ya got another skinny boy." Mammasayra said. A worried look crossed her face. "Anythin' I need to know Skinny Boy? Not got yourself a boy have you?"

"No darling." I sighed. "He's helping me out on this, and like he said, we need evidence to show they are behind the purchase of property, anything they have on Faust Genetics and a schematic of the building. Normal sort of thing."

"Five minute. Get yourself a coffee."

With that her face vanished and was replaced by her screen saver, a photograph of her, myself, Peter, Sid and the rest of the band. I felt a twinge at seeing Peter's non-smiling face. Time to mourn later.

"I saw Mel." Pete said out of the blue. He was staring straight ahead.

I tried to keep agitation and worry out of my voice. Maybe I succeeded. "Where?"

"Going into the building. She was wearing Jeans, a T-shirt with a loose blue fabric jacket and trainers. She was being accompanied by twelve men. All wearing long black coats and sunglasses. Do you

360

suppose they have some sort of uniform? No. There was no sign of Cadell or Whisper."

"Lisper."

"Sorry. Lisper. She did not look happy. She did however look alive. Are we going in after her?"

"Not yet." I said. Hard to say, as every part of me wanted to go charging in, get the girl, deal with the bad guys and probably get us both hacked to death in the process. It was the last thought that stopped me.

"If we go in without a plan, we are dead."

"I thought she was important to you?" Pete asked. There was no accusation in his voice, but a straightforward question.

"She is, but all of us stand a better chance of getting out if we go in carefully. There's an old phrase…"

"Fools rush in where Angels fear to tread."

"I was thinking more of the one that goes 'If you don't want to be a Vampire's lunch don't lie down wearing a push up bra, open a vein and shout The Drinks are on me.' That one."

"Ah. The Faustus humour. I hold my sides with laughter. Oh, the pain. Please stop. That is Mel in there. We should do something."

"And we will." I rested a hand on his forearm. "Don't go looking for revenge. You probably won't get it and if you do it really isn't worth it. Nor will you save the day. Best you can hope for is to walk away in one piece with some justice."

There were a few moments of telling silence.

"That was quite clever."

"For me you mean. Peter taught me that. And I learned the hard way."

"Will you two stop chatterin' and get back to your office. You don't wanna talk 'bout this atta bus stop."

"Do you really want to be talking about this at all?"

Well, it wasn't Mammasayra's voice, and it wasn't Pete's voice. I was pretty certain it wasn't my voice, so using a detective's deductive power I worked out that it had to belong to someone else.

I looked up.

Yep.

Steam heads.

Chapter Forty Two: The Dick Dallies with Dangerous Decrepit Dispatchers of Death

The Steam Heads

'Mickey The Boy', 'Tony the Tugger' and 'The One They Only Call John'.

'Mickey The Boy was the youngest of the three at two hundred and ninety seven. He had fought in all the major conflicts Britain had had over the last two hundred and fifty years including The War Against The Welsh. Not one you'll find in your history books. He had been decorated for bravery seventy one times and shot for desertion twice.

Big and round all over, with jet black hair that's the bane of his life. He can't wait for the first grey flecks so he can get taken seriously.

'Tony the Tugger' didn't like his nickname. He much preferred being called 'Tiger', but due to a cereal manufacturers record of litigation and his personal habit the name was irreversibly engraved on him.

Stick thin with thin wisps of hair plastered to his mottled scalp. A real 'hot' look. Women would fall at his feet.

A lover and a fighter (sometimes simultaneously) at one thousand, two hundred and sixteen he had experienced an eventful life that included holding the ink bottle for Prince John whilst signing the Magna Carta, to disproving Lizzie the First's nickname. A Taurean.

'The One They Only Call John', was called John. Nearly two thousand years in search of a nickname.

They looked like three harmless old men, not the battle hardened hitters they were. The Strong arm of the council, you'd go up against a twenty foot rabid skunk before you tried your luck against them.

"Here. Faustus. Pull my finger." John said. "Go on. It'll be a gas. Gas. Wind. Get it?"

Because it's best to humour him, as I value my teeth, I pulled The One They Call John's finger. He duly farted and all three fell about laughing like schoolboys.

The Steam heads were all Old Men. They took advantage of the fact whenever they could. Fortunately, due to my relationship with Peter they viewed me as a sort of Grandson by adoption.

Tony The Tugger came and sat next to me, recovering his breath. He clamped an iron hand on my leg and sighed.

"E.M. Good to see you again. Good to see you. Not got yourself killed yet then?"

"Not yet Tony, but I'm working on it." I said. Nice line, I should write that down.

Pete stood up and gestured to his seat. "Would you two gentlemen like to have a seat?"

Mickey the boy walked over to him and stood far too close for anyone's safety.

"So he's the half-breed then. Doesn't look that tough." Mickey the Boy said. "Daemons? I've shit 'em."

"Play nice Mickey." I said.

"Oh he will." Tony said. "Just for now though. You see E.M. The Council has asked us to have a bit of a look at what's going on. There are some very upset people on The Streets. Very upset."

"I've some tissues somewhere if anyone wants a good cry." I said popping a smoke into my mouth. The One they Call John reached over and took it out, crumpling it in front of my eyes.

"Bad for you." he said, smiling like he meant it.

"You ever spent time in jail sonny?" Mickey the Boy asked Pete. "You look like you enjoy a good shower."

"Sit down Mickey." I said. "I've seen him pull the head off a Daemon. You wouldn't worry him."

Mickey the Boy didn't even attempt to discuss things, he just let rip a punch that can go through a brick wall. Pete caught it with ease and slowed it down, rather than stop it dead and break Mickey's wrist. Mickey smiled and slapped him on the back.

"Nice one son." he said as he moved straight to where Pete had been sitting.

"Now E.M. "Tony the Tugger was the designated talker of the group. The others were there as muscle. "This whole bit of bother you've got yourself into."

"That's an understatement." I said. Tony squeezed my leg hard to let me know that while my participation in this conversation was appreciated, I should really desist. Or... No one ever explains the 'Or'.

"Now," Tony said tugging away at his ear, "E.M. we think it would be good for you to take a little trip somewhere. Somewhere warm maybe. Reflect on the money and properties Peter left you and decide what you will do with them. Perhaps visit your friend Mammasayra. Encourage her to take a few days off. What do you say E.M? What do you say?"

"Bollocks" I said using tact and decorum.

"Now, E.M." John interrupted, "You need to be sensible and let us deal with this."

"Double Bollocks." I continued my argumental theme.

Tony tugged his ear hard enough to pull it off. John shifted his weight slightly on the balls of his feet. Mickey the Boy simply chambered a round.

"You are leaving us very little room to maneuver E.M." Tony said. He'd lose that ear if he wasn't careful.

"We have to report to Council when we find you E.M. As soon as we find you." John said taking out his mobile phone and waving it at me.

"And what will you do Tony, John, Wild Bill?" I snapped. "Because someone has decided to make their move and they're doing it as we speak. By the time you catch up it'll be too late."

"Now, E.M." Tony warned.

"And as someone has decided that it's open season on Old Men, you three had better watch your backs"

"Would you like me to take that gun from him Faustus?" Pete asked.

"Best not Kid." I replied. "He'll kill you." That was more to massage Mickey the Boy's ego, but there was the possibility.

"Well. E.M." Tony said. "No choice really. Mickey, Kill him."

The gun was silenced and I heard the barest cough, followed by a gentle sigh.

Then a dead wizard was lying at my feet. John poked him with the toe of his shoe.

"They think that just because they wear a cloak of invisibility that cuts out the smell of their bloody terrible aftershave." John said.

"Course, I remember the days when they all had great long beards." Tony said. "Before your time Mike,"

"They die just as quick though." Mickey the Boy said, holstering his still smoking gun.

"Bloody council." Tony said. "Paranoid as it gets."

"Imagine getting a wizard to spy on us." John said.

"Do you know E.M., they even have a girl at Table now? A girl. I bloody ask you."

I happened to know that 'girl' was over two hundred years old. As sneaky and dangerous as a bag of rattlesnakes. Luck pushing time.

"So when you find us, you ring the council?" I asked.

"Faustus there is a dead wizard on the floor." Pete said.

John put a reassuring hand on Pete's shoulder.

"No there isn't lad. Because if there was it would mean we had been here, and if we were here, I'd have to make a call to Council and then you two would have to be dead. See what I mean?"

"There is no dead wizard at your feet Faustus, but I suspect it is time we left."

Tony smiled at Pete. "I will like him E.M. When we find him. He looks like he could plate with us."

"I like him too." Mickey the Boy said, standing and squaring up to Pete. "He's not as stupid as he looks."

Pete held his hand out for Mickey the boy to shake.

"It has been a pleasure not to meet you, and I look forward to meeting you for the first time in the future." Pete could be quite quick on the uptake.

Tony stood up. John grabbed hold of the feet of the wizard.

"Funny old world E.M." Tony said. "If the Council hadn't sent him to spy on us, you two would probably be dead by now. Funny old world."

"Nothing personal mind." John said. "Here E.M. Pull his finger. Go on. He won't bite."

I slowly reached down and took hold of one of the corpses fingers and gave it a firm pull. John pulled the other way and the corpse expelled a lot of air. The three of them laughed themselves silly.

"I'm thinking of writing a book." Mickey the Boy said. "A thousand laughs you can get from a corpse."

"You're a sick man Mickey." I said.

"That is the truth. I'll see you E.M. You won't necessarily see me, but I'll see you."

Now that's a threat to make you wee yourself.

I liked The Steam Heads. I was also somewhat nervous of them. You would never think that three old men who owned a model railway shop would be so effective as heavies.

Funny old world, ain't it?

Chapter Forty Three: The Dick Dresses for Danger.

Back at the office we were looking at the building's schematics. The place was wall to wall sensors and cameras. It would be impossible to break in unnoticed. Even with IMF help.

"What are they?" Pete said pointing at small squares along the wall.

"Tazers" Mammasayra's voice echoed. "Big electrical dart guns. Nasty. More than legal voltage too."

"That would cause me to explode. I would not like that."

"Oh. Sort of power they's got in 'em, much worse than that. That's not da worse of it." Mammasayra was enjoying this. "They's got lasers, machine guns, spikes an deadfalls thada squish you likea bug. Bid like tha film wit tha ma widda hat."

The screen changed to a photo-image of a console.

"The plus side is Skinny Boy, I can work it all off dis. Simple enough to create it. Course I can do notin about people, but I can stop dem shooting you fulla lectricity. How about dat?"

"I think we have ourselves a plan Mammasayra. A plan or something like it."

"You know this voltage." Pete said.
Wimp.

A few arrangements with Mammasayra sealed the plan. Pete still was not happy about the possibility of radical electric shock therapy, but never mind. That was the least of his worries.

I made a couple of phone calls and dug out my spare body armour (you need a spare while the other gets laundered).

"Will this protect me from electric death?" Pete asked.

"No." I was being honest. I lied to him about so many other things. "But it will keep a lot of the bits in one place. Now let's sort out your uniform."

"Uniform?"

I reached into my wardrobe and grabbed the emergency suit. The one I only wore when there were no other options. The funeral suit.

Best not to tell him it's use.

"I really don't see why I need all of this." he said putting the vest on back to front. "I heal rapidly after all."

"You're not bullet proof any more. Remember." I passed him the suit.

"But I should still be just as fast and strong so…"

So…I hit him. A proper punch, full in the face. I have to admit there was a small degree of satisfaction in there. He promptly fell flat on his backside. Blood dribbling from his bottom lip. I rested the suit on the bed and watched his lip.

"What was that for?" Pete tried to get to his feet, I pushed him back to the floor. Blood still kept dribbling. I passed him a handkerchief. He dabbed at the blood and looked at it.

"I'm bleeding. I don't bleed. Not like this." I offered a hand and helped him to his feet. "And it really hurt."

"And?" I asked.

"And I will wear the vest. Possibly a helmet too?"

I threw him my spare hat. "Don't push it. I want to try something else." I stood rigid. "Hit me."

There were becoming many things which, in retrospect, I wish that I had not said to Pete.

"Are you alright? I pulled the punch. I was careful not to hurt you."

Two or three visions of Pete danced in my vision. My jaw hurt and I seemed to be cuddling the wall.

I think it would be fair to say that he is still strong.

"And look." Grinning like a Cheshire cat he showed me a set of bruised and slightly grazed knuckles. "I cut my hand. And it really hurts."

"Good for you." I climbed up the wall, shrugging off Pete's attempt to help and blinked focus back into my eyes.

"Can I ask you something Faustus?" Pete asked trying to turn the vest around while still wearing it.

"Well you're going to anyway, so go ahead."

"Will the dogs be safe with Sid? I have read about Trolls and they do eat…people."

I pressed my forehead against the wall.

"That old story. Well he doesn't. Let me tell you a story about Sid."

I sat down on the flat's only chair and dug a cigarette out of my pocket. I needed to pick some more up. I was running low.

"Long, long, long, about three years ago, Sid was tailing me for Ti. He was human looking and doing so good a job of it I hadn't spotted him."

I lit up.

"Well some kids, eighteen, nineteen years old, had stolen a car, got wired on something and gone joy riding. They came tearing down the street playing knock down with the doors. That's where you open a door as you drive past someone and try to beat them to the ground with it. Well the passenger had hit three pedestrians by the time they got to me."

"And Sid pulled you out of the way?"

I looked at him. He was sat on the floor, half dressed, knees up to his chin and hugging them with both arms.

In so many ways I was actually dealing with a child. The file showed he was only five years old. Here he was sitting as if I was reading him a bedtime story.

"What happened next?" he asked.

"Well," I had the urge to turn a page, "There was a small boy in the street. Couldn't have been much more than five. I got to him and grabbed him, but I was going to get hit myself, so I braced myself and..."

"Yes?"

"Nothing." I relaxed at the memory. "Sid had caught the car and ripped the door off, pulling the kid out with him. Then he stopped the car by..."

"How? How did he stop the car?"

"He leaped on it, punched through the engine block and slid off, grabbing the car and dragging it to a stop. Then he flipped it onto its roof."

"What happened to the driver and the others?"

"They ran away." I was lying. You attack people from and on The Streets...The Streets fight back.

The car had been reported as abandoned and as a child had been involved, well... The Night Feeders fed well that night.

Eventually.

Me. How did I feel?

They got what they deserved.

I never claimed to be a nice guy.

"So you trust him because he saved your life?" Pete said.

"I trust him because he's my friend. I would walk into Hell with that man, and him me. The fact he's also shit hot on a piano helps."

"Would you prefer him to be going with you tonight?" Pete asked. He wasn't fishing for a compliment or reassurance. It was a straight question, so it got a straight answer.

"No. He's my friend and I trust him totally, but he has no... 'vested interest' in this. We do. Like it or not I'm saddled with you kid. So you and I, we go and kick some arse. Get Mel out and hopefully get our hands on Cadell and Lisper."

There was one of those significant pauses. Long enough for Pete to pull on his trousers.

"Are you going to kill them?" he asked.

The thought had crossed my mind. A lot. But I'm a detective not an assassin. I may have killed people, on The Streets sometimes you have to, to survive, but only when there's been no other choice.

That's what you tell yourself late at night.

"I'm going to arrest them." I may have surprised even myself. "People like Cadell and Lisper think they are above the law. They can just smile a winning smile, say 'no comment' and with a good lawyer, and I suspect they have very good lawyers, walk away with no charges. A bit of political clout and they think they can get away with murder."

I took out another cigarette and lit up. I must have some in my desk drawer. I always get twitchy when I start to run low.

"I want them to see the inside of a cell for a very long time, know their hope is dwindling away, day by day, minute by minute, second by second. I want them to be scared and bored. No liberty to do what they want. People telling them what to do and when to do it. I'm a detective. I want them nicked. Then the law can eat them alive."

I had been ranting come the end. Pete just stood and looked at me.

"I got the impression that there was no law on The Streets, just people looking out for each other."

"Oh there's law, the kind that goes 'We know you did it, so you're dead', but then there's me. I have rules and I don't break them. I follow the law. Maybe not to the letter all of the time, but the spirit. The law says they should stand trial and they will. Maybe they get sent down, maybe they don't, but they won't be untouchable any more. Kill them and five more spring up in their place. Send them down and people are so worried about their own nasty little secrets the bad guys keep a low profile. For a while. So we arrest them."

Pete looked at me in silence.

"I want them dead." he said slowly and carefully.

"And they'll be dead soon enough, but you let the machine eat them first." I snapped back at him. In temper I kicked the wall "We do this my way. The plus of it is you might just get to go back to Dog. Your way we both end up dead. I plan on booking a holiday tomorrow, so alive is good."

"And what about Peter?" This time there was accusation in the voice.

"What about him?"

"He wanted revenge."

"No." I shouted. "He wanted the right thing to be done. He could have sent any nasty thing to kill them. He could have killed them there in his shop.

He was powerful enough. Don't you know what he was?"

"He was my friend." Tears were welling up now.

"And mine, for the best part of twenty years, so I know him a little better than you do. He was like a second father, he got me straight and made damn sure I stayed that way and knew right from wrong. So don't tell me what he wanted. Get dressed."

Pete moved forward, the look on his face somewhere between anger and fear.

"Faustus. Wait." he said.

"No. No more talking. And the name's Mr Faustus. Don't use it unless you have to. And do up your zip."

Chapter Forty Four: The Dick and The Duck Debate Drivel

I sat in the office sipping instant espresso when the office door opened. Well, I say office door, it was more a bit of old blanket I had pinned into place.

"Can I come in?" Sid asked, still in his George Formby look.

"Sure.

Sid came through the door and flopped himself onto the corner of my desk.

"You mind?" he asked.

"Feel free." I said. There was a brief pull on the air and Sid the Duck was standing on the desk. He settled down and stared up at me.

"Thanks. That feels so much better." He preened for a second or two. "I settled the dogs down at Peter's shop then came over to see if you needed any muscle."

"I'm fine mate, but thanks for asking."

Sid cocked his head to one side and stared in the way only a duck can stare.

"What's going through that head? It normally means trouble."

"How was the shop?" I asked as innocently as I could. Probably not very.

"Tidy, apart from the spiders' webs. It didn't feel the same though."

I knew what he meant. Take the person out of the equation and the place loses its atmosphere.

"You still unemployed?"

"Ah yes." Sid gave a little shudder of his feathers. "I received notification that my 'work' for the Fae has been appreciated, but due to restructuring my role within the organization is no longer relevant and they wish me well in my future. That came straight from the Big O himself."

"Your fired then?"

"Redundant, please."

I was taking a chance, and risking our friendship, but Sid needed somewhere to work and stay, otherwise he'd become just more hired muscle on The Streets. After that he would end up truly on the other side.

"Ever thought of going into the retail industry?" I asked as innocently as possible.

"What?" Then the penny dropped. "Oh no. Not this duck. I could never run that place. It's too weird, and I know weird. I lived with The Fae, so don't tell me about weird. I could write you a book on weird. Want to know how I spell Weird. I spell it W.W.W.W. E.E.E.E.E.E.E.E.E.E. I. I. I. I.I. I. I. R. R. R. R. R.R.R.R.R.R.R.R.R.R.R.R.R.R.R. D.D.D.D.D.D.D.D. So I know Weird. Oh yes. Ben there and bought the armour plated T shirt that says 'Don't ask me about WEIRD! OK? I mean it Because I. Know. Weird. Alright?"

"So you'll do it then?"

"Yeah. OK. Got nothing better to do."

I took a piece of paper from my desk and picked up a pen, scribbling;

"Sid runs the place now.
No arguments. It is his."
Signed E.M.Faustus.
Fabricati Dieum.

Sid peered at the note and gave a little sniff.
"Is that legal?" he asked me.

"Legal enough." I said. "It even has some Latin in it."

"I could have been a Judge you know. But I didn't have the Latin."

"Can't be a Judge if you don't have the Latin."

We paused for a few seconds, listening to the sound of The Streets. Nice quiet and easy. Neither of us wanting to say much. Just two old friends reliving a little, tiny bit of their youth.

"Sure you don't need muscle tonight?" Sid asked eventually.

I wanted to say yes.

So I said no instead.

"Could get nasty." Sid wanted to come along and watch my back. I couldn't afford to let him.

"Someone has to stay behind and wear the Hat Sid." I finished my espresso, upended the cup and rested it carefully on the saucer.

"No chance. I'm more of a cape and rubber suit duck myself."

"Super Duck."

"Exactly."

Again there was another long pause. Long enough to pour myself another espresso and put some into a saucer for Sid.

"You are planning on coming back from this one?" He asked. I didn't reply. "Well?" Sid pushed.

I took a long breath in and let it out.

"I want to. I really do, but I'm not sure if it's my time." I said. "Still, I have to see it through to the end. Finish it. One way or another."

"Why you?"

"Because it has to be someone. I wouldn't ask anyone else to,"

Sid sipped from his saucer. Not easy with no lips, but he managed.

"You die, I'll come find you and kick your arse."

I smiled. "Better bring an army."

Pause time.

"Story with the Kid?" he asked.

I lit another. Thank gods for a spare pack in the office desk drawer.

"I still don't know how he's in on this. Not fully. Medical experiment gone wrong, or maybe right. He was important to Peter. Peter trusted him. I trusted Peter. And he's handy enough with his fists to help out if there is any 'unpleasantness'."

"Who else you got with you?" Sid was normally not this pushy. Even when he was worried.

"Just him. I'll put no-one else in harm's way."

"Weapons?"

"Only what's inside the hat."

"Ah. The dangerous ones." Sid smiled wide enough to show a perfect set of white teeth.

"Good trick." I said.

"Thanks." He said chomping his teeth, "It takes practice. Works well with the ladies too. See you."

"See you."

Sid jumped off the desk and waddled to the door without looking back. A waft of air drew the curtain back, he walked through and was gone as the curtain fell back into place. Nice trick.

After a moment, a full drag after Sid had left there was a knock on the blanket. It's impossible to knock on a blanket, but Pete was giving it a damn good try.

"May I come in?" Pete asked from the other side of the fabric.

"Might as well." I said, fixing a glare onto my face so when he entered he had a rough idea of my general mood.

He had finished dressing and looked half- way presentable. He was wearing the funeral suit well enough. The trousers were a little short, the waist band a little big. A belt had fixed that. The jacket was big on him as well, but short of sticking a surprisingly thin pillow up his shirt, there wouldn't be much that could be done there. Couple that with the black tie and he was ready for a funeral.

Shame it was going to be his.

"The hat was too big." he said.

I sat and glared a really good glare.

"Can we talk?" he asked.

"If you can vibrate your vocal chords you can talk Kid, so make with the tremolo."

"We are going after them? Still?" He asked, sitting on the corner of the desk.

"Yep."

"Are we going to be doing it without help?"

"Yep."

"Are the police going to be brought into it?"

"Nope."

You can really carry off these monosyllabic conversations if you leave a smoke dangling between your lips.

"You are sure you don't want to bring in the police to do the arrests? He repeated.

"Yep."

Probably shouldn't have lit the fag though as ash fell onto my shirt. I brushed it off nonchalantly.

"Then firstly, I would like to apologize for my comments earlier." He did look sincere, and as I didn't think he was that good an actor I was gracious. I nodded.

"Secondly, I feel I should say something about the police and their involvement, as they already have lines of pursuit with the deaths of Jo-Jo Mar and poor Miss Kat. It is logical that they will become a part of this whether you wish them to or not."

"I said. No. Police."

"Mr Faustus." Pete said. "There comes a time during troubles when it is necessary to call for police assistance." Pete raised a hand to stop the interruption he could see coming. "Personally, I would like to make my suggestion."

"Go on."

"Fuck the police. Let us kick their fucking teeth in."

"Let's roll and rock."

I paused a moment.

"You know we may well die." I said.

"At least it won't be boring. Roll and rock as I believe the saying goes"

"Roll and Rock Kid. Roll and Rock"

"No Mr Faustus. Let us Mambo!"

Pete stood up and looked out of the window.

"Mr Faustus, there seem to be some people in the street."

I slowly got to my feet, dusting remaining ash from my trousers.

"That's not abnormal. It's a street." I said.

"But these ones are holding flaming torches and pitchforks, well one has a garden rake, but the rest all have pitchforks."

I looked out of the window as a pitchfork imbedded itself in the window frame.

"Burghers." I said. And meant it.

Chapter Forty Five: The Dick Dances

Excerpt from
Angels, Daemons and other realm beings.
By E.M Faustus
(unpub)

The Burghers

Burgher- A formally defined class in medieval German cities, usually the only group from which city officials could be drawn.

Well that's what my dictionary says anyway.
As we no longer are in the middle ages and indeed not in Germany, The Office of Burgher is one that's rarely visited.

However, it must be an old tradition of some of the more 'ethnic' Street People that a good pitchfork waving, flaming torch wielding crowd gives you a feeling of a homeland you never knew.

Because of the need for an almost effective police force for people on The Streets, the rank of Burgher was reintroduced in the 1930's. Those in charge decided it would be helpful to have their own arm of the law that could enforce the Law of The Streets.

Admittedly the Law of The Streets depended upon the whims of the Council, but they did represent an enforcement arm of the Law, not just legalese.

A mix from all species, they were based strongly in old traditions. Where most policemen carried truncheons and whistles, they carried flaming torches and pitchforks. They were secretive and dangerous to cross.

Sort of a cross between the Stasi and Morris Dancers.

On The Streets they are the ones who keep people in line. You don't cross them, ever.

Ω

The conversation ended with a scream of agony,
That was alright.

I wasn't the one screaming.

The conversation started as Pete and I stepped outside the office building.

"Take your hand from my jacket or I'll rip off your ear." I said.

The Burghermiester was fifty and fat. His balding pate showed a few old scars, but more of a livid case of dandruff. His red nose sat on his swollen face, with two swollen red patches on his cheeks, covered with scarlet veins. Obviously not a man who ate his five a day.

He was out of breath just ascending the few steps to the door.

"We want the aberration." Burghermiester said. "Hand him over or it will be the worse for you Faustus."

"Is that worse than fingernails being pulled?" I asked. "Worse than the trick with the trained rats? Worse than a little attention on the joints with a small hammer? Worse than the bone needles? Worse than the ginger beer trick? Stop me if I get close."

The Burghers are tough and when they surface to the light tend to expect people to give into their authority. They simply can't handle it when you stand up to them. They only have two responses.

384

Back down or stick you with a pitchfork. So far I had managed to avoid the pitchfork.

So far.

"Man with shiny shoes send you Burghermiester?" I said "Or would you prefer me to call you Hilton? Hilton."

Hilton Oswald Greetstanley. Current head of the Burghers round the Fens. Fat racist bully. Sort of man that spells 'black' with an 'N'.

The Council can surely pick them.

"It will be decided at Council what will happen to It." Greenstanley spluttered, obviously surprised I knew his name. "Hand It over."

"You could try to take me I suppose." Pete said, stepping forward. "But you could find a certain difficulty in my cooperation. You may even encounter some belligerency on my part. I would like to apologize for any 'unfortunate circumstances' that may occur if you try."

I stepped forward and Greenstanley backed away rapidly. NBC. Natural Born Coward. Hands began to tighten on pitchfork handles and a torch was thrust towards me. I took out a cigarette and grasped the handle of the torch. Tilting my hat back I leaned close to it and lit up, never once taking my eyes from those of the thug wielding it..

I only singed my eyebrows a little but the move drew gasps from the rest of the Burghers.

This was not meant to be how it went.

It was supposed to be that they intimidated, we adopted a Victim Mentality and were appropriately intimidated. It wasn't meant to be me using them as a lighter or Pete breaking off a corner of one of the buildings steps and handing it to one of them.

Greenstanley's second in command, Herbert Morris, a not quite so fat, not quite so alcohol sizzled bully.

"You may find this useful if you decide to resort to projectile weaponry." he said, with a cheerful smile of pure helpfulness.

I leaned in towards Greenstanley. With nowhere else to back up to he leaned back. It was a reciprocal movement that left half the crowd getting ready to limbo.

"Don't bring our attention down on yourself Faustus." Greenstanley wheezed.

"Gods' forbid I draw the attention of a bunch of Fascist thugs Hilton. I lie awake at night shivering at the prospect of getting noticed by your bunch. Hilton" I said. Near death experiences always bring on a confidence that sensible people don't have. "Believe me Hilton, I'm shaking in my shoes. If you listen carefully you can hear my knees knocking with fear."

Greenstanley's deputy stepped up. There was a man bucking for promotion. Greenstanley would need eyes in the back of his head. Pitchforks can point in all sorts of directions.

"We are operating within the remit of The Law and The Lore Faustus. Walk away now." Morris said.

"The Lore ought to buy a dictionary Morris. The Lore is just an excuse for whims and bigotry. Right here, right now I'm the closest thing The Street has to Law. How many of your people have a little extra change in their pockets nowadays? Handed out by a man with shiny shoes?"

"We are beyond reproach Faustus." Morris protested. "We do not accept bribes."

Morris said it with the conviction of a fanatasist, but the faces of several of the Burghers twitched just enough to see who had a healthier relationship with the bank than mine.

I turned to face Morris and to his credit he didn't flinch.

"No one is beyond reproach Morris. Not even Hilton here." I turned back to Greenstanley. "Still beating your wife Hilton?" I said softly, but it drew an intake of breath from those nearest.

"Don't talk rubbish Faustus and step back." A small amount of pointed pressure was applied to my stomach.

"You first." I said reaching down and grabbing hold of somewhere he would rather I hadn't. In truth, I wished that I hadn't either. I'd never bleach my hand clean.

"Let me spell this out to you." I said, giving a little squeeze. He, obligingly, gave a little whimper.

"I'm human. He's human. You can thank one of the Gods for that. Worse than that, you'll have to justify to the Council killing me if you try to take him. Well someone will. You won't be able to on account of your being dead. And devoid of your wedding tackle. If you understand give a little whimper."

Squeeze. Appropriate little whimper.

"Good." I know it's wrong but I was sort of enjoying this. "Now. What is The Music of the Spheres?"

"What?" Greenstanley squeaked.

"The Music of The Spheres." I repeated. "Do you know what it is?"

Greenstanley nodded frantically. Maybe I'd increased pressure a little. Just a little.

"It's the music of Creation. The Music that started the world." Greenstanley managed.

"Good." I got nose to nose with Hilton. "Now who can reproduce it?"

"Gods and Senior Wizards." He squeaked.

I popped my lit cigarette into his trouser pocket. He squirmed a bit more.

"And Me." I said, smiling a little too widely to be fully sane.

My spare hand shot straight up into the air, with the arm following closely behind.

The crowd held its collective breath. Bar one voice.

"What? Where's the light show?" Said the voice who watched too much TV.

I gave a firm good crunch of Greenstanley's meat and two veg and he let rip a scream that ended the conversation.

In the background a dull thudding began, slowly growing to a strong beat. I let go of Greenstanley and he visibly sagged. I wiped my hand on his coat held my hand up and snapped my fingers.

Music began, a driving beat with guitars. It came from everywhere. The walls, pavement, windows. Every surface vibrated with the slow beat.

I turned to Pete.

"Get the gun cases." I said. "We're wabbit hunting."

Pete held up both hands. In each hand was a Dreadnought guitar case. Two big cases, capable of holding lots and lots of weapons. A lot of big guns.

A shocked look spread across the faces of The Burghers. They knew my reputation, and that included not using guns. Ever. Well, almost. They could see the cases and a little imagination allowed them to figure out roughly how many guns there would be in there. Lots. They backed away. The smarter amongst them covered their ears as the beat grew and the singing came into its own. Pete walked down the steps and stood next to me, passing me a case. I took it with ease, and may have accidentally caught Greenstanley with it as he was sobbing and squeaking on his knees. Behind him stood Morris, smiling slightly. He may even have winked at me.

We turned and walked off down the street, slow and easy to the sound of 'celestial music.' Well, 'Fat Boy Slim' doing 'Wonderful Night'. A classic to leave a murderous crowd behind.

As we walked through the crowd it parted to let us past. Then I saw it. On the head of one of the Burghers, I stopped in front of him and beckoned him closer and without control of his own legs he shuffled towards me. I held out my hand and he stared at it for a moment before placing his pitchfork in it. I dropped the fork and looked at the top of his head. His eyes turned up and he understood. Eventually. Reaching up with both hands he lifted his fedora from his head then passed it to me.

I nodded my thanks and spun it quickly in my fingers and dropped it onto the top of Pete's head. He adjusted it 'til its Angle was the same as mine, and kept on walking until we turned a corridor into an alleyway.

Then we ran like hell.

Chapter Forty Six: The Dick's Driver Drives…Dangerously…Deliberately.

"Did you just confront a crowd of forty six people?" Pete asked as we sat waiting for a taxi.

"Well, as there's snipers watching the back door the front seemed the best option." I gasped. Maybe I should cut down on the smokes.

"Are you some sort of Wizard?" he asked sucking breath in. Maybe he had acquired my lung capacity as well. Could be passive smoking I suppose.

"No." I said, sticking a smoke in and firing up. "I have the use of a ladder, some high quality speakers and a stereo. Good. Huh?"

"Then it was a trick?"

"Yeah." I replied taking another drag. "Although it probably wore off when the next track came on. David Bowie singing 'The Laughing Gnome.'"

"I hate that song." Said a passing gnome of the non-laughing variety.

"Sorry." I said. I thought about the look on the faces of the Burghers when the music came on, and imagined it when the track changed. "That cess-pit we're in. I may just have made it deeper."

"When you are drowning in cess, dog paddle and do not attempt to light a pipe." Pete said. "Peter used to tell me things like that. I do not know if it proves helpful."

"No." I said. "He used to make that stuff up you know."

Pete may have looked crest fallen, but Enid pulled up and I was too busy sticking the cases into the boot to notice or care.

As soon as we got in Pete lay straight down on the floor and closed his eyes. He did indeed learn quickly.

"Where to this time?" Enid asked. "But I do insist upon one or two things, firstly, no dogs, secondly no blood, brain matter or any other body parts not fully attached to the passenger, no becoming unwell in the back or next to the car and finally payment up front due to the possibility of you not being around to pay the fare later. No offence young man, but given your reputation I don't want to see you in the hospital or waiting room."

The funny thing about being dead is the ability to follow a sentence through without taking a breath.

I handed Enid a twenty as it was just a short trip. She kept her hand outstretched. I dropped in another twenty. The money disappeared. I was going to have problems explaining how I couldn't pay the rent this month.

I told Enid where we were heading.

"I know that industrial site." She said. They have lots of guards there, fences and a big metal gate to limit access."

I took the hint and handed her another twenty. That left me enough for a coffee and a packet of twenty when this was all over.

"Thank you. The gates won't be a problem then." she said, and we pulled away.

I got my eyes closed just in time.

About a minute later Enid spoke.

"You might want to open your eyes young man."

I did as the lady asked just as we hit the gates at about one hundred miles an hour.

I may have screamed a little.

The gates didn't so much burst open as shatter, My mind fell into two different states at that moment. One said that the shattering was probably due to the ghost presence of the car super-cooling the air around the gates just before impact so that the actual striking of the metal caused it to shatter rather than bend.

The other state went 'Ohmygodohmygodohmygodohmygodohmygod. I'mgonnadieI'mgonnadieI'mgonnadieI'mgonnadie.'

Once the gate was left behind us in little pieces, we encountered the guards. They stood out in front of the car and were quickly left in little pieces too.

"This is unlike you Enid." I squawked as we came to a shuddering halt.

"Some people came and wanted to buy the taxi office." Enid said getting out her knitting. "They were not very polite."

That seemed to bring a full stop to the conversation along with the click-clack of needles. I let the seatbelt go and prodded Pete from his prone position.

"Get the cases." I said. "We're here."

As we got out of the car things were very quiet. Apart from the ranks of close circuit cameras whirring on their pivots to keep track of us. I gave them a little wave.

No one waved back.

Chapter Forty Seven: The Dick Deliberatley Deceives

The industrial estate was blank and soul-less. White concrete buildings, one or two storied save the eight story one we were standing in front of that seemed whiter, blanker and more soul-less than the rest.

Call me a traditionalist, but I do think that if you go to a vampire lair it should have the decency to be an old ruined castle, or a ruined church at least. Maybe a few hundred bats flying about and an armadillo or two. It should not be an eight storey white building on an industrial estate. With a big glass entrance. No place to confront a villain.

We walked up into the vampires' functional building where the rent was cheaper than in town and had a large car park.

Just not the right ring to it at all.

Surprisingly the two big glass doors were unlocked and swung open for us as we approached. Sat behind the desk in the lobby was a security guard. I knew he was security because he was wearing a jumper that said 'SECURITY'. I'm a detective. I notice these things.

We walked up to the desk as the Security man put down his 'Woodworking Weekly' magazine and fixed on his smile.

"Can I help you gentlemen?" he asked.

He was big. Crew cut head and hair to match. A low forehead and single eye brow that was stretched across it. About six-nine, six-ten, and wide enough so that I'm not sure how he fitted inside his clothing let alone behind the desk. Muscle on the hoof. I glanced down at the desk and there was a script. How to answer every possible simple question. Someone had been very precise in what they wanted from this guy, even laminated the sheets so he wouldn't get a coffee stain on the paper.

"Hello" I said, going for polite. "Can I see your I.D please?"

"I.D?" he said.

"I.D." I said.

"I.D?" he said.

"I.D" I said. "The little card with your name on it."

"Oh. That." The Mountain reached into his pocket and came out with a small laminated card that revealed him to be 'Robert Simple. If ever a name was appropriate. The corner of the card had even been chewed in boredom.

"Ah. Mr Simple. We have the right man. We are your unemployment counselors."

"Unemployment?" Give him time and it would sink in. I momentarily missed the gay wit and repartee Richard had provided earlier in the day.

"That's right Robert. May I call you Robert, Bob?"

He scratched his head. A small avalanche of dandruff made drifts on his shoulders. He automatically dusted them off

"I suppose so." he was working the little grey cells. "But most people call me Nelly."

"Why Nelly? Nelly." I was actually curious.

"I dunno. So, have I done something wrong?"

"No. No. Far from it." I said putting a reassuring hand on his shoulder. "Did Mr Campbell not take you through this?"

"No."

"Well, I am not surprised." I shook my head in disappointment. "He is very busy with his Health and Safety audit after all. Between you and me," I said leaning a little closer, "I don't think he's up to the job."

And people say I don't plan in advance.

"I am sorry to tell you, Nelly, that your job has been terminated." I should hate this but I was doing the guy a favour.

Nelly's brow knit even further.

"Was it something I did?" Poor guy was worried.

"No, no, no. Your work has been impeccable. Unfortunately the company that owns the lease on the building is about to undergo radical closure, so it seems best to discontinue your contract so that you can leave with a positive reference before the company is unable to provide you one."

"What should I do?" Poor Nelly was close to tears.

I gave him my card.

"Go and see this chap in a couple of days and he should sort you out with some work, all nice legal and above board." Assuming that he wasn't dead, or worse.

A big smile spread across Nelly's face. Ah. He looked just as sweet as a nut.

"Really?" he said.

"Really really."

"Do I…would I need to hit anybody?" Poor lad was worried again. He would be really confused if he saw me again. I would have to pretend to be my identical twin brother…again.

"No. Something nice and easy."

"Could it be doing knitting? I love knitting. And woodwork." His hobbies lit his face up. "I like knitting more though."

I don't get too many bursts of inspiration. I'm much more of a plodder, but now I had one.

"Can you drive Nelly?" I asked.

"I got a license but no car." he was getting confused again.

I turned him around to the doors, where the top of Enid's car could just be seen.

"You see that car out there?" Nelly nodded. A slow process that needed quite some time to complete. "Well you go out there and introduce yourself to Enid. She's a friend of mine. Have a chat with her."

"Shouldn't I finish my shift?" Nelly asked.

"No." I said. "You go have a chat with Enid. I believe she's working on a cardigan at the minute. You could hold her wool."

Nelly's face lit up again.

"Great. Thanks sir." Nelly trotted towards the door then suddenly stopped. He turned around slowly. I heard Pete's hand tighten on the handle of the guitar case. "Is she working on seamless or sections?"

We both relaxed.

"You'd have to ask her. Go on now."

Nelly trotted out the doors and into a better life.

Pete tapped me on the shoulder.

"What happened to a good whack on the head, hiding him in a cupboard and locking the door?" he asked.

"I don't think there's a cupboard around here big enough to take Nelly."

Above us cameras whirred. The phone on Nelly's desk rang. Pete picked it up.

"Hello." he said. "Lunatic vampire zombies or us?" Kid was catching onto the lingo.

"I see. I see. I see." Pete gave a little laugh. "Actually I am not sure that what you suggest is physically possible, but we can only see." Pete gave a little nod of his head. "Well I do look forward to meeting you. Which floor?" Pete picked a pen from the table and wrote the number eight on Nelly's laminate. "Yes. I have that. Any message for Mr Faustus?" He started writing again. "Oh no. Now where would his parents get a gorilla from at this time of night? But I will pass on the gist of your message. Take care." Pete hung up the phone and looked at me. "Wrong number."

I started walking towards the lift. Pete trotted along behind me.

"I gather Lisper was not too happy then." I said.

"Somewhat."

"Nice banter." I said pressing the up button. But you could have done better on the name though."

"Oh, such as?" he asked as the lift arrived and we stepped in.

I pressed the button for the floor we wanted.

"How about 'Vampires under Threat'."

"Power crazed leeches requiring salt?"

"Psychotic blood drinkers awaiting staking?"

"Try 'Antisocial recidivist sociopathic egomaniacs' herald omnipotent liberation, successful."

Pete looked confused. "I don't get it." he said.

"It's an acronym." I said.

"Ah." He nodded his head, "Accurate and pretentious at the same time." Pete leaned the guitar cases against the wall, giving them a little pat.

The lift shuddered to a halt a few moments later.

As the lift doors opened to the eighth floor shotgun fire really destroyed the cases.

"And that's why we got off on the seventh floor." I said to Pete.

"I had wondered how we were going to get through unmolested." He replied as we reached the top of the service stairs at the eighth floor.

"Now Darling." I said.

Several thousand miles away Mammasayra pressed a couple of keys at her station, activating the wall Tazers in floor eight's walls. On floor eight, covers popped off and little metal prongs shot out, either imbedding in flesh or the floor. Another button was pressed and the fire sprinklers came on drenching the hall and its occupants and nice wet water dropped down. The wires were kind enough to transmit several hundred volts of electricity. The water that had sprayed anyone shooting into the lift (courtesy of two guitar cases filled with plastic bottles of water) aided the journey of the electricity right into the subjects of Doctor Baldy's experiments.

There were several big splattering noises from the hallway. I was right about the electricity working then.

I slowly edged the service door open and saw that the hallway was a mess of splattered bodies. The clothing they wore had contained most of the viscera, but a certain amount of brain matter meant that they would have to pay a fortune to re-decorate.

We stepped out into the hallway and walked down towards the fire doors at the end.

"Any idea how many were...dealt with?" Pete asked.

"Not enough." I said, passing through the fire doors and coming face to face with eight shotgun barrels and Cadell applauding.

"Very good Faustus." Cadell said. "Very good. I do not know how you did it, but I am truly impressed."

I took out a smoke and did what I do.

I took in the faces of Cadell's goons. They were all vacant and dead. Possibly because we'd killed some of them in a café. Great. Zombie Vampire Goons.

"Thanks Cadell, but don't go hugging and kissing me yet. People will talk."

Cadell waved his arms and the guns were all lowered.

"People are already talking Faustus." Cadell said, grinning ear to ear. "You simply refuse to die. God knows I have tried, but you are possibly the luckiest man I know."

"Must be the rabbit's feet. I keep four on me in case one fails."

"I hope you removed the rest of the rabbit first." Cadell said.

"Actually that seems particularly cruel." Pete said. "Not nice at all."

"And you brought the Whitlow with you. How nice. Just what we wanted." Cadell clapped his hands and the guards all stood to attention.

"If I give them a dog biscuit each will they do tricks?" I asked

"Oh yes."

Cadell snapped his fingers and a cord snaked around my throat, pulling tight. Immediately I felt my breathing restricted and my face began to redden. I managed a glance at Pete who was also wearing this season's look, of a vampire with a garrotte.

"Nithe to thee you again Fauthtuth."

I slowly took a limited drag on the smoke.

"Glad you're here Lisper. The old gang wouldn't be the same without you." I exhaled as best I could.

"Careful not to kill them." Cadell said, smiling. "I believe there are plans for both." Cadell nodded his head and two goons lowered their shotguns to the floor and came forward. Neither of us struggled as a very proficient frisk was carried out, although possibly too much attention was given to the trouser region. Still at least they didn't dig out the rubber gloves.

A small shove in my neck indicated that I should move forward. I did so and Pete followed suit. Cadell walked down the corridor until we came to an anonymous door with a brass sign screwed onto it announcing it to be 'The Board Room'. Cadell turned to us smiling.

"Now you two are going to behave when we get in there I hope."

"Hell no." I said. "I'm going to burn your playhouse down."

"And I'll pass him the matches." Pete said.

Cadell smiled. He tousled my hair. A uniquely unpleasant experience for a man of my age.

"You two are such little scamps." he said. "Even captured and under threat of…"

I raised a hand and shook my head. Not a clever thing to do with a garrotte about your neck.

"Wait a minute." I said. "you have some of that wrong."

Simultaneously Pete and I drove our heads back, making contact with the softer parts of the face on the heads behind. There was the satisfying crunch Lisper's nose makes when you break it…again, followed by the low pitched scream when his teeth are broken…again.

One thing this rejuvenation serum has got working for it is the ability to hurt Lisper again and again and again. He just bounces back for more. The one thing the scum bucket has in his favour.

The hands holding the garrottes let go and turning around a second head butt drove all thoughts from the two vampires' heads apart from the universe encompassing pain as two knees were brought to two groins.

Get down and boogie.

Well, we would have, but we were cooler than that. We straightened our jackets, adjusted our hats and turned Cheshire cat smiles towards Cadell.

"Shall we go in?" I said.

Slowly Cadell shook his head.

"As entertaining as I find your antics Faustus, it would not be good to the morale of my men, and we understand that I use the term loosely, were I to let that little assault go unanswered. You understand?"

"Your men are all dead Cadell." I said.

"Mere technicalities." Cadell said, beckoning his goons closer.

I raised my hands in resignation. I shot Pete a look and he did the same.

"What would you say the protocol is in these circumstances Faustus?" Pete asked.

I looked at the Vampire Zombie crew getting ready to dish out some retribution. Briefly I saw the face of Angel Mickey flash across all of their faces.

"We take a kicking Kid. We take a kicking." I replied. "Legs open or closed?"

Ouch!

On the plus side, Cadell's little band could not give out a kicking. Too uncoordinated and not enough power. Half the time they were kicking their own legs. About a quarter hitting the floor.

So we each took a quarter kicking, slowly helped each other to our feet and dusted off. I reached down, picked up my hat and put it on. One of the Vampires picked up Pete's and popped it on his own head, smiling.

"That's my hat." Pete said.

"Tho?" said the Vamp. It seems they all had some of that 'special' work done on them.

"I would like it back please." Pete tried politely.

"Thuck…"

One blow shattered his jaw, sent the hat flying into the air, where Pete caught it and dropped it onto his head, adjusting the Angle to match mine. He turned to Cadell.

"So shall we go in Mr Cadell, or will there be some more pointless, and in my case, ineffective violence?" Damn. Pete was being 'cool'.

Cadell's face was totally passive as he looked at Pete, deciding what he would do next, then he broke into a grin and laughed. He took a deep bow and swept a hand towards the doors.

"Gentlemen," he said still laughing, "after you."

Chapter Forty Eight: The Dick Deduces, Destroying Delusions,Dancing with Danger and Demolishing... Oh Sod it...He makes one shit load of a mess.

As we walked through the doors a couple of sniffs confirmed what I suspected.

"Hello Mel. Hello Belfast." I said, but my heart really wasn't in the casual manner I had in my voice.

Mel was sat behind a long oak desk while Belfast lounged against the left hand wall, next to the door of the adjoining office. Mel stood up as we walked in.

"Actually Faustus..." she began

"Actually 'Mel', I am addressing The Lady Simone Marie Mellasaundre Duche de Malsaunte, founder and architect of The Streets system, while the scruffy baggage in the corner calls himself 'Pythorax of The Seven Wands'. Real name Kelvin Taylor. Warlock for Hire. In the nineteen thirty's he was even quite popular in the war effort. For the Nazis."

"Hey there Big Man." Belfast said, grinning too wide for my liking. "Youse takes the work you can get."

"I can go on at great length about who you both are and what you have done." I went on. "But I won't. I just wish people would remember I'm a detective, and quite clever."

"Not so clever that you didn't walk in here Faustus." Mel said. "Oh relax. No one's going to kill you."

"Not yet." Cadell said, tapping me on the shoulder as he walked past to sit on the edge of Mel's desk.

I took out a packet of smokes.

"Anyone mind?" I asked

"Well actually I do." Cadell said.

"Shame we're not on a date then." I said popping one into my mouth. "Light me." I said and in a fraction of a second a naked flame appeared in Pete's hand. Admittedly it was coming from a cigarette lighter, but near enough.

Cadell applauded again. It was getting on my nerves.

"Very good." He said. "You have taught him tricks. But will he do this one." He pointed at one of his goons. "Out the window."

The vampire walked over to a large window that gave a panoramic view of the estate, opened it and jumped out. After a moment or two there was a splatter-crunch noise.

Cadell closed the window.

I nodded slowly.

"Nice trick." I said. "Pointless, but nice. But can you do this one?"

I reached under my jacket, around the back and pulled out a .45 semi-automatic pistol. There was an understandable and underrated pregnant pause in the room.

I was mid-wife and delivered the sprog by throwing the gun onto Mel's desk.

I know her name's Simone Marie Mellasaundre Duche de Malsaunte, but she'd been Mel to me for over two years. I take time to get used to changes.

Who she was had been easy to figure out. When people change their name, they often keep some of the old one.

"I took it from one of the gentlemen who let loose the kicking. They may do what you tell them, but they ain't that clever." I said.

"Are you two finished with this macho bullshit posturing?" Mel asked. She was right. But it was just a thing you have to do. She should have got with the genre.

"Why don't you two have a seat?" Mel asked, "But do try not to bleed on the upholstery. It is rather old."

Mel gestured to two armchairs in front of her desk. We walked over and sat down. Pure spite caused Pete to draw the back of his hand on his split bottom lip and wipe it on the arm rest.

"My apologies." Pete said. "After you had been so kind to me as well. Would you like me to pay for the dry cleaning?"

Cadell moved to stand next to Mel. Belfast rolled himself a cigarette. Lisper moved to stand behind Cadell. I took a lungful.

"You may be wondering why I let you come in, Faustus." Mel said. I did make a mental note that the statement reduced Cadell and Belfast to the status of hired help. I hoped their fragile little egos could handle it.

"Not really." I said. "You need me for something, or I would be dead by now. Something tells me you didn't stop the attempts because you have any affection for me."

It was quite crushing when she nodded.

"And you would also have taken your best shot at me." Pete said. I really hoped he didn't believe this 'I am invulnerable' stuff he was coming out with. That could be a problem.

"You have been buying up great chunks of The Streets all over the world for the last few years." I continued. "Probably because you experienced a serious shrinkage in your own power base in the community since The Second World War. Really should have sided with the winning side."

"One could argue that I did, in the long term." Mel said. I also filed away that Mel was now speaking a lot more precisely and educated, devoid of affection and focused on the job in hand. Obviously everything I had read and heard of The Lady Simone was true.

We were in such trouble.

"That is why you are here Faustus." she said as a cup of coffee materialized on my right. "I wish to continue my good fortune and indeed powerbase by buying Peter's shop and all of his other properties, totaling about one half of those I do not already own. As it is well known how fond he was of you, he will have left you those in his will. I am therefore offering to make you very rich indeed."

Cue the smile of the liar. Ah. There it was.

"How rich?" Well, you have to ask.

In reply Mel did that thing I hate. She picked up a pen and a slip of paper from her desk, wrote a number on it and slid it across to me. I picked it up and looked at it. It was a big number. A very big number. Certainly more zero's in it than I am used to seeing. I slid it back.

"That's no use." I said.

"Why?" Mel asked. She was very good. No hint of frustration or annoyance in her voice.

"It's just a slip of paper with some numbers on it." I replied. "Rich to me is lots and lots of big folding notes. Plus coins. Just for parking change."

I thought for a second. "Also I would need a big bag to put it in. Oh and it would need to be double the amount, so two bags. Got an ash tray?"

"It is a no smoking building." Mel said.

"Fair enough." I dropped my stub to the floor and ground it out with my shoe. I took out another. Pete lit me while never taking his eyes off Cadell or Lisper.

"So you want a big bag of cash for all of Peter's properties." Mel said. There was a little confusion in her voice. "It's as simple as that?"

"Not quite. I want two big bags of cash. And don't say you don't have it, because it's all in your safe in the next room."

"I won't ask how you know because I get the feeling you are enjoying this."

"Time of my life." I said. "Even if you ignore the joy of getting beaten up, shot at and attacked by killer clones, I got to see my best friends killed, maimed and tortured to death. My office is trashed, I've had to get a lot more nasty than I'm used to and I have not seen a decent coffee in over an hour. And I have a contract out on me. You know how to show a man a good time Mel.."

Mel sat back in her chair and stippled her fingers.

"It is the Catholics who put the contract out on you." she said. "Not me."

"No." I leaned forward. "You faked it so the Catholics would get the blame. After all I did take out one of their short eyes last year, and they don't forgive or forget. Nice work on that by the way."

"Thank'th." Lisper said. "Firtht nithe thing you ever thaid."

Now that took me back a lot. I had him down as just a thug. Still, skilled workforce or not, he's going down.

"Now onto the subject of my cash." I said.

"Are you seriously going to sell?" Mel asked. "I don't have to blackmail you or resort to physical violence?"

Lisper looked so disappointed. Ahh. Shame.

"I'm getting tired of being shot at." I replied. "Time to retire. I've been waiting for a big payout for years." I smiled and took a bow. "Hello big payout."

Mel clicked her fingers and nodded to the door. Two of the Vampires walked over to the door to the next room, opened it and went in. The door closed behind them.

"Five minutes." Cadell said.

"Neat trick Cadell. So much less terminal." I tapped a little ash onto Mel's desk. "I suppose you would like me to sign some forms?"

"You read my mind." Cadell walked over to the filing cabinets and took out a folder. He placed it in front of me and placed a pen next to it.

"Just sign where the little crosses are." he said, stepping out of my reach as I picked up the pen. I looked up at him.

"What did you think I'd do Cadell?" I said. "Stab you in the throat with your pen?"

I read on through the folder. I hadn't realized how many properties Peter had owned. It came to about a sixth of the whole town, with some rural properties as well. I twiddled the pen in one hand and my smoke in another. I felt an arm rest upon my smoking arm.

"You are not seriously going to sell. Are you?" Pete asked. He looked very worried.

"Two big bags of cash for some crumbling old buildings?" I said. "In a second I'd sell."

"What would Peter have said?"

"He would have said, 'Give me more money'". I turned to face Pete. "Greed probably got him killed. Have you no idea about him?"

"He was my…father." Pete said, tears welling up in his eyes.

"Now, listen Kid." I began, allowing the anger to rise. "He was a nasty old bastard. He had done things in the past that would have made you run for the hills if you knew. You think he was all nice and good because he took you in? Please! He saw the commercial potential in you from the start. A walking abortion. If he could have sold you he would. He got himself killed because he wanted to haggle over the price. Me? I have enough sense to take what I can get and run like hell. There's a beach and a packet of cigs with my name on it. You're just my errand boy."

The two Vampires emerged from the next room. Each was carrying a very large shoulder bag. Big enough to fit a body in.

Well, you might have to fold it a little.

"Hello payday." I said, dropping my smoke to the ground. "Now the paperwork. I turned back to the folder and began to sign. Pete stood up.

"And you pretend to be such a moral man," he said, "with all your rules of who you work for and what you will do. And to think I decided to side with you. I would have been better to side with The Fae."

"Shut your mouth Kid and take the bags to the car. Then get back here." I snapped hard at him. He stepped back. "Put your morals to one side and you get a decent cut. That should let you and the mutt live comfortable for the rest of your life. Now go."

Cadell stepped in front of the door.

"I don't think anyone will be going yet." he said. I stood up and turned to him.

"Listen Cadell, I want out of here fast when it's done, so money, car, sign and gone. Understand."

Cadell glanced at Mel, then stepped out of the way. Pete picked up the bags and walked out of the office, casting back a look that combined disapproval, anger, despair, betrayal, or possibly constipation.

"Use the stairs." I shouted after him. "You could use the exercise."

I turned back to the desk sat down and began to sign papers.

"So where do you fit into all of this Belfast?" I asked. "Funding the cause?"

"No." Belfast said, pushing himself from the wall. People relaxed as the rest of Cadell's vampire crew slipped out of the room. "Just paying my way and securing my place in the order of things."

"Taking over the world, you three?" I asked.

"Nothing so melodramatic Faustus." Mel replied. "Simply exercising good business principles and creating a monopoly of power. Eradicate the competition"

"So you buy up the land and houses, rent them back to people at a low rate, everything goes on the same, but you have a ready bunch of supporters should you need them? Even if you have to threaten them with eviction to get your way. And in the process net all the profits from thieving, drugs and women too?"

"Oh too right." Belfast said. "An we all end up stinkin' bloody rich in the process Big Man. You too."

"Just don't count on my support." I said. "I'll be on a beach with an iced coffee and a hot lady." I looked up at Mel. "No blondes though. I have bad luck with blondes"

"You wound me Faustus." She said. Shame she was still smiling.

"You'll live." I said. "After a fashion."

Belfast walked towards me and sat on the desk next to me. He still had the smell of shit on him. Nice.

"I really don't understand this antagonism Big Man." he said. "Youse in a perfect position to make a lot more money than that. Business is business after all. Look at me." Why he felt the need to point to himself with both hands I don't know. "I invest with m'Lady here an next thing you know I'm a millionaire."

"Why the shop then?" I asked.

"Oh, it's amazing what people will tell you while they's waitin' for a bite to eat. Youse get to hear all about their troubles. Marital problems, trouble with kids, trouble at work and the debts they get themselves into. Especially the debts. All this info…"

"Lets you know who to target." I finished. "The most vulnerable."

"Too right." He slid the cigarette into his mouth and the end burst into flames. Cheap parlour trick. "After all we's doing them a favour. Buys up their houses, pays their debts, gives them a nice little rent theys can manage." Belfast gave a tobacco stained grin that made me think about giving up smoking. "Then inna year or so, move's 'em out whilst we's rebuild."

"After a nice big tower are you Belfast?" Why wizards like towers I have no idea. It's a Tolkien thing.

"I'm more of a mansion kinda guy." He stood up and strolled behind Mel, making himself part of her power play. He wouldn't last long.

"That why you set up the coffee shop Mel? To gather information?"

"Partly." she said. "That and to integrate myself into the community." Good old Mel. Gives you a decent cuppa, bit of credit on prices here and there. Sad life, but she's doing well for herself now. If only the ants knew. Do you know, even Peter didn't recognize me until I turned up at that dirty little shop with my offer. Of course when he did it was time for him to leave this realm. Sorry, but that's modern business. After all, we had so much dirt on each other going back over the years. I couldn't have people knowing. Not yet anyway."

"Everything a lie." I made the statement because I was curious. I had invested two years of lust in this woman. "Your violent boyfriend. I assume you got Shadwell to take care of him. Looking after a friend. Coming onto me. Heavy duty glamour even I couldn't see through. All to get info on Peter, and in turn Pete. Shame I was too nervous to ask you out earlier."

"Yes." She said matter of factly. "I had to get close enough to find out who was most usable. You were a problem though. It seems that even though you knew so many women, you wouldn't get up the nerve to ask me out. So I had to push things a little."

"You came to me." I said. "You must have got a shock when you saw Pete walk in. He could have recognized you. I assume you were there when they tested and experimented on him?"

"True." She said taking out a cigarette and holder from a desk drawer. If I had known she'd smoked I wouldn't have brushed my teeth so much. "That was quite fun, all those needles and scalpels, and he would have proven quite profitable. Then he went and escaped."

"Has no one heard of the dangers of passive smoking?" Cadell asked, opening a window. Some standards then.

"It's all about business and money sweetie." Mel took out a jelled lighter and lit up. "Even my little clones are business. Once perfected they will be an invincible army. Very sellable commodities, and useful to have around. We have a lot to thank your little friend for."

I finished signing the last document and closed the folder. I rested my arms on it while I spun Cadell's pen in my hand.

"Nice story." I said. "It does bring me onto my next offer."

"You have something else to sell?" Mel asked. Her voice and face was calm, but her eyes were hungry. "Your little friend perhaps?"

"Of course." I smiled back. "He is the base line from which all the rest came from. Without him you don't get any more little dogs- bodies. And I figured all that out on my little lonesome. He is vital to your plans. Or is that an understatement?"

414

"True enough." Belfast said. "Just like a spell, without the basic conjuration youse can't do shit."

"Nicely put." I said. "But there are conditions."

"Beyond the money I take it." There was that smile on her face again. The one that said 'I've won'.

"You don't kill him." I leaned closer. "You can do whatever you want to him, experiment, probe, even shove a live snake up his bum for all I care, but you don't kill him."

"I could do that dead easy." Belfast said leaning against the window. "Course getting it out's more difficult."

Mel sat for a few moments pretending to think. She had already decided, she was just playing for the crowd.

"Agreed." she said. "Will a cheque do? You seem to have cleared me out of walking about money."

"Secondly, I get to walk out of here with the money, and alive." It didn't take a lot to figure that as soon as I left the office I'd be jumped and all that lovely money gone. I would not have come off well.

"Agreed." Mel said. That's it lover. Show what you meant to do. "So what's the price for him?"

"One of these three guys." I said taking out another smoke and using the quiet pause to light up in.

"Are you serious Faustus?" Mel asked. "They are all very important to my organization."

For all her words Mel was calculating which of the three would be most easily replaced. Belfast was looking relaxed. Lisper looked worried while Cadell was expressionless, but he had dropped his left shoulder just a fraction of an inch and pulled it back to allow his jacket to hang open a little. He rubbed his chin with his right hand, putting that hand nearer the gun in its shoulder holster. He was the most professional of the three, I'd give him that.

"Deadly serious." I said. "We need a fall guy for the killings that have happened. Someone to give to the law."

"I've bought the law." she said. "That won't be too much of a problem."

"You can buy a couple here and there, but not them all." I said. "Now, Peter's body's gone, but Jo-Jo Mar was killed by your stooge Kat. You used her well. Must have had something good on her, after all she let your men into the Fae's sanctuary. So I'd say whoever killed Kat would do nicely."

"Do you know what we had on her? You. A simple threat to kill you and she did whatever we wanted. Little puppet on a string. So. A fall guy. Who do you think it should be then?" Mel said, a small smile on her lips. Humouring me.

"Well, while Kat opened the doors and provided the invite you needed, there were still Wards to deal with. Belfast dealt with them. The centaur in the hallway, well. I know how much it would have taken to take him down. That would have been Cadell. Probably a shotgun with an iron load in the rounds. That leaves Kat. Lisper killed her. It was such a vicious job, so messy, only a bloody crazed bloodsucker would do that. Very hands on. Very nasty. What did you do Lisper? Wait till her back was turned? If you'd faced her head on, she would have done much worse to you."

I took a deep drag and waited. After a couple of heartbeats Lisper filled the silence. No way I was going to let him live after what he did to Kat. Right and wrong would have to take a back seat to my law…and survival.

"Yeth." he sprayed. Those teeth really got in the way. "Thee made fun of the way I talk. Bethides, who'd mith another cheap thlut?"

I slid the papers on the desk to my right.

"Me." I said, fixing his eyes to mine. "For the rest of my life."

Cadell reached down for the papers with his left hand and I drove the point of his pen straight through it. He didn't scream or shout, simply reached for his gun with his right. My hand met his on the shoulder holster. My finger reached the trigger and pulled it once. The bullet slithered down the side of his body armour and shot him in the hip. His leg gave way as I stepped behind him and hauled him upright by the throat.

"Mind if I borrow this?" I asked Cadell, as I drew his gun from its holster.

"Feel free." he said, his leg sagging. He was exaggerating the injury. I didn't fall for it and hit him in the ear with the but of the gun.

"Behave." I said.

Belfast's shotgun was in his hand, pointed at us, but unsure whether to fire and risk hitting Cadell.

"You too Belfast." I said. If you try to fire you'll have to lower your shield first and I'll get you, besides you had best look at the end of your gun first."

Belfast risked a glance down and saw that the end of his shotgun had been squeezed shut. A smile spread across Belfast's face.

"Neat trick that Faustus." He said. "Don't suppose you'd like to tell me how youse did it?"

"Don't suppose I would. Maybe I'm a wizard." I said. "Now drop your shield or I'll bounce one off the wall behind you."

"Well youse could try, but it's a window. Don't think that would work."

I squeezed the trigger and the bullet hit the glass causing fractures to spread out, but the window stayed mostly intact.

I did have the satisfaction of seeing Belfast jump though.

"Jeez Faustus." Belfast shouted then turned and looked at the squashed bullet lodged in the glass. He gave a little laugh. "Bullet proof glass big man. Works. It works."

On a roof outside the building, looking up was a man wearing full evening dress, with an opera cloak. Drawing back the string on a very big bow, with a very big arrow notched. Using my bullet break to sight on while sucking a sherbet lemon.

"Faustus." Mel shouted at me. "That was my window."

"I'll be round tomorrow to fix it." I said, swinging the gun back towards Lisper. "Ah-ah" I said as he began to reach for the gun in his waist band.

"Faustus. No." Mel shouted, slamming her hands onto the desk. "He is like a son to me."

"Adopt." I said and shot Lisper in the throat.

The bullet slammed straight through Lisper's Adams apple and burst out the back of his neck, taking chunks of his spinal column with it. A second bullet in his chest stopped Mel from going to him.

"Naughty." I said, and Mel moved back to her chair and sat down. "Hands on the desk." I said, and she promptly followed my call.

"Hell on wheels." Cadell said, drawing a knife from a leg sheath and ramming it into my trouser leg. It skittered off the chain mail and he dropped it.

"Get some rest." I said tightening my arm around Cadell's throat until he started twitching and passed out. I pushed him face down onto the floor, took off my hat with my left hand and tore the inner free, taking out some plasti-cuffs and tying him up. I kept the gun on Mel the whole time. We didn't bother speaking. Cadell was just coming to when I finished. I kicked him in the head. More for fun than anything.

I stood up, gun pointed squarely between Mel's eyes. She turned a little towards Belfast.

"Kill him slowly." Mel said. "Turn him inside out."

"Sorry Big Man." Belfast said. "But you did start this."

I put another bullet into the glass behind Belfast. This time he didn't jump.

"Bullet proof. Sees." Belfast said, raising his hands. "This'll hurt."

I only said two words. They should have checked for a wire.

"Open window." I said

Far across the seas Mammasayra pressed a little button.

The window shot open on a motorized hinge, showing Belfast's back to the world.

The arrow burst through the open window and lodged in Belfast's back. The second arrow went straight through the body and came out of his chest.

The cord on the second arrow went tight and four large barbs snapped out of the arrow head. The barbs stopped it being pulled back through. Then one tug and Belfast was gone, leaving only the wind behind. Slowly Mammasayra pressed some more buttons, thousands of miles away and closed the window.

If Belfast lived, maybe he'd become another Renfield to brush up the icing sugar.

One thing they teach aristocracy in the old country is archery. And the Count was good.

Good old Vlad.

"Now me? Is it Faustus?" Mel asked. She was quite calm considering everything.

"Not yet." I said. "Have a seat, and don't pretend you are worried about Lisper there. We both know he'll be up on his feet soon enough. He was the only one the serum worked on?"

Mel sat down, hands on table and looking at Lisper.

"Yes." she said. "Poor Andrushka. Such a beautiful boy. My sweet boy."

"He was a psycho." I snapped. "First time I met him he was about to feed on a three year old girl."

"You broke his teeth, face, arms, legs and hands. He begged me to kill him at one point. That's when I decided to kill you instead." Mel was talking matter of factly. "You made the trip here part of the plan all along. Now what Faustus? Do you wait until he comes back and then kill us both. How long can you keep that up?"

"You have goons in the building Mel." I said sitting down, but keeping the gun on her. "They should have heard those shots. Why don't we just sit and wait? See what happens."

"What is it you want Faustus? Revenge. You can kill us both again and again, but one day I'll get to you and treat you in ways you can't believe."

"Please don't include me in the killing Faustus." Cadell said. From the corner of my eye I could see Cadell had got out of the cuffs and was sitting up against the wall, pressing both hands onto his bleeding hip.

"By the window Cadell." I said.

"No more arrows I hope." Cadell said, shuffling over.

"No." I said. "A friend of Peter's. Just wanted a little payback."

Cadell looked out of the window and pulled a face.

"That's not pretty." he said. "And all of those people. Are they with you too?"

"Any carrying flaming torches or pitchforks?" I asked.

"Not that I can see. Got a bandage?" he asked.

"Not on me." I said. "Sounds like The Fae have arrived."

Mel stood up and walked to the window. She looked worried when she turned back to me.

"So you decided to side with that bitch did you? She's worse than I am and that's saying a lot."

I took out a smoke and lit up.

"Not with me. I suspect they were waiting for your little house to come tumbling down. Don't worry yet. They can't come in unless you invite them. Rule of propriety mean a lot to them. Why did you go against them Mel? You could have bought the whole world up and they wouldn't have cared so long as they were entertained. Instead you started a war with them."

"They are scum Faustus. All they care about is being 'entertained', and that Bitch has spent too many decades around humans that she doesn't even know who she is any more, let alone what." Small dribbles of saliva were starting to form on the corners of her mouth. And to think I fancied her. Mad as a box of Frogs.

On speed.

Lot of frogs.

Small box.

Very, very mad.

"I wanted them gone Faustus, from my towns my cities, my property. They were like wasps in the attic, always getting into things and even if you swat one or two they keep coming back. They need to be eradicated. Poisoned off. Destroy the nest and get rid of that bitch of a queen before she lets any more through. I wanted that Church and she wouldn't give it to me. I wanted the Tree and she wouldn't part with it. Bitch deserves to fucking die in it."

Wild guess. She didn't like Ti.

"You have a foul mouth on you Mel." I said

"You fucking cunt." she snarled.

Mel threw the ashtray at me. I moved not an inch, but caught it with my free hand and put it on the desk in front of me. I tapped a little ash into it.

"And you." Mel rounded on Cadell. "You took the contract off him as soon as I'd put it on. Brkzth kdlmmthrth…" Mel lapsed into the old tongue and raved at him. Cadell looked up at me.

"I don't understand a word of this but I suspect there are some very bad words in there." he said.

"Your right." I said as Mel suggested I did something that was physically impossible and very painful.

"Why did you take the contract off me?" I asked. I was curious.

"Survival." Cadell said. "Plus she told me what her plans were. They included a descent onto a primary school. She talked very matter of factly about killing children. Even I knew she had to be stopped. As I hadn't managed to kill you, I guessed that you at least stood a chance. I'm a lot of things Faustus. I run drugs, women, guns, sell my 'expertise', but I don't touch children."

I looked at him. He meant it.

"Even guys like us have to have standards." I said.

"Even guys like us." Cadell said. "I am sorry about the old man."

"Best not go there." I raised my voice a little as Mel's raving was getting noisy.

"We should." Cadell said. "Whether I live or die tonight, I want you to know I was too late to stop Lisper and the Irishman. They got, carried away."

"But you still killed him and left him for me to find." I said. Surprisingly I wasn't angry. I was saving it till later.

"That's right. I killed him. He wouldn't have lived and was in too much pain. Best thing I could do for him was kill him. I quite liked him."

I sat for a moment, putting the pieces together.

"Got your back up piece Cadell?" I asked.

"Of course."

"Go. You get a head start. I'll find you later."

"I almost look forward to it." Cadell struggled to get to his feet. "Any chance of you helping me up?"

I surprised myself by standing up and walking over to him. I held out a hand. He took it and pulled himself up. He stood face to face with me for a moment.

"Take care E.M. Faustus." he said and limped out of the door, closing it behind him. It wasn't the way I had thought things would go but you can't have everything.

Mel had got some of her composure back and was seated again.

"So you have it all worked out then? Now you just sweep up the mess." she said.

"Smoke?" I asked, rolling one towards her. She picked it up and lit it without bothering with a thank you. I lit another from the remains of the last.

"You wanted land, you wanted an army. You wanted revenge. You wanted control. You wanted things back the way they were. The old system where the lord of the manor, castle or whatever, says something happens and it does. You're insane, so it's pointless trying to guess your motives, but you've hurt too many people to get away with it."

"I 'get away' with anything I want, Dick." Mel smiled. "I am The Lady Simone Marie Mellasaundre Duche de Malsaunte, and I can do what I want when I want. I built these streets, made it all happen. Now it bores me and I want to start again with a new idea. My people will come to know Us again. I will be their God, and they will pay homage to me. My people, mine, answerable only to Us, honouring only Us, with slaves to follow Our will."

Very, very small box and an infinite number of frogs.

I looked at Mel. She looked older, manic and barely in control. Dried spittle on her chin had a faint pink tinge to it, which is more than her face. As she looked at me, she looked hungry.

"If you're that desperate to eat there's always Lisper." I said.

Without missing a beat Mel fell onto Lisper's body. He did manage a limp 'No' as she used her nails to tear a hole in his neck. She fastened her lips to the hole and sucked.

When you watch a horror movie, the director either tries to create a gore fest when vampires feed or lapses into old fashioned erotica. In this case it was like listening to someone trying to unblock a drain with a plunger.

Mel wasn't even drinking, she was sucking in mouthfuls of blood and swallowing whole. He'd not be in a very good mood when he came back.

Then things changed. With a final swallow Mel's body relaxed. Slowly she turned on me, hatred and fire burning in her eyes. I wondered if one bullet would stop her. Then I got lucky.

The door to the office opened and in walked two of Mel's goons. Between them they dragged a limp body. Tell-tale red stains soaked the body's hair and shirt. Pete.

Oh Goody. A reunion.

"How are you feeling?" I asked.

"Fine. Thanks for asking." said Sid.

"Oh, not too bad." The Other Sid said.

"Tired." Pete said. "Can I get up from this ridiculous pose?"

Mel glared at the group.

"You two." she screamed. "Tear that thing apart. Hold Faustus still and make him watch."

One Vampire head turned to her.

"I don't think that would be a very nice thing to do at all." Sid said.

Mel almost ran around the desk. I took a step back and pointed the gun at her head.

"I don't think you were introduced." I said. "This is Sid, and his brother. The Other Sid. Pete you know and if you look behind you, you won't see one of your friends."

"Hello Mel." Shadwell said.

All credit to her, she did try to bring him in on her side.

"Shadda's". She said, turning around and grinning. "I'm so glad you're here. You won't believe what Faustus did to me."

A breeze from a shadow stroked her hair.

"Say nothing Mel." Shadwell said. "I've been here since you first walked into the office. I heard more than Faustus did. Who do you think blocked the Irishman's gun?"

Mel did keep trying. Without a beat she turned and ran towards the window, planning a leap for freedom. Shadwell was a lot faster and blocked her path. The Window went dark and he threw her back onto the floor.

"You don't understand." She said.

"You still have blood on your chin." Shadwell said.

Mel got to her feet and turned to face me.

"So you are the clever one Faustus. A big medal and reach around and give yourself a big pat on the back. Good for you. So kill me. Get it over with, put a bullet in my head, go home and have a nice sleep because it will be your last. Even if you burn me and scatter the ash I'll come back for you, for all of you. I will destroy your lives, kill everyone you love and leave you broken. The last thing that you will see is my face as, old and broken, I watch the life slip away from you. You'll be old and broken and dry, and I will be as strong and young and beautiful as I am now. Fuck you all."

With that she walked back to her chair and threw herself into it.

I turned to Pete.

"O.K. What if we kill her?"

"Well morally it is a mortal sin to take a life. On the other hand there are circumstances under which it is necessary to take a life in order to prevent suffering of oneself or others. Then…"

"Pete."

"…there are also the legal implications to be considered as…"

"Pete."

"…..most of the major religions…"

"Pete. Look at her."

"You shoot her in the head and I'll dismember the body."

There was another one of those significant pauses. Everyone was waiting for me to do something. I raised the gun and took the Weaver stance. After all no-one wants to miss an important shot.

I was just a tad annoyed.

Every detective, good or bad, wants the disclosure. That bit at the end of the case where you get to show how clever you are and how you worked it all out.

And I had.

Mel was barking mad, but so far gone it was almost extreme sanity.

She had what we all get. A fit of nostalgia. While the rest of us go out and buy the music we used to listen to, contact friends we haven't seen in years or dig out clothes we haven't worn in years, Mel had decided to reshape The Streets into the old feudal kingdom she used to rule.

That meant she had to remove the new and get a fresh set of indentured serfs. A new army of thugs. More money than you could shake a stick at. She had to build herself a power base. So she decided to take her pet project, The Streets, and shape it into what she wanted.

She got the Serfs by becoming peoples' landlord. She got the money from the rent of millions of homes. The army was tougher.

She had managed to gain access to The Fae lands and sent a brilliant geneticist to get his hands on the poisonous membrane that keeps The Tree's victims alive while digesting them. The equally mental geneticist was able to take cells from The Tree's membrane and shape it into a weapon.

He had used Angel and Daemon cells to produce an embryo. That cell he managed to splice with a cell from the tree and one of his own. Gods alone knew how, but the twisted nutter had done it. He got himself a perfect individual. Pete. He would regenerate super-fast, be as strong as it gets and have the killer instincts of both Angel and Daemon.

The down side was he got a sweet guy. Not so much a natural born killer, more a natural born cuddler.

From Pete he developed the army of vampires for Mel and a couple of bodyguards for himself. Unfortunately he couldn't get the polarity of the cells right, making them 'overly susceptible' to a big electrical shock.

The Mad Doctor kept himself a couple of playthings for himself. Left over from his experiments. Part protection, part toys. No brains, just pretty bodies.

The Mad Doctor also managed to splice up Fae and Vampire genes. Gods know how many of them he'd produced, but you could bet Ti would find each and every one.

The only two decent results Mad Doc got were Pete and Lisper. Nice to know we'd done a public service and stopped him before it was too late.

Probably.

From invading The Streets Mel had not just acquired housing and business's but moved in on illegal trades as well. Drugs, prostitution, guns, gambling. All the big money enterprises. She got rich.

Enough to get herself a toy boy in Lisper and pour enough money into fixing him up after I messed him up.

She had done this over years, careful not to draw attention to herself. But someone noticed. Peter noticed. Peter put the pieces together and knew something had to be done. So Peter got himself a weapon of his own.

Peter found a young down and out drunk. Sobered him up, taught him about The Streets and how to survive. It was important to use an outsider to the vampires, werewolves and all the other species. An independent hitter. Unfortunately he liked him, then he became the son he could never have.

Then it kicks off. All because Peter helped Pete to escape. I had seen the cages in that lab. They could only have been opened from the outside. He had to have gotten Pete out of there. He had enough tricks

429

about him to keep him calm and quiet, probably using a cute little dog to keep him calm and help him relate to others and give him 'humanity'. Of course Peter wouldn't have done that himself. He'd have used his man on the inside. His own mole. Someone he could trust enough, and who had access without inciting curiosity.

Cadell.

Cadell.

No one walks away.

"Bang!" I said.

I'm no killer.

"Fucking idiot." Mel said laughing.

I wouldn't make it that easy on her.

Not after Peter.

Not after Kat.

Not after Paul.

Not after Pete.

Not after everything she had done.

Damn. I even let her sing with me. At least she'd never been to Film Night.

"I'm giving you a chance." I said. "Go out with dignity."

Mel stood up and smiled.

"A little suicide Faustus? Maybe a wrist, couple of pills? What do you suggest?" Smug cow.

"Walk outside. On your own." I said. "Walk or be carried by him." I nodded at the Other Sid. "Your choice."

A large finger poked me in the shoulder.

"Excuse me." The Other Sid said. "I have a name you know."

I turned and looked into the face of a vampire goon, with the eyes of a gentle troll. "Sorry Sid. You walk out with The Other Sid carrying you."

"Thank you." The Other Sid said. "Don't get me wrong F. I don't mind letting my hair down and clearing this lot out, but I did close up the Nursery for this. Bit of recognition." The Other Sid gave a little shrug. "You know. It's appreciated."

"Sorry The Other Sid." I said.

The Other Sid's hand rested on my shoulder. "Thanks' man. I just get ignored a bit, that's all. By the way, she's got a gun on us."

I kept looking at The Other Sid. There was some frantic clicking going on behind me.

"It's all right. No bullets and no firing pin." I turned to Mel. "I've been careful. So. With honour or not. Face it babe. It's all you have left."

"How much to let me walk away?" she said, drawing herself up.

"I don't think you could pay me anything sweetie. Your broke."

"I have money and property. Tell me what you want."

"Your bank accounts have been emptied, your deeds returned to the people you stole them from, all their debts paid off and some charities made happy. And your Vampire Zombie army?"

Pete held up a hand held tazer and pressed a button. A small electrical arc shot between it's two probes.

"They all look like porridge." Pete said.

Mel gave a smile and a half laugh. "Not much choice then."

"None." I said. "Only whether it's on your own feet, or under The Other Sid's arm pit."

"I'll be back for the lot of you."

"I doubt it Mel." I said. "You might be able to come back from a lot of places, but not Ti's new gardening project."

Mel's face dropped.

"No." she whispered. "Faustus. You cannot do that to me. Not to me."

I took out two cigarettes and passed her one. She took it with shaking hands.

"Faustus." she said. "You cannot give me over to the Queen Bitch."

"I won't." I nodded at The Other Sid. "He will." I lit her smoke, then mine. "You should have stuck to business and stayed out of my town."

"What did I ever do to you?" Mel said.

Slapping a lady is never the done thing. I settled for a head butt instead.

"Get it out of my sight." I said. Sid and The Other Sid both took an arm each,.

"See you at Film Night E.M." The Other Sid said on his way out.

I turned to Sid.

"Thanks for doing this." I said.

"No trouble at all F." he said.

"Faustus." Pete said

I turned to Pete.

"All over Kid." I said.

"Cadell and Lisper Faustus." he said.

"Go home." I said. "It's over."

Pete let out a long sigh.

"Faustus, forgetting for a moment that I don't actually have a home to go to, Cadell has got away, as has Lisper"

"Cadell's around somewhere." I said. "Lisper crawled out when you three came in. He thought I was distracted."

I reached into my trouser pocket and took out my front door keys. I passed them to Pete.

"You know the rules." I said. "You can stay with me till you get things sorted. Keep the dogs off the furniture and out of my room. Go home. I'll deal with them."

Something occurred to me.

"We should find a last name for you. I can't just keep calling you 'Pete', besides we'll need something to stick on your papers."

"Did you know that they all mispronounced what they thought I was. The runt of a litter is referred to as a 'whittle'. A whitlow is a small annoying infection that gets in the way."

"I don't get you." I said.

"Pete Whitlow." he said. "A good enough name."

"Good enough." I said.

"Sid talked me out of my first choice." he said as my heart sank.

"What was it."

"Pete Chlamydia." Pete took the keys and put them in his pocket. He shrugged. "I saw the word on the television and liked the way it sounded."

"Go home Pete Whitlow." I said. "My case to finish, so I'll finish the job."

Pete looked down at the gun.

"You're out of bullets. I counted."

I tossed the gun away.

"Lend me your sock." I said.

Chapter Forty Nine: The Dick Deals Death and Destruction

The blood trail led up the service stairs and onto the roof.

I was a good bloodhound and followed them.

Why do they always run for the roof?

When I kicked the door open the rain had started. How atmospheric of it.

The roof was…a roof. Flat with grey felt and some chimney vents. It was a roof.

The swinging sock, loaded with Mel's ashtray, found Lisper behind the first chimney.

I think it may have hurt him because he screamed.

I liked the sound.

"Thtop it. Leave me alone." He sounded like a bullied schoolgirl.

I kept bullying.

Lisper crawled out from behind the chimney vent. His chest and shoulder were covered in his own blood. The hole in his throat had not properly healed, and the tear in his jugular was just an open gash with flaps of flesh unable to properly knit together.

Maybe if you damage him enough he won't heal.

My foot conducted a scientific experiment and stamped on his left hand. The fingers snapped like burnt wood.

Nice.

He screamed something, but I wasn't in the mood to listen. I was in the mood to break a leg. So I did.

"What do you want?" He shouted. "Thell me what you want and I'll give you it. What do you want?"

The sock and ashtray answered him. I couldn't be bothered.

He crawled across the roof up to the fence that surrounded the roof.

"The children. The children. I'll tell you what thee planned to do with thee children. I'll tell you where the other tholdiers are being developed. I'll give evidenth againtht her. Jutht tell me what you want."

"Guess." I said. I kicked him hard enough to send him through the fence and over the roof.

I don't know how he managed it, but he got hold of the edge with his right hand. He tried to grab on with his shattered left, but had no chance. I dropped the sock and crouched down to see him.

He didn't look too happy.

He looked down and looked less happy when he saw the gathering of The Fae below him. All of them had very sharp and pointy looking spears. Another group was holding Mel and walking her towards a limo. At least she was going out in style.

"You can't kill me Fauthtuth. You won't do it. You're a good man. You're a dethent man. You're not a killer. You're not an athathin. You won't kill me. Help me up. Pleathe."

Technically, the fall shouldn't kill him. Hurt him. A lot. Not kill him.

Technically, the Fae spears shouldn't kill him. Hurt him. A lot. Not kill him.

I took a risk.

I'm not a killer. Not a murderer. Not an assassin. But I am a bastard.

He screamed all the way down.

Two very large shadows fell over me. I stood up slowly and picked up the sock.

"Very Laz." Sid said. "Roof top confrontation and all."

"Didn't know you were a fan Sid."

"Greatest detective the world has ever seen." Sid said smiling. "No offence." Sid popped a smoke in my mouth.

"None taken." I said. "Light me."

A lighter appeared in a shadow tentacle and lit me.

"We were talking Faustus." Sid said.

"Quite a bit." Shadwell said.

"And?" I asked.

"Well, we were wondering if you had any job vacancies?" Sid asked.

"Due to us both finding ourselves embarrassingly, temporarily, unemployed." Shadwell finished.

"It seem's that our respective employers no longer require our services." Sid continued.

"That's because Ti's trying to protect you Sid, and Fats Boy is a malicious piece of crap Shadwell." I said.

"Thought you could use some occasional muscle." Shadwell said.

"After all, lots of people do seem to want to kill you." Sid went on. "Often." And on and on.

"How does 'Proprietors Shadwell and Drake' sound?" I asked.

"No. Lost me there boy." Shadwell said.

"Me too." Sid followed.

"How do you two feel about partnerships?" I asked. "Never mind. You'll learn."

I found Cadell in the alleyway. He was bleeding. Quite a lot.

"You found me then." Cadell said.

"Yep."

"I heard you found Lisper first. Probably a good thing." Cadell was limping away from me, dragging his left leg. His shattered hip must have been causing him no end of pain. I resisted the temptation to smile.

"You don't want to go that way." I told him. "You're walking straight into The Fae. I don't think they're in the mood to take prisoners."

"Thanks'." Cadell winced, slowly turning around to face me.

"Sit down man." I said. "Your hip's shattered." I walked over to him and lowered him to the ground.

"Thank you." he said. "Again. By the way, what happened to you arresting us? Just curious."

"That was all said for the benefit of the parabolic mikes you had trained on the building." I said, pressing a handkerchief onto the wound to slow the bleeding. "Did you think I wouldn't have anti-surveillance kit in the office?"

"Never occurred to me. You looked so low tech. Plus someone seemed to have dropped your office and broke it."

"That's the idea. Let's get you to a hospital." I picked him up in my arms. He was as heavy as he looked. His back up piece was jammed under my chin. His finger rested on the trigger.

"Do you think it's possible that jail time may be involved here?" Cadell asked.

"Almost certainly." I said. "After all you'll be coughing to at least maiming Paul."

437

"Now that is fair enough. Probably get five for that. In all honesty I don't think I killed anyone on this job."

"Apart from Peter."

"Apart from Peter." he said. "I'll hold my hands up for that, if they find the body."

"Cough to it anyway." I started walking. Gods the pain in my knees. "What will you tell them about the rest?"

"Close to the truth. I may not mention the vampire bit. Why didn't he tell you I was working for him?"

"He was a sneaky old bastard. Never put all of his eggs in one basket and never told anybody everything."

"You would have thought though, that at least he'd let you know you weren't alone. Tell me. What happens if I pull this trigger?"

"No one can tell the court how you blew up a genetics lab rather than let them experiment on children. Or took on all of Mel's heavily armed crew by yourself to stop them running rampage through the town."

"I did all of that then?"

"You did." I said.

"Ah." Realization dawned as a bright shining light. "I am the flawed hero. A man who does the 'right thing' in the end. At great personal cost."

"Someone has to explain all of the explosions." I was giving Mammasayra her cue. She didn't disappoint.

It wasn't just the Vampire lair whose windows blew out. It was all of the buildings on the entire industrial estate. While Mel had everybody watching me with every kind of electronic gismo they could get their hands on, no one noticed the little notes passed between me and Sid. By the sudden rise in temperature my helpers had been very busy indeed.

"You knew about the good doctors other labs then."

"Yep." I wheezed. "So bang goes your idea of making money out of this."

"Fair enough. Remind me what happens if I pull the trigger?"

"I drop you."

"And that will not be a patch on what I will do to you before his heart has stopped beating."

A pair of heads turned to see Pete walking four paces behind us. I hadn't noticed he was there and I am real good at spotting a tail. Real good. He gave me a small nod which I returned.

I could get used to back up.

"I'm the stooge then. The fall guy to explain all this away." Cadell gave a small laugh. Eventually he had realized.

"If I didn't need one Cadell, I wouldn't be looking after you so well."

"Yes you would. You're one of the Good Guys." Cadell said, lowering the gun. "So am I it seems. In return then, allow me to let you in on a secret. The Catholic church has indeed put a contract out on you. Lisper just upped the price. He was never that good."

I wondered why the Catholics would put a hit on me. Then stopped wondering. Between ruining their image in nicking short eyes, bent and brutal nuns and that time I beat up a Cardinal, there was quite a bit for them to be irked about.

Add on to that I'm one of the few humans ever to have met Jesus Christ… Nice girl, even if she does like a drink a bit.   And she can really shift those pies.

"A good guy eh." Cadell whispered. "That's my reputation ruined. I may never work again. I think I'll pass out now. Wake me when we get to the hospital."

He did and I did.

Chapter Fifty: The Dick Delivers

"So it's all sorted then? All 'taken care of'? Faustus?" Malder was rubbing his knuckles in an especially threatening manner.

He can do that. He's a cop.

It's not intimidation or anything.

Maybe he has rheumatism.

"All sorted, plus you have a confession, which includes, I happened to notice, his admitting to breaking Schoone's nose. Lucky break eh?" I said.

"Very lucky." Malder said flopping down in my semi-destroyed sofa. "Mind you, it seems that no one saw anything. Must have been a glare from all of those lights."

"It was bright in there." I said. "Where did they take Kat's body? I want to make arrangements."

"Get some sleep." Malder said. "It looks like you could use it. When did you last sleep?"

"About four days ago." I said rummaging in my desk drawer. "Got a smoke?"

Malder took out a packet and threw them onto my desk. I nodded my thanks and took one out, throwing the pack back to him.

"Got a light"

Malder made with the matches.

"Who's the tall guy hanging around with the two dogs?" Malder did a thumb jerk towards the hallway. I'd told my new partner (Thank you Peter for including THAT little codicil in your will) to wait there.

"It seems I have been left a partner by Peter." I said, forcing sleep away with some heavy blinking. "I got left him in his will."

"Funny. My Auntie Maureen left me a soup tureen. He left you anything else?" Malder asked.

I slid some papers towards Malder, plus a memory stick loaded with all the dealings Mel's company and shell companies had made.

"Should keep you busy for a few years." I said. "You might notice that I took out references to a couple of bent coppers on her payroll. Not so much bent as bruised."

Malder swallowed and stared at me.

"Why would you want to do that?" he asked.

"Sometimes bad coppers stay bad. Other times good coppers make small errors of judgment. Doesn't stop them being good coppers."

"Schoone has a lot to learn." Malder said. "He could make a good copper."

"With the right guy to show him how." I said. "I think he's got it."

Malder brought himself to his feet. He threw the smokes onto the table.

"See you around Dick." He said. "Keep an eye on Freak Street and keep me informed." With a friendly wave he was gone.

Rain was coming through the broken windows. I'd have to get that sorted. New furniture. New doors and new equipment.

No idea how I'd pay for it, but somehow I'd get by.

Peter may have left me money, but it wasn't my style. I'd keep it tucked away for when I needed it. Funerals and rehab I suppose for old friends. I might even contribute to Cadell's defence fund. Providing he pleaded guilty.

I had about twenty minutes left before I passed out so I picked up the telephone to call Ti.

Just to see how she was.

That's all.

"Mr Faustus?" A melodious voice said.

"That's the name. Don't wear it out." reflex said.

"Your chap outside suggested I come in." the voice said again.

I looked up.

A tall man, dressed in a dark three piece suit. Yellow handkerchief in pocket with matching tie. He wore a grey fedora to suppress his buoyant hair. The smell of chocolate drifted over.

"My employer felt that you may be able to help us with an item that has become, shall we say, mislaid?"

I held up my hand to pause the conversation.

"Pete." I shouted. "What are the new rules?"

"Hang on. I wrote them down." Pete shouted back. "Here they are.

1)   Respect the confidentiality of the client.

2)   See the job through to the end.

3)   Make sure you know who your client really is and never   work for the Bad Guy.

4)   Always get paid in cash.

5)   Never, ever work for fairies.

6)   They are your fucking dogs. You fucking walk them and don't forget to pick up after them. No they can't have chocolate. It's mine and keep them off the fucking furniture.

I looked at the Angel.

I looked at the broken windows.

I thought about my bank balance.

I remembered Angels had wings.

"Check out the rules. Rule five should apply to you too." I said. "Pick a window. You're leaving."

443

Keep
Reading

Everybody else plugs the next book at the end of the
First.
Did you expect this to be different?

Hmmm?

Well?

Did You?

Sometime Much Later

"Pete. Put the gun down."

"Faustus. You idiot."

"Pete. That gun is loaded with armour piercing rounds. They'll cut right through my vest. Please. Put it down."

"Look around you Faustus. Look at the dead."

"Their choice Pete. Not mine."

"You. They listened to you. Now look at them. I listened to you. Look at Me. I'm nothing when I could have been a God."

"Pete. Don't."

"Your turn to die, Faustus. My turn to be a God."

"Pete."

Bang.

Made in the USA
Charleston, SC
30 October 2012